Buckskin Pimpernel

the Exploits of Justus Sherwood,
Loyalist Spy

by Mary Beacock Fryer

Dundurn Press
Toronto and Charlottetown
1981

General editor: J. Kirk Howard
Design and production: Ron and Ron Design Photography
Typesetting: Howarth and Smith
Printing: Editions Marquis, Montmagny, Quebec
Cover illustration: John Lasruk

The publication of this book was made possible by support from several sources. The author and publisher wish to acknowledge the generous assistance and ongoing support of the Canada Council and the Ontario Arts Council.

We are grateful as well to the Toronto Branch of the United Empire Loyalists' Association of Canada for the members' financial support and enthusiasm for this project.
J. Kirk Howard, Publisher

Canadian Cataloguing in Publication Data

Fryer, Mary Beacock, 1929-
Buckskin pimpernel

Bibliography: p.
Includes index.

ISBN 0-919670-57-1

1. Sherwood, Justus, 1747-1798. 2. American loyalists - Vermont - Biography. 3. United States - History - Revolution, 1775-1783 - Biography. I. Title.

E278.S53B42 973.3'14'0924 C82-094320-7

Contents

List of Maps

Photographs

Preface

In July of 1790, my great great great grandfather, Caleb Seaman, left his blacksmith's shop in the village of Lyn and journeyed twenty kilometres into Augusta Township. He appeared before the Luneburg District Land Board and with a petition as a "U.E. Loyalist" applied for a grant of land. He got his wish, for the land board record shows "Certificate granted 6th July 1790, 200 Acres." The chairman of the land board, who signed the certificate wrote "Sworn before me Justus Sherwood Esq. this fifth day of July at Augusta." After seeing this certificate, I wanted to know more about Justus Sherwood, my ancestor's benefactor.

A plaque at the foot of Merwin Lane, west of Prescott, Ontario, hints at a neglected hero. It reads:

> Justus Sherwood 1747-1798
>
> Born in Connecticut, settled in Vermont in 1774. On the outbreak of the Revolution he was arrested as a Loyalist, but escaped to join the British at Crown Point. He was taken prisoner at Saratoga in 1777, and after being exchanged was commissioned as a captain in the Intelligence Service. From 1780 to 1783 he had charge of secret negotiations which, it was hoped, would result in Vermont's rejoining the British Empire. Sherwood, who took up land in this township in 1784, played a leading role in its settlement. One of the District's first magistrates, he was also a member of the local land board until his death.

A second plaque at Blockhouse Point, North Hero Island, in Lake Champlain, tells the story from the American point of view:

> On this site was erected in July 1781 Loyal Blockhouse by Justus Sherwood, Captain, Queen's Loyal Rangers. This spot was a stopping place for British

> refugees during the American Revolution and from here were conducted the negotiations between the Republic of Vermont and the British Government. This tablet was erected September 1912 by the Vermont Society, Sons of the American Revolution.

Clearly, Sherwood was an interesting man, and if I could find enough material, I wanted to make his story into a popular biography. I did find the material, although some interpolation was necessary because there were gaps that needed to be filled. When I started this book I had already explored the loyalist era as it pertained to Ontario and the war years, and had the confidence to interpret what was happening when the sources were slim.

I want to thank the people who have made the publication of this book possible. My husband, Geoffrey, is tolerant of a wife who spends hours immersed in the eighteenth century, neglecting the twentieth. Gavin Watt, who has re-created a detachment of the King's Royal Regiment of New York, was generous in sharing his own findings. Professor Ian Pemberton, of the University of Windsor, was a valuable correspondent, and Norah Hugo-Brunt typed the manuscript and offered advice on the weaknesses in my prose. Ron Rochon designed the book, and Kirk Howard, of Dundurn Press, agreed that a Sherwood biography fitted in with his policy of publishing new approaches to Canadian history. Lastly, we owe a debt of gratitude to the Toronto Branch, United Empire Loyalists' Association of Canada, for generous financial support.

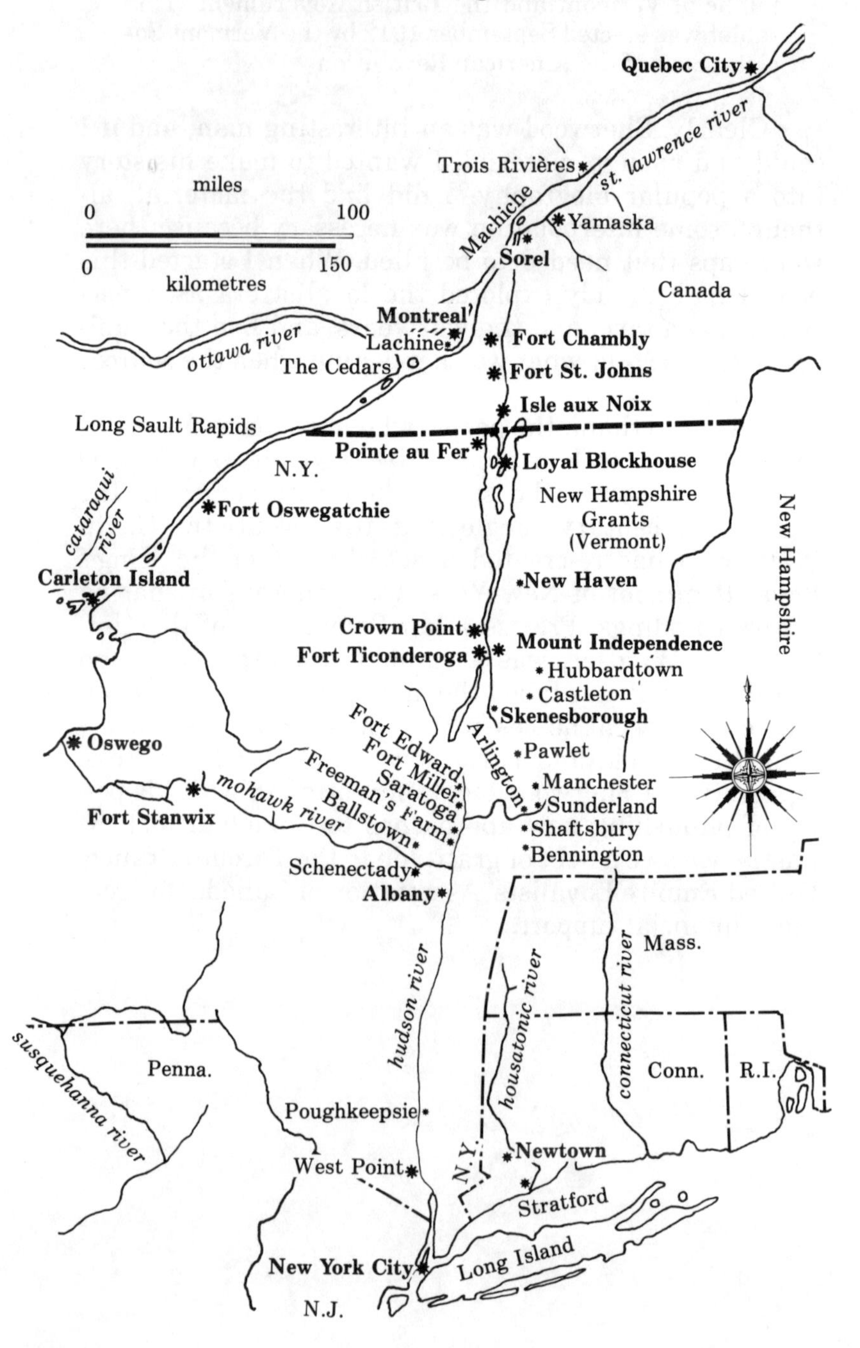
Place Names Relating to Justus Sherwood
Quebec City
st. lawrence river
Trois Rivières
Machiche
Yamaska
Sorel
miles
0
100
0
150
kilometres
Canada
Montreal
Lachine
ottawa river
The Cedars
Fort Chambly
Fort St. Johns
Isle aux Noix
Long Sault Rapids
Pointe au Fer
Loyal Blockhouse
N.Y.
New Hampshire
Grants
(Vermont)
New Hampshire
Fort Oswegatchie
cataraqui
river
Carleton Island
New Haven
Crown Point
Fort Ticonderoga
Mount Independence
Hubbardtown
Castleton
Skenesborough
Oswego
Fort Edward
Fort Miller
Saratoga
Freeman's Farm
Ballstown
Arlington
Pawlet
Manchester
Sunderland
Shaftsbury
Bennington
Fort Stanwix
mohawk river
Schenectady
Albany
Mass.
hudson river
housatonic river
connecticut river
susquehanna river
Penna.
Conn.
R.I.
Poughkeepsie
Newtown
N.Y.
West Point
Stratford
Long Island
New York City
N.J.

Prologue

From a Fate Worse Than Death

The trussed prisoner thrashing softly in the box of the wagon that October day of 1776 was slim and lanky. His face, gaunt and pale after more than a month in confinement, was set in determined lines, the mouth thin and taut. Even in his present state of helplessness he drove himself relentlessly, an indomitable will forcing him to press for release. He had to escape and soon. A few kilometres farther and they would be out of the Green Mountains into settled country, where he would make a fine target if he tried to dash for freedom.

The hideous spectre of Simsbury Mines, in far away Connecticut, loomed before his eyes. Only hours ago the rebels' Grand Council of Safety had passed the sentence of life imprisonment on him for his so-called crimes. The mines were, he knew, an appalling place — a prison built into an abandoned mine shaft — where men were confined in dank, rat-infested darkness. Such a fate was not for him, not Justus Sherwood, only 29 years old, with family responsibilities and in the very prime of life!

At last the ropes began to give and he freed his hands. He glanced anxiously at the backs of the three armed men crammed on the seat at the front of the wagon. His keepers were more concerned with what might lie ahead than with their handiwork when they bound Sherwood. Their eyes, glued on the trail in front, were watching for the prisoner's friends, who might appear, firelocks raised, to rescue him. Justus started on the ropes that pinioned his ankles, momentarily grateful that leg irons had been unavailable in Bennington, where, for want of a gaol, the rebels had held him in the stable of the Green Mountain Tavern.

In seconds he was free, and he rubbed his ankles vigorously to restore the circulation. He shot another cautious glance at his guards and silently let himself down over the rear of the wagon. Sprinting towards a thicket he rose and ran into the depths of the forest which extended up the slopes of the Green Mountains, until he was winded and had to pause to regain his breath. Now he felt safe, for he knew these woods well. Moments after Sherwood had dropped from the wagon his guards discovered his absence. Gloomily they turned back for Bennington to raise a posse, knowing too well that their search for the prisoner would be in vain.

Justus hurried to the house of his father-in-law, Elijah Bothum, whose farm was in the Township of Shaftsbury, 16 kilometres above Bennington. There he knew he would find his wife Sarah and their nearly two-year-old son Samuel. Sarah, who was seven months pregnant, had gone to her father when Justus was imprisoned. She greeted him with a shout of delight, thinking he had been released by the rebels and they could return to their own farm in New Haven Township, 150 kilometres to the north.

Her face sobered when Justus informed her he had escaped, and could only linger long enough to sign over the title of their farm to Elijah. By doing so Justus hoped that the rebels would not confiscate it and leave Sarah homeless.[1] Then he must be on his way. Sarah's father's farm was the first place a posse would look for him. Sarah's eldest brother, Elijah Bothum Jr., 20 years old, a heftier man than Justus with a bluff heartiness that matched his bulk, wanted to know where his brother-in-law was going.

"To the British army at Crown Point where I'll be safe," Justus replied impatiently.

Young Elijah begged him to hide out in the woods while he contacted other loyalists who were living in fear of the rebels. If they knew that Justus had escaped and was willing to be their guide, Elijah was certain they would follow him. Justus had been taking timber rafts down Lake Champlain and the Richelieu River to Sorel, and he knew the way better than most men in the New Hampshire Grants.

Sherwood agreed to wait three days on the mountain beside the Battenkill River overlooking a tract of land he owned in Sunderland, a township north of Shaftsbury. Elijah Jr. saddled a horse and went off to inform other loyalists, while Sarah and her mother, Dorothy Bothum, assembled a week's supply of provisions, and his father-in-law pressed a rifle on Justus. He bid a sad farewell to Sarah and his son and went off to his mountain hide-out, 11 kilometres to the northeast.

Within the allotted time men began to arrive. At the last moment Elijah Bothum Jr. joined the party, now twenty strong, pleading that he would be in deep trouble if the rebels learned of his part in assembling the men. He was also looking for adventure not to be found on his father's farm. Guiding the men northward Justus set a grueling pace, keeping well away from the scattered farmsteads of that wilderness frontier, making for his home in New Haven, where Elijah's younger brother, Simon Bothum, had gone to take charge of the farm after Justus' arrest.

Justus was heartened by the response to his call to join the King. All these men were known loyalists, in danger of being imprisoned; nevertheless they were making a great sacrifice, leaving their wives and children and all they possessed to serve a cause. He, too, was a prey to thoughts of what might happen to his property, which he valued at 1,200 pounds in New York money, about two thirds the value of sterling.[2] He had signed the 50 acre (20 hectares) farm in New Haven to Sarah's father, but he owned nearly 3,000 acres (1200 hectares) all told, a farmhouse in Sunderland as well as the house in New Haven, furniture and other personal effects. Marching along, his rifle over his shoulder, he prayed fervently that the rebels would take their time about any more confiscations.

His mind flew back to the times when he had ridden with his companions, nights when the Green Mountain

Boys chased New York settlers out of the New Hampshire Grants. Those New Yorkers had been trying to drive away his fellow New Englanders, claiming they did not have valid titles to the farms they owned and worked with loving devotion. His thoughts were interrupted by the sound of running feet and he halted. Someone called his name and Justus recognized Edward Carscallan; other men were popping from the undergrowth, all familiar. Carscallan was Irish, a veteran of the Seven Years' War who had settled some years earlier in the Camden Valley, not far from the farm in Sunderland where Justus had lived until 1774. The others were Irish-born men who spoke German among themselves. Justus knew them because they had been present at Anglican services in Arlington, which he had attended before he moved to New Haven.

At any other time the men from the Camden Valley would have clashed with the New Englanders in Sherwood's party. The former were tenants on a large estate, deliberately planted there by a landlord in New York City because these sturdy German-speaking people would stand up to the Green Mountain Boys. Now, however, they forebore because they needed help. They had set out to join the British but had become lost. Willingly Justus agreed to lead them, setting aside his private aversion for the good of the cause.[3]

Each night his party, which now numbered forty, bivouacked in the woods. At the farm in New Haven Simon Bothum gave them provisions for the rest of their journey. Simon was working the farm with the help of Justus' two slaves, until Sarah had had her baby and would return home. With her in Shaftsbury was Justus' third slave, a boy named Caesar Congo, her house servant.[4] From New Haven Justus led his men 32 kilometres through the forest to the east shore of Lake Champlain, opposite Crown Point, his mind on Sarah.

Her time was drawing near, but surely he would not be away long. The rebels' Army of the North was stationed at Fort Ticonderoga, the stone stronghold 16 kilometres south of Crown Point that overlooked the lake. Once the British army captured the fort the rebellion in the north would be as good as over, and he should be home before winter set in. Ticonderoga was garrisoned for the most part by ill-disciplined militiamen, and the British would not have difficulty dislodging them.

The closer to Crown Point his party marched, the more wary Justus became, lest he encounter rebel patrols spying on the British position. Near the shore he ordered the men to hide, and taking only Elijah he went in quest of a boat to cross the "quarter mile" of water between himself and the fort at Crown Point. Above it, to his delight, the red jack was flying. The two men soon found a skiff and pushed off.

Crown Point was a charred ruin, burnt, Justus guessed, by the rebels, either after Benedict Arnold's fleet had been destroyed only days before, or during their retreat in the spring of 1776, following their failure to capture Canada. Reporting to the officer of the day, Justus requested bateaux to bring his party across the lake, pointing out the danger of their tangling with rebel patrols. The officer dispatched red-coated soldiers to man the bateaux, and Elijah went with them as their guide.

The officer ordered Justus to wait upon His Excellency, Governor Sir Guy Carleton, who wanted to see newcomers of stature — which Sherwood appeared to be — to receive any intelligence they might bring. The governor's headquarters was aboard the schooner *Carleton*, a small vessel of twelve 6-pounder guns riding at anchor offshore. Visitors were taken over in a ship's boat rowed by sailors with greasy pigtails, clad in blue jackets and loose canvas trousers. Justus would soon be meeting a man who already knew something about him, for secret agents had carried his reports from New Haven to Carleton's headquarters in Quebec City.

Thus, on an October day in 1776, Justus Sherwood began his service as a provincial soldier with the British army. In a memorial he wrote ten years later, Justus stated that he had exerted his influence to prevent the people in New Haven from taking up arms against His Majesty:

> For which your Memorialist was in Augt 1776 taken by order of the Committee by an armd compy from his House and Farm in New Haven who wantonly destroyed and took away the Household Furniture Wearing Appl and provisions & belongings to your Memt

breaking open his Chests taking tearing and trampling under foot all his papers and writings which they could get hold of, your Memorialist procured Bail at that time and permission to go to his Family and Continue under certain restrictions untill further Orders from the Committee, But the same night on which Your Memorialist came to his Family he was taken out of his Bed by an Armed Force, who kept him under a Guard of Insulters for some time obliging him to bear his own and their Expences.[5]

Sherwood's escape while under sentence to Simsbury Mines ended a short history of persecution at the hands of the rebels in the Green Mountains. It began when he resolved to turn his back on certain of his fellow Connecticut-born men. Because of his earlier associations, he was destined to become, two generations later, the villain of song and story, not only to mythmakers but to early historians.

For example, in 1839 there appeared a book entitled *The Green Mountain Boys — A Historical Tale of the Early Settlement of Vermont* by Judge D.P. Thompson. In his foreword the judge proclaimed that he was 'Sensible of no violations of historical truth. The arch knave of this romance is a resident of New Haven named Sherwood. In the best tradition of nineteenth-century novels, Sherwood is all bad, responsible for every dastardly misfortune that befalls the handsome, manly hero, and his beautiful, vulnerable lady.

Sherwood is the miscreant Tory, 'who, through the inscrutible ways of Providence, was permitted to live, Cain-like to old age, found his way at the close of the Revolution, to the common refuge of American Tories in Canada, where he finished his days in poverty and disgrace.[6] That Judge Thompson could conjure up such an ogre indicates how thoroughly the Vermonters perverted, or eliminated, Sherwood from the early histories of their state during the American Revolution. Even in more recent times, as Vermont writers examine the period with less jaundiced eyes, Sherwood is miscast as a sophisticated British officer being outwitted by a pack of shrewd rough diamonds — with one exception. Louise Koier, writing in 1954, praised Sherwood for sparing Vermont some of the worst horrors of war.[7]

Justus was a British American who espoused a losing cause, one that failed through British bungling and French military intervention, not because of adroitness on the part of the rebels. Like other loyalists, Sherwood had to be erased from American history because he detracted from the myth of oppressed colonists seeking justice through rebellion. The Canadian reaction has not been much better. The myth that all the loyalists came to Canada after the revolution refuses to die. It overlooks the presence in Canada of provincial soldiers like Sherwood from 1775 onwards, and the refugee camps.

Loyalists wrote very little about themselves, and biographies of individuals are rare, and frequently brief because of a dearth of information. One exception is William Smith, later Chief Justice of Canada. He left private letters and diaries that invoke the portrait of a man in satin, powdered hair in side curls, queue tied with a velvet ribbon. Imagine instead a man sporting a frontier crop, hair barely touching his collar, clad in buckskin leggings and a knee length fringed hunting shirt, gazing over Lake Champlain. Such a man was Justus Sherwood.

Confusing to many students of loyalists was the fact that there were two named Justus Sherwood. Both were secret agents and some writers have lumped them together as one man.[8] The other Justus Sherwood was from Westchester County, New York, and after the American Revolution he settled in New Brunswick. The subject of this biography settled in what became the Province of Ontario, and his extensive correspondence is preserved in the papers of General Frederick Haldimand.

What events in Sherwood's early life made him fitted for the role he played? One quality shines clear. He was a dominant male in a frontier society where strength ruled. Since by his own admission he was not a 'burly fellow',[9] he had about him an air that could make men wary. He was forthright, brave, inclined to speak up before weighing the consequences. His handwriting reveals a man whose thoughts raced, but whose excellent co-ordination allowed his pen to keep pace. Warmth and ability to show affection were strong qualities, but coolness and practicability are to be found in certain of the strokes.[10]

British regular officers were inclined to sneer at mere provincials, but most made an exception of Justus Sherwood. Here was one colonial who impressed them by his bearing, and none ever cast aspersions on him after meeting him face to face.

Chapter 1

Outlaw, Rebel, Loyalist

Justus Sherwood was descended from Thomas Sherwood and his wife Alice who left England for Massachusetts Bay in 1634.[1] With the founder of the American branch of the Sherwood family, a behavior pattern emerged that surfaced in Justus himself. Thomas found the rule of the Massachusetts leaders onerous, and he soon moved to Connecticut, settling in Fairfield. The Puritan ideal was a form of communism, where all worked for the good of the whole. Dissidents were encouraged to depart and found their own settlements in what they called the 'howling wilderness'.

John Sherwood, Justus' father, was born in the seaport of Stratford, Connecticut, one of several sons of a Dr. Thomas Sherwood. John settled in Newtown, 50 kilometres from the coast, up the Housatonic River, where, on April 6, 1717, at age seventeen years, eight months, he married Hannah Patrick, a maid of only sixteen years. Justus was their tenth child, his date of birth March 7, 1747. His father was a farmer, but he had other business interests. In soil exhausted, over-crowded Connecticut, he had to turn to many pursuits to support such a large brood. In order of age the Sherwood children were: Sarah (1728); John Patrick (1730); Rachel (1732); Ebenezer (1734); Hannah (1736); Bethuel (1738); Samuel I (1741-1753); Jemima I (1743-1754); Abigail (1745); Justus (1747); Daniel (1749); Joshua (1751); Samuel II (1754); Jemima II (1756).

Justus' training in leadership began when he was

six years old. With the premature death of his elder brother Samuel, he lost his natural protector. Bethuel was fifteen at the time and rarely on hand when his small brother needed him. At the village school Justus had no big brother to run and stand beside when someone decided to punch him. He had to fight his own battles, and those of the three young brothers who came after him.

His writings indicate that he received a better education than was available in Newtown, which had six school districts but no grammar school. Justus never used classical allusion characteristic of men educated in grammar schools and colleges, but his father sent him to Stratford, a longer settled community that had a grammar school. Two of Sherwood's journals reveal a knowledge of coastal fisheries, sailing and ships, and an eye for a good harbour, skills he would never have acquired had he lived only in Newtown before he left for the New Hampshire Grants.

Colonial grammar schools offered Latin and Greek, but they also trained boys in writing, arithmetic and practical subjects for a lower fee. As a matter of economy Justus was relegated to the English side of the school, and he studied surveying. This training spared him seven years as an apprentice, and he was able to earn his own living before he was twenty-one. His drive and ambition were evident early. By the time he was old enough to hold property he was ready to buy a small farm.

On August 31, 1768 — the year he came of age — Justus purchased a ten to twelve acre parcel (approximately 4 to 5 hectares) with a house on it from his brother Ebenezer for 14 pounds. In October 1769 he bought six acres (2½ hectares) for 50 pounds that had thirteen rods of frontage on Cranberry Pond, a better investment for it had access to water. Then in February 1771, with his brother Daniel, he bought six acres for 50 pounds. In October he sold his interest in this latter parcel to Daniel for 25 pounds because he was planning to move to the frontier, where, for similar sums he could buy acreages by the hundreds.[3]

The appeal of cheap land was a strong motive, but Justus had another for leaving his native province. The

Congregational Church had held sway since Connecticut was founded, although Anglican parishes were forming, and Baptists were making inroads on hitherto solidly Congregational ranks. This church, the established one, was itself torn by dissent. Certain of Justus' attitudes indicate that he was raised a Congregationalist, but religion was not very important to him. Secretly he longed to join the Anglicans, mainly because the Church of England demanded less of its members. In the part of the New Hampshire Grants where Justus later settled were many others who had fled the rigours of Congregationalism.

Attendance at the Newtown Meeting House each Sunday was an ordeal. Women and girls sat together, separate from the men, while the boys were placed on the steps leading to the pulpit under the eyes of the minister and the entire congregation. Each week the minister preached the virtue of diligence and proclaimed avarice a sin, as Congregational preachers had done for more than a century. During Justus' youth these words had lost some of their original fire, but the sight of the community leaders, all of whom had achieved material success — a possible consequence of avarice — was a lesson not lost on young Justus Sherwood.

Then, too, the magistrates who were elected to preside over the courts were invariably men of wealth. Regardless of the theme of the sermon, Justus could see which men were the most godly in the eyes of the whole community. In short, Justus' background had made him an ambitious Yankee, but one whose actions were tempered by a Puritan conscience. After Yankee diligence and frugality brought security, Justus believed that a man had a responsibility to look to the public good and show concern for the less fortunate.[4]

Once he resolved to leave Connecticut, Justus had to decide where he would settle. Two of his uncles, Adiel and Seth Sherwood, had taken their families to Fort Edward on the upper Hudson River, an area that did not attract Justus. Most New York farmers leased their land, for that province was feudal, with great estates and a landed gentry. In the New Hampshire Grants, so Justus understood from other people whose families had gone there, a man could buy land outright.

Connecticut men had been freeholders since the time King Charles II toyed with the notion of giving part of the colony to one of his brothers as a dukedom. When it was rumoured that land not in private ownership would belong to the crown, the Puritan leaders distributed parcels to individuals. Over-night freeholding became the goal of every freeborn man,[5] and Justus had no intention of working land he could never own. In the course of the winter of 1771-1772, he made his way to the frontier. By the spring he had been established long enough to have made an impression on the local people. He had met his future wife, Sarah Bothum, and made an enemy of a local law officer.

Not far from the Bothum farm in Shaftsbury Township dwelt a Scots veteran of the Seven Years' War named John Munro. He was an unpopular man with the Yankees, especially after he accepted an appointment as a magistrate from New York's latest royal governor, William Tryon. His Excellency had recently arrived in New York City to take up his duties, and he was determined to bring law and order to certain remote parts of his realm.

On March 22, Magistrate Munro was passing the Bothum farm in a sleigh with a prisoner with the memorable name of Remember Baker. Sarah's sister Dolly noticed the sleigh and recognized the prisoner, his hands bound and bleeding, and gave the alarm. With thirteen men Justus rode in pursuit to effect a rescue, and the posse accompanying Munro fled into the woods. Recognizing Sherwood, Munro ordered him to come to his aid, but Justus was assisting the prisoner. An irate Munro hurried to Albany to complain to the sheriff about the wickedness of certain folk in the Green Mountains.[6] For this and other instances of rioting Justus found himself an outlaw with a price of 50 pounds on his head.[7]

He did not hesitate to embroil himself in the quarrel on behalf of his fellow Yankees, for he had bought 100 acres (40 hectares) from Samuel Rose, which fronted on the Battenkill River in Sunderland Township, a short distance from the village of Arlington.[8] Justus was scarcely settled before he made an alarming discovery.

The title to his farm was not secure. At any moment a New York owner might claim the land — a discovery that left him momentarily stunned.

Connecticut was a charter province where the members of the legislative assembly were elected, as in other colonies, but so were most officials and the governor himself. New York and New Hampshire were royal provinces, where the governors and other officials were appointed by the crown — men who could not be turned out of office at the will of the enfranchised citizens. In leaving Connecticut Justus had forfeited some of his God-given democratic rights. The situation in the Grants did not permit a man to be neutral, and an aroused, worried Sherwood sided with his own people.

The source of the trouble lay back in the 1740s, when the Province of New Hampshire was separated from Massachusetts. That started the struggle between successive royal governors of New York and the new province. The governors of New Hampshire awarded grants of land between the Connecticut and Hudson Rivers, hence the name New Hampshire Grants. New York also claimed that territory, and the royal governor of the day complained to the British government. Meanwhile, New Hampshire went on granting land in the expectation that the only peaceful solution would be to place the Grants under that jurisdiction, until, in 1764, the home government decided in favour of New York's claim.

This ruling was disturbing to farmers with little cash, ruinous to large land speculators. The governors of New York refused to recognize the New Hampshire titles unless the holders paid them quit rents. These amounted to two shillings, sixpence per 100 acres (40 hectares) per annum,[9] the rate in other parts of New York. Most New Englanders refused to pay. Small farmers felt abused; land speculators were unable to raise large sums. On lands where New Englanders had not paid their rents the governors of New York issued patents for large estates to New Yorkers, without regard to whether the land was already occupied. Into this situation Justus Sherwood stepped, to discover that his title was originally from the governor of New Hampshire, and no quit rent had ever been paid.[10]

Appalled at the prospect of losing his hard-earned investment, Justus contacted the ringleaders in the fight against New York. These were two remarkable brothers, one a blaspheming giant who scorned hellfire and damnation; the other small, soft spoken, observant and a skilful plotter. Big Ethan and little Ira Allan were speculating in land under New Hampshire title, and, hellbent on opposing New York's claims, had already done much to reduce the leaders of that province to hysterics. Ethan, the man of action, was the colonel of an illegal army called the Green Mountain Boys, but the strategy was the work of diminutive, thoughtful Ira — nicknamed 'Stub'. They were aided by their four brothers and an array of cousins, including Remember Baker.

Justus could find no peaceful alternative to their reign of terror that discouraged New York settlers from occupying the lands they had leased. But, the terrorism had to stop short of serious acts of violence. The Allans calculated, correctly, that a dead man, or a seriously injured one, might provoke retaliation, whereas a humiliated man would be laughed at. The game called for self-control, and Justus agreed. If the Green Mountain Boys started a shooting war, the governor of New York might be persuaded to send in troops and quell their movement.

Justus joined the Boys on what Ethan called a wolf hunt — an euphimism for an attack to drive away settlers brazen enough to take up land under New York title. Faces blackened, clad in garments intentionally ridiculous, they descended on their hapless victims. The mere sight of them was often sufficient. If not, a barn might be burnt, and to the stubborn a flogging on the bare back with a green beech rod which the Green Mountain Boys called impressment with the beech seal, or chastisement by twigs of the wilderness. Through name calling, bluster and threats and bravado, they were able to keep New Yorkers at bay while making their royal governor look foolish. A wolf hunt over, the Boys congregated at the Green Mountain Tavern in Bennington, the hub of political and other activities in the New Hampshire Grants.

One such rowdy session followed the rescue of Remember Baker. The landlord's son, Dr. Jonas Fay, attended to Baker, for in the struggle to subdue him one of Magistrate John Munro's men had hacked his thumb off. Justus and the other deliverers gathered round Landlord Stephen Fay's flowing bowl to toast another successful wolf hunt against New York. The concoction in the bowl was called a 'stonewall', a mixture of rum diluted with almost equally potent hard cider which did wonders for Remember Baker, while raising the spirits of the others to a level that fairly rocked the sign in front of the tavern. On a tall pole it stood, surmounted by a badly stuffed mountain lion, locally called a catamount, panther or painter, fangs grinning, head facing New York in a gesture of defiance.[11]

Not long after the rescue of Remember Baker, while chatting with Seth Warner, another of the Allen brothers' cousins, Justus witnessed a second discomfiture of Magistrate Munro. Some Green Mountain Boys playfully fired shots into the upper storey of Munro's house in Shaftsbury. Later, according to Ira Allen, when Munro:

> Met Captain Warner and Mr. Sherwood, some provoking words were passed and Warner drew his sword and smote Munro on his head, but his thick hair and scull saved his brains and broke Warner's sword.[12]

Justus and his associates in the New Hampshire Grants continued to elude Governor Tryon's men, and they built blockhouses in preparation for a showdown that never came. The rebellion intervened.

In 1774, Justus and Sarah were married by a Baptist elder in Shaftsbury, the denomination to which the Bothum family adhered. Soon afterwards they rented out the farm in Sunderland and set off on a trail blazed through the woods, driving their cattle before them, to the land Justus had bought in New Haven Township, 150 kilometres north of his Sunderland property. When they arrived the place did not have a cabin to shelter them, but it was safer from the governor's agents. This tract was gently rolling, much better than Sherwood's hill farm in the more southerly township.

Because Justus quickly demonstrated that he was a man on whom others could rely, the settlers voted him their Proprietors' Clerk, responsible for presiding over town meetings and keeping the township records. Meanwhile, the relations between Governor Tryon and his obstreperous Green Mountain subjects had worsened. About the time Justus moved to New Haven, the New York assembly passed an edict that forbad gatherings of more than three persons anywhere in the New Hampshire Grants. Officers of the law would be absolved of any responsibility if they killed or injured people in the execution of their duty. At the same time the governor raised his reward for Ethan Allen to 100 pounds.

Ethan, an inveterate scribbler, wrote a pamphlet denouncing what he called 'The Bloody Law', and toured the Grants gathering support. In February of 1775, he visited Justus to ask his advice on what should be done.[13] Although Justus claimed in his memorial that he had advocated loyalty from the start of the rebellion, at first his vested interests lay with the rebels.

By April, Ethan was thinking of capturing Fort Ticonderoga, on Lake Champlain, from its British garrison of 47 retirement-aged men. He and Ira had vast holdings on the Onion River, north of New Haven, and had formed the Onion River Land Company. Whenever Justus had the spare cash, he bought lots from the company and intended buying more. Ethan called a meeting of the leaders of his band, at which he proposed taking over the fort. Justus agreed, because rumours circulated that the British were planning to strengthen the garrison. If that happened, the troops would impose law and order — New York law, since the New Hampshire Grants were supposed to be under that jurisdiction. Justus felt that he had nearly as much at stake as the Allens, and he could not afford to let Ticonderoga be reinforced.

Before the local men were organized, Benedict Arnold arrived with permission from the rebels in Massachusetts to capture the fort. The Green Mountain Boys were keen, but only if Ethan led them. Arnold, the egomaniac, was infuriated, but he had the choice of sharing the command — and the glory — with Ethan or abandoning the scheme, since he had not brought enough troops of his own. When Allen's summons to a wolf hunt reached Justus in New Haven, he set out on horseback with a party of friends, making for the rallying point at secluded Hand's Cove, on the east shore of Lake Champlain, a mile north of Ticonderoga. By dawn on May 5,

Ethan had 200 eager volunteers gathered at Hand's Cove. As soon as others brought enough boats, 80 men set out across the water for 'Ty' as locals called the fort.

Riding south as fast as he could, Justus reached Hand's Cove at noon, by which time Allen and Arnold had captured the fort. The 80 men sent in the first wave was sufficient to force the garrison into submission. Justus was pleased with the results, disappointed at missing the action, and disconcerted over the looting spree that met his eyes. Meanwhile, Seth Warner had taken a group to capture the ten British regulars that made up the garrison at Crown Point. Remember Baker had occupied Skenesborough, which had a dockyard and was a potential naval base. The village was on a large estate owned by the wealthy Philip Skene, a leader of the Tory party which opposed independence. At the time Skene was on a visit to England. By late afternoon Lake Champlain was entirely under the control of men from the New Hampshire Grants.[14]

To Sherwood's amusement Ethan Allen and Benedict Arnold were soon squabbling. Arnold was determined to take the heavy guns from Ty to Boston, where the rebels needed them to drive the British army out of the city. Allen wanted them at the fort so that his Green Mountain Boys could remain in command of the lake, and incidently protect the interests of the Onion River Land Company. The excitement over, Justus rode home to New Haven. Throughout the summer he pondered the situation in the Thirteen Colonies. By the autumn, when he discovered that the rebels were forming an expedition to capture Canada and were calling for volunteers, he had decided where his priorities lay.

The capture of Ticonderoga had been protection for his holdings, but an attack on one of the King's provinces was a much more serious matter. For pragmatic reasons Justus had to support his sovereign. To avoid a confrontation, he arranged to be absent in the woods, cutting timber, whenever he heard that agents were in the neighbourhood in quest of recruits, until the expedition had left Lake Champlain. Carefully he laid his plans.

Since 1774, when the Continental Congress first met in Philadelphia, the Yankees in the New Hampshire

Grants had been petitioning the Congress to establish a separate state. The New York delegates were opposed to surrendering any territory, and nothing had happened. Justus reasoned that his fellow settlers would be shrewd if they adopted the opposite stance to the Congress. The British government might reward the people in the Green Mountains by setting up a separate province — provided enough of them stayed loyal.

From friends in Bennington, Justus learned that Ethan Allen had lost the command of the Green Mountain Boys. He had asked the men of the Grants to proclaim his band of roughnecks an official militia, and the matter was put to a vote. It carried, but the older men feared Ethan's rashness and demanded another vote on who should lead the regiment. It went in favour of Seth Warner, Ethan's younger but more conservative cousin. Seth had taken the regiment to Canada, while Ethan had gone along as a volunteer, rather than miss a good fight.[15]

Meanwhile, in New Haven, Justus soon heard that Remember Baker had met a sad end. Sent to spy on the British outposts along the Richelieu River, he was shot by some Indians scouting for Governor Carleton. They removed Baker's head, carried it to Fort St. Johns and mounted it on a pole. The horrified British officers ordered it taken down and given a decent burial.[16] Also, in the fighting outside Montreal, Ethan had been captured. Justus pitied him and hoped that most of his friends would escape and reach home safely.

In the spring of 1776, resentment ran high in the New Hampshire Grants. Aided by Ticonderoga's guns, taken through the woods during the winter, the rebels had chased the British troops out of Boston, but the expedition to conquer Canada was a dismal failure. Then word reached the Green Mountains that Ethan had been clapped in irons and shipped to England. Not long afterwards Justus went on a business trip to Bennington, and he chose the wrong time and place to speak his mind freely. Entering into a discussion on the Canadian misadventure in the Green Mountain Tavern, his companions demanded to know why he had not gone with the expedition. Seizing the opportunity, without weighing the consequences, Justus put forth what he thought were sound reasons for evading rebel exhortations to join them, and voicing the case for supporting Britain. The atmosphere became electric, then the mutterings became a rumble rising in crescendo to thunder in his ears.

He tried to back out of the tavern but a gang of rebels subdued him and brought him before Judge Charles Lynch of the Grand Council of Safety, a zealous foe of the Tories. Justus watched warily, knowing he was in for some humiliation but confident the rebels would never dare harm him. His father-in-law was only 16 kilometres away, and he had many friends around Arlington, nicknamed 'Tory Hollow', who would march in and do battle. The judge thought so, too, for the sentence, while unnerving, was only twenty lashes. Justus Sherwood, the former Green Mountain Boy, was about to taste the twigs of the wilderness. He was led shirtless to the village green, and the strokes were laid on with a beech rod before a jeering crowd.[17]

Flinging his shirt over the bleeding stripes, feeling as though his back had been set on fire, Justus stumbled blindly towards the stable in the tavern to fetch his horse. Galloping towards the Bothum farm, his sense of outrage mounted to fever pitch. If the damn rebels thought they could intimidate him they were mistaken. After Dorothy Bothum had put salve on the wounds, he wrote a letter to Governor Tryon, offering his services, arranged to have it carried to New York City by someone he could trust, and set out for his farm in New Haven.

In due course he received a packet containing a letter bearing the governor's seal. Tryon expressed surprise at the prospect of assistance from an unlikely source, and recommended that Justus remain at home, supplying information to scouts working for Governor Carleton in Canada, whose residence in Quebec City was more secure. Below his signature the governor had written 'Aboard the *Duchess of Gordon*'. His Excellency had taken refuge on a ship of war to elude the rebels marching in the streets of New York City.[18]

By the end of August the local Committee of Safety had become suspicious, and sent an armed force to storm the Sherwood house in New Haven. While they ransacked his papers they did not find the township records. These Justus had buried in a potash kettle beside his house,[19] lest the content of the discussions at town meetings incriminate him or any of his friends. After his arrest the rebels took him to Bennington, and lodged him in the only prison available, the stable of the Green Mountain Tavern. For a month Justus fretted in his prison. As his fortunes declined, those of Governor Tryon improved. In September a large British army occupied Manhattan, Staten and Long Islands, and Tryon was once more ensconced in his mansion.

Later that same month came Sherwood's trial before the Grand Council of Safety and Judge Charles Lynch. While Justus admitted only that he was accused of sending information to Carleton, the rebels' decision to send him to Simsbury Mines indicates that he was spying, and they had made their decision on what to do with him after some deliberation. They had evidence and felt justified in hanging him, but fear of retaliation hung over their heads. His friends might march on Bennington to rescue him, or hang someone in revenge. If the council removed him from the scene, his supporters would expend their energies scheming to have him set free. Judge Lynch chose Simsbury Mines because they were secure and 100 kilometres south of Bennington. Albany had a gaol, but prisoners sometimes escaped; besides, the Green Mountain men did not want to call upon New York for assistance. The trial over, the Grand Council arranged for Sherwood's journey to Connecticut with discretion.

Mob rule was commonplace in the Green Mountains, and the members knew they must move quickly. For that reason they assigned only three guards to the wagon. When Justus escaped he made his furtive visit to Shaftsbury, signed his farm in New Haven over to his father-in-law, and after some friends joined him, marched to Crown Point.

Justus was impressed at the sight of the army, 8,000 strong. The British regulars were in red coats, the artillerymen in blue. The Germans were also in blue, except for companies of green coated riflemen — troops rented from several German principalities for service in America. Disparagingly called mercenaries by the rebels, the Germans were for the most part trained professional regulars, proud of their abilities.

With Sir Guy Carleton were several subordinates who would have direct dealings with Justus Sherwood in the near future. General John Burgoyne was Carleton's second-in-command. Also present was Brigadier Simon Fraser, under whom Justus would see most of his active service, and the Baron von Riedesel, the commander of the German troops. Justus assumed that this well equipped army would continue up Lake Champlain and occupy Fort Ticonderoga. The time was ripe for the rebel garrison, although about as large as Carleton's army, was ill prepared. The very occupation he had dreaded in May of 1775 would now be his salvation and he could soon return to New Haven. Then, to his dismay, he heard that Carleton had decided it was too late to proceed that season, and had ordered a withdrawal to Fort St. Johns, on the Richelieu River inside Canada.

Among the loyalists who went into winter quarters near Montreal were several with whom Justus would have a close association. Sir John Johnson, the heir of the late Superintendent of Indian Affairs, had permission to raise a battalion of New Yorkers from among the tenants on his estates in the Mohawk Valley. John Peters, Connecticut-born, from the part of Gloucester County that lay on the east side of the Green Mountains, had come with the rebels to Montreal the year before in order to defect. Edward Jessup was there with his brothers, Ebenezer and Joseph. Men with business interests in Albany and Charlotte Counties, the Jessups had also brought a party of men. Francis Pfister, a former British officer who lived near Bennington, had come with some followers. John Peters, Francis Pfister and Ebenezer Jessup had received permission from Governor Tryon to raise battalions, and this was to have serious consequences later on. All these leaders would be Sherwood's colleagues in the months and years that lay ahead.

Chapter 2

Secret Mission

Sir Guy Carleton was anything but delighted at the arrival of Sherwood and the other loyalists eager to enlist. Writing to Brigadier William Phillips, the commandant of Fort St. Johns, on October 29, 1776, he said he would have been happier had they remained in their homes until he was ready to start another campaign in New York in the spring of 1777.[1] The governor-in-chief was not certain he had the authority to let loyalists enlist or allow them pay. The decision to allow Sir John Johnson to raise a battalion had been an easy one, for he was wealthy and could outfit a regiment from his own purse. At first, Carleton ordered the Jessups, Francis Pfister and Justus Sherwood, with the men they had piloted to Crown Point, to join Sir John Johnson's battalion, the King's Royal Regiment of New York.

Ebenezer Jessup, John Peters and Francis Pfister maintained that they had permission from Governor Tryon of New York, to raise battalions, and Sir William Howe, the commander-in-chief at New York City, had already approved the appointment of some officers. Justus was confused. He wanted to serve under John Peters, a Yankee he thought he would find compatible. All the men who had followed Sherwood, Jessup and Pfister insisted that they be commanded by officers of their own choosing. Such had been their right in the colonial militia, but Carleton deemed this nonsense.

At length, to quell the disturbance, he ordered all the loyalists placed under Sir John Johnson so that they could be provisioned and paid. All were to report to Major James Gray, Sir John's second-in-command, and they were to march to Pointe Claire.[2] Except for the men who had been promised commissions by Tryon, and those already appointed by Howe, all would be paid as privates — sixpence a day with deductions for rations, clothing and hospital expenses. Those who were willing to work could do fatigue duty on the defences around Montreal. Carleton wanted to ensure that the city would never again be vulnerable to attack by the rebels.

Willingly Justus agreed to do fatigue duty. Chopping down trees for fortifications was little different from building his first cabin in New Haven or constructing timber rafts, but his mood was bleak. His thoughts were ever in the Green Mountains. What was happening to his property? How was his beloved Sarah, who would have her baby soon, without any moral support from him? He prayed the rebels would not harass the Bothum family because he had escaped and taken Elijah with him.

With the coming of spring, a new mood of optimism was alive in Canada, and Justus believed that his exile was nearly over. Sir Guy Carleton was preparing his invasion of New York State, stock-piling supplies at Fort St. Johns, which the regulars had been strengthening all winter. General John Burgoyne, who had gone to England on a leave of absence, was expected any day, with new instructions from the colonial secretary, Lord George Germain, and the War Office. Late in March, Major James Gray sent for Justus. Gray was in charge of the loyalists for Sir John Johnson was on a visit to New York City. The major ordered Justus to proceed to Fort St. Johns and report to the commandant, Brigadier William Phillips, for a special assignment.

Justus travelled on a stage-coach along the road from the south shore of the St. Lawrence River overland to the Richelieu River, a distance of some forty kilometres. From Phillips, dressed in the blue coat and red facings of an artillery officer, Justus learned that Governor Carleton wanted him to take a party of five men who knew the country and go on foot to Fort Ticonderoga, to reconnoitre the fortifications. Afterward they were to go as far as Albany and report on all the rebel fortifications in the British army's path, information vital to the success of the expedition soon to embark.[3] The men to accompany Justus were chosen by Major Gray, and late in the day they arrived at Fort St. Johns.

Armed with orders from Brigadier Phillips, Justus approached the Quartermaster's Department and the Commissary for equipment and provisions, and to draw warm clothing — blanket coats with bright coloured strips, knitted caps, buckskin leggings to be worn over breeches and stockings, and fur-lined moccasins. Each man would carry a firearm, a tomahawk tucked into his belt, a knapsack of provisions, a blanket rolled up and secured with twine, and a pair of snowshoes. Justus required a spyglass, quills, a block of ink, a note-book, and a white sheet from the officers' stock to serve as camouflage — this last wrested from the Quartermaster after an argument. Although he had many friends in rebel territory to help him, Brigadier Phillips supplied him with a list of names of people who provided safe houses for secret agents which Justus was to memorize and destroy.

After a night in the barracks Sherwood's party of spies marched thirteen kilometres to Isle aux Noix, the next outpost to the south, where they were taken aboard a bateau for the journey to the outpost at Pointe au Fer. From there a trail through the forest led to Crown Point, on Lake Champlain, and between that ruin and Fort Ticonderoga was a military road of sorts. The time of year was wet and sloppy. The sun melted the snow during the day though the temperature dropped below freezing after sundown. Snowshoes were necessary for travel through the deep snow in the bush. Justus was accustomed to bivouacking outdoors and he knew how to keep his men warm and dry. From Crown Point onward they had to be cautious. Rebel patrols were likely to be scouting along the military road, or lying in wait in the woods, aware that Carleton must have agents out gathering intelligence.

Overlooking Fort Ticonderoga was a small steep mountain called Sugar Hill because it resembled a loaf of sugar. To Justus it was better known as Rattlesnake

Hill, and the perfect vantage point from which to view the rebel position, provided they had not fortified it. Justus reckoned, by scaling the side of the hill that faced away from the fort and creeping carefully over the summit, he would have an excellent view of the rebels, but there were risks. With no foliage, a man moving on the hill might be spotted by watchers in the fort. Here the white sheet would come in handy. He made a short reconnaissance himself, leaving his men concealed, and could find no evidence that the rebels had put a battery on the summit of Rattlesnake Hill.

He guided his party inland through the trees and they began climbing, pulling themselves up by means of saplings, digging the toes of their moccasins into the soft snow. Below the summit Justus stopped and cut a hole in the white sheet for his face, and donned it before executing the next phase of the operation. Alone he went to the top, and descended slowly until he had a good view of his objective. He removed the spyglass, noted that the sun was behind him and his glass would not flash and alert the rebels, and began examining what lay below him.

Fort Ticonderoga guarded the best route between the settled parts of New York State and the Province of Canada. On a promontory facing the east side of the lake, it was set against the backdrop of the Adirondack Mountains, where the lake was scarcely 400 metres wide. Built by the French, it had been captured by the British in 1759, had been held by the rebels ever since the escapade with Ethan Allen two springs ago. On the east side of the lake, facing Ty, were huge new fortification which had not existed when the Green Mountain Boys captured the fort. A log boom, with a row of bateaux tied along it, lay across the narrow waterway linking the two fortified sites, and Justus could see men crossing over it.[4]

The rebels had done a lot of building on the east side of the lake, but the walls of Ticonderoga were crumbling and had had no repairs. While Ty was a massive stone structure with inner and outer walls and elevated gun batteries, the new fortifications were of sod and earthwork with wooden stockading. It looked promising. Back at Fort St. Johns, Carleton's new frigate, the *Royal*

George, lay at anchor. From his knowledge of ships Justus thought she was about 400 tons (this was long tons, equal to about 41 metric tons), a large vessel for Lake Champlain, and she carried 24-pounder guns which would easily reduce these forts.

Justus needed more information on the size of the guns the rebels had, and the strength of the garrison. From Rattlesnake Hill he could tell that the rebels had not brought the big guns back from Boston. Only eight cannon were visible on the batteries, 16-pounders, he reckoned. He also noted six smaller guns mounted at the old French redoubt. Now his party must move in closer, and he would have to visit people he could trust. The following morning, despite all his precautions, suddenly behind them in the deep woods a party of rebels appeared. Because they were not wearing snowshoes, Justus ordered the men to run towards the lake where they could make better time on the thin skirting of ice not yet melted. Cursing the lack of foliage for cover, they hoped to outrun their pursuers. Justus explained:

> Your Memorialist was 41 days on this Scout and lost two of his party taken prisoners by a Rebel Scout on the Coast of Lake Champlain and your Memorialt escaped with the rest of his party by seizing the Rebel boats which lay on the Shore and pushing into the Lake.

Rowing hard, Justus decided to quit the area and complete his observations around Ty later, when the grass would be green, the trees a haze of buds and young leaves which would make concealment easier. He agonized over the fate of his lost men, well aware that they might be coerced into revealing why they were there, and who their associates were. First, however, he wanted news of Sarah and he thought a quick visit to New Haven would be safe. Simon Bothum would know whether she had borne a healthy child. His party concealed the boats on the east side of the lake opposite New Haven, and they set out on snowshoes through deep bush towards his farm.

Simon Bothum was there, and so, to Justus' surprise, was Sarah. Proudly she showed him his new daughter. They named her Diana — the Huntress — from Greek mythology, a fitting name for a frontier girl.

That night his party had beds on the second storey while Sarah and Justus were in their ground floor bedroom. As Samuel and the baby slept, the two had a passionate reunion on the mistaken assumption that nursing mothers did not conceive. Justus set out before dawn, little realizing that he had left his wife in an awkward predicament. Apart from her immediate family, Sarah could hardly explain that Justus had visited her, and would have to pretend she had been unfaithful or risk being interned for aiding the enemy. In his memorial Justus said he scouted as far as:

> Shaftsbury opposite Albany for Intelligence and returned in the beginning of May to Genl. Philips at Montreal with an Account of the Rebell Troops from Albany Northward and a Sketch of the Fortifications at Ticonderoga and Mount Independent.

His memory was playing tricks. Brigadier William Phillips was the commandant of Fort St. Johns, and Brigadier Allan Maclean was in command at Montreal. Also, Shaftsbury is 25 kilometres north of Albany and to the east. He travelled southward through the New Hampshire Grants and from the neighborhood of Bennington turned towards Albany. That town was surrounded by a high wooden stockade inside which the rebels were stock-piling supplies that would be safe from raids by loyalists.[5]

Justus led his party up the Hudson River, and at Fort Edward they visited the safe house of an Irish born lawyer, Patrick Smyth. His brother, Dr. George Smyth, a valuable contact for the British in Canada and at New York City, lived in Albany. The lawyer warned Justus to be careful of his uncles, Seth and Adiel Sherwood, both zealous rebels, an unnecessary warning for he intended to avoid them. He went instead to the house of his cousin Thomas — Seth's son — because he needed provisions. Thomas, two years older than Justus, had loyalist sympathies, and found the unexpected arrival of his cousin timely. Since the British expedition would soon be setting out, Thomas decided to accompany Justus back to Fort St. Johns. He left his wife Anna, and children Reuben and Anna, behind, confident that Seth would protect them from reprisals.

Near Crown Point with his remaining three men

and Thomas, Justus took stock of the intelligence he had acquired. At Mount Independence, the new fortifications opposite Ticonderoga, the rebels had placed their only big guns — one 32-pounder, some 24- and 18-pounders. At Fort Edward, Uncle Adiel was repairing the old citadel on the bank of the Hudson, and he had two 9-pounders mounted. A dozen other guns lacked carriages. The barracks near the fort could house 1,000 men. A storehouse on the beach was filled with flour and beef, and the rebels were building a hospital in the village.

The garrison at Fort Ann, above Fort Edward, was thirty men, and sixty were stationed at Skenesborough, which was to be a naval base. The rebels were hauling timber for six vessels, and sailors to man them were expected from New England by the summer. Most of the soldiers were at Ty and Mount Independence, 1,350 men, but Mad Anthony Wayne, the commandant, expected to be reinforced by General Arthur St. Clair and five fresh regiments. Albany, with its stockade and supplies, and the Ticonderoga-Mount Independence complex were the strong points on the rebel line of defence. The report as complete as Justus could make it, he headed north along the west side of Lake Champlain making for Pointe au Fer. He gazed longingly in the direction of New Haven but dared not go there for fear his house was being watched.

At New Haven Simon carried on looking after his brother-in-law's interests. Owing to Simon's presence Justus did not lose all his livestock. Shortly after his arrest, the rebels stole two of his cows and seventeen hogs, but his horses and a yoke of oxen had not been taken.[6] Thanks to Simon, Justus' farm was intact, ready for him once the coming campaign had ended. Surely, by the autumn, Carleton would be in control of Albany, and if Justus succeeded in enlisting for the expedition, his term would end once the governor achieved his purpose.

By early May his party reached Fort St. Johns. He found the fort bustling with activity as he went to hand in his report to Brigadier Phillips. Many British and German regulars had arrived since Justus had set out for Albany, and all around he saw signs of preparations for the coming expedition into New York. Of Brigadier Phillips, Justus asked help in obtaining the return of his two men who were captured, but the time was inopportune for a prisoner exchange. Neither the brigadier nor the rebels wanted flags of truce approaching the sites of their activities. For the moment nothing could be done. Because Sherwood had shown concern for the captives' welfare, Phillips resolved to do what he could to see that this colonial received a commission. He had the makings of a fine officer. On his part Justus was grieved at Phillips' refusal, and he decided to take initiatives when the opportunity arose.

The briefing over, Justus enquired whether Governor Carleton was planning on taking any loyalists on the expedition. Phillips assured him that the governor wanted the services of every man who had come into Canada, and was honouring the promises made by Governor Tryon at New York City and Sir William Howe, by allowing the leaders to raise battalions. Justus told Phillips he wanted to join John Peters, and the brigadier gave him permission to report to Peters, whose corps was mustering on the south shore of the St. Lawrence opposite Montreal. Finding the stages full, horses impossible to borrow, Justus hurried there on foot.

Peters was delighted, because the former Green Mountain Boy had led 40 loyalists to Crown Point the autumn before. Now Peters could lay claim to them and Justus would be their captain. Commissions were to be awarded on the basis of the numbers recruited, and Peters promised to ask Carleton to make Justus' appointment official. He should not have difficulty recruiting the men he needed to complete the company to 60, as required under the terms of the warrant for the regiment. Thus far, Peters had scarcely 200 men, and his rank as their lieutenant-colonel was only a provisional one. All his officers' commissions would be signed when the battalion reached two thirds strength.[7]

Peters also told Justus that Ebenezer Jessup had permission to raise a battalion and had enlisted 80 men. Others hoping to raise corps were Francis Pfister and Daniel McAlpin. Both were former British regulars, as was Samuel McKay, whose home was near Fort St. Johns, and who wanted to accompany the expedition.

Samuel Adams, a doctor from Arlington, had permission from Carleton to raise some companies.

Sir John Johnson had 133 rank and file and they were to go to Oswego as part of a small expedition under Colonel Barry St. Leger, 34th Regiment. Major John Butler, of the Indian Department, with a large party of warriors and some loyalists who had fled to Fort Niagara, were to join St. Leger and Sir John. They were to capture Fort Stanwix, at the western end of the Mohawk Valley, and march to meet the rest of the British army at Albany.

Early in June, Justus learned that Carleton would not be leading the expedition. General John Burgoyne, who had spent the winter in England, arrived in Quebec City with a commission to command the army in the field. He was now the military governor of Canada, while Carleton remained the civil governor. The British government felt that Carleton had been too hesitant in taking the offensive against the rebels, an opinion Justus shared. Perhaps Burgoyne's appointment would be a blessing, for the faster the army moved towards Albany, the less opposition it would encounter. The more time the rebels had to prepare, the larger the army opposing Burgoyne would become.

Time was passing quickly for Justus. The men of his regiment were to serve as foragers under the Quartermaster's Department.[8] Tailors at Fort St. Johns were sewing uniforms, and Peters was assigning weapons to his officers and men. Burgoyne had sent ahead muskets, bayonets, swords, officers' spontoons and sergeants' halberts. Peters decided that the short spontoons would be useless, and ordered his officers equipped with muskets and bayonets, or rifles if they owned any. The regular officers would be mounted, the loyalist officers on foot since there were not enough horses to go round.

On June 11, General John Burgoyne reached Fort St. Johns, and the following day Peters received orders to march his corps there.[9] The regiment arrived on the 13th, and a few days later Sherwood's commission, approved by Carleton, was received by Burgoyne. However, Peters warned Justus that none would be signed until the corps reached two thirds strength. Neither officer was disturbed, although the corps still stood at 200 men. Once the army was on the move, recruiting agents would have no difficulty bringing in 200 more, and the commissions would be signed. Burgoyne named Peters' corps the Queen's Loyal Rangers, and Jessup's the King's Loyal Americans, while the group commanded by Francis Pfister was the Loyal Volunteers.[10]

William Phillips, now a major-general and Burgoyne's second-in-command, assigned the men Justus had piloted to Crown Point to his company, and Colonel Peters chose Edward Carscallan as the lieutenant, John Wilson the ensign. At that, Carscallan and the men he had been leading when Justus found him in the Green Mountains, complained to Peters. They had promised to join Colonel Pfister before they left their homes, and they wanted to honour that commitment.

Peters maintained that since they had accepted Sherwood's help they had a prior obligation to the Queen's Loyal Rangers. They disapproved of Justus' former association with the Green Mountain Boys, and wanted nothing to do with him after the storm his kind had stirred up in northern New York. At length, Peters reached a compromise. In a memorial Ensign John Wilson wrote later, he explained, 'That your Petitioners agreed to be under the command of Colonel Peters on condition of leaving him if they thought proper'.[11]

The matter was settled for the moment, and Justus had no time to worry about what might lie ahead, for he was busy helping drill the men in firing their weapons as rapidly as possible, imitating the training of the regulars. Justus had reservations about those tightly packed lines of regulars, a formation unsuited to forest warfare, but speed in loading the muskets was essential.

He was disconcerted by certain restrictions which Carleton and Burgoyne were placing on his regiment. All units raised in the British colonies were to be known as Provincial Corps of the British Army. These were inferior to regiments of the British regular establishment, and officers of provincials would be ranked one grade lower when serving with regulars. Furthermore, a provincial was inferior to a regular of the same rank. He would have to take orders from lieutenants of regulars, and officers of provincial corps could not have permanent rank and half-pay when their regiments were reduced.[12]

Nevertheless, at Fort St. Johns confidence was infectious. A sea of tents spread out all around the village that encircled the fort, and the fort itself was stockaded on three sides, open on the fourth where it faced the Richelieu River. There armed vessels of the Provincial Marine guarded the site. Officers of all nationalities were resplendent in gold and silver lace.

Justus thought the Brunswick Dragoons looked ridiculous in their thigh high leather boots and enormous plumed hats. That they were unmounted did not disturb him. The army would move by water, and only on the sixteen kilometre portage between Lake George and the Hudson would the men be on foot. This large, magnificently equipped army should have no difficulty capturing Albany. Burgoyne could not possibly fail.

Gentleman Johnny, as the regulars dubbed Burgoyne, was an elegantly attired man whom Justus remembered seeing at Crown Point the autumn before. The new commander-in-chief was popular with the regulars, who cheered lustily when he addressed them, with good reason. Gentleman Johnny did not allow corporal punishment for the men in his ranks.[13] Back in Quebec City, Carleton had resigned, affronted by his demotion, but he was remaining at his post until the home government had sent his successor.

Soon after Justus' captaincy was approved he went to be measured by the tailors at the fort. In a few days his uniform was ready, and his red coat had green facings, the colour Burgoyne had selected for all his provincial troops.[14] His small clothes — breeches and waistcoat — were of white linen, although he noticed that some of the enlisted men were issued with overalls of the same material. He also received short spatterdashes of white canvas. His hat was a black bicorne edged with silver lace. A single silver epaulette on his right shoulder held his sword belt in place, and the red silk sash knotted round his waist bespoke a commissioned officer. The sword by his side had a silver hilt to match the lace, epaulette, the buttons on the coat and small clothes, and a silver gorget stamped with the royal coat of arms lay

Uniforms of provincial troops, 1775-1784

shimmering on his chest, flanked by pink rosettes. Because he had a rifle, he received the bulky black leather cartridge case carried by the rank and file.

Justus thought this attire absurd for the campaign ahead. A red coat was practical for open fields where, after a musket volley, smoke obscured everything. The red made it easier for officers to rally their men back into formation as the smoke cleared. What lay ahead was a guerrilla war in the forest, waged against riflemen who would not expose themselves. He resolved to tuck the shiny gorget in the pocket of his coat tail before going into battle. No rebel marksman was going to aim at such a tempting target!

On June 17 the army embarked for the journey onto Lake Champlain. The impressive flotilla carried some 9,000 persons, including 300 women to do the housekeeping, and a few children. The troops rode in bateaux with gunboats along the flanks, war canoes of painted Indians beyond them. The frigate *Royal George* led the way, carrying Burgoyne, his staff officers — and apparently his mistress. Sitting in the bateau, Justus listened to the strains of martial music that floated over the boats, brass bands of the Germans, whistling fifes and drums of the English, bagpipes of the Scots Highlanders. By the 30th, the two kilometres-long flotilla had reached Crown Point.

Seven kilometres farther, Burgoyne began landing his troops, British regulars, Pfister's and Adams' provincials on the west side of Lake Champlain, Germans under the Baron von Riedesel on the east, with Peters' and Jessup's corps as their vanguard.[15] Justus knew his side would have more difficulty making their way on land. Apart from the dragoons' heavy boots, the east shore of the lake was swampier.

At last he would soon see action, and he had scant cause to worry about Sarah's safety. New Haven lay to the north of the British army. Then a new recruit for his company arrived from New Haven and informed him that the Bothum family had packed and left Shaftsbury to stay with Sarah. Except for Elijah Jr., his wife's relatives were at his farm. His mind at rest, Justus could get on with the job of soldiering, free of other worries.

Chapter 3

Rattlesnake Hill

In organizing his fledgling battalion, Colonel Peters decided that Sherwood would be in command of the third company. The first was Peters' own, and he was reserving the second for a major when he found the right man. The Queen's Loyal Rangers marched in single file, the only practical method Peters could devise for travelling over such difficult terrain. Leading his company, Justus could hardly contain his enthusiasm for the campaign ahead. He was unaware that since leaving Canada his regiment had come under a different administration. To conduct the military operations against the Thirteen Colonies, the British government had established military departments. The Province of Canada was the Northern Department, Nova Scotia was the Eastern Department, New York City the Central Department, and Florida, the other place where the British were in control, the Southern Department.

Burgoyne had set out with instructions that once he reached Albany he was to place himself under Sir William Howe, in command of the Central Department. All the provincial troops serving with him, even units authorized by Carleton, were no longer the concern of the Northern Department. Sherwood's future now lay directly in Burgoyne's hands, indirectly in those of Governor William Tryon, who had once outlawed him, and Sir William Howe, whom he had never seen. None of the provincials were aware of their changed situation as they marched towards Fort Ticonderoga and Mount Independence those sweltering days of early July.

Burgoyne sent some of his provincials to the rear to bring up supplies and maintain a link with their base at Fort St. Johns. Because the Queen's Loyal Rangers promised to be the largest corps, Burgoyne decided they would remain in the vanguard of his army throughout the campaign. Justus stated that he was, 'Employed on various Scouts and services under Genl Burgoyne and was in every Action a [nd] Skirmish thro' that Campaign'. John Peters confirmed the position of his corps in a letter he wrote after the war, 'as my situation was generally in the advance party, my men were killed off not quite so fast as I enlisted them'.

Scrambling through dense forest, wading through swamps, Peters and Jessup had to halt their men frequently, to allow the struggling Germans to catch up with them. A red-faced, perspiring Baron von Riedesel, leading his horse, attempted to march after the loyalists. Behind him, his officers were trying to maintain a tight column four abreast — quite impossible in that country. It was also dangerous, Justus muttered to Peters as the provincials stood about after having lost sight of the German advance party for the tenth time. If the rebels had the foresight to ambush them, the slaughter would be horrendous.

Suddenly a story from his youth returned to Justus with stark clarity, of how Robert Rogers, the ranger leader in the old war against the French and Indians, had kept his men spread out while in the forests. His rangers could not be surrounded and not more than one man could be a target. He mentioned this to Peters, who admitted that both he and Jessup had the same thought when they ordered the Queen's Loyal Rangers and the King's Loyal Americans to go in single file. Peters chose German-speaking John Dulmage, from Sherwood's company, to take a message to the Baron von Riedesel, suggesting that his men would make better time if they abandoned their columns. A few minutes later Dulmage returned, a sweaty, panting von Riedesel following him. The Baron, Dulmage explained, would have none of Peters' suggestion. If provincials wanted to behave like Indians, that was their affair, but his officers knew how to conduct a war, and Peters had no business offering advice.

Frustrated at the bogged down state of the army on the east side of the lake, Justus longed to know what was happening to the redcoats across the water. Peters, curious himself, dispatched a scout in a bateau to find out how the others were progressing. Returning two hours later, the scout reported that Brigadier Simon Fraser, who commanded Burgoyne's vanguard, had led the light companies of several regiments around the back of Rattlesnake Hill and taken up a position guarding the entrance to Lake George. Here was strategy Justus could not fault. The vanguard had cut off the rebels' most advantageous line of retreat. Lake George reached well into the heart of New York State, with only a sixteen-kilometre portage to the Hudson. Burgoyne was now in a position to bottle up the entire rebel army in Fort Ticonderoga and Mount Independence and capture all of them.

On July 2 Peters ordered Sherwood to go to General William Phillips' tent near Rattlesnake Hill for an assignment; a bateau was waiting to take him across the lake. Once over the water, Justus found the tent easily. With Phillips was another officer, restlessly pacing up and down the small space. Justus noticed his report lying on the general's cot. Phillips introduced him to the officer, Lieutenant William Twiss, of the Royal Engineers, who had been scouting around Rattlesnake Hill and was intrigued by the possibilities it offered. He wanted to mount two 12-pounder guns on top, and he was certain that both Ticonderoga and Mount Independence would be within their range. In fact, he told Justus, he thought it strange the rebels had neglected to fortify the hill.

"I fancy they think only a mountain goat can scale it," Twiss said, turning to Phillips.

"Where a goat can go a man can follow, and where a man can go he can drag a gun," the artillery officer replied.

Justus, who had reservations about a gun, assured the two officers that a man could get to the top. Phillips had three reports on the defences of the two rebel positions. One was from Dr. Smyth in Albany, another from Captain Samuel McKay, and Sherwood's. Smyth was still in Albany. McKay, who had recently joined Burgoyne, had been sent to the rear with his company to bring up supplies. Captain Sherwood, Phillips decided, would accompany Lieutenant Twiss. They were to find the best path for the guns.

Twiss agreed, a trifle haughtily, Justus thought, and the two officers left the tent. In short order Justus showed the engineer — his superior officer on the mission — the place where he had started his climb when preparing the report on Ticonderoga's defences in April. Together they scrambled upward, removing their coats and tying them round their waists. Gaining the summit they crouched low, using the underbrush as cover, edging forward until Twiss had a good view. Grudgingly he praised Sherwood, for the spot was perfect. This provincial had led him along a path out of sight of the enemy inside the forts. Once the guns were on top, the rebels would know what Twiss was about, but he wanted to give them as little advance warning as possible. Back down the hill slid the engineer and the one-time Green Mountain Boy.

As they parted, Twiss was issuing orders for oxen to drag the guns forward, and for axemen to start cutting a path up Rattlesnake Hill. Justus returned across the lake to his regiment, feeling that he had done more good in the last few hours than during the struggle to advance towards Mount Independence. For three days, as the Germans consolidated their position close to the sod and stockaded fortress, Justus could not keep his eyes off the top of Rattlesnake Hill. He tried to picture the axemen, the ropes and pulleys, the sweating soldiers heaving those lethal pieces of iron up that steep slope. At last, towards noon on the 5th, his watchfulness was rewarded; both guns were on top and the soldiers were moving logs to serve as carriages.

Late in the afternoon he heard the first boom and saw the blue smoke rising from the top of the hill. He longed to know what the rebels thought of Twiss' cleverness, proud of his own part in the business.[2]

As darkness fell, Justus settled down in his tent, fully clad, with orders to rise at three o'clock. Before the drums could sound a note he was aroused by orange light penetrating the white canvas tent. Outside, brushing sleep from heavy eyes, he beheld flames rising from Mount Independence. Soon everyone knew that the rebels had set the fire, and that Ty was empty. He grabbed his accoutrements and ordered his company to fall in.

From a deserter, Colonel Peters learned that General Arthur St. Clair, the rebel commander, was hurrying up Lake Champlain with his fleet, his troops fleeing overland through the New Hampshire Grants. St. Clair's orders from his superior, General Philip Schuyler in Albany, were to save the rebels' Army of the North to fight another day. The previous afternoon, Lieutenant Twiss' gunners were firing into his fleet and that was enough for St. Clair. With Fraser's vanguard blocking the entrance to Lake George, the rebel general had taken his fleet along the inferior waterway towards Skenesborough. The two 12-pounders atop Mount Defiance, as Twiss' gunners rechristened Rattlesnake Hill, had done their work well. When he heard the news from Peters, Justus was gratified. Beyond the handful who had encountered rebel patrols beforehand, Ticonderoga and Mount Independence had fallen without the loss of a man in Burgoyne's army.

The Queen's Loyal Rangers, King's Loyal Americans and the German troops occupied the charred ruins of Mount Independence, but Justus longed to be with the troops marching into Ty. This time, he thought there would be no looting spree such as had followed Ethan's capture of the fortress. British soldiers were professionals whose officers would keep them under control.

He did not have long to ponder. Brigadier Fraser arrived with part of his vanguard, and he wanted 300 Queen's Loyal Rangers to accompany him in pursuing the rebel army, because they knew the country.[3] Justus overheard Fraser telling Peters that the 24-pounders on Burgoyne's frigate *Royal George* had made short work of the log boom the rebels had strung across the lake, and the commander-in-chief was sailing after the rebel fleet.

The vanguard set a brisk pace, and before long the brigadier rode back to confer with Colonel Peters. He wanted a scouting party to go ahead, and Peters recommended that Captain Sherwood be given command of it.

He was to take some former Green Mountain Boys from his company and a party of Indians, to find out where the rebel army was. Some might be lying in ambush, and if not, Justus was to establish where the rebel rearguard might be posted.

Leading his party a few miles, Justus visited a friend, who told him that Seth Warner and his regiment might be at Hubbardtown. Indian scouts operating ahead confirmed this, reporting that the bulk of the rebel force was ahead of Warner. Satisfied that Warner's men were the rearguard, Justus began retracing his steps, when some Indian scouts appeared with four civilians. If he let them go, they might warn Seth Warner that he was lurking nearby. If possible, Fraser should surprise Warner. Such caution, and his natural urge to lead, made Sherwood a good soldier and an officer whose capabilities were coming to the attention of his superiors.

Late in the afternoon Justus' party, with the prisoners, rejoined Fraser, but this provincial officer had more to do before he could retire. When darkness fell that night of July 6, he led some of his men away from camp. If General Phillips thought it was too early to exchange the men he lost while scouting near Ty that spring, Justus would arrange one himself. Silently his little band approached the farmhouse of Elijah Kellogg. As Justus had once been dragged from his bed, so now was Mr. Kellogg.

From there, Justus went to the farm of Henry Keeler and repeated the operation. He chose these men because he knew them for insane rebels who were a threat to local loyalists. He instructed Mrs. Keeler to send a message to Seth Warner. Kellogg and Keeler could be exchanged for the men taken from his party near Ty. His two prizes secure, Justus led his men back to Fraser's camp.[4]

When the advance party was stirring at three o'clock in the morning, Justus discovered that one of the civilians captured the day before had escaped. Brigadier Fraser sent the other captives, including Kellogg and Keeler, under escort to Ticonderoga, where Burgoyne had left a garrison of the battalion companies of the 53rd Regiment under their lieutenant-colonel commandant,

Brigadier Watson Powell, and a detachment of German Troops. There, to his astonishment, Powell received a flag of truce from Seth Warner, and a prisoner exchange took place. Powell was impressed. When prisoner exchanges began in earnest, as they must, for Burgoyne was certain to lose some of his troops, this captain of provincials might be useful.

The next day Fraser sent Justus forward with a small party, to forage and bring back whatever supplies he could wrest from local farmers. The first homestead Justus chose belonged to Samuel Churchill. In an effort to make him reveal where he had hidden his flour, Justus had him tied to a tree, and with his best bluster threatened to set him aflame. Then in true Green Mountain fashion, he stood by praying that Churchill would not be stubborn, thinking of something less dire which he really would carry out if Churchill remained steadfast.

When Churchill gave in and told him where the flour was, Justus heaved a sigh of relief. Then he insisted that the Churchill family come with him. He could not afford to have anyone riding through the countryside warning others that he was in the vicinity, plundering farms. He continued on his mission, capturing more civilians after robbing their premises.[5] When he rejoined Fraser's advance party near Hubbardtown, large numbers of German soldiers were standing about. Reporting to Fraser and handing over his loot, Justus discovered that he had missed a battle.

Fraser's men had surprised some New Hampshire militiamen who had bivouacked without posting guards and were routing them when Seth Warner and his rebel Green Mountain Boys appeared. Warner almost had Fraser's flank turned, when the Baron von Riedesel arrived with reinforcements. When the blue coats hove into view, the Boys of Sherwood's former regiment ran away, but the casualties had been heavy for a minor encounter.

Reporting to Colonel Peters, Justus found that none of his company had been wounded. Lieutenant Carscallan was a good officer, and Justus prayed he would never lose him nor his followers to Colonel Pfister. At dawn on

July 8, the advance party turned back towards Lake Champlain. Fraser and von Riedesel did not have enough supplies to continue their pursuit of the Army of the North, and ordered a march to Burgoyne's new encampment.

Justus was bitterly disappointed. Surely supply wagons could have been sent after them. Besides, more provincials might have been used to forage for the food the advance party needed. He thought Fraser might have kept up the pressure on the rebel army until it surrendered. Sadly, he admitted that professional soldiers were a stodgy lot, and not involved in the life and death struggle that had overwhelmed the loyalists.

In sight of the lake the advance party turned south to catch up with Burgoyne. After leaving the garrison at Ticonderoga, Burgoyne followed the rebel fleet, which he found in flames, the crews nowhere to be seen. The commander-in-chief sailed on to Skenesborough, twenty kilometres south of Ty, and there the veterans of the Battle of Hubbardtown and Sherwood, the forager, hastened.

When Justus arrived, Skenesborough was surrounded by tents. Burgoyne was staying in the large fieldstone house that overlooked the village, as the guest of Philip Skene, the proprietor who owned the land for miles around. When the Green Mountain Boys captured the village two years before, Skene was sailing home after a visit to England, with a commission as commandant of Ticonderoga and Crown Point.[6]

Skene landed at Philadelphia, and was seized and transported to a prison in Connecticut. After a year in confinement he escaped and made his way to Canada. Now he was with the expedition as Burgoyne's chief adviser on local conditions. Justus suspected that Skene was a poor choice and his doubts were well founded. Colonel Peters said Skene was telling Burgoyne that the northern frontier was peopled by 'Friends of Government', as Tories called themselves. If Burgoyne took that landed gentleman seriously, he would be in for a shock. Hubbardtown had convinced Justus that the expedition might meet considerable resistance along the way, and he extended his estimate of the time Burgoyne would need to reach Albany.

Days passed, Justus wondering when Burgoyne would pack up and return to Ty for his ascent of Lake George. Finally he confronted Peters, who informed him with a grimace, that Burgoyne was having his troops build a road from Skenesborough to the Hudson, and had no intention of returning to Ticonderoga. Burgoyne feared that withdrawing to the fort might be construed as a retreat, which would dishearten the rank and file. Privately, Peters had another suspicion. Was Philip Skene guilty of persuading Burgoyne to build the road to have his property improved at the expense of the British army?

To Justus that explanation made more sense than the excuse that returning to Ty would be hard on morale. Skene was a damned rascal, Burgoyne a fool for being taken in. The best way to reach the Hudson was through Lake George, and the portage that already had a decent road. If the commander-in-chief knew what he was doing, he would have sent a vanguard along the better route to seize Fort Edward ahead of the rebels. The fleeing Army of the North had to use the longer, more difficult route by land through the New Hampshire Grants, and Burgoyne was throwing away an opportunity to put a strong detachment between the rebels and their base of supply in Albany.

Justus was alarmed that his cause might be going awry. He was familiar with the country where the troops were building that foolish road. It was filled with swamps over which long causeways of logs were required. Furthermore, he knew the value of a surprise attack. Ethan had used these tactics with great success in his many wolf hunts against New Yorkers. Pondering the situation, Justus tried to convince himself that Burgoyne could not fail. The commander-in-chief's strategy was making the expedition's task more difficult, with unnecessary sacrifice of lives.

Justus knew his own people, and he realized that rebels not yet in the Army of the North would come forward in ever greater numbers as the British and Germans neared their homes. With each day that Burgoyne dallied, the ragged army of rebel frontiersmen that opposed him must be growing larger.

Casting aside this gloomy prediction, Justus found some grounds for optimism. With each day's delay, scouts came in with more recruits for the Queen's Loyal Rangers. Men were arriving for the other units, although Colonel Ebenezer Jessup was not faring very well. His agents were recruiting in Albany County, where the rebels were massing, and loyalists had more difficulty leaving the area.[7]

Justus took advantage of the delay to do some recruiting himself. From friends, he discovered that the rebels' Army of the North reached Fort Edward on July 12, its lines of supply back to Albany intact. Another blow was the capture of four of his men while looking for recruits. Nevertheless his company now numbered 46 rank and file.

On July 23, Colonel Peters mustered the Queen's Loyal Rangers, which stood at 262 men, not including agents out looking for recruits. Peters had appointed Jeremiah French, Francis Hogel and David McFall as Sherwood's fellow captains. As the commander of the third company in the regiment, Justus was senior to them, but the second company was still reserved for a major of Peters' choosing. He hoped that an old friend and neighbour, Zadock Wright, would come and fill that appointment. After giving some thought to non-commissioned officers, Justus selected John Dulmage, German-speaking and three years his senior, as his first sergeant.

Thomas Sherwood and Elijah Bothum were looking for recruits, hoping to win commissions, while the colonel's son, John Peters Jr., fifteen years old, was the only ensign appointed thus far — contrived but not surprising. Peters had assigned his son enough recruits as a way of taking care of him.[8] Colonel Francis Pfister had three companies, while Daniel McAlpin had two. Ebenezer Jessup's corps stood at 172 men.[9]

An important part of each muster was paying the rank and file. On July 28, Justus drew 23 pounds 6 shillings and 8 pence from Peters for his men's service since June 25 — thirty days.[10] Peters assured him that as a captain he would receive 10 shillings a day, but he did not know when the money would be forthcoming. The rank and file had received New York currency, but Justus would be paid in the more valuable sterling.

Finally by July 26 the road was ready and the vanguard was ordered to march. To Justus' delight the Queen's Loyal Rangers were assigned to Brigadier Fraser instead of to General von Riedesel. Remembering the speed at which Fraser had marched towards Hubbardtown, Justus thought working under him would be a joy, but to his dismay, even Fraser now moved at a snail's pace. The vanguard was bringing too many heavy guns, more than would be required to reduce Fort Edward if the rebels made a stand there. The redcoats had constructed hundreds of two wheeled carts, but the entire army was short of draught animals. Burgoyne's plan to move the army by road seemed more dim-witted than ever.

Fraser posted the Queen's Loyal Rangers forward as his advance party and Justus found the countryside nearly deserted. General Schuyler, in command of the rebels' northern military department, had removed known loyalist families and lodged them in a barracks in Albany to prevent them giving aid to the British army, while rebel families had fled. The fields were bare of crops, and the cattle and other livestock had vanished. Clearly Schuyler intended Burgoyne to be dependent on his lengthening lines of supply stretching back to Fort St. Johns. When they neared Thomas Sherwood's farm, Justus gave his cousin permission to seek out his family, and he returned to report that his house, like the rest was deserted, his fields naked. Thomas was perturbed, but Justus was certain Seth Sherwood had taken Anna and the children somewhere for safety, and he probably had Thomas' livestock, too.

On July 30 the Queen's Loyal Rangers reached Fort Edward, and were soon joined by the rest of Fraser's vanguard. The village was deserted, and Justus realized that the Army of the North intended making a stand much closer to Albany, the base of supply. He wondered where Patrick Smyth, his loyal informer, had gone, and scouts informed him that his friend had been taken to gaol in Albany as Burgoyne's army marched south.[11] When the main body of the army arrived, Burgoyne settled himself in the Smyth house, the best one in the village.

Then Justus was appalled that there would be a further delay. Belatedly, Burgoyne admitted the folly of trying to bring all the heavy baggage and artillery by road, and he sent some of it back to Ticonderoga to be brought along Lake George. Two weeks might pass before the army could advance again — time Justus feared Burgoyne did not have. Autumn would soon be upon them and the troops had no winter clothing.

His company was now close to full strength, and Justus longed for the opportunity to strike back at the rebels who had wronged him so shamefully. Then a party of Indians came into the village and the whole camp was thunderstruck with horror. One of them displayed a scalp of long blond hair. Lieutenant David Jones, of the King's Loyal Americans, recognized those tresses as belonging to his betrothed, Jane McRae. After questioning the Indians, his fears were realized. In due course Jane's body was found. Burgoyne's Indians were out of control, marauding in the woods, caring not whether families they attacked were rebel or loyalist.

Heartsick, Justus wished Burgoyne would send all his native allies back to Canada. They were doing more harm than good, driving into the ranks of the rebels many who were wavering over which side to choose. He was certain the rebels would be quick to use the murder of Jane McRae to their advantage, ignoring the fact that she was engaged to a hated Tory officer. Thank heaven Sarah and his children, and the rest of her family, were safe in New Haven.

While he was trying to recover his balance after this tragedy, Colonel Peters told him that the Queen's Loyal Rangers would be going on an expedition in the course of which, Burgoyne hoped, the regiment would be brought to full strength.

Chapter 4

Bennington Bloodbath

Because of the supply situation, General Burgoyne decided to send a detachment of his troops across the Green Mountains to the Connecticut Valley. This expedition would be commanded by Lieutenant-Colonel Friedrich Baum, who would lead 500 German troops, including those clumsy Brunswick Dragoons, 300 of Peters' Queen's Loyal Rangers, all of Pfister's Loyal Volunteers, and one company of British riflemen led by Captain Alexander Fraser, the brigadier's nephew. Baum's purpose was threefold: to requisition horses for the dragoons, to forage for provisions, and to obtain recruits to complete Peters' corps.[1]

That foraging might be incompatible with inducing recruits to come forward did not enter the commander-in-chief's head. Philip Skene, who would be going on this foray, had assured Burgoyne that the land was occupied by loyal colonials. Such would welcome an invasion by foreign troops, helping themselves to precious horses and the food they were storing against the coming winter. Peters suggested that not less than 3,000 men should be sent, but Burgoyne informed him that when he wanted advice he would ask for it.

Justus grimaced at the prospect of serving again with the Germans, and Peters was no more enthusiastic. Both men would have preferred to see the task assigned to Brigadier Fraser, but Burgoyne's decision was a matter of etiquette. Since the Germans were encamped to the east of the British, Burgoyne could not offend the

Baron von Riedesel by sending his redcoats across the German position so that they could reach the New Hampshire Grants. Loyalists were another matter, especially the Queen's Loyal Rangers and the Loyal Volunteers; both corps had been recruited mainly among New Englanders in Charlotte and Gloucester Counties. They knew the country, and von Riedesel had requested that provincials be Baum's vanguard, together with some Indian scouts.

In preparation, Colonel Peters ordered Justus to lead a party to obtain intelligence on the strength of the rebels at various posts, and to bring back as many recruits as possible. Peters was convinced that Baum would not have nearly enough men in his detachment, and he was sending most of his agents in search of volunteers, praying they would return in time to join him on the march. On August 1, Justus left with six men, all in their civilian dress. In his absence, Garret Miller, a quartermaster sergeant for the regiment, reported that of Captain Sherwood's company, 11 were absent on missions, 5 were sick in quarters, and 4 were prisoners of the rebels.[2] Edward Carscallan was out after recruits and he brought back 20 men, some for Sherwood, the rest for Pfister, news Justus heard at a safe house near Arlington.

His host told him that Seth Warner, with his Green Mountain Boys, was at Manchester, and Justus' onetime band of roughnecks was now part of General Washington's Continental Army. Justus went on to the vicinity of Bennington, where he found that the rebels had a huge stock-pile of supplies, guarded by only 400 militiamen. He sent a courier to suggest that Burgoyne stage a quick raid on Bennington without delay.[3]

Meanwhile, Colonels Baum, Peters and Pfister, were about to leave Fort Edward, but when Sherwood's message reached him, Burgoyne, whose orders were for Baum to march towards Manchester, changed his instructions. Baum was to raid Bennington, and he should march as far as Arlington, and, 'take post there until the detachment of Provincials under the Command of Captain Sherwood shall join you from the southward'.

After sending his message to Burgoyne, Justus continued keeping his ear to the ground while gathering recruits. He went north to the Bothum farm to get provisions from his father-in-law's slaves. There, to his surprise, he found Elijah Bothum Sr., who had come from New Haven to reassure himself that his property was safe. He chided Justus mildly for his indiscretion last April. Sarah was carrying their third child, and Justus was overcome with remorse. He could only murmur that he was sorry, but after a winter without his wife he was desperate, and he loved her very much. Asking Elijah to forgive him Justus resumed his scout. For reasons he could not fathom, hundreds of rebel reinforcements were pouring into Bennington.

On August 12 his party met Peters and his Queen's Loyal Rangers leading Baum's column, on the road a few miles north of Cambridge. A look of relief swept over Peters' countenance at the sight of his senior captain. He introduced Justus to Major Zadock Wright, who had finally taken up his appointment, but his face darkened when he described the way the Germans were behaving. Baum's men marched at the rate of "one mile an hour", ranks meticulously dressed, a band playing most of the time, dragging two brass 3-pounder cannon, followed by a tumbrel full of powder and a train of supply wagons. Baum thought he was travelling light, for he had not brought tents.

Uneasily Justus enquired whether the expedition's destination was Bennington. Upon Peters' assurance that Burgoyne had changed his orders, Justus' heart fluttered. He admitted that he had suggested a quick raid, but now it was too late. Baum's leisurely and noisy march had warned the rebels, and they were reinforcing Bennington. Reporting this to Colonel Baum, with John Dulmage as his interpreter, Justus received orders to go immediately with 80 men in quest of supplies. He set out with his party, and when he had acquired several carts, wagons, horses to pull them, plus a fair number of cattle, he turned back to meet the expedition.

This time, opposition marshalled, and his party was fired upon. In the scuffling, Justus' men took five prisoners, but none of his side was scratched. Late the following day, he found Baum still at Cambridge, having marched only a short distance in the twenty-four hours Justus had been absent. From the prisoners he discovered that General John Stark, of New Hampshire, had marched into Bennington with 1,800 rebel militiamen. Seth Warner was marching from Manchester with a small detachment of his regiment, and the main body of his Green Mountain Boys was to follow as soon as possible. Colonel Baum dispatched a rider to inform Burgoyne that he would need reinforcements before taking on the rebels at Bennington.

On August 14 several small parties of loyalists joined the expedition along the road. Before long the Queen's Loyal Rangers and Loyal Volunteers far out stripped the German column. Peters asked Justus to go back and see if he could persuade the Germans to hurry, as he had done many times, praying that Sherwood, who knew what was happening, might have more effect. Taking Sergeant John Dulmage as his interpreter, Justus obeyed. They found Baum a mile behind, and while Dulmage was relaying Peters' message a party of men in frontier dress, with white paper in their hats, suddenly appeared. Philip Skene shouted to the men to hold their fire. These men, too, were loyalists. Unable to restrain himself Justus called Skene a blockhead, but his words were drowned when the newcomers opened fire, and one casualty was Skene's horse.[5] When the smoke cleared, the rebels had vanished.

An unnerved Colonel Baum promised Dulmage that he would speed up the pace, and the two loyalists returned to the Queen's Loyal Rangers. Upon enquiring of Peters, Justus learned that the provincials had not received any unwelcome visitors. The rebels had let the spread-out loyalists pass by in order to concentrate on the closely packed German column. The rangers reached White Creek, where the rebels had destroyed a bridge. Waiting for the arrival of the Germans, Peters, joined by Pfister, had their men repair the damage. The entire expedition marched as far as the Walloomsac River, seven kilometres from Bennington, and they found the bridge there intact.

Here Baum, who had arrived soon after his provincials, decided to dig in and await his reinforcements, but he made the fatal mistake of scattering his force, which Justus viewed with alarm. Baum selected a hill around which the Walloomsac River wound for his Germans, with an outpost of Brunswick grenadiers and Captain Fraser's marksmen halfway down the slope, and more regulars at the bridge. He divided his provincials in half. Peters, with Wright and most of the Queen's Loyal Rangers, were placed in the rear on the road from Cambridge. Pfister's men were sent forward across the Walloomsac with orders to build a redoubt, but the Loyal Volunteers only had 200 men. To placate those in Sherwood's company who wanted to serve under Pfister, Peters assigned his third company, now at full strength, to serve with the Loyal Volunteers at the redoubt.[6]

Justus noticed an old cabin near the bridge, and after eyeing the storm clouds creeping across the sky, he decided to station some of his company within it. He would remain at the redoubt, regardless of the elements. He arranged for a few of his men to be with him in shifts, while all had orders to quit the cabin and join him at the first sign of an enemy approach.

During the night of August 14, heavy rain fell, and the downpour continued all the following day. The Germans and loyalists tried to pile earth on their barricades, but it slithered away. Justus and the men on duty at the redoubt huddled together in misery, rivulets of water pouring from the bicornes of the men in uniform. Like Justus, some were in civilian clothes, because they had been scouting, or were recruits acquired after the expedition left Fort Edward. Meanwhile, the Indians who had come as scouts vanished, which pleased Justus. Loyalists were capable of being the eyes and ears of Baum's force.

August 16 dawned sunny but damp, and Justus discovered that the cartridges in his men's pouches were wet. Fortunately the powder in Baum's tumbrel was dry, as was a supply of cartridge paper from the wagons. The troops were busy in the early hours making fresh ammunition, ever on the alert for signs of a rebel approach. The men had breakfast, and at nine o'clock the rebels attacked from three sides. New Hampshire militia came towards the German position on the hill from the northwest. General Stark, with the main body of New Hamp-

Battle of Bennington August 16 1777

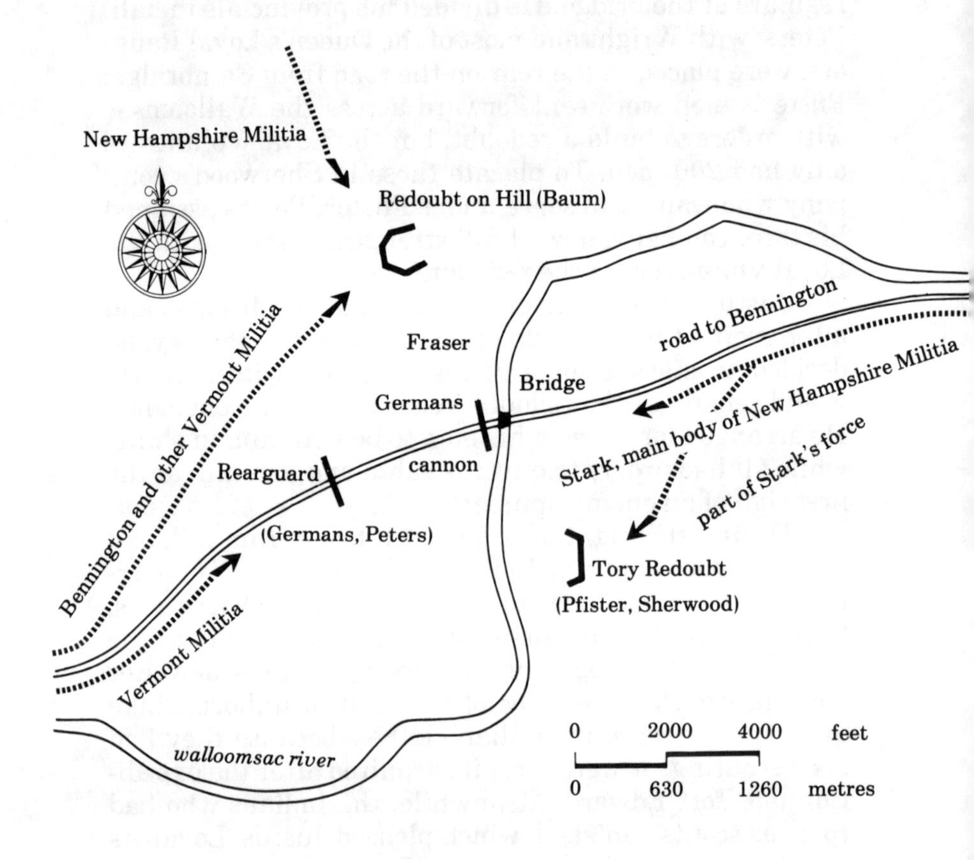

shiremen, moved in from the east towards Pfister's redoubt. Meanwhile, a larger force of Bennington militia had crossed the Walloomsac River on a ford farther downstream, and had circled round to attack Baum's Germans on the hill, out of sight of Fraser's riflemen and the Brunswick grenadiers.

Justus could not tell what was happening; smoke from firelocks and Baum's cannon obscured everything. The men fired and reloaded, missing most of Sherwood's and Pfister's orders as the cannon boomed. Then Robert Leake, Pfister's senior captain, shouted that his colonel was mortally wounded. Justus moaned. This was no way to be fighting when there was plenty of cover only a few yards off in the woods. He ordered everyone to abandon the redoubt and shelter behind trees. Captain Leake agreed to let Sherwood command, and all took cover, firing hour after hour of that fateful day.

Suddenly he heard a thunderous explosion, and Elijah Bothum, hands as powder-blackened as Justus' own, came running to report that the rebels had blown up Baum's tumbrel of powder. Like Pfister, Baum was mortally wounded, and but for what each man carried in his cartridge case, the Germans and provincials were out of ammunition.

Around four o'clock, with Leake in agreement, Justus ordered a retreat. He led the way because Leake, a former British regular, was a New Yorker who did not know the country. With the help of Lieutenant Carscallan, Ensign Wilson and Sergeant Dulmage, Justus collected his company, while Leake marshalled Pfister's survivors. Justus avoided the main battlefield and led all the loyalists through the woods, joining the road "a mile away", from the carnage. "One more mile on", they found out what had happened to the reinforcements. The road was littered with dead men in blue, and some abandoned field guns. In spite of the grisly scenes of the dead and dying, both at the Walloomsac River and now, Justus had to think of the living. His belly was numb with hunger, and he looked in vain for supply wagons, but found none. Stoically the survivors marched up the road, many of them walking wounded.

At Cambridge Justus met Colonel Peters and a detachment of his men, waiting to remove the bridge when he thought those lucky enough to be alive had joined him. Peters was limping from a ball that had grazed his foot, and he had a bayonet wound in his chest, bestowed by an old schoolfellow, a cousin of his wife. Justus ordered his men to rest, and taking a long drink from a stream, he sat down to hear how Peters and the rest of the regiment had fared on their part of the battlefield.

Peters had retreated earlier than Sherwood, after horrendous losses. More than 200 Queen's Loyal Rangers were dead, wounded or now prisoners of the rebels, receiving God knew what harsh treatment. Only a handful of men left the scene of the disaster with him, and while Major Wright and John Jr. were safe, his other three captains were missing. Assessing the situation, Sherwood's company had fared much better than the others because he had taken his men into the woods. From the sixty men that he had at the start of the day, forty-six were left.[7]

All told, four lieutenants and three ensigns were safe, and some seventy rank and file. As the shadows lengthened, Captain Fraser arrived with the survivors of his company, and a few blue-coated Germans joined them. Then, fairly certain no more would follow, Peters ordered some of the able-bodied men to dismantle the bridge. The night was clear as the provincials and regulars continued their march up the road, until they were too exhausted to go on.

With Peters, Wright and Sherwood walked Captains Fraser and Leake, deploring Baum's tactics that had led to the slaughter. Fraser felt that the force should have been deployed closer together, where fire power might have saved the troops until the reinforcements arrived. Peters and Sherwood disagreed. Had the men been deployed in the woods, more would have survived. Peters, who had withdrawn early enough to meet the reinforcements as they were being attacked by the rebels, was convinced that Colonel Heinrich von Breymann, in command of them, had been in no hurry to reach Baum. In any case, the road had been a quagmire during the heavy rain, and the reinforcements had not been able to make good time. In the attack on von Breymann, Peters had recognized Seth Warner, and it was his regiment, the rebel Green Mountain Boys, that had dispersed the German column.

When the first light streaked the sky, the survivors struggled on, unable to find any food because the country had been stripped bare during Baum's march southward. Mercifully they did not have to walk all the way to Fort Edward. Before Peters had set out with Baum, Burgoyne had ordered his army to march to Fort Miller, thirteen kilometres closer, where he would be encamped when the incursion into the Green Mountains was over. The fifty-eight kilometre trek to Burgoyne's new encampment seemed the longest walk of Sherwood's life. The reasons for the disaster preoccupied all the men as they dragged themselves along. The defeat at Bennington, they decided, was because of Baum's ignorance of local conditions, the ponderous performance of the Germans, who had no idea of how to conduct a hit and run operation, and the cunning of John Stark, a ranger officer in the Seven Years' War.

Justus voiced his agreement, and even Captain Fraser was in accord. The provincials and his riflemen would have fared better on their own. Light troops — and no brass band — might have reached Bennington before the rebels were alerted. Sadly, as he arrived at Fort Miller, what Justus remembered best about Baum's column was the lumbering Brunswick Dragoons, each carrying a halter in case he found a horse. Now most of those comrades in arms, unsuitable as they were, lay dead on the hill above the Walloomsac River. Worse still, so were many of Sherwood's own kind, red-coated provincials whose mangled bodies were sprawled in Pfister's redoubt.

His only solace was that he had saved most of his own men. All told, he soon learned that 1,500 men had been sent towards Bennington — Baum's 500 men, von Breymann's 500 reinforcements, and some 500 provincials. Of these, 1,220 were lost at Bennington.[8]

Chapter 5

Saratoga

At Fort Miller, Brigadier Simon Fraser received the remnants of the Queen's Loyal Rangers kindly, assuring them that they were not to blame. He ordered the wounded Peters to rest in his own bed until tents could be erected for the men who had returned with him. Before Justus had recovered from the shock of the battle and the drain of the walk to the British camp, he discovered unrest in his company. On August 22 Lieutenant Edward Carscallan and his two sons, as well as Ensign John Wilson and most of the German-speaking Irishmen, in all twenty-five officers and men, were asking permission to transfer out of the Queen's Loyal Rangers and serve under Captain Samuel McKay, who had taken command of Pfister's corps.

One exception gratified Justus. Sergeant John Dulmage, so valuable in communicating with the Germans, was standing by him, although David Dulmage, his brother, and Paul Heck, his brother-in-law, were among those who wanted to leave. If they did, Justus would have only nineteen men on his muster roll, and of these, four were prisoners of war, one had deserted, and another was with the bateaumen because he was unfit for duty with Fraser's vanguard. If the dissenters transferred to McKay, Justus would have only thirteen men on duty with him at Fort Miller. Questioning them, they admitted that McKay had told them they could be discharged sooner if they joined him, although their dislike of Yankees was the real reason for their desire to leave the Queen's Loyal Rangers.[1]

Justus confronted John Peters, who summoned the would be defectors before him. With Justus standing by, he said they could remain with the regiment or face arrest. To Sherwood's chagrin all chose the latter, and were marched off to the guardhouse. He appealed to Burgoyne and was granted an interview in what locals called 'the Duer House', where the commander-in-chief was staying. He found the general sympathetic but unbending. Justus explained:

> the General said it was never his intention that they should leave me. . .. Desired me to make myself Fast and said that I should have Employ and Receive Capt. Pay wheather I had men or not I was obliged to put up with the wrong done me.

Burgoyne felt he could do no less, for he had received many reports of Captain Sherwood's valour. Writing his own account, the general noted that Sherwood was forward in every service of danger to the end of the campaign.[2] Finding Lieutenant Carscallan and the others adamant, Burgoyne ordered them sent to Captain McKay as the most expedient way of making them return to duty. With rations so short he could not afford to have men gobbling up food when they were not doing any work.

Grieving and angry, Justus returned to the tents where his regiment was encamped. There Colonel Peters, irate at losing so many men to that scoundrel McKay, promoted John Dulmage to be Sherwood's lieutenant, and assigned Joseph Moss to replace John Wilson as the ensign. The Queen's Loyal Rangers had been decimated at Bennington and further depleted by losses to other units. Summing up the situation, Peters told Justus that before Bennington the regiment had had, in addition to himself as the lieutenant-colonel, Major Wright, four captains, two lieutenants, two ensigns and 311 rank and file. Of these, 111 all ranks had been killed or captured in the battle, leaving him with 200 officers and men once the stragglers reached Fort Miller. At the fort Peters discovered that Gershom French, Captain Jeremiah French's brother, had arrived there on August 16 with ninety recruits and three other officers, all of whom had received appointments from General Sir William Howe. That made a total of 294 men, but with the loss of those sent to Captain McKay, and others who had been relegated to the bateau service bringing up supplies and protecting the route back to Fort Ticonderoga, Peters was left with only 172 effectives.[3]

Of some consolation was a general order from Burgoyne on August 25, by which all officers of provincials were to draw the same pay as the King's regulars. Justus received 61 pounds sterling for his services from June 25 to October 24 — 122 days at 10 shillings per day.[4]

By the 26th, Burgoyne had sufficient supplies brought forward and he ordered the vanguard to break camp and resume the southward march down the Hudson. Ponderously the entire army moved, dragging too much artillery, Justus thought. He counted no less than forty-two guns, many of them 24-pounders. Time was running out and the nights were growing chilly. In spite of food shortages, the women who had come from Fort St. Johns remained with the expedition, and their ranks had been reinforced at Fort Edward. On August 14, the eve of the slaughter at Bennington, the Baroness von Riedesel had driven into the village with her daughters, aged six, three and one year, and an entourage of nurses, servants and baggage. The Baron had written from Skenesborough informing her that the country was quiet and it would be safe for her to join him. So it was, Justus reflected, then.[5]

As August drew to a close, news arrived of another setback to Burgoyne's aspirations. Colonel Barry St. Leger, in command of the small expedition through the Mohawk Valley, could not reduce rebel-occupied Fort Stanwix, about 170 kilometres west of Albany. With his regulars, Sir John Johnson and his men, Iroquois warriors and loyalists led by Major John Butler, St. Leger had withdrawn to Oswego to await the arrival of heavy guns from Fort Niagara. Burgoyne sent him orders to abandon the Mohawk Valley venture and come to reinforce the army on the Hudson River. He also sent urgent appeals to Sir Henry Clinton, in command at New York City, to dispatch what troops he could spare northward towards Albany.

Each day refugees arrived at the British camp, to be

sent on to Fort St. Johns, where Sir Guy Carleton's officers would make arrangements for their welfare. Among them came Paul Heck's wife, Barbara, driving a wagon loaded with five small children and a large grandfather clock. Paul was one of the men who had defected from Sherwood's company and joined Captain McKay.

By September 13, the Queen's Loyal Rangers again with Brigadier Fraser's vanguard, Justus and his men crossed a temporary bridge built by Lieutenant William Twiss, the engineer. Now they were on the west bank of the Hudson above Saratoga, and when every man and piece of equipment belonging to Burgoyne's army had joined them, the bridge was removed. Now retreat meant handing the rebels a handsome gift of heavy artillery. Their fate was Albany or surrender. Again, as on the march to Fort Edward, Justus found the countryside bare of anything that could be of value to the British expedition. From scouts Fraser had sent towards Albany, Justus learned that General Philip Schuyler had been blamed for the loss of Forts Ticonderoga and Mount Independence. General Horatio Gates, a one time major of British regulars who had served under Burgoyne, had been given command of the rebels' Army of the North, but Schuyler remained in command of the military department in Albany. He had made sure that the British force would be entirely dependent on the long lines of supply stretching back to Fort St. Johns.

Their dwindling provisions in bateaux, the army marched down the Hudson Valley, a long height of land to the right. In his red coat, Justus felt dangerously conspicuous. The regulars were puzzled by the lack of opposition, but Justus was not fooled. The rebels were waiting on the heights for the right moment to strike with effect. Then parties of rebels began appearing to fire a few rounds, answered by Justus, who led his company in small skirmishes that helped chase them away.

At night, the enemy began launching small raids against the margins of the British and German encampments. With food not plentiful, parties of foragers left camp without permission, sometimes never to return. When a party of thirty regulars was captured by the rebels, Burgoyne ordered that any man caught leaving camp would be denied a soldier's rights. Instead of a firing party, he would be hanged like a common criminal. Justus, who had led parties himself when hunger drove him to it, admitted that the risk was now too great, both from within and without.

On the afternoon of September 18, Burgoyne halted his army, now strung out along the Hudson forty kilometres north of Albany. In the lull Justus and the other officers of the Queen's Loyal Rangers enquired of Colonel Peters what was to happen next. From scouts Peters had learned that the enemy was encamped five kilometres ahead, on high ground overlooking the Hudson at a place called Bemis Heights. Then the colonel received orders from Brigadier Fraser for his regiment to make camp. Burgoyne intended to attack the rebel position at first light.

As September 19 dawned, fog blanketed the landscape. While waiting for the mist to lift Burgoyne divided his army into three columns. When the visibility allowed, von Reidesel began his march along the Hudson, while Burgoyne and Fraser marched their columns up on the heights, moving due west. At an open valley Burgoyne and the men of his centre split from Fraser's right wing and turned south down this valley. Fraser directed the Queen's Loyal Rangers to follow a small party of Indians onward towards the west, and to send scouts to report any sign of the rebels. Then the brigadier rode back to the head of his regulars.

The rangers spread out in three lines of widely spaced men, Peters' company followed by Major Wright's, and then Sherwood's. On they marched until they heard the boom of cannon from below them and, breaking into a clearing Justus beheld smoke rising. Fraser, with a small escort, rode in shouting orders to follow him with all speed. Peters ordered a close formation and his men jogged after the brigadier, the regulars close behind them. Burgoyne had engaged the rebels in overwhelming numbers at Freeman's farm, and had ordered Fraser to come and reinforce him. Down the slope the Queen's Loyal Rangers ran, keeping right behind Fraser. Through the woods they dashed, deafened by the noise of the guns.

Justus saw Fraser astride his horse, waving his sword and bellowing at Peters to place his men on the flank. The regulars ran past the Queen's Loyal Rangers and formed into tight lines, firing their volleys in support of Burgoyne, while Peters led his men and some Indians into the woods, picking off rebels who were trying to turn the British flank. Justus and his company aimed at men in frontier dress or the beige, gray or blue coats of men in the Army of the North.

They found many opportunities to skirmish, for small parties of rebels were trying to reach the rear of Burgoyne's lines. Then suddenly the firing ceased and Captain Alexander Fraser came riding through the woods ordering all the provincials to come to the battlefield. The rebels had taken to their heels and Burgoyne controlled Freeman's farm.

Arriving with his company Justus was grieved but hardly surprised to discover that many of the officers, mounted on horses, gorgets flashing in the sun, had fallen. Such offered frontier riflemen targets they could not miss. Burgoyne was proclaiming a victory, but Justus suspected that the battle statistics were not impressive. Darkness fell as the army waited for the return of the rebels. The men lay beside their arms, listening for any signs of a pending attack until dawn.

After touring the field with Colonel Peters and Major Wright, Justus counted 57 Queen's Loyal Rangers among the dead.[6] Several were his own men and he ordered a detail to bury them. Once all the dead had been counted and the toll of prisoners taken, Burgoyne had lost 600 men while another 200 had been captured; the rebel losses were 65 killed, 300 wounded, some of whom were now prisoners. Justus and his fellow provincial officers were dumbfounded. A few more such victories and Burgoyne would not have an army.

Next, Burgoyne ordered the troops to dig in and build barricades, despite the fact that the land around Freeman's field was an exposed position where rebel snipers would have a heyday. While his men were starting on a barricade, Justus faced the truth. The rebels were little more than thirty kilometres from Albany, their source of supply. Burgoyne's lines now stretched nearly

350 kilometres back to Fort St. Johns. The British expedition was doomed. Burgoyne should abandon his heavy artillery while he still had time and withdraw to Ticonderoga. After the losses at Bennington and Freeman's farm, the rebel army must now outnumber the British force. If Burgoyne surrendered, Justus and all the other provincials were as good as dead. His only salvation was desertion, unthinkable for he was an honourable man.

September 20 dawned foggy and this time the mist did not lift. The 21st was sunny, disturbed by sporadic bursts of firing from the trees around the British encampment. The other provincials heard that Burgoyne had sent Joseph Bettys, of McAlpin's unit, south in search of news of Sir Henry Clinton. Bettys was from Ballstown, north of Schenectady. A member of the rebel militia, he was captured while serving with Benedict Arnold's fleet in October of 1776. Wearied of life as a prisoner of war, Bettys offered his services and McAlpin vouched for him. Justus thought Bettys a buccaneer, but if anyone could get through the rebel lines that man was Joe Bettys.[7]

On October 4 Bettys returned, and reported that Sir Henry Clinton was moving north, with a small force but only as far as Forts Montgomery and Clinton, near the mouth of the Hudson. All Sir Henry could do was try and lure away some of the swarm of rebels then menacing Burgoyne's army by staging a diversion against these forts: one named, Justus learned, after the general's own first cousin, George Clinton, the rebel governor of New York State. Justus thought of his own family, his uncles Seth and Adiel, zealous rebels, all their sons except Thomas on the rebel side. Sir Henry Clinton, too, came from a family divided by rebellion.

Three days after Bettys' return, Colonel Peters received orders to prepare his remaining rangers for a reconnaissance near the rebel position at Bemis Heights. With 1,500 men and two 12-pounder guns, Burgoyne would lead the attack from his centre. Brigadier Fraser, with companies of light infantry and the remaining provincials not bringing up supplies, was to move by secret paths through the woods behind the rebels' position and engage them from the rear, to prevent too much strength being thrown against the centre of the British line. Again, Justus found himself close to the front, with Fraser behind the Queen's Loyal Rangers at the head of his regulars. They had not gone far when Peters received orders to turn back. The enemy had broken through Burgoyne's line, and the men of the 24th Regiment — Fraser's own — were keeping a path open for their commanding officer's men to regain the British camp at Freeman's farm. In the headlong dash Justus noticed Fraser, bleeding from a wound in his stomach, being held on his horse.

Towards dusk the Queen's Loyal Rangers and the other provincials were sent to reinforce Colonel von Breymann — the officer who had been leading the reinforcements near Bennington — at a redoubt on the north side of the British camp. The Germans were under attack by Kentuckian Daniel Morgan and his corps of riflemen, and a few snipers of provincials might help turn the tide. As night fell the rebels overran the men at von Breymann's redoubt. Justus was ordering his men back within the camp when he felt hot iron pierce his thigh and he staggered and lost his balance. Lieutenant John Dulmage, swimming before his eyes, aided by a German soldier, was lifting him from the redoubt. As the second Battle of Freeman's Farm was ending, Dulmage, aided by men from the company, carried Justus past Burgoyne's own headquarters to the hospital tents on the north side of the camp, near the bank of the Hudson where the provision bateaux were tied up.[8]

The hospital was a madhouse of shrieking men, surgeons sawing shattered limbs on tables slimy with blood. Dulmage found an empty straw palliasse, and joined by Thomas Sherwood and Elijah Bothum, both very alarmed, they laid Justus down gently. With a knife his lieutenant cut away the breeches from around the bloody hole. In his agony Justus heard John say that he had stopped a musket ball but the bone was intact. Elijah brought a tumbler full of rum, which Justus sipped while awaiting a surgeon to attend to him. Dulmage left to look after the company, while Thomas and Elijah sat with Justus and held him steady until the surgeon had extracted the ball. With teeth clenched, Justus wondered why the rum was doing so little good.

Throughout the night Justus lay comforted by more doses of rum. In the morning Thomas Sherwood came in, and on asking about Brigadier Fraser, Justus was saddened to learn that he had died before dawn at the house where the Baroness von Riedesel was staying. The army's present predicament was not Fraser's doing. After a moment's silence Thomas reported that Burgoyne had ordered a withdrawal up the Hudson. The vanguard was leaving, although rain teemed down, beating on the walls of the tent. Outside the road was a sea of mud, guns towed by emaciated horses and oxen, pushed by men who had scarcely the strength to walk, let alone salvage the artillery. The most severely wounded men would be left behind, but John Dulmage had men making a litter for Justus. All refused to forsake their captain.

Early on the morning of the 9th, Dulmage, Thomas and Elijah carried Justus, praying that he would have the strength to reach Ticonderoga and the garrison Burgoyne had left there. The rest of the company in command of Ensign Moss had set out with the first wave of Burgoyne's rearguard, trudging through the mud after the rest of the army. Twelve kilometres to the north they found the army halted at the village of Saratoga, the troops digging in. After the retreat under such appalling conditions, Burgoyne had decided they could go no farther.

When they reached Saratoga, John Dulmage, Thomas and Elijah took Justus to the newly pitched hospital tents and found him another pallet. There an anxious Colonel Peters visited him. Burgoyne was ordering his provincials to escape in small groups and try to reach Ticonderoga, for he was fearful he might not be able to protect them at the inevitable surrender. Many had already left, but Peters was hoping that Sherwood and ten privates who had also been wounded might be able to march soon.

On the 14th, Peters visited Justus again. The colonel had procured written permission from Burgoyne to remove the Queen's Loyal Rangers, for the rebels would slaughter them after the capitulation. While others had left, Peters decided to seek the permission in writing lest superior officers he might encounter on the way to Ticonderoga consider his men deserters. Justus could walk a little, but a long march was out of the question; his wound was healing slowly owing to inadequate food and the rawness of the weather.

Sorrowing, Peters told him that the Queen's Loyal Rangers were now reduced to 62 all ranks. At the second battle around Freeman's farm, 80 more had been killed or captured.[9] Also, 24 had been discharged, two had died and two had deserted. All told, in the course of the campaign, Peters' officers and agents had recruited 643 men, more than full strength for a regiment, although so many had been lost. Peters would try, on the basis of total numbers, to have all the officers' commissions signed.

Peters was about to set out with 34 men, Major Wright and John Jr. The other able-bodied men had already left with Lieutenant Dulmage, although he had been unwilling to leave Justus. The colonel, too, was bereft at abandoning any Queen's Loyal Rangers, but he held out one note of hope to his doomed senior captain. General Phillips had told him Burgoyne and his officers would rather die than hand over a single provincial to the mercy of the rebels.

Ebenezer Jessup and his two brothers, Edward and Joseph, were going to remain with Burgoyne. Some King's Loyal Americans had left, but the Jessups had kept a detachment of volunteers. These men were running bateaux of supplies past General John Stark and an army of New Hampshiremen who had moved in from the north to intercept the retreating army, and still had useful work to do.

Justus bade Peters farewell, limping out of the tent to watch him on his way, appalled at what he saw around him. The whole camp stank. Many animals that had died for want of forage lay where they had fallen. Men had scarcely the strength to bury their own dead. Feeling utterly depressed, Justus returned to the tent to await the next news of Burgoyne's plans. As the hours dragged by, a long rejected Puritan doctrine helped sustain him. God had placed him on this earth for a set purpose and predestined time. If his time had come he should accept his fate with resignation. Yet he resolved to escape if any means came his way, and Peters had told him that Burgoyne intended to protect his provincials.

The day after Peters left, Justus was startled by the unexpected appearance of Elijah Bothum. He had set out with John Dulmage, but had turned back because he could never look Sarah in the eye if he deserted his brother-in-law. He told Justus that the staff officers had accompanied Burgoyne to the new encampment of the rebels, to the south, to discuss surrender terms with General Horatio Gates. Justus pictured Gentleman Johnny treating with a man who had once been under his command, but after his poor performance Burgoyne deserved the humiliation. Justus felt sorrow only for the tragic souls who were dead or dying because of poor generalship. Soon Edward Jessup came to see him with news that the provincials were to be protected under what Burgoyne called the Saratoga Convention, because words like capitulation and surrender offended him.

All persons were to be regarded as British subjects, and none were to be treated as traitors to the Continental Congress.[10] The British and German regulars were to march to Boston where they would embark on transport vessels for Britain. All would be prisoners of war on parole, ineligible for future service in America. The provincial rank and file were to sign paroles to take no further part in the hostilities, after which they would be escorted to Fort Ticonderoga under a flag of truce and handed over to Brigadier Powell. Most of the women and children had already left for that post.

The provincials who would march to the surrender ceremony the following morning would carry muskets. All were officially privates and eligible for parole because Burgoyne had never signed any officers' commissions. If he had, Edward explained, the officers would have been held until prisoner exchanges could take place, which might have been a long time since the rebels had so many more prisoners than the British. Grateful for the reprieve Justus decided to attend the surrender ceremonies.

On the morning of October 17, he washed, dressed in his shabby uniform, and joined the other able-bodied provincials for the march to the village where Horatio Gates and his officers waited. He could have stayed in the hospital tent, but if he had to face any of his former associates from the Green Mountains he intended to be standing on his own two feet. He did not want his enemies to know how bunged up he was.

The provincials formed two companies, Ebenezer Jessup leading the first, Justus the second. With Ebenezer went his brothers, the King's Loyal Americans, and the remnants of Captain Daniel McAlpin's men. None of Samuel McKay's who were fit to march had been left behind, for the scoundrel had cleared out the moment Burgoyne had given the order. Samuel Adams and a few of his men who had not escaped joined the company Justus was leading. The two companies followed after the regulars into Saratoga, where General Gates and his officers stood in front of an inn, the rebel troops lined up along the road, a band playing 'Yankee Doodle'. By the time it was his turn to lay down the musket he carried, Justus' strength was spent.

Thus far the rebels had been quiet, standing beside the captured army's route. Then some of them recognized the Jessups and a rumble ran through the crowd. This was mild compared with the volley of abuses and insults that arose when some Green Mountain Boys recognized Sherwood. They rushed forward shouting his name, and Benedict Arnold was calling for a hangman's rope.

General Gates, the one time British officer, would not allow a breach of the rules of war, and he dispatched men he trusted to guard the provincials and escort them to a safe place. Through all the hubbub Justus tried to steady himself, knees weak, body trembling. His worst thought was that someone might construe his wobbliness as fear. Heaven forbid! Justus was not afraid of Arnold nor anyone else in the damned rebel army.

The loyalists were assigned tents near Gates' own, under guard, and given a decent meal, the first in three weeks. At dusk General Phillips arrived with a junior officer bearing a Bible, paper, pen and ink. Ebenezer Jessup hesitated when Phillips wanted him to take the oath, but Justus and his two brothers urged him to comply. This was a stay of execution, and Ebenezer was a fool to stand on his dignity. Once all the paroles had been signed, Phillips took leave of them. Guarded by some of Gates' Continentals, the paroled loyalists marched to the bank of the Hudson, where bateaux were waiting. As the escort rowed away from the rebel camp, Justus caught sight of the lonely figure of Phillips waving to them. That haunted him. The general faced a long march to Boston through unfriendly territory.

All night the provincials and their escort rowed, passing the camp fires of General Stark's New Hampshiremen. By the time they reached Fort Edward, Justus was feeling stronger, for the food continued to be adequate. With help from Elijah Bothum he hobbled the sixteen kilometres to Lake George, where more bateaux waited. They passed several small British outposts, and because many in the bateaux were wounded, the officers waved the rebel flag past. By October 22 they were outside Ticonderoga's walls, waiting while Ebenezer Jessup informed Brigadier Watson Powell that the rebels were ready to hand over the prisoners of war. Jessup returned with a British flag and escort, and the formalities were soon completed.

At the fort, Colonel Peters was overjoyed to see the men he had left behind, and he told Justus that having the written permission from Burgoyne had been worthwhile. Captain Samuel McKay, who arrived with no written permission, was in disgrace with Brigadier Powell for deserting his commander-in-chief. The garrison was preparing to withdraw, and Powell had orders to destroy anything that might be of use to the rebels. Justus spent the next few days resting, and then the remnants of Burgoyne's once proud army wound their way in bateaux towards Fort St. Johns.

The 62 Queen's Loyal Rangers were reunited, Justus, Elijah and ten privates prisoners of war, the rest able to do duty and recruit to fill the depleted ranks. All told, of 796 provincials known to have survived Burgoyne's campaign, 272 officers and men could be active, 196 were prisoners under the Saratoga Convention, while 328 were being held prisoner by the rebels.[11] The most battered corps was the Queen's Loyal Rangers, many of whom had been with the vanguard. The units that had brought supplies forward had suffered fewer casualties.

Relaxing in the bateau after his long ordeal, Justus' thoughts turned to Sarah. He would not be going near New Haven for some time. Once the baby she would have about the beginning of January was old enough to travel, he wanted her to join him in Canada. He would find some means of livelihood around Montreal when he was well enough, and take care of his family until the war came to an end and all could return home.

Chapter 6

Under Convention

In New Haven, Sarah Sherwood soon learned that Justus had been wounded. Some of Seth Warner's men had reported, in the presence of loyalists, that he had been among the prisoners at Saratoga, and that he had a painful limp and wasted features. Soon after the news that Burgoyne's army was encircled reached New Haven, the Bothum family returned to Shaftsbury, but Simon had remained to help Sarah run the farm. When she heard the distressing news about Justus she begged Simon to escort her and the children to Ticonderoga, but he cautioned her against rushing there like a refugee. To be sure, Ty was only forty-three kilometres away, but if she simply packed up and left, Justus' property might be confiscated. The proper procedure was for her to go to Bennington and request a safe conduct on compassionate grounds.

Sarah allowed Simon to drive her to Shaftsbury in a chaise to see whether their father agreed with him. They packed a supply of clothing and set out with Samuel and Diana, accompanied by Caesar Congo, for the 150 kilometre journey to the Bothum farm. Elijah Sr. was in full accord with his second son. Sarah must see the Grand Council of Safety in Bennington and Elijah would accompany her.[1] He was in the council's good graces, for the situation in the Green Mountains had changed by the time Burgoyne's expedition had set out in June. The people of the New Hampshire Grants had proclaimed themselves the independent Republic of Vermont, and were defying both the Congress and Britain.

While Seth Warner and his rebel Green Mountain Boys and the Bennington Militia had rallied in August to drive the invaders away, to the people of the illicit republic the Continental Congress was as much the enemy as the mother country. Loyalists in the Green Mountains were having a breathing space, and now the leaders of the secessionist movement were resisting demands from Albany that Seth Warner take his regiment to join the Continental Army. Seth himself was ill from severe sunstroke he had suffered during the battle near Bennington.

Sarah had not been pressured to leave, and many women in her situation were living quietly in their homes, unmolested. The rebels had stopped evicting loyalist families, and only the properties of those who had already fled were being confiscated. In deciding to ask for a safe conduct Sarah was casting aside concern for her own welfare, thinking only of Justus. On October 24, Sarah and her father drove to Bennington and appeared before the Grand Council of Safety in the Green Mountain Tavern, the seat of what passed for government in Vermont. At that time Major Joseph Fay, landlord Stephen's younger son, wrote to Colonel Samuel Herrick, the commandant of Fort Vengeance, half way between Castleton and the shore of Lake Champlain:

> Whereas Capt. Sherwood's wife had applied to this Council for Liberty to go to her husband at Ticonderoga, the Council would Recommend to you, or the Officer Commanding at Pawlet or Skeensboro to convey her (by a Flagg) if you think most Expedient. Her necessary clothing and one bed is to be allowed her.

In Shaftsbury, Dorothy Bothum selected the bed, secreted a few useful items into Sarah's baggage and added some provisions. Then with the children and Caesar Congo, her father drove her to Fort Vengeance and entrusted her to Colonel Samuel Herrick — a onetime friend of Justus. That officer arranged for her to continue by wagon as far as Skenesborough. From there a bateau took her to the vicinity of Ticonderoga, which her escort found deserted.

Sarah's was an epic journey, for the rebels panicked and left her on the west shore of Lake Champlain, fifty kilometres from the British post at Pointe au Fer, lest a patrol operating from that base capture them. The wagon trip left Sarah aching down both sides. Well into the seventh month of her pregnancy, each sway of the wagon had torn at the muscles that supported her swollen abdomen. Now, aided by Caesar Congo, himself only a boy, Sarah cached her belongings and marked them. The little party walked slowly along the trail, Sarah carrying Diana, holding three-year-old Samuel by the hand, while Caesar Congo carried provisions and blankets. On they trudged, pausing frequently for Sarah to rest. Sleeping rolled in blankets at night, they reached the British post. Sarah waited in relative comfort while Caesar went back along the lake with some bateaumen to retrieve the bed and other baggage.[2]

Even the remaining part of the journey to Fort St. Johns by bateau was miserable for Sarah. Early November was damp and raw, and snow filtered below the canopy that was her only shelter. Her arrival at the barracks where Justus was living startled him. He never dreamed she would try to leave New Haven until after the birth of the new baby. Yet he was relieved that they were together again, sharing his exile. While Simon was looking after their interests in New Haven, the immediate future was far from rosy. For the present, Sarah and the children were dependent on provisions from the government and she would be housed in the barracks with other families until he could find better accommodation. That posed a problem, for Justus could not draw his captain's pay of 10 shillings a day, because he was not allowed to be on duty. He hated to think of the Queen's Loyal Rangers who were active. The regiment now mustered over 100 men, for many of those who had been removed for other services during Burgoyne's campaign had been returned to Colonel Peters.

Soon a little help came for Justus' financial embarrassment. Governor Carleton allowed him a pension of 30 pounds per annum to support his family.[3] This was a paltry one shilling and eightpence a day, and his family was in for a thin time. Justus resolved to seek some employment as soon as his leg had healed fully, to add to his light purse and to help him forget his frustrations at being unable to serve the cause he had embraced at such cost.

His immediate concern after he received the first installment of his pension was a decent place to live. He found a small house for rent in the village of St. Johns, and for some time he was very busy with domestic affairs, making furniture with the help of Caesar Congo, and doing a lot of baby sitting for Sarah. Then, to his alarm, Sarah's labour pains began on December 12, three weeks too early. Fearful that the journey from Bennington had been too much for his wife, Justus ran to fetch one of the military physicians.

The baby was a boy whom they named Levius Peters Sherwood — the middle name in honour of Justus' commanding officer.[4] Despite the furtive circumstances of his conception, the fears that haunted his mother during the absence of his father, her exhausting journey to Canada and his premature arrival, Levius was a healthy boy who closely resembled his father, ruling out any gossip that he might not be Justus' son.[5] Like Justus, Levius was long-boned and slender, with blue-grey eyes. Justus was delighted with all three children, but there must not be any more, until they were resettled in New Haven.

By early March, his wife was able to cope at home, and Justus rode to Montreal to purchase items which he and Sarah could not make. Then, too, he needed to escape from the military comings and goings at Fort St. Johns, a constant reminder of his own impotence as a soldier. While in the city he wrote a memorial to Governor Carleton, pleading that the men who had joined Captain Samuel McKay be returned to his company, which at that time stood at twenty-four men.[6] He claimed twenty-three of McKay's, ignoring Edward Carscallan and John Wilson because he had satisfactory replacements in Lieutenant Dulmage and Ensign Moss. He needed men desperately to fill his ranks, especially when they rightfully belonged to him. He complained to Carleton:

> I think no man has had so much Fatigue and Risque as I have to Bring those men into His Majesty's Service that are now with Capt. McKay. I humbly Pray Your Excellency to Consider my case and if in your wisdom it seems meet which Please to Grant me those men for

the Ensuing Campaign.

Back at Fort St. Johns he met some refugees from Fort Edward who complained about the way Brigadier Watson Powell had received them. Powell, the commandant of the fort because General William Phillips had been captured with Burgoyne, suspected all refugees of being rebel spies unless they could prove otherwise. Much embarrassed, Justus asked Brigadier Powell to permit him to interrogate newcomers, for he could distinguish between genuine loyalists and spies. Frowning, Powell shook his head. Any involvement with incoming refugees might be viewed as a violation of his parole by the rebels.

Meanwhile, Thomas Sherwood and John Dulmage were frequently out in New York and Vermont, carrying dispatches and bringing in recruits for the Queen's Loyal Rangers. Returning from a mission in April, Thomas had news for Justus. His youngest brother, Samuel, had left Connecticut and leased land in Kingsbury Township, not far from Thomas' own farm.[7] Furthermore, Samuel was a loyalist, and had provided Thomas with information on rebel activities. That alarmed Justus, and he prayed Samuel would be cautious, but at least his brother was working for the cause.

To supplement his meagre income Justus looked for work, but he found that his surveyor's training was of no use. The Province of Canada was divided into seigneuries that were scantily populated. Seigneurs merely allotted each tenant a narrow frontage on water, and an American surveyor was not needed to lay out townships and lots. Work always available was loading and unloading bateaux, and Justus accepted this lowly employment.

As April turned into May, Justus suffered another staggering blow to his pride, not to mention his purse. Scouts returning from Vermont informed him that on April 23 the rebels had confiscated his property, except for "400 acres" in New Haven where many people still held him in high regard.[8] These tracts were the 50-acre farm occupied by Simon Bothum, and three others close by. Here was some consolation. When the war ended Justus would have his home intact, but all his other wealth was lost, the years of hard work that had gone into accumulating his thousands of acres wasted. He longed to strike back at the men who had wronged him. That damned parole! If only he could be active and feel that he was working for the cause. He paced the confines of St. Johns like a caged catamount from his beloved Green Mountains, longing to pursue his prey.

He felt disgraced over the loss of his property. He was a failure. His Puritan upbringing taught him that to have reached the age of thirty-one, with family responsibilities and so little to show for his life's work was degrading, humiliating. Back of those confiscations he suspected Ira Allen. Little Stub, very active in the affairs of the illegal republic, might be the man who dreamed up the method of raising revenue for the provisional government that operated from Landlord Stephen Fay's tavern in Bennington. Selling off the property of absent loyalists was a tidy way of side-stepping the issue of taxes that had started the rebellion, while making the government solvent.

Justus had yet another nagging worry that was keeping him awake at night. At some point, Colonel Peters might decide to give the twenty-four men of his company to an active officer. Thus far, John Dulmage had been in command of the men and doing a competent job. The big thirty-four year old farmer from the Camden Valley was invaluable, and Justus forgot that he was a Yorker, the kind of man despised by Ethan Allan and his band.

As May slipped by, intriguing hints reached Justus that his precarious existence as a prisoner on parole might be ending. On the 11th, Governor Carleton ordered Colonel Ebenezer Jessup to bring the King's Loyal Americans from Fort St. Johns to Quebec City to work on fortifications. The order applied to the entire corps, regardless of whether the men were on parole.[9] For the rest of the month Justus waited impatiently. When would Carleton remember that other provincials were on parole? Nor had he received a reply from the governor's headquarters on his petition to have the men Samuel McKay had stolen from him returned.

In Quebec City, Carleton had ignored the petition. If

the men did not want to serve under Captain Sherwood, ordering them sent to the Queen's Loyal Rangers would only mean more quarreling. Besides, he had no plans for a new campaign against the rebels. It did not matter which officer had the men as long as they were doing something to justify provisioning them. As far as Carleton was concerned, the provincial troops who had been with Burgoyne were the latter's responsibility, and belonged to the Central Department. The returns he ordered kept on their numbers were only a temporary list. Burgoyne's men were refugees in Canada, nothing more, entitled only to food, clothing and shelter. If they could be employed for their keep, Carleton was willing to use them, but placating provincial officers was unnecessary.

However, Carleton had received news from London that would release Sherwood and all the paroled prisoners of war. On June 1, 1778, the governor issued an order from his residence, the Château St. Louis, stating that since the Continental Congress had broken the terms of the Saratoga Convention, all the King's troops were to regard it as invalid.[10] When this order reached Fort St. Johns, Brigadier Powell called a meeting of all commissioned officers who were under convention and announced that they could return to duty, their pay restored.

Justus was overjoyed. Now he could go after recruits in Vermont and on the frontiers of New York, and start building his company to full strength so that his commission would be signed. The struggle to keep his family fed and clothed was over. After blessing Sir Guy Carleton, Justus could not resist asking Powell why the governor had had a change of heart.

When the first supply ships of the spring reached Quebec, Powell explained, His Excellency discovered that the rebels had not sent the captured British and German regulars to England, as General Gates had promised at Saratoga. The regulars had marched to Boston, but the only men sent home on parole were General Burgoyne and some of his staff officers. The others had been marched off to prison camps in the southern colonies, where food was more plentiful than in the north. The Continental Congress had repudiated the terms

Gates had signed, for if Burgoyne's men were sent home they could be used in Europe. That would release other troops for service in America.

While he felt some regret for the men of that army whom he respected, Justus was elated as he left Powell's headquarters. The lanky loyalist hurried to his house to unpack the regimentals he did not feel entitled to wear when he had no military duties. The uniform was in poor shape after the campaign, but with Sarah to patch and brush it while he polished his silver accoutrements, he would not look any shabbier than the other officers of his corps. After a flurry of activity at the house, Justus went to spend the evening in the mess used by officers of provincials. They ate separately from the regulars, who were inclined to look down their noses at colonials.

Justus and the other convention officers received a royal welcome from Colonel Peters and their brother officers, even though all were on the temporary list and none had signed commissions. All made merry, with many toasts to the next campaign, and the King. This time, the Lord willing, the British brass would show that they had learned from Burgoyne's muddle and use more effective tactics. Justus pressed Peters for permission to go after recruits, but his colonel said he must see Brigadier Powell before setting out into enemy territory. Swaying a little but very happy, Justus left the mess with the others and made his way home, resolved to see the fort's commandant at first light.

Powell's attitude had changed for the better, and he agreed that Justus should interrogate prisoners and refugees. He had time to talk to only a few before Powell had a mission for him. A dispatch was ready, and Justus was to carry it into Albany County, after which he could go recruiting. Governor Carleton wanted to begin exchanging prisoners, and Powell asked Justus to spread the word among people he could trust in Vermont that His Excellency wanted the men taken at Bennington returned. Immediately Justus thought of Ira Allen. If anyone could initiate such arrangements it was Ethan's small brother. Before Powell dismissed Justus he gave him a packet to be delivered at a safe house near Albany, where a scout would collect it and carry it to Sir Henry

Clinton's headquarters in New York City. General Sir William Howe had been recalled recently, and Clinton was now the commander-in-chief of all British forces in the Central Department.[11]

Justus set off from St. Johns, dressed in buckskin leggings and a fringed hunting shirt, moccasins on his feet, long-barrelled rifle over his shoulder, a knapsack of provisions on his back, the dispatches secreted on his body. He rode in a bateau as far as Isle aux Noix, close to the exit to Lake Champlain. From there he went aboard a vessel of the Provincial Marine that dropped him on the east side of the lake opposite New Haven. A furtive visit to his farm to reassure himself that his remaining property was safe in Simon Bothum's care, and he made for Shaftsbury, using safe houses for shelter along the way, storing his memory with intelligence to report to Carleton and Powell.

To his in-laws, Elijah and Dorothy Bothum, he brought news of Sarah, Elijah Jr. and the grandchildren. Then, feet propped, sipping a stonewall, he heard the latest developments in the new republic. The governor was one-eyed Thomas Chittenden of Arlington, illiterate, and a man Justus knew well. Ira Allen and Jonas and Joseph Fay had sent a message to the Continental Congress asking to be admitted as the fourteenth state. If the members refused, Vermont would remain an independent republic, and she already had her own constitution, under which she would be governed by the laws of God and of the State of Connecticut, until the founders thought of something better.

Justus blinked. They could not be serious. Connecticut law was harsh, and the men of the Green Mountains lived by more mellow dictates. Those who framed the constitution had made a meaningless gesture. Connecticut law had never been enforced on the frontier, and he was certain nothing would change merely because the regulations had been written into law. However, Justus was disturbed when Elijah told him Vermont had abolished slavery for all women over eighteen and all men over twenty-one. That meant he might lose his other two slaves.

Elijah smiled complacently. Liberty for all folk was

as hollow a gesture as Connecticut law — Green Mountain bluff. Elijah had other news of interest, for Ethan Allen had arrived recently in Vermont. After confinement in England, he had been sent to New York City and kept on parole until General Washington arranged to have him exchanged for a British officer. Now Ethan was living in Sunderland and had brought his wife and children from Connecticut. When Justus first knew him, he kept his family in the older province so that he would have a place of refuge if Governor Tryon sent troops to capture him.

Ethan was also quarreling with his brother Levi, and proclaiming that Levi was a Tory whose property ought to be confiscated.[12] That was fascinating, but Justus had questions of a more immediate concern. What would happen if the Congress tried to force Vermont to reunite with New York?

Elijah laughed. No one worried about that. George Washington was occupied watching Sir Henry Clinton, who had evacuated Philadelphia and was entrenching his grip on New York City. There was precious little the Congress could do to coerce Vermont, not while the Continental Army was a rag-tag and bobtail collection of poorly armed, underpaid rebels.[13] The day might dawn when Vermont would reunite with Britain, and Justus could come home, his confiscated property restored. The mood of the people in the Green Mountains was changing. Elijah felt secure because he kept a low profile. Occasionally he had to pretend that he thought Justus and Elijah Jr. a pair of miscreants, but he was surviving nicely by being in favour of Vermont's independence from New York.

On his way, spirits raised by what he had heard, Justus had much food for thought, as well as the mission for Carleton. Prisoner exchanges had to be started, and soon. At safe houses he learned that loyalists captured at Bennington were hitched to the traces of horses, in pairs, and forced to run or be dragged. Now some were in Bennington, where the rebels had built a gaol, but others were aboard a prison ship in Boston harbour. The Germans were treated as prisoners of war, but the provincials had been regarded as traitors.[14] With a friend near

Bennington, Justus left a message for Ira Allen asking that exchanges begin. Shuddering at the fate that might have been his had he not escaped from the battlefield nearby, Justus turned eastward with his dispatches, planning to look for recruits in Albany County as soon as he had delivered his packet.

Chapter 7

A Pimpernel Emerges

At the safe house near Albany where he delivered his packet, Sherwood's host described the widespread distress among loyalist families whose men had gone to Canada or were in prison. Many of the wives and children had been removed from the Hudson Valley when Burgoyne's army approached. After his surrender they were allowed to return home, but having lost their harvests and livestock, they were unable to feed themselves unless they had relatives to assist them. Justus was torn. He wanted to get recruits, but he could not leave the dependents of men he respected to suffer. They should be in Canada receiving government rations.

Near Saratoga he visited some of the wives, who confirmed the appalling stories he had heard. Taking what slim provisions they possessed, they left their homes and followed him. When he had six women and fifteen children, almost more than was safe, he started north along forest trails, walking in the moonlight when the local residents were abed. Making slow progress, often carrying a small child, he headed towards his cousin Thomas Sherwood's farm. There Thomas' wife Anna and his children stayed, protected by his father Seth, and Justus knew he could get provisions. Hiding his charges he went to see Anna by himself, making certain no one saw him, especially his uncle.

Thanks to Seth, Thomas' livestock had been brought back to the farm. Anna was well supplied with food, and Seth had sent servants to do the spring planting. He had not forgiven Thomas, but he did not want his grandchildren to suffer.[1] From Thomas' farm Justus led his refugees to the farm of his brother Samuel, where he met his sister-in-law, Eunice, for the first time. When Justus had left Connecticut, Samuel was seventeen and single. From there Justus made his way into Vermont, where he had more friends who could provide his party with food.

At a safe house Justus' host told him that Major Zadock Wright, of his regiment, had been scouting near Albany when a rebel patrol captured him and carried him to Massachusetts. Now he was in Springfield Gaol in irons. Shuddering Justus resolved to beg Governor Carleton to initiate a prisoner exchange as soon as he reached Fort St. Johns.

Next Justus made for New Haven to get provisions from Simon Bothum. Then, with Simon and his slaves carrying the smallest children, Justus' party began the twenty-five kilometre trek to Lake Champlain. He hoped to signal a vessel of the Provincial Marine to take his people aboard, or find boats left by local settlers which they could row to Pointe au Fer. He was in luck, for the schooner *Maria* was cruising off-shore. Simon started a fire, and when the smoke rose Justus saw a cutter being lowered. To his immense relief, the ordeal was nearly over. The *Maria* dropped Justus and his refugees at Isle aux Noix, and a bateau took them to Fort St. Johns.

By this time the children, rested and comfortable, had revived. They had grown fond of their lanky protector and insisted on climbing all over him. He felt like smacking them but he restrained himself since their mothers were looking on. He was delighted when he could hand them over to the nearest British officer and hurry home to Sarah. But, as she remarked when he was relating his experiences, he would do it all over again if the need arose.

She brought Justus up to date on developments during his absence, and of greatest interest was the arrival in Quebec City of General Frederick Haldimand to replace Sir Guy Carleton as governor. Everyone expected Haldimand to come up the St. Lawrence soon to inspect the province's defences.

After changing into regimentals, Justus went to report to Brigadier Powell. The commandant ordered him to put his findings in a letter to Carleton. Although Governor Haldimand was now on duty, Carleton was completing his reports on all the work he had initiated. Before Justus could finish his letter, Powell asked him to assess a number of intelligence reports other scouts had brought in, and he was to incorporate any useful information he found into the report he was making for Carleton.[2]

For the next few days Powell had Justus interrogating loyalist refugees and rebel prisoners who had been brought to Fort St. Johns. Some of the prisoners were vowing that they were loyalists, captured by mistake, or coerced into joining the rebel militia. When Justus thought a man was reliable, he recommended that he be allowed to join one of the provincial corps. Brigadier Powell sent New Yorkers to Colonel Ebenezer Jessup or Sir John Johnson, the New Englanders to Colonel John Peters.

Where Justus was suspicious that so-called refugees might be spies, Powell recommended internment. He allowed the less dangerous to be confined in Montreal, where Sir John Johnson or the commandant, Brigadier Allan Maclean, decided which ones could be free on parole. Others were sent down the Richelieu River to Fort Chambly, a stone walled edifice from which escape was more difficult.

While Justus was absent carrying dispatches and rescuing women and children, the Queen's Loyal Rangers had moved to Lachine. Under Lieutenant Dulmage his company was working on fortifications there. Early in August, Justus' work was interrupted by the arrival of Colonel Peters, who wanted him to be his guide on a small expedition authorized by Major Christopher Carleton, 29th Regiment, the new commandant at Pointe au Fer. The major was also Sir Guy Carleton's nephew, and he wanted Peters to destroy a new blockhouse the rebels had built on the Onion River in Vermont, north of New Haven, an area Justus knew well.

The Onion River raid was a success in the style of Ethan and his Boys. With thirty-four Queen's Loyal Rangers and a party of Indians, Peters and Sherwood travelled in bateaux, and after leaving the boats at a safe distance they advanced through the woods. They captured the garrison, removed everything of value, and turned the blockhouse into a gigantic bonfire. By August 3 the raiders were back at Fort St. Johns with their loot and with prisoners who could be exchanged for some of the provincials and regulars captured the year before.

A few days later, Brigadier Powell had yet another mission for Justus, this one a meeting with rebel emissaries from New York to be sent by General John Stark. Justus was to open negotiations for a prisoner exchange. Stark, then on duty in Albany, had sent a messenger to Fort St. Johns to inform Powell that he wanted to discuss the return of civilian sympathisers and rebels who were being held in Montreal. Justus was to take an escort of regulars and meet Stark's representative under a flag of truce at Ticonderoga.[3] He left Fort St. Johns in full regimentals, a British officer albeit a shabby one. His escort consisted of men from the 34th Regiment, assigned by the commandant of Isle aux Noix, Major Alexander Dundas of the same unit.

Provincial troops were never used as escorts, Major Dundas informed Justus. Loyalists might lose their heads when coolness was mandatory, and might not be protected by the flag of truce. Noticing Justus' knitted brows, Dundas hastened to reassure him. He was a British officer on an official mission, and since the regulars would be there to witness any violations of the rules of war there would not be any. As his party went aboard a vessel of the Provincial Marine, Justus prayed Dundas was right. He was, nonetheless, a provincial officer with a temporary commission, which struck him as a trifle flimsy. He was relieved that he was to meet New Yorkers who might be deluded into accepting him as a British officer; Vermonters would burst out laughing at the very idea.

When the vessel reached Ty, Sherwood's party was put ashore, and he found the flag from General Stark waiting. Head high, Justus played out a role that called for considerable bravado. The rebel party was commanded by a captain, who proffered Stark's list of prisoners while Justus handed him Powell's. Carefully he perused the list of prisoners; then the dickering began. Rank should be exchanged for like rank, but many of the prisoners held by both sides were civilians. The rebels had loyalists interned or under house arrest, while in Montreal were American businessmen under suspicion of aiding the rebel cause. The New Yorkers agreed that some civilians could be exchanged for enlisted men. Civilians held in Montreal might be allowed to return to the United States if they gave their paroles not to take part in further hostilities. Also, some loyalists would be allowed to leave for Canada under safe conducts. Obviously, each exchange would have its own terms of reference — a fine task for a Yankee trader.

The bargaining over, Justus and his escort returned to the British vessel. Sailing towards Isle aux Noix, Justus reflected that the British and loyalists were at a disadvantage. The rebels held more prisoners — a situation that could be remedied. Some of the privates might be exchanged for civilians, but Justus was desperately short of rebel officers. Abductions of important rebel leaders would help, but for this work he would require the co-operation of the various post commanders, Majors Carleton and Dundas and Brigadier Powell. They would have to allow him to call upon the services of reliable men in the provincial corps who knew the country.

His plotting was interrupted when he noticed the crew lowering the ship's cutter. When the boat returned from the shore of the lake it brought a large party of refugees. At Isle aux Noix Justus went to report to Major Dundas on his mission, and upon reaching Fort St. Johns he repeated his story to Brigadier Powell. Post commanders had to know what intelligence anyone coming from rebel territory had brought, but to his dismay, so did everyone else. Brushing aside all the eager interrogators, Justus strode angrily towards his house. Almost immediately Powell sent for him again.

Major Christopher Carleton had received orders to destroy some blockhouses and mills on the Vermont side of Lake Champlain, and he wanted Justus to serve as one of his guides. Carleton's force consisted of 327 regulars with 31 officers and a surgeon, as well as 30 of Sir John Johnson's men, and several officers from the temporary list who were from the area. Justus' role was to guide Lieutenant Farquhar and 30 regulars to Moor's sawmill on Putnam's Creek, a few miles south of Fort Ticonderoga.

After rowing in bateaux down the long arm of Lake Champlain in the direction of Skenesborough, Justus ordered the regulars ashore, and after a short march inland they burned the mill and made prisoners of the employees.[4] Then the expedition returned to Fort St. Johns.

Reporting to Brigadier Powell, Justus discovered that all the provincials had been ordered to Sorel, where Governor Frederick Haldimand wanted to inspect them. Lieutenant John Dulmage had already marched his company to Sorel from Lachine, and Justus was to follow as soon as possible. Noting how gaunt and exhausted Captain Sherwood appeared, the commandant procured a horse for the journey. Gratefully Justus accepted the mount, and after taking leave of his family he rode at the head of the little column of provincials who had been on Major Carleton's expedition. Justus' thoughts were on the new governor as he travelled the seventy-five kilometres to Sorel, where the Richelieu flowed into the St. Lawrence. Would Haldimand carry on in the style of Carleton or make upsetting changes?

Reporting to Colonel Peters when he reached Sorel, Justus learned that Governor Haldimand, a Swiss professional soldier, had paraded and inspected all the provincial troops on October 16. The men who had served with Burgoyne had put on the poorest show. As well as their depleted numbers, they were the shabbiest. Sir John Johnson's King's Royal Regiment of New York, and Brigadier Allan Maclean's Royal Highland Emigrants — both members in good standing of the Northern Department — had been impressive. The two corps were only two-thirds strength, and Haldimand was signing commissions as each company was completed. This procedure was different from Carleton's, who had agreed to sign all the officers' commissions when a regiment reached two-thirds full strength.[6]

Peters wanted Justus, as senior captain of the Queen's Loyal Rangers, to be his second-in-command until Major Wright could be exchanged. The regiment was to remain at Sorel, working on fortifications, because Haldimand wanted to seal off that route to the rebels. A large force had penetrated Canada by the Richelieu in the spring of 1776, something that must not be allowed to happen again. Justus was willing to remain at Sorel, but he wondered whether Brigadier Powell might raise some objections. The work with the prisoners and refugees at Fort St. Johns was more important than supervising a below strength corps this far inland. His prediction was correct, for soon after his arrival Peters received a message for Captain Sherwood to report to Haldimand's headquarters.

Making his way to the château where the new governor was in residence, Justus fairly cringed when he spotted Samuel McKay, who still had the men he had seduced away from the Queen's Loyal Rangers the year before. Then Justus recognized someone, the sight of whom made him freeze in his tracks.

Marching at the head of a full company of Sir John Johnson's regiment was John Munro, dressed as an officer and in the captain's spot, no doubt with a signed commission, too. Seeing his old adversary from the Green Mountains gave Justus a nasty jolt. How that dour scotsman with the thick skull — the magistrate escorting Remember Baker to gaol six years ago — had done so well was downright incredible! Relieved that Munro had not noticed him, Justus slunk past and soon found himself in front of the governor's residence.

He was ushered into the governor's presence by Captain Robert Mathews, 53rd Regiment, who warned Justus beforehand to speak distinctly. His Excellency's first language was French, and he spoke fluent German, but he had some difficulty with English.

Frederick Haldimand, a major-general with the British army, was a man of vast experience in North America. He had come, at the outset of the Seven Years' War in 1756 to command a predominantly German-speaking battalion of the Royal American or 60th Regiment. As lieutenant-colonel of his battalion, Haldimand was stationed in Albany when he was a brother officer of Philip Schuyler, now a rebel general. Later, Haldimand was at Oswego, and he was with Lord Jeffrey Amherst's expedition that captured Montreal.

In 1773, Haldimand was commander-in-chief of British forces at New York City. At that time Governor Tryon begged him to send regulars into the Green Mountains to deal with Ethan Allen's Boys. Haldimand refused on the grounds that Tryon ought to be able to keep order on the frontier.[8] The new governor had been with the British army in Boston until 1775, and after three years on duty in Britain he received his present appointment.

After reading Sir Guy Carleton's reports, Haldimand decided to interview Captain Sherwood. The governor did not trust anyone unless he had just cause, and his previous experience had left him wary of all colonials, whether Canadian or American. He was having houses built for loyalist families across the St. Lawrence from Sorel in the parish of Machiche. Very few French-speaking inhabitants lived there, and the women and children would be close to their husbands and fathers. They would also be well away from the Canadians, which suited Haldimand, lest spies be sent with them to stir up trouble among His Majesty's francophone subjects.[9] But Captain Sherwood might be a colonial he could trust. He had already demonstrated compassion for refugee loyalists and an ability to secure information from prisoners, and Haldimand suspected he might be useful.

Captain Robert Mathews, newly commissioned in Brigadier Powell's 53rd Regiment, had come from England with Haldimand, and had not been part of the garrison during Burgoyne's campaign.[10] Both the new arrivals were sizing Justus up, and both were inclined to be impressed with the lanky frontiersman, who spoke with a Yankee twang but otherwise showed some vestiges of refinement.

On his part Justus was doing some assessing of his own. Mathews was a sturdily built man in his red coat and red facings and single gold epaulette, standing beside the governor, who was seated behind a massive oak desk. Haldimand appeared slightly built with a receding hairline and snapping, penetrating eyes. This meeting must be important, Justus reckoned. Surely it was not usual for a mere captain of provincials to be called before so important a person as the governor. Mathews began the conversation, and prisoner exchanges were the first item on his agenda. One major difficulty was the shortage of appropriate prisoners to offer for the return of provincials and regulars the rebels were holding.

Justus recommended sending parties of kidnappers into New York State to abduct important rebel leaders, but the governor urged caution. Mathews stepped in, warning Justus that relations with France were a tricky matter, and these might affect his cause. When Burgoyne's army had taken to the field, the French were watching. When that army was defeated by the rebel frontiersmen, Britain's traditional enemy decided that the Continental Congress had some hope of success. In February, the French had formed a military alliance with the rebels. Soon French troops would be in the colonies, and in a position to retake Canada, a possibility, His Excellency admitted, that was giving him sleepless nights.

If an army of rebels appeared on Canada's borders, as had happened in the autumn of 1775, the governor thought he could rely on some support from the Canadians. But if the rebels were supported by French troops, the Canadians would return to their former allegiance, and Canada would be doomed. Haldimand's first duty was to Canada, and he reminded Justus that keeping the province out of rebel hands was in the best interests of the loyalists in the northern colonies. Haldimand's domain was their place of refuge.

After commending Justus for the work he had done thus far with the prisoners and refugees, Haldimand ordered him to return to Fort St. Johns, but under no circumstances should he try any kidnapping without His Excellency's consent. And he was to remember that the governor would not tolerate atrocities by any of his provincials. All prisoners were to be treated with the greatest civility and humanity.

Feeling as though his wings had been clipped, Justus returned to Colonel Peters to inform him that he would not be remaining at Sorel. He expected him to be disappointed, instead Peters was downright angry. He was also jealous of his subordinate, who was being given the important task of working with prisoners and refugees, receiving special status. Saddened and a trifle bewildered by Peters' fractiousness, Justus mounted his horse for the ride back to Fort St. Johns.

Trotting his horse along the bank of the Richelieu, Justus pondered the status of Butler's Rangers at their base, Fort Niagara. Butler's was the only provincial corps that had not paraded at Sorel. Justus had heard that independent companies were operating from Fort Niagara with Butler's Rangers, and under the auspices of the Indian Department. When he reached his house, he wrote to Captain Mathews, requesting permission to transfer his company to the Indian Department. This would remove him from the temporary list and ensure that his men became part of the Northern Department. He might not be able to go to Fort Niagara for a while, but Lieutenant John Dulmage could lead the company, and the men would be happier serving on the frontier than building fortifications at Sorel.[12]

The letter in the post, Justus resumed his duties at Fort St. Johns. He was tired, and looking forward to some well deserved rest, but he was soon disappointed. Brigadier Powell ordered him to go to Pointe au Fer and take some scouts then at Isle aux Noix with him. Major Christopher Carleton wanted Justus to accompany him along Lake Champlain, to see whether the Vermonters were rebuilding the outposts which the regulars and provincials had destroyed during the late summer and early autumn.[13]

Justus gathered his party at Isle aux Noix, among them Joseph Bettys, who had gone scouting for information on Sir Henry Clinton during the last days of Burgoyne's campaign. Bettys had been journeying back and forth between Isle aux Noix and Albany with dispatches, and Justus wanted to know him better. He would be useful whenever Haldimand gave orders for abducting rebel leaders.[14] From Pointe au Fer, by bateau and on foot, Justus and his party guided Christopher Carleton to all the posts, and they found them exactly as the major's foray had left them, charred, empty shells. Returning to

Pointe au Fer, Justus went aboard a vessel with his scouts for the journey back to Isle aux Noix, and leaving the scouts at that post he proceeded on to Fort St. Johns.

Meanwhile at Sorel, certain of his brother officers were looking for a way to escape from the Central Department. On November 21, John Peters and some other leaders sent a petition to Haldimand asking to have their men incorporated into a second battalion, King's Royal Regiment of New York.[15] His Excellency refused. Since Burgoyne's provincials belonged to the Central Department, Haldimand had no authority to take them into his own Northern Department.[16]

For the same reason he ignored Captain Sherwood's request to join the Indian Department. Besides, Justus was doing excellent work with the prisoners and refugees. Some of Carleton's reports indicated that this captain of provincials was a gallant officer, but he would be of greater service at Fort St. Johns than in the employ of John Butler, a man Haldimand did not like very much.

For Justus and Sarah, the winter of 1778-1779 passed quietly. The tranquil time was important, the opportunity to make things his family needed, to sit by the fire in the evening, smoking his pipe, reading Pope, Swift and other popular authors, chatting with Sarah as she wove linsey-woolsey. Occasionally a party of refugees arrived, or Brigadier Powell asked him to choose men for scouting parties that left the fort on snowshoes, but most of the time Justus could relax, and admit that he could not drive his less than robust body indefinitely. Elijah Bothum had leave to join them at Christmas, and Thomas Sherwood called in on his way to Fort Edward for one of his frequent clandestine visits with Anna and his children. Justus treasured the quiet time, certain his activities outside the home would soon be even heavier than during this last summer and autumn.

Chapter 8

Banished Yankee

In February 1779, a scout returning from the Green Mountains informed Justus that the Vermont Legislature had passed an order of banishment against him.[1] The scout had visited Elijah Bothum Sr. in Shaftsbury, who sent a warning to his son-in-law not to attempt to visit the illicit republic. If caught, he might be hanged on the spot. This news numbed him momentarily. To be sure he had enemies in Vermont, but he still had many friends there as well. He wondered what effect his banishment might have on New Yorkers. As the snow began to melt he half suspected that his brother Samuel's days in Kingsbury Township might be numbered.

That spring Justus received two appointments of importance from Haldimand. The governor made him Commissioner of Prisoners, responsible for negotiating exchanges, and also Commissioner of Refugees, to assist distressed loyalists trying to reach Canada.[2] As soon as travel was feasible, Justus carried out his first prisoner exchange, after making arrangements through correspondence with General Stark in Albany. Using passwords and countersigns, loyalists with letters were conducted safely into Albany, rebel scouts to Isle aux Noix. Brigadier Powell ordered Justus to see a tailor for new regimentals. He wanted to be represented at the exchange by an officer who looked the part, not a tattered scarecrow.

Justus assembled the prisoners at Fort St. Johns, making sure that each was searched from the skin out. If they gave the enemy any information it would be verbal. Meanwhile, the rebels were bringing their charges northward towards Skenesborough, soon to be the scene of many negotiations of this nature. While Justus was preparing to set out, a rebel prisoner named Andrew Stephenson escaped and reached Albany. To General Stark, Stephenson reported overhearing Captain Sherwood boast that if he did not have enough prisoners to exchange for 'Major French and other worthy gentlemen' he would go out and catch some if he were permitted. For the benefit of the rebels present, Justus had boosted Jeremiah French's rank.

His expedition, guarded by British regulars, went as far as Isle aux Noix in bateaux, where the whole party went aboard an armed vessel for the journey to Ticonderoga. There they went in bateaux for the rest of the ride to Skenesborough. Ships of the Provincial Marine could have reached that village, but they were reluctant to enter the narrow arm of Lake Champlain where they had less room to manoeuvre if attacked.

Justus was shocked at the condition of the men he received. Some had been held in the holds of ships on the Hudson River; others had suffered close confinement in irons. Still others had been performing hard labour. He looked in vain for Jeremiah French, and only when he called his name and received a reply was he able to discern that this was his brother officer. All the exchanged men were provincials. Some of Burgoyne's regulars had been exchanged earlier, but they had been sent to New York City.

Returning to Fort St. Johns with the freed prisoners, Justus was soon given more responsibility by Brigadier Powell in the selection of scouts who went in quest of intelligence or carried Haldimand's dispatches. The governor depended on Sir John Johnson for information from the Mohawk Valley and Albany, where Dr. George Smyth was a reliable resident agent. Justus was more familiar with loyalists in Vermont and New Hampshire, but he was accumulating considerable intelligence on New Yorkers like Smyth, who signed his messages 'Hudibras'. He had also heard something of a man of mystery the rebels called Hans Waltermyer, a friend of Joseph Bettys, who carried dispatches between Albany and New York City.

On May 6, 1779, a scout named Caleb Clossen arrived from Fort Edward, bringing a newcomer whom he introduced to Justus as John Walden Meyers. The latter had a dispatch that he would surrender only to Brigadier Powell.[3] He spoke with a German accent, towered well over six feet, and had shoulders so broad they dwarfed his massive height — a mountain of a man.[4] He glared at Justus disapprovingly, who reflected that the mere sight of him was sufficient to make others wary. While Meyers was closeted with Brigadier Powell, Clossen informed Justus that he had just met the legendary Hans Waltermyer, who had recently anglicised his name.

Meyers had come all the way from New York City with his dispatch from Sir Henry Clinton, and Clossen had guided him the last stage of the journey because Meyers had never been north of Skenesborough before. Meyers was a tenant farmer from an estate near Albany. Clossen had noticed the look Meyers gave Justus, and he assured him that the scout was a gentle soul.

When Meyers emerged from Powell's quarters, Justus invited the two scouts to dine at his house, hoping to mend some fences with Clossen as the go-between. Grudgingly Meyers accepted, for he had to eat somewhere. Over the meal, mellowed by generous servings of rum, the big German peasant admitted that Powell had ordered him to go to Quebec City to discuss the contents of his dispatch and his own verbal report with Haldimand. He would say nothing more, and Justus respected his reticence.

While they managed a measure of cordiality, Meyers and Sherwood instinctively disliked each other. To Justus, Meyers was a poor-spirited apolitical Yorker. To Meyers, Justus was a despicable rioter who had persecuted his fellow tenant farmers and refused to let them live in peace on acreages they had received from their landlords. Despite Clossen's remark that Meyers was gentle, Justus resolved to handle him with great care. If he were roused he was one man Justus could not defeat in a fair fight.

Meyers had been discreet and after he left Fort St.

Johns Caleb Clossen told Justus why the German had been sent to Quebec City. His intelligence conflicted with the message he carried from Sir Henry Clinton, and Brigadier Powell was worried over the discrepency. Clinton warned Haldimand to expect an attack on Quebec City from the Connecticut Valley, a fairly direct route. Both Meyers and Clossen had seen thirty-five Onondaga prisoners in Albany, captured when the rebels had sent 500 men to destroy the Onondaga settlement to the west of the Mohawk Valley.

Another message Meyers had carried from Clinton informed Haldimand that the rebels planned to attack Fort Detroit, and would make a feint up the Susquehanna Valley to distract the attention of John Butler at Niagara from the real target. Meyers was convinced that the rebels were about to move up the Susquehanna in force, to destroy the Iroquois Confederacy and capture Fort Niagara, and that Clinton had been duped. Apart from some of the Oneidas and Tuscaroras, most of the Six Nations had sided with Britain, although the Onondagas, the first to be struck, had been trying to stay neutral. Justus sent his cousin Thomas Sherwood to find out what the true situation was. His wife Anna was having a baby in May, and anxious to keep in touch with her, Thomas was only too pleased to be asked to go after intelligence.

On May 16, Haldimand announced that all the men who had been with Burgoyne would be regarded as one corps under the command of Daniel McAlpin, who would hold a provisional rank of major of provincials. Captains would receive nine shillings a day, lower wages than they had received under Burgoyne. Justus' pay was reduced, but he did not mind. Brigadier Powell was allowing him extra for the time he spent in rebel territory, which made up the difference.[5] Hitherto, Sir John Johnson had been responsible for the small units, and he had asked the governor to make other arrangements for these troops. Haldimand had more faith in McAlpin than in the other leaders, because he was a half-pay officer from the 60th Regiment, of which His Excellency was the colonel-in-chief.[6]

By the middle of August, John Walden Meyers had

returned to Fort St. Johns, with orders from Haldimand to wait there until he had dispatches for Sir Henry Clinton. Throughout the summer Justus had ample opportunity to observe the hostile scout. Haldimand did not send any dispatches for months, and the hefty German-speaking man was livid.[7] In the interval many reports on developments near Fort Niagara reached Justus.

The feint up the Susquehanna Valley to distract John Butler was a massive attack on the Iroquois Indians by a rebel expedition more than 5,000 strong that was moving towards Fort Niagara. Butler was begging for reinforcements, but Haldimand felt helpless. His supply ships had not arrived by the beginning of August, and until they did, Haldimand felt he could do little to help the Indians.[8]

Early in September, Justus discovered that Haldimand was discouraging recruiting for all but Sir John Johnson's King's Royal Regiment of New York and Brigadier Allan Maclean's Royal Highland Emigrants. The governor claimed that he was having difficulty procuring men to complete these two corps, and he feared that agents trying to complete other regiments might interfere with Johnson's and Maclean's efforts. This was a blow to Justus' hopes and a source of frustration as he worked at Fort St. Johns. Between June 25 and August 24, 337 men had arrived to join provincial corps, of which 61 were for the Queen's Loyal Rangers.[9] After Haldimand's new orders, Justus might never get enough men for a signed commission.

Finally the supply fleet arrived, and on September 13 Haldimand ordered Sir John Johnson to leave Montreal for Niagara, and the loyalist from the Mohawk Valley set out with 201 men.[10] Haldimand dispatched 90 Royal Highland Emigrants to strengthen the garrison at Niagara while Butler's and Johnson's corps were in the field against the rebels. It was too little, too late. The rebel expedition had wrought havoc, but Fort Niagara was saved because the rebels ran short of provisions and turned back.

At Fort St. Johns, Justus had a clear picture of the situation near Fort Niagara, and had had some discussions with John Walden Meyers, still stranded because

Haldimand had failed to send dispatches. As Meyers' frustrations mounted, so did his willingness to talk. Haldimand's restrictions on recruiting made no sense at all. He should have sent every available man to aid Butler and the Indians. The fact that the governor sent only men from the two regiments he was trying to complete was not lost on Justus, and he smoldered as the weeks went by. Why had the governor ignored Meyers' warning? If Haldimand was so callous over the fate of his Indian allies, could loyalists expect more consideration?

On October 6, Brigadier Powell wrote to remind Haldimand that Meyers was still waiting for dispatches, and soon afterward a packet arrived for the sturdy man to take to New York City.[11] A few days later Thomas Sherwood arrived from Fort Edward with his wife Anna, children Reuben and Anna, and a new son, Adiel, born on May 16, 1779. Unlike other loyalists, Thomas' family did not come with only what they could carry and the clothes on their backs. He set out by wagon with a load of household goods for Skenesborough. From there he arranged for a bateau to carry the family and possessions to Fort St. Johns.[12] Anna and the children stayed with Sarah. Thomas was employed mainly on scouting missions; if his family went to the main refugee encampment at Machiche he would be very lonely.

Justus was delighted with Reuben, who had just turned eleven. Stalwart and self-reliant, this young cousin would be an ideal protector for Samuel, now five years old and nearly ready to trade petticoats for small clothes and attend school. Classes were held at the barracks by the Reverend George Gilmore, a chaplain to the regulars. The parents paid 48 pounds to the Anglican clergyman, and Haldimand allowed him some subsidy, as he did Josiah Cass, the schoolmaster at Machiche.[13]

The weather grew cold, the ground snow covered, and the work of interrogating prisoners and refugees nearly came to a halt. Once again Justus could relax and restore his vitality. While Thomas was building an addition to the house so that the two families would have sufficient room, Justus had time to get better acquainted with his children. Diana was three, Levius two, but there must not be any more, not until he knew what the future held. In the house, surrounded by his family, Justus could almost believe that they were back in New Haven, the disruption in their lives merely a bad dream, and Thomas and Anna had come only for a visit. Someday, somehow, they would have a home and a good piece of land. He prayed it would be in Vermont, with the magnificent view of the mountains, amidst scenery that could inspire poetry in the most prosaic of men.

Inside on a winter night that order of banishment ceased to bother him. The temporary commission seemed less important. A few sips of rum to dim reality, and Justus could believe that some day the people of Vermont would welcome him back. Meanwhile, miles away, other men were conspiring to send him home, to a bizarre reception.

The intrigue that eventually sent a banished Yankee captain to Vermont — a pigeon among the cats — began at Sir Henry Clinton's headquarters in New York City. As the year 1780 opened, Colonel Beverley Robinson, of the Loyal American Regiment, who handled some of Clinton's secret correspondence, suggested making an overture to Ethan Allan, now a general in Vermont's army. On March 30, with the approbation of the colonial secretary, Lord George Germain, and Clinton, Robinson wrote a letter to Ethan.[14] It was forwarded to Albany, to be sent on to Vermont by Dr. George Smyth, the reliable resident agent, code name Hudibras.[15] Robinson said he was aware that Ethan was not in sympathy with the rebels' desire to separate from Great Britain, and proposed through correspondence or visits by trusted emissaries, that they discuss the benefits of Vermont's reunion with the mother country.

Robinson was well aware that Ethan and Ira Allen and Governor Thomas Chittenden were conspiring to ensure Vermont's continued independence from New York. The Continental Congress had refused to admit Vermont as the fourteenth state, because that might upset relations with France. The French had made their alliance with thirteen states, and turned balky when the Congress suggested extending it to include a fourteenth, one that bordered on Canada, which the British might easily occupy.

British propaganda had been successful. The rebels in the northern states were convinced that Haldimand had 10,000 crack regulars standing by to invade Vermont at any moment — which was exactly what the Swiss professional wanted them to believe. In fact, Haldimand had less than 5,000 British regulars, which included the Royal Highland Emigrants, recently put on the British establishment as the 84th Foot. In addition, he had 2,000 Germans, some 1,500 provincials, and 17,500 Canadian militia. In the latter two groups he placed scant confidence. A neutral state on Canada's border would be a blessing.[16]

With the security of Canada in mind, as well as the future of British North America, Robinson had written on March 30 to Ethan. For Vermont, Robinson's suggestion had two advantages. It would rid the Green Mountain people of domination by New York and make it difficult for the Congress to use coercion — because of the danger of tangling with Haldimand's mythical army — and ensure that the same mythical army did not descend from Canada and put an end to the rebellion in Vermont. That Haldimand lacked the troops was irrelevant. The threat was what counted.

Early in April, Ethan was accosted in Arlington's only street by a man dressed as a farmer, who shoved a letter into his hand. Ethan glanced at it, sent the messenger away, and hurried to the home of Governor Thomas Chittenden.[17] Later, Ethan claimed that he did not receive this letter until July. He did not reply, and Haldimand sent a letter to Sir John Johnson, asking his opinion of Dr. George Smyth, who had been responsible for delivering the message to Allen. The doctor worked in the rebels' military hospital in Albany and might be a double agent. Sir John assured Haldimand that Smyth could be trusted and had already suffered greatly for the cause.[18]

In July, after much furtive shuffling, the Vermont leaders wrote to the Continental Congress in Philadelphia, pointing out that the republic had never waged war against Britain, nor joined the Congress by confederation. (They overlooked the Battle of Bennington, almost three years before, when Seth Warner's regiment and the militia had taken part.) The letter was written by Ethan for the illiterate Chittenden, its meaning deliberately opaque — part veiled threat, part a declaration that Vermont was at peace with Britain. If the Congress would not admit Vermont, she was free to make her own terms with the mother country.

Justus had some inkling that these machinations were taking place. One of his sources was a half-Indian scout named Corporal David Crowfoot, whom he described to Captain Robert Mathews, the governor's secretary, as 'a man of no great penetration but sincerely honest and true'.[19] Frequently near Arlington in search of intelligence, Crowfoot returned with the story about Ethan receiving a letter from the mysterious stranger. Although the big mountain chieftain denied it, several people had noticed, and no one believed him.

Meanwhile, anxious as he was for news from Vermont, Justus was occupied with his usual duties. Joseph Bettys came in with twelve prisoners, the most impressive tally to date by any scout. With two Canadians and 58 Indians, Bettys had captured a rebel patrol near Skenesborough, and marched the captives to Fort St. Johns. Brigadier Powell sent them to Montreal, where they were placed in a house under guard. Two of the rebels removed a window grating, lowered themselves on blankets to the ground and escaped, but the others would be used in a prisoner exchange.[20]

Also, to Justus' satisfaction, Haldimand lifted the restrictions on recruiting. Johnson's and Maclean's battalions were close to full strength, and a general order from Quebec City announced that the officers of all provincial corps would have permanent rank in the army, as well as half-pay when their corps were reduced.[21] Now Justus had real incentives for completing his company, and several refugees who reached Fort St. Johns agreed to serve with him.

In the Mohawk Valley, Butler's Rangers and the King's Royal Regiment of New York were laying waste to all the frontier settlements, burning crops, driving off livestock, forcing the farmers to seek shelter in Schenectady and Albany. In fact, they were winning the war in the north and the rebels were utterly demoralized. On

July 13 Haldimand gave Sir John Johnson permission to raise a second battalion.

Another encouraging sign was the arrival at Fort St. Johns of James Rogers, the major of a new corps called the King's Rangers. Almost at once this news turned sour. The lieutenant-colonel of the corps was James' brother, Robert Rogers of Seven Years' War fame, who had received his warrant to raise the regiment from Sir Henry Clinton in New York City. The King's Rangers belonged to the Central Department, and from Quebec City Governor Haldimand ordered James to return to New York City. James had hoped to get recruits along Canada's frontiers, but Haldimand wanted all such recruits for his own regiments.[22]

Late in July Major Daniel McAlpin died, and Haldimand placed all the below strength units again under the command of Sir John Johnson. Sherwood's company was at Sorel with Lieutenant Dulmage, and he learned that all was well with his men when Captain Jeremiah French, now recovered from his long confinement at the hands of the rebels, visited Fort St. Johns.

As the summer passed, the juggling continued in Vermont. Brigadier Powell sent Justus a note enquiring how much he knew about Ethan Allen. Justus replied that he was well acquainted with Mr. Allen, and with most of the leaders in Vermont. He was certain they would accept any proposal rather than give up their lands to New Yorkers, adding:

> I should be extremely happy to be in some Measure instrumental in bringing deluded people to their right senses and the allegiance they owe their Sovereign which I think may be done by buying their leaders.[23]

He was being cynical, but the thickness of their pocketbooks was of great significance to the plotters in the Green Mountains.

Late in August, to Justus' surprise, his brother Samuel arrived at Fort St. Johns, accompanied by his wife Eunice, year-old-daughter Rachel, and a slave.[24] Samuel had decided to leave when he found that the rebels were suspicious of him. He agreed to join Justus' company as a volunteer, hoping to bring in enough recruits to qualify for a commission. He would remain at the fort as one of his brother's scouts, making himself useful in a number of ways. Eunice and Rachel stayed in the house with Sarah and Anna, for like Thomas, Samuel wanted to see more of them than would be possible if they went to Machiche with the other refugee families.[25]

Justus soon felt the effect of the scurrying in Vermont. Loyalists were arriving from there, and he learned that Governor Chittenden was issuing passports to all who wished to join the King's troops in Canada. Many of the families brought slaves, for Vermont's sincerity over abolishing bondage was one more example of Green Mountain bluff.

Among these loyalists came Captain Samuel Wright, who had been captured at the Battle of Bennington. Wright was released to carry a letter from Governor Chittenden to Governor Haldimand. As the paroled officer was setting out for Quebec City, Justus could hardly contain himself. Chittenden must be proposing that Vermont rejoin the British Empire. Why else would the governor of the republic want to communicate with the governor of Canada?

Chapter 9

With Fife and Drum

On August 24, from Fort St. Johns, Justus sent a message to a friend in Vermont named Hawkins, telling him he thought reunion with Britain could be effected because the people in the republic were disenchanted with the Continental Congress.[1] Late in September, Samuel Sherwood, who had been scouting for his brother, returned and reported that Hawkins had been arrested and spirited to Albany before the message reached him.[2] The imprisonment of Hawkins forewarned Justus that some people were opposed to the plotters in Bennington and Arlington. Reunion would not be effected without overcoming some obstacles. The inhabitants on the east and west sides of the Green Mountains were not united.

Those on the west side were mainly Connecticut-born, and Baptist or Anglican. To the east were more Congregationalists and a few pockets of New Yorkers. The Congregationalists wanted to continue the rebellion, and the Yorkers wanted no quarrel with their own kind. The instigators of the plot for reunion were nearly all on the west side — Chittenden, Ethan and Ira Allen, the Fays, the Brownson brothers of Sunderland, and Samuel and Moses Robinson. The latter, a judge, was the only ringleader who lived on the east side. The clique planning to open negotiations with Haldimand had to keep their intent a secret from many people in Vermont.

Nevertheless, as the autumn progressed Justus was feeling optimistic. If the plot succeeded he could go home when hostilities ended. Then, too, Benedict Arnold had reached New York City after his unsuccessful attempt to hand over the fort at West Point to the British. In the southern colonies, from all accounts, a large British expeditionary force was doing well, clearing more and more territory of rebels. Not only that, Haldimand had authorized Major Christopher Carleton to lead an expedition of provincials and regulars 800 strong to destroy outposts along the west side of Lake Champlain, on New York territory. The men assembled at Fort St. Johns on September 27, and the following day the expedition set out, accompanied by 100 Indians. As the men were leaving, Justus was disappointed that Carleton had not asked for him to join as a scout.[3]

He soon learned why he had been passed over. Early in October, he received a summons to wait upon Brigadier Powell, and their very private meeting left him elated, if a trifle apprehensive. The letter from Governor Chittenden, which Captain Samuel Wright had carried from Skenesborough to Quebec City, did propose a truce between Vermont and Great Britain. Some months before, in anticipation of such a proposal, Haldimand had written to Lord George Germain, the secretary of state for the colonies, for instructions. Towards the end of September, by order of Germain, Haldimand accepted Chittenden's offer, and agreed to talks under a flag of truce. While these talks, disguised as prisoner exchanges, were taking place, Chittenden promised that Vermont would be neutral.

As commissioners to represent the republic, Chittenden appointed Colonel Ira Allen and Major Joseph Fay, of the Vermont army. As his commissioner, Haldimand selected Captain Sherwood, assisted by Major Alexander Dundas, the commandant of Isle aux Noix. Reflecting that Chittenden was more generous with promotions than Haldimand, Justus almost missed Powell's next pronouncement. The Green Mountain conspirators assured Haldimand that despite the order of banishment, Captain Sherwood would be in no danger. Justus had some reservations, but risking his life was a small price to pay for the chance to bring Vermont back into the British fold.

While Justus waited for orders to set out to meet Ira Allen and Joseph Fay, reports on Carleton's expedition poured into Fort St. Johns. The major's force had struck Fort Ann, Fort Edward and Fort George, and taken many prisoners, who were being sent to Canada. At the same time an expedition was sent through the Mohawk Valley, under Sir John Johnson, and a smaller one led by Captain John Munro was to raid Ballstown, Joe Bettys' home village north of Schenectady. Carleton's raid, and to some extent Johnson's and Munro's, were staged in preparation for a mission Haldimand had formulated for his commissioner to the Vermont ringleaders. The aggressive behavior was directed against New York, but the governor was using it to put the folk next door in a co-operative frame of mind.

On October 24, Justus received instructions from Brigadier Powell to leave for Miller's Bay, a cove on the west side of Lake Champlain eight kilometres north of Crown Point, where the ships of the Provincial Marine often took shelter. There he would meet Major Carleton, and proceed to Castleton, where Ethan Allen had his headquarters. Justus' mission would be concealed under the guise of a cartel to open negotiations for prisoner exchanges. He left Fort St. Johns with an escort of regulars and Captain John Chipman, the commandant of Fort George who had been captured by Carleton's raiders. After giving his parole, Chipman was to be exchanged for Captain Samuel Wright. Chipman was a Yorker, but Haldimand felt that the Vermont leaders would be pleased if he released a man of like rank.

Travelling in an armed vessel, Justus and his party reached Miller's Bay on the 26th, where Major Carleton had halted his expedition after the tour of destruction against New York. The weather was bitingly cold. Lieutenant John Enys, of the 29th Regiment, recorded in his journal:

> On the 26 we all got under way to return to Canada but to our great disappointment had not gone more than two leagues before we Met an express from the Commander in Chief ordering us to keep on the Lake as long as possible. . .. we again return'd to our old Station in Mill Bay. As Soon as we had arrived in our Camp, one Capt. Sherwood of the Roialists, was sent

with a flag of truce to the State of Vert Mont.

After conferring with Major Carleton, Justus asked for a cutter, eyeing the strong wind blowing straight from the south. When Carleton offered a bateau Justus reiterated his request. The lateen sail on the bateau would only run before the wind, but a cutter was sloop rigged. He intended to sail against those headwinds, for rowing would be nearly impossible. After Justus persuaded Carleton that he was a seafaring man, the major reluctantly handed over the ship's boat belonging to the sloop *Lee*, begging him not to smash it. Setting out, Justus ordered his regulars to row the cutter into the wind while he unfurled the main and jib. Taking the tiller, he instructed his landlubber crew to hoist the canvas. Throwing the tiller hard over he ordered the others to row across the wind until her sails filled. Happily he beat back and forth, impressed with his own skill after so many years. The cutter was a joy to handle.[4]

Justus' journal began:

> Received His Excellency's Instructions for a Negotiation with the State of Vermont, and Major Carleton's order to proceed to that State with a Flag — Sett off at 7 o'clock in the evening with a Drum, Fife and five Privates, with Capt. Chipman & his Servant in a cutter — went about six miles in a strong head Wind.[5]

He was in full regimentals, quite unlike his furtive visit of June and July, 1778. He continued:

> 27th. Imbarked at six o'clock — still a head wind — encamped six miles above Ticonderoga.
>
> 28th. Imbarked at four o'clock — at one landed Chipman & his Servant and Baggage at Skenesborough. Then proceeded to the head of East Bay.

East Bay was a long creek that ran northward from its mouth on Lake Champlain for sixteen kilometres, then swung west. Justus had the men row the cutter to a point where Castleton was about twenty kilometres inland:

> Landed at four afternoon, set off immediately with the Drum, Fife and two Men: leaving a Flag and three men with the Cutter — Arrived at 7 o'clock at Col Herrick's Camp — a frontier post of 300 men, at Mills about four miles west of the Blockhouse at Castleton, was blindfolded and led to Col. Herrick's Room. . .. Genl Allen commanded at Castleton and that my Dispatches would be forwarded without delay — at about

11 this evening received a Message from Genl. Allen.

The blindfolding was a charade. Justus knew the area well, and if he needed information on Fort Vengeance, Herrick's camp, he would have sent a scout for it. Herrick was the man who had sent Sarah Sherwood towards Ticonderoga when she left Vermont under her safe conduct. Justus handed over his official dispatches, those which pertained to an exchange of prisoners, keeping back some top secret ones he was to disclose only if Ethan consented.

At eleven o'clock on the morning of October 29, Justus was escorted to the home of Major Isaac Clarke, in Castleton. Ethan was there, and a sight to behold, resplendent in a pale blue coat with two huge gold epaulettes that made his already massive shoulders look as wide as his more than six foot height, dazzling yellow breeches, and a cavalryman's sword that clanked every time he moved — larger than life he was. The slender Justus, in his red ranger coat, sporting one modest silver epaulette, seemed a discreet shadow of his former friend and leader. With Ethan were his council of ten officers, to whom he introduced Captain Sherwood as a British officer. That raised some eyebrows. How many of that ilk had once been outlaws in the Green Mountains?

"Members of the Council" boomed Ethan, who was incapable of modulating his stentorian tones. "Captain Sherwood's instructions are somewhat discretionary. I wish to have a private word with him so that I may be of assistance in explaining the business to you." The council agreed to allow Justus and Ethan to hold a short conference. Justus reported:

> after much conversation informed him that I had some business of importance with him, but before I communicated it, must request his honor as a Gentleman that should it not please him, he would take no advantage of me, nor even mention it while I remained in the Country — He said he would if it was no damned Arnold Plan, to sell his Country and his own Honour by betraying the trust reposed in him. I replied that my business with him was, in my opinion, on a Very Honourable Nature, but as I did not know how far his opinion and mine would differ, I should insist on his most sacred promise that in whatever light he might view it, he would not expose me — To this after some Con-

sideration he consented.

"His Excellency," Justus said, "is well aware of all that has passed between Vermont and the Congress, and he views this as a favourable opportunity for you to cast off the Congress yoke and resume your former allegiance to the King of Great Britain. By doing which, you would secure for yourselves those privileges you have so long contended for with New York."

Justus' journal resumed:

> I then made known to him the Generals proposals, then expressed my own anxious desire that they would accept them informing him, that it was not from any selfish motives of my own, but the tender Sentiments of regard and friendship which I felt for the People of Vermont, that induced me to wish them to accept of those proposals

Sherwood was being generous, or at least tongue in cheek, and he was not a man who held a grudge. After the abuse he had suffered, the public flogging, imprisonment, and the sentence to Simsbury Mines, he was putting his head into the lion's mouth, willing to paint a situation any colour to achieve his goal of living in New Haven once more. Ethan replied:

> that the proposals, so far as they concerned his personal promotion had not the weight of a straw with him, and that he was not to be purchased at any rate, that he had been offered a lieutenant-colonel's commission on condition of changing sides while in Captivity, which he had refused as he ever meant to be governed by the strictest rule of Honour and Justice, but that since the Proposals seemed materially to concern the whole People of Vermont whose liberties and properties for a number of years past were much dearer to him than his own life, he would take them into very Serious Consideration

Then Ethan recommended returning to his council, lest some become suspicious. Justus asked him whether he could raise the question of reunion, but Ethan gazed at him vaguely. For the present only the cartel for the exchange of prisoners should be disclosed. When the two rejoined the council, Justus laid the letters pertaining to the public part of his mission before the members, and Major Joseph Fay read them aloud. Justus recorded:

> They appear well satisfied with the contents of them, except that part of Maj. Carleton's letter respecting

> the limits of the Truce — Some of them suspected a design on the Frontiers of New York, while the negotiation was on foot with Vermont — to this I became a Pledge on the part of the Government, that no movement would be made on the offensive by Maj. Carleton, and informed the Major of it in a letter by Genl. Allen's Flag — After this Genl. Allen wrote circular letters to all his officers commanding Frontier Posts informing them to call in all their Scouts and not to suffer any more to be sent out during the present truce — These Letters were read to us in Council — about one o'clock the Council broke up and Maj. Fay was sent express with my dispatches to Bennington — Had another short conversation with Genl. Allen this evening.

Thus ended October 29. During their short conversation, Justus did most of the listening, allowing Ethan to ramble on, giving free rein to his highly controversial notions of the nature of the universe and the wickedness of the Congregational ministers, who maintained that a man had access to God only through them. Rum flowed freely and both men were somewhat intoxicated, enough so that Justus could believe Ethan was serious in his intellectual pursuits, although in the former's experience, the eldest of the Allen brothers had been a war-horse all his life.

On October 30, Sherwood and Allen met again, and conversed 'free of any restraint'. Justus told Ethan he had brought written proposals and had secreted them, but could procure them if the other thought proper. Ethan said he would send Ira Allen and Joseph Fay to Canada with him to read them on safer ground. At that time, it would be unwise to let anyone suspect that more than neutrality was involved. Ethan was surrounded on all sides by enemies, the most inveterate being New York. To Justus this seemed incompatible with the council of officers' insistence that the truce also cover parts of New York. Behind his hand, Ethan admitted that Vermont had designs on that territory, which clarified certain underlying motives for Justus. Ethan vowed that he was 'heartily weary of war, and wished once more to enjoy the sweets of peace and devote himself to his philosophical studies'.

Again the rum was flowing, and both men were inebriated. Since Justus was taking Ethan seriously, he was not quite himself. Ethan said that while he could never betray Vermont, he was inclined towards Britain, rather than the Congress, but it was not within his power to speak out at present. His own people, he claimed, would cut off his head! He told Justus that the neighbouring states could send 30,000 men into Vermont in thirty days' time — a whopping over-statement of rebel strength then available to crush Vermont.

Congress, Ethan maintained, was bound to support New York, and he boasted that he would soon publish a manifesto declaring Vermont neutral. 'Free and independent of any Power on Earth, and will invite all People to trade with her'. Also, should he decide to raise his own brigade and occupy Albany, he was confident thousands from the neighbouring states would join him. If he were obliged to retreat to Ticonderoga, Haldimand should send a force to help him. The governor should then establish outposts at Albany and Bennington, and would need at least 20,000 men. Clearly Ethan had no accurate information regarding British strength in Canada, and Justus was leaving him in the dark.

If Haldimand did not wish to occupy these posts, he should offer other proposals for Vermont to consider, and Ethan spelled out his demands:

> He expects to command his own forces, Vermont must be a government Separate from and independent of any other Province in America — must choose their own Civil officers and Representatives; to be entitled to all the Privileges offered to other States by the King's Commissioners

Ethan was asking for a government based on Connecticut's charter, and Justus, with the same background, agreed, seeing nothing out of order in the other's aspirations. Ethan said 'a revolution of this nature must be the work of time; That it is impossible to bring so many different Minds into one channel on a sudden'.

He dared not at present send to or receive any letters from Major Carleton or General Haldimand, and he wanted to keep open the negotiations under flags of truce. Such flags should always have some business with New York to allay suspicions. As a parting shot, Ethan said that if Congress should grant Vermont a seat in its assembly, all negotiations would be ended and kept secret by both sides. However, the cartel to exchange prisoners should go ahead and be observed 'with honour'. Vermont officers then prisoners in Canada, if not exchanged before winter, should be given as much freedom as could safely be arranged.

These demands were heavily weighted on the side of the republic, but Justus was convinced that the Congress would never agree to Vermont's proposals, and there was hope for the British province he so earnestly desired. The most dramatic part of the journal lies in Sherwood's account of what followed his meeting with Ethan – a tale of hours of trauma, infuriating frustrations and backbreaking toil:

> About three this afternoon Genl. Allen parted with me for Bennington, left me with one Cap. Parker, a very civil Gentleman, with instructions to treat me with all possible politeness – This evening, I had notice that Maj. Eben. [Ebenezer] Allen's Scouts had discovered that Maj. Carleton had returned with his whole detachment from Miller's Bay to Tyconderoga, and was drawing some boats over the landing, had sent a Detachment on the East side and I was soon after put under strict charge of two Centinals — some said my life should answer for the Consequences, some said one thing, and some another, but all conspired to make me very uneasy

Major Ebenezer Allen, another of Ethan's cousins, was in command of Castleton during the other's absence. Ebenezer led a faction that had no desire for dealings with the British, whether for prisoner exchanges or deeper plots, and he did his best to the point of insubordination to frustrate the conspirators. He spread false information, seizing the opportunity Ethan's absence afforded to have Sherwood murdered. If British emissaries were not safe under their flags of truce, Haldimand would not send any more of them. Ebenezer was also lying, for Major Carleton had not been near Ticonderoga and was still at Miller's Bay, abiding by the truce. Justus acted quickly, sending a letter to Ethan's truculent relative:

> wrote to Maj. Allen assuring him of Maj. Carleton's good Faith, informed him that disputing his good Intentions, was disputing the Faith of Government, as

he acted by the Generals order – As to the Indians, if there had been any then they must be straggling . . .. if so they would not attempt anything except hunger precipitated them to it, advised him to watch their motions and rest assured that if they destroyed any property belonging to the Inhabitants I would give security for the payment

He did not receive a reply, and on the 31st began a nerve-wracking nightmare. By order of Ebenezer, Justus and his party were placed in charge of Captain Brownson and twenty men. The captain told Justus he could not speak to anyone without his knowledge. That day they marched forty-six kilometres to Pawlet, and Justus found the populace very alarmed because of Ebenezer's insistence that Carleton was marauding nearby. Through the long hours, Justus refused to be intimidated as he marched, an embarrassed, protesting Captain Parker by his side. Again a Calvinistic determinism sustained him. If God had decided his time had come, there was nothing he could do to save himself. Ethan and his talk of free will could go hang. He hoped Haldimand would allow Sarah a generous pension, or failing that she would find a husband worthy of her. Murder was not the way of the Green Mountain people, but only one itchy finger on a firelock was sufficient to send him to meet his maker. People were 'rabid and insulting to me' he commented, adding:

Nov. 1st. Marched 10 Miles in a tedious snow storm. 2nd Marched 20 Miles to Arlington, This morning received a Message from Gov. Chittington [sic] expressing his disapprobation of Maj. Allen's Conduct, and his orders to Cap. Brownson that I should be treated in a manner that an officer of a Flag had the right to expect

On November 3, Major Isaac Clarke returned from a 'Flag to Maj Carleton' and his report much calmed the doubts of the populace. The following day, November 4, Justus received permission from Governor Chittenden for his departure. Three more days passed before his party set out for Castleton — days wasted while Chittenden and Ebenezer wrangled and called each other every name in the book. At length civil authority triumphed over the military, and on the 7th, Justus and his escort, accompanied by Captain Brownson, set out for Castleton on hired horses.

Meanwhile, Governor Haldimand had begun to worry about Sherwood's safety. The news that Major John André of the Queen's Rangers, had been caught after leaving Benedict Arnold's headquarters at West Point was well known. Rumours that he had been hanged had reached Quebec City. Writing to Major Carleton on November 8, Haldimand said that the fate of Major André 'shows the fatal consequences of being frustrated'. Mr. Sherwood being in the 'Enemy's Power strengthens this Necessity' and he recommended that Carleton withdraw Justus as soon as possible.[6]

The entry in Justus' journal for November 9 read:

> A Snow storm this day, arrived at Castleton. 9th. Col. Allen and Maj. Fay arrived as Commissioners to negotiate the Cartel – forbid by Maj. Allen to proceed till the 11th towards night, then set off and went to East Bay – found it frozen about two inches thick.

Momentarily Justus wondered why Ira Allen let Ebenezer push him around when he outranked him. Joseph Fay answered him. If Ira came down too hard on behalf of Haldimand's commissioner, Ebenezer might become even more suspicious. Besides, as he had demonstrated, Ebenezer commanded the loyalty of far too many men of the Castleton garrison, and could flex his military muscle.

At East Bay the cutter was entrapped, and Justus' only entry for November 12 was 'Broke the Ice about three miles'. He wished he had left the boat on the shore of Lake Champlain and walked the few extra distance to Castleton.

While Justus and his escort worked feverishly to reach the open lake, Major Carleton and his expedition remained encamped at Miller's Bay, with an outpost at Crown Point. Rations were short, the men crouching round campfires, shivering in bitter cold. The sloop *Lee* patroled offshore looking for Sherwood and the cutter. By November 12, Carleton felt he could hold out no longer, convinced that the Vermonters had double crossed Haldimand. Justus must be a prisoner by now, if indeed he was still alive. Reluctantly the major ordered a withdrawal. His men took to the bateaux, while parties of refugees who had joined them went aboard the sloop for the journey to Isle aux Noix.[7]

The following day, the 13th, Justus and his men broke the ice another three miles. By that time Ira Allen and Joseph Fay had become restive. The journal continued:

> 14th. Allen and Fay turned back and said they would come to St. Johns by ice as soon as possible – I had the day before shown them the General's proposals, after perusing them and discoursing largely on the subject – we burned them.

On parting, Justus promised Allen and Fay that when they came to meet him at Isle aux Noix, he would show them Haldimand's orders empowering him to act as his commissioner. He agreed to use his influence to have Vermont officers in Canada freed on parole. The two conspirators handed over ten days supply of bread and beef for Sherwood's party, and took leave of him. The rest of the day passed breaking ice another 'three miles, and on the 15th yet another three'. Justus' journal resumed:

> 16th. Three miles to Fidler's Elbow. From the 17th to the 19th Break the Ice about eleven Miles, to the open Lake. This evening sent the Cutter forward with orders to proceed as fast as possible to Ty – and there wait for me.

He wanted to be away from the vicinity, lest Ebenezer Allen make more mischief. With the time consumed breaking ice, his party was again short of provisions, and accompanied by one man, Justus set out on foot for Skenesborough. There he bought 'five bushels of Indian corn' and other food. Out of cash, he borrowed '30 pounds of pork from Ensign McDonald'. The two carried these heavy loads on their backs 'three miles to South Bay', where they appropriated a skiff and left a message for the owner. Mr. Ephriam Jones of the Commissary Department would pay him, or Justus would send him as good a one in the spring.

Rejoining the cutter on the 21st, Justus sailed as far as Chimney Point, on the east side of Lake Champlain opposite Crown Point, where he waited for Captain McDonald's family. The captain was in Canada, and his wife and children wanted to join him. Towards dusk, near Miller's Bay, Justus took aboard two men, four women and four children who had been four days without food. Now his enlarged party was short of provisions, and his people had been on half rations before the newcomers joined him. With ten more mouths to feed, and a total of twenty-five persons, he had only 'thirty pounds of bread and meat and half a pint of Indian corn per day to each person'.

On the 22nd they went 'two miles' against a strong headwind, snow swirling about the cutter, and had to lie up for most of the day. His entry for the 23rd read 'A Favourable Wind – Run about sixty miles to Tea Kettle Island'. The tail wind was gratifying. The cutter sped down the lake, main and jib winged — a blessing for the starving soldiers and refugees aboard. By the 24th the ordeal was ending: 'Arrived at Point au Fer and rowed this night to Isle aux Noix – 26th, about ten o'clock this morning arrived safe at St. Johns, waited on Maj. Carleton, delivered him my Dispatches'.

Christopher Carleton was vastly relieved when he saw Justus. The two officers held a conference with Colonel Barry St. Leger, the new commandant of Fort St. Johns. Brigadier Powell had been sent to Fort Niagara. On the 28th, Carleton and Sherwood set off in a sleigh for Quebec City to confer with Haldimand, a Canadian driver at the reins, stopping each night at an inn. The sleigh followed the snow-covered road northward and turned at Sorel to follow the St. Lawrence. On December 1 they reached the outskirts of Quebec City.[8]

Chapter 10

Justus Smells Success

Towards evening on December 1 the sleigh carried Justus and Major Carleton past the barricades and batteries that protected the Lower Town. The driver stopped at an inn for a fresh horse before attempting the stiff climb to the Upper Town, and the two officers had some food. Back in the sleigh Justus looked about him as the driver guided the horse across Notre Dame Street and up the winding hill to the Place D'Armes, at the corner of which stood the citadel. Passing a sentry at the gate the sleigh came to a halt before a vast, dreary looking edifice — The Château St. Louis, the governor's residence.

Inside they stood in a drafty, gloomy hallway awaiting Captain Robert Mathews, Haldimand's secretary. Justus shuddered, and was not surprised when Carleton observed that the governor hated the uncomfortable mansion. When Mathews arrived he gave them an appointment to see His Excellency early the following morning. Major Carleton left to join his wife at a house where she rented rooms, while Mathews escorted Justus to the officers' quarters in the barracks at the end of Baude Street.

Justus was awake early after a night of fitful sleep, and Major Carleton arrived in a sleigh to accompany him back to the Château St. Louis. The meeting was brief, for Haldimand had many commitments. He ordered Justus to remain at the barracks, and he would send for him when he had more time. He was hoping for dispatches by way of the Saint John Valley from Sir Henry Clinton, apprising him of information on Vermont that had reached New York City. Before dismissing the two officers, he warned them that they should expect to be in the city for at least three weeks. Carleton was delighted, but Justus fumed when he left the château. Damn Ebenezer Allen for the trickery that had held him up nine full days. Without that piece of duplicity, he might have got the cutter out of East Bay before it iced over and been home two weeks sooner. Now he would miss spending Christmas with Sarah and the children.[1]

Haldimand summoned him occasionally for discussions at which Captain Mathews was always present, and occasionally Major Carleton. In between times Carleton entertained him frequently, and Captain Mathews, who lived at the same barracks, did his best to cheer him up, taking him to social affairs when he was off duty. By December 20, Haldimand had digested Justus' report, and he wrote to Sir Henry Clinton to inform him that he was optimistic about Vermont.[2] Whenever the governor had time, he and Justus speculated long on whether any of the Allens could be trusted. They might be using the threat of reunion only as a weapon to force the Congress to grant statehood.

Much as Ethan bragged of being a man of honour, Justus suspected him capable of double dealing, but as he had told Brigadier Powell, the Vermont leaders could be bought. There was also Ira, with his secretive ways, his face a mask as he burned Justus' top secret letters from Haldimand back at East Bay. Tom Chittenden, too, feigned artlessness. He might pose as a half-wit farmer, but he was one of the shrewdest men in the Green Mountains. Ethan was easy to read, but he was only one of the conspirators, a man of action in a game that called for delicate manoeuvres.

Haldimand was prepared to suspend all discussions if he suspected duplicity, but Justus pointed out another reason for continuing. A truce and Vermont neutrality were useful ends in themselves, a help to loyalists, his own people and his first concern. Furthermore, Ethan had warned him that it would take time to persuade the people of Vermont to accept reunion as an alternative to statehood. A neutral Vermont was a guarantee that a rebel army could not sweep up the Connecticut Valley and attack Quebec. Then, too, the adjacent parts of New York were to be included in the neutral zone, and there was a possibility of extending the truce into New Hampshire. By stopping the war in the northern colonies, victory might be won through negotiation, without further bloodshed.

When not closeted with the governor, Justus found the social life dazzling. Each night there was a ball or a dinner party or the theatre to attend. Popular London plays and ambitious Shakespearian productions were staged by members of the garrison. As Christmas drew nearer the pace quickened, and he found the food almost more than he could endure, still recovering from his days on short rations.[3]

At the nightly festivities the red coats outnumbered the ladies' gowns by three to one. In that setting Justus felt he could identify with little Cinderella. Like her, he had been cold and hungry, and now he had been catapulted into the lap of luxury, amidst the most influential people in the province, waiting for a midnight that would thrust him back into reality. Before introducing Justus into the officers' mess, Captain Mathews had a word with some of the snobbish young regulars. The tall provincial in worn regimentals with the Yankee twang would not be visiting a tailor before mingling with them. Captain Sherwood was not a poorly educated younger son of the country gentry whose father had bought him a commission and was sending him an allowance to pay his gaming debts. To overcome the effects of gluttony and indulgence in wine and spirits, Justus needed long walks in the sub-zero cold that left his breath frozen on the hair close to his face.

At one of their last meetings Haldimand informed Justus that in addition to being a Commissioner of Prisoners and Refugees, and his role in the Vermont negotiations, he was to be in charge of sending out all scouting parties from Isle aux Noix. Haldimand would continue to rely on Sir John Johnson for information on the Mohawk Valley and Albany, otherwise Justus was to be responsible for the scouts around Lake Champlain. On matters that concerned Vermont, Justus was to talk only with

Major Dundas, the commandant of Isle aux Noix. For greater security, Dundas would be the sole British regular officer involved in the discussions soon to take place with Ira Allen and Joseph Fay.[4]

On New Year's Day, Justus and Major Carleton set off up the ice of the St. Lawrence in a sleigh. They stopped at Sorel so that Justus could see the men of his company and confer with John Dulmage. From Dulmage Justus learned that his superior officer was now Major John Nairne, 84th Regiment, appointed to replace the late Daniel McAlpin.[5] As the sleigh carried them along the Richelieu, Justus knew that this winter would be different from the two previous ones, and he would have less time to devote to his family. Yet he was not downhearted. The work he was doing might lead to Vermont's reunion, and his near and dear would one day return to New Haven. Haldimand was optimistic, Justus bursting with enthusiasm.

On January 6, 1781, replying to a letter from Mathews, Justus wrote that he could easily find three trusty guides to accompany Caleb Clossen and David Crowfoot whenever Colonel St. Leger gave the order. Justus also wanted to move his entire scouting operation to Isle aux Noix, because Haldimand wanted him to report only to Major Dundas. Since some of the information the scouts brought in concerned Vermont, Justus assumed that Dundas was his superior, and his reports should be forwarded to him. For some time he remained at Fort St. Johns, because a mild spell and unsafe ice made travelling nearly impossible.

On the 18th, Colonel St. Leger ordered him to take six scouts and accompany Lieutenant William Twiss, Royal Engineers, along Lake Champlain. Twiss had asked for Captain Sherwood, but Justus felt he must stay in case Ira Allen and Joseph Fay arrived. Nor could he produce the other scouts. He had only six men at Isle aux Noix, but all were about to depart for Albany and Vermont. All the other scouts were already in rebel territory.[6]

Colonel St. Leger was furious, and demanded to know why he had not been informed about all parties leaving Isle aux Noix. No scouts should go into enemy territory without his permission since he was senior to both Major Dundas at Isle aux Noix and Major Carleton at Pointe au Fer. Justus felt he had too many masters, and did not deserve St. Leger's wrath. A week later he received Mathews' reply. His Excellency was pleased with Justus' work, but Mathews did not say which of the post commanders was his superior.[7]

He was also disgruntled with the results of Haldimand's latest recruiting drive. His company was little more than half strength, and agents were no longer finding Vermont fertile ground. Other corps commanders were constantly bickering over the few recruits that had come, and the situation was enflamed by the efforts of Major James Rogers to fill the ranks of the King's Rangers. Because his home was in Londonderry, Vermont, Rogers had the same appeal as John Peters to loyalists in that area. However, Ebenezer Jessup had complaints about Rogers, and so did most of the other commanders of small units. Haldimand had established a Board of Officers which met periodically to deal with the complaints, and decide where each recruit would be assigned.[8]

As soon as the weather turned cold, Justus drove in a sleigh to Isle aux Noix, to see whether Major Dundas had news of Ira Allen and Joseph Fay. The major had not heard a word, and while Justus was there, hoping that a message would arrive, the Board of Officers held a meeting at Fort St. Johns. Justus' claim was neglected, for on the board was Lieutenant Edward Carscallan, who had led the exodus from Justus' company after the Battle of Bennington. On February 19, Justus returned to Fort St. Johns to discover that James Rogers had succeeded in claiming some of his men. Writing to Captain Mathews, Justus stressed that he would be on his guard when the Vermont Commissioners appeared, and ended his letter:

> P.S. I understand that I have lost some men that I claimed to Rogers' Corps by not being there to support my claim, or rather to state it, as it seems Col. Peters has left them off his List[9]

Colonel Peters was jealous of his junior officer, and had deliberately overlooked the men. Now that Justus was occupied with prisoners and refugees, Vermont and the scouting missions, he was unable to do duty with the Queen's Loyal Rangers at Sorel. Then, one of the scouts,

Captain Azariah Pritchard, King's Rangers, informed Justus that the majority of the people in Vermont favoured neutrality, while a minority was in 'the utmost Confusion and undetermined what course to take'. Justus sent Pritchard on a scout towards the Connecticut Valley to see what else that officer could glean.

On the night of March 9, Pritchard returned with a prisoner named Thomas Johnson, a resident of the eastern part of Vermont, and a lieutenant-colonel in the rebel militia.[10] Colonel St. Leger entertained him to dinner, and afterwards gave him the freedom of Fort St. Johns. He asked Justus to chat with the distinguished captive to see whether he was reliable. Johnson was offering to become a resident agent if he were allowed to return home. Justus was impressed, and admitted to St. Leger that he thought Johnson was trustworthy.

A few weeks before, Colonel Peters was ordered to move his Queen's Loyal Rangers to Verchères, and when he got wind that Thomas Johnson was at Fort St. Johns he warned Justus not to be hoodwinked by this turncoat:

> Don't think I take too much on myself when I tell you that M. Thomas Johnson will, if possible, deceive you, he is very subtle, will not stick at 50 guineas or pounds to give intelligence to his rebel friend Bailey, the Deacon; at the same time will speak light of M. General Bailey to you. I am not prejudiced against M. Johnson as an Individual, but a Rebel he is

Justus enclosed a copy of Peters' letter, adding 'N.B. M. Johnson Knows nothing of this letter, nor does M. Peters know anything that M. Johnson has said to me'.[11]

Deacon Jacob Bailey, whom Peters mentioned, was a general in the Vermont army and a member of the Grand Council of Safety. This same Bailey had evicted Peters' wife and eight children from their home in the Connecticut Valley in February, 1777. Justus did not want Peters' resentment to cloud his own judgement, but Haldimand should know about the colonel's reservations. If Johnson could be trusted, he would be useful.

The letters posted, Justus went to attend to the scouts at Isle aux Noix. David Crowfoot and Samuel Rose were in quest of information about Vermont. Crowfoot was around Arlington and barely eluded capture by the rebels.[12] Rose, who had sold Justus his first piece of land in the New Hampshire Grants, had travelled to New York City to see Colonel Beverley Robinson. That officer, optimistic when he first contacted Ethan Allen, was now disillusioned and called the big mountain chieftain a 'Damn'd Rascal'.[13]

Justus stayed at Isle aux Noix, dispatching scouts, and on April 9 he sent Mathews a letter he had received from Colonel Thomas Johnson, who asked that it be forwarded to His Excellency. Johnson pleaded again to be allowed to return home, and before sealing his own letter Justus added 'I thought it my duty to forward it without any Comments or Remarks'.[14] Now the matter of releasing Johnson rested with the governor.

Justus stayed at the outpost until May, sifting through the information his scouting parties brought in. Back at Fort St. Johns, Colonel St. Leger persisted in sending out couriers without informing him. One he dispatched was John Walden Meyers, now recruiting for the King's Rangers and hoping to qualify for a captaincy. Justus fumed. His scout, Richard Ferguson, was looking for recruits near Ballstown, and he prayed Meyers would not use that route. A manhunt for the hefty German might entrap Ferguson. Scouts should operate at safe distances from one another, and Justus feared that Meyers might go through Ballstown if the way along the Hudson River was heavily patrolled.[15]

In spite of these worries and irritations, Justus' spirits were soaring. To the devil with St. Leger. The war was as good as over. A scout brought him a gold mine — a revealing packet of letters on their way to the Continental Congress that had been intercepted by Dr. George Smyth's agents around Albany.[16] One was an extract of a letter Haldimand had sent Sir Henry Clinton, originally in cypher, dated February 28, 1781, in which he admitted that a 'Staunch friend in Albany' had warned him against the people of Vermont. That sort of warning was to be expected, Justus knew, but it was the other letters that excited him. One told of a scheme to unite the New Hampshire counties of Cheshire and Grafton with Vermont, because the local people envied the republic's neutrality. Another warned the Congress of the danger that individual states might make separate arrangements with Britain. Also, deserters from the Continental Army, malcontents and loyalists were flocking into Vermont. The Congress should admit Vermont without delay, lest others follow her example and the war collapse completely. Neutrality was having a beneficial effect on his cause. The northern states were ready to sue for peace, and from reports reaching Isle aux Noix, the British army was doing well in the south.

Justus went about his duties with a new air of confidence. Haldimand was also pushing recruiting to fill the ranks of the below strength provincial units, and men on the temporary list were no longer regarded as the property of the Central Department. In spite of Haldimand's requests for reinforcements to Lord George Germain, he had received only a few fresh regulars. Since Haldimand mistrusted loyalists less than Canadians, he was increasing his provincial force. He was offering a bounty of twenty-two shillings and sixpence for each new recruit, money that volunteers like Samuel Sherwood were holding out as inducements.[17]

While Justus remained at Isle aux Noix, Lieutenant John Dulmage took the company to Yamaska to rebuild an old blockhouse which would guard the route into Canada by way of the Yamaska River.[18] With Samuel's help Justus thought he would have a full company by the end of the year. He prayed that Colonel Peters was having as much luck in filling the other companies. Under the latest regulation, if the regiment could be brought up to strength, officers were entitled to half pay when the corps was reduced, and any who were maimed in the lime of duty would receive compensation.[19] Not even word of the latest piece of Vermont skullduggery could daunt Justus.

Although Governor Chittenden had stopped confiscating loyalist property, his government had passed an Absentee Act which imposed a special tax. Any landowner not in residence to pay it could have his property forfeit to the state.[20] Justus' remaining land was safe because Simon Bothum was on the spot, looking after his brother-in-law's interests. In spite of the Absentee Act, Vermont was offering sanctuary to loyalists. For this reason alone, negotiating with Ira Allen and Joseph Fay was worthwhile, if only they would come to Isle aux Noix.

Tired of waiting for them, Justus returned to Fort St. Johns to spend some time with his family. At his house, a dispatch marked top secret was delivered from Captain Mathews. Governor Haldimand had appointed Major Richard Lernoult, his adjutant-general, as Sherwood's assistant in the Vermont negotiations. Major Dundas was to be excluded, except where prisoner exchanges were involved. However, Dundas was to read all correspondence leaving Isle aux Noix.[21]

On May 8, Dundas informed Justus that Ira Allen had arrived at his post. Justus hurried to Major Lernoult's quarters, but found him ill and unfit to accompany him. Later in the day he left alone by bateau from Fort St. Johns.[22] At Isle aux Noix Justus reported that Ira was accompanied by an oaf named Lieutenant Simeon Lyman. Ira was remarkably circumspect, even for him, Lyman a plagued nuisance:

> M. Allen has brought a subaltern officer with him, who is not connected with the Business of the Truce; but has the Charge of the Escort – He is quartered in the Same room with Allen and myself and being a downright Illiterate Zealous-pated Yankee, is a very great embarrassment, especially as Allen is very cautious not to mention a syllable of any kind of Business in his presence; When we walk out he most commonly attends us closely, and has just breeding enough to listen and look over a man's shoulder when he is writing.[23]

Justus could not decide whether Ira had given Lyman orders to hover, or was as disturbed as he over the lieutenant's conduct. It was also possible someone else had told Lyman to spy on the two commissioners. Whatever the cause, Ira refused to discuss anything but prisoner exchanges. When Justus persuaded him to write down counter proposals, Ira refused to sign them. In desperation, Justus presented Haldimand's terms for Vermont: namely a separate province within the Empire, plus 3,000 troops to go up Lake Champlain and protect her territory. If the Green Mountain people were accepted into the United States, all these negotiations were to be kept secret. Ira hedged and said he would present these terms to the legislature when it met in

July. When he had something to report his signal would be three puffs of 'smoak' and at the middle puff a small white flag.[24]

Dissatisfied, Justus sent Ensign David Breakenridge, King's Rangers, to Bennington to 'Procure intelligence' from his father, James Breakenridge Sr. Justus explained 'Perhaps the Old Gentleman's opinion of Vermont policy may be worth sending for'. His letter ended on a note more cheerful than he felt:

> P.S. I have been informed that the General wishes to procure a young Moose Deer, and I would be very much obliged to you to inform me by the next post; as my Men have taken a young one which I can procure – Have directed them to keep it here and supply it with Milk till I hear from you[25]

Justus and Ira held other discussions, all along the same lines. Ira said any talk of reunion was premature, and Major Dundas was eyeing Justus oddly. Haldimand had ordered Dundas to take no part in the negotiations with Ira Allen, and yet had ordered him to read all dispatches before sending them to Quebec City. The governor's instructions left Justus bewildered and frustrated, since he could not send any secret reports to Haldimand. Fortunately, Major Richard Lernoult recovered enough to join Justus, and he had one person in whom he could confide. In a dispatch dated May 21, Haldimand ordered talks on prisoner exchanges suspended until Vermont stopped stalling on reunion.[26] When this message reached Isle aux Noix, Ira announced that he was leaving. The whole visit had been a waste of time.

On June 2, in a final letter from Isle aux Noix before setting out for Fort St. Johns, Justus informed Haldimand that Vermont was planning to annex the land to the west as far as the entrance to the Mohawk River, and General Philip Schuyler, the rebel commander in Albany, half-heartedly agreed, to prevent the wholesale movement of loyalists and the war weary from that territory into Vermont. Elijah Bothum and Thomas Sherwood reported that Schuyler had been burning boats along the Hudson River to check the exodus.[27] After handing this letter to a fast courier, Justus hurried to Fort St. Johns, planning to write a more detailed report for the governor, which was exactly what His Excellency wanted. Letters were more likely to be intercepted around Isle aux Noix.

At his house he found Anna Sherwood in charge, for Sarah had taken to her bed. The physicians at the fort could not identify the cause of her illness, but thought a good rest would help her.[28] Justus had scarcely reached home before he received an order from Mathews to come to Quebec City and confer with the governor on what had transpired during Ira Allen's visit. Reluctantly he left Sarah and travelled by express, riding hard, stopping to change horses at inns, napping when he could ride no farther. When he reached the Château St. Louis, he learned that Haldimand had decided that he would no longer be subordinate to the commandants of Fort St. Johns, Isle aux Noix and Pointe au Fer. Justus was to be the head of the British Secret Service, Northern Department, reporting directly to the governor, and in command of all scouting and gathering of intelligence, except for the western posts,[29] since placing these under Sherwood's jurisdiction would be impracticable.

Before he left, Justus had permission for a private headquarters, where his agents could come and go, free of the gossip that was such a curse at Fort St. Johns. Isle aux Noix was better, but Justus wanted complete secrecy. The place he recommended was a secluded bay on Long Isle, which some Vermonters were calling North Hero Island in honour of Ethan Allen.[30]

When Justus reached Fort St. Johns he found Dr. George Smyth, the valuable agent from Albany. He had arrived on June 14 in company with a scout named Mathew Howard, whose home was at Pittstown, near Bennington. Howard had rushed Smyth through the forest, well aware that the rebels were desperate to capture the master spy. On the 15th, Smyth had written Haldimand:

> Yesterday I arrived at this post, much indisposed. The Climbing of Mountains & Rocks, & travelling thro' Swamps & Thickets renders me incapable at present to pay my personal respects to your Excellency, but when my health is restor'd will do myself the Honour of waiting on you when I shall inform you of the cause of my flight &c'[31]

Anna Sherwood, who was well acquainted with the doctor, had invited him to stay at the house to convalesce. Justus approved, for he wanted to get to know Smyth personally. The man who had signed his letters Hudibras loved to talk, and he launched into a recital of his experiences without probing. Born in Ireland, the doctor emigrated with his wife and sons, Terence and Thomas, in 1770. For a time he practiced medicine at Fort Edward, near his brother, Patrick the lawyer, then he moved to Claverack, south of Albany. He was questioned many times by the rebel committees, arrested and taken to Albany when Burgoyne's army set out from Canada in 1777. After eighteen months in gaol, Hudibras was released on parole, but he had to stay within the confines of Albany. For some time he had worked in the rebels' military hospital.

Despite the restrictions placed on him, Hudibras continued passing information, keeping a network of men spying, aided by his wife and sons. On August 1, 1780, he was charged with sending one, Peter Cohoun, through the country, and was arrested and confined in irons. When he became ill, the rebels released him and placed him under house arrest.[32] On May 28, 1781, the Albany Board of Commissioners for Detecting and Defeating Conspiracies issued warrants for the arrest of Hudibras and his son Terence — code name Young Hudibras. Terence was captured and placed in Albany gaol, but the doctor had vanished. He succeeded in reaching Bennington, hoping for sanctuary from Joseph Fay, but he was captured by rebel sympathizers and marched back inside New York. A party of rebels from that state was escorting Smyth to Albany gaol when Mathew Howard, on a scout, overtook the doctor and his escort and rescued him. Thus the spy who called himself after the hero of a satirical poem by Samuel Butler reached safety.

Justus thought Dr. Smyth a delightful man, witty and at least as knowledgeable as himself on many of the characters he had to deal with. Not only that, Smyth was keeping an eye on Sarah, assuring Justus that rest was all she needed. Like many young mothers she was finding the care of three children taxing. When Smyth reached Fort St. Johns, his younger son Thomas was serving as a lieutenant in the King's Royal Regiment of New York. Mrs. Smyth was still in Albany, very worried for their other son Terence, and passing messages, as she had done during the doctor's two periods of confinement.

From Smyth, Justus learned that John Walden Meyers had been at the house during his absence. Meyers had returned from carrying dispatches to New York City, bringing fourteen recruits for the King's Rangers, a British regular who had escaped from a prisoner of war camp, and four rebel militia officers which his party had kidnapped at Ballstown. Colonel St. Leger was elated at Meyers' success, Smyth jubilant, Justus livid. As he feared, Meyers had travelled south through Ballstown, and had accompanied his scout Richard Ferguson. On his return journey, Meyers decided to stage his own raid.

He did not have permission and he might have endangered other scouts near Ballstown, for the rebels would have gone in force after him. For the moment Justus could not take Meyers to task because he was on his way to Quebec City to confer with Haldimand.[33] Yet one aspect of Meyers' caper amused Justus. Two of his recruits were French regulars, deserters whom St. Leger refused to allow to join a provincial corps, even the King's Rangers, which belonged to the Central Department.

Justus was favourably impressed with Dr. Smyth, despite his irritation over Meyers' insubordination. In his own way, Hudibras, too, was a dominant male. A small man who wore spectacles, Smyth was wily, loved intrigue and could achieve through manipulation what Justus accomplished by being forthright. However, Justus had to establish his new headquarters, leaving the doctor at his house recovering his strength. He sent a request to Colonel Peters at Verchères for his company to join him at Fort St. Johns as soon as possible, but received a refusal by the earliest post. Lieutenant Dulmage and the men had recently returned from working on the blockhouse at Yamaska, and Peters declined to release them.[34]

On June 28, Justus set off for Long Isle, accompanied by twenty-three men, loyalists not attached to any provincial corps and hefty youths, to build a blockhouse at a spot known as Dutchman's Point.[35] Pondering his poor relationship with John Peters, Justus longed to transfer his company from the Queen's Loyal Rangers so that he could serve under a more reasonable officer.

Setting of the Loyal Blockhouse

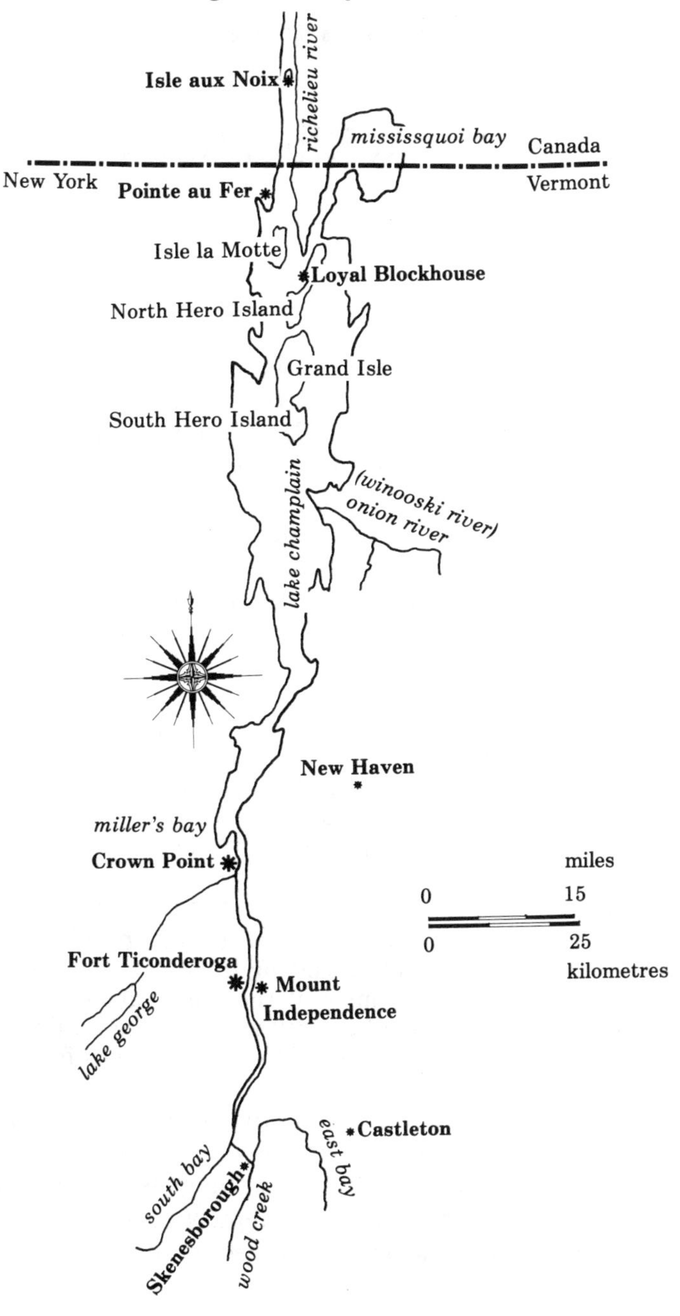

Chapter 11

The Loyal Blockhouse

Justus decided that the headquarters of the British Secret Service, Northern Department, would stand on some high ground at the end of Dutchman's Point, which jutted into Lake Champlain on the west side of Long Isle. It was an ideal defensive site with a view far up the lake, but which could not be seen from either shore. To the north lay abandoned, flat farmlands, once the property of a Dutch family for whom the point was named. The post would be known as the Loyal Blockhouse, to emphasize that this was a loyalist operation. On July 1 he reported to Mathews:

> I arriv'd here yesterday with 23 men including old men, Boys and unincorporated Loyalists. I am now Building an Oven & Hutting the men, shall tomorrow begin felling timber for the block house. Timber is not so plentiful here as I expected & we must draw it a mile at least.

He made bricks of local clay, drying them in the sun and firing them to make them hard. He continued:

> The spot on which I propose setting the Block House is a rise just at the extremity of the point, about five yards higher than the other ground & may be fronted with Abbitis [abatis] of about 50 yards in length from water to water.

While Justus was busy working on his blockhouse, Dr. George Smyth made a journey to Quebec City to meet Haldimand. During this visit the governor decided to appoint the doctor Sherwood's deputy in all four matters that were his concern — the secret service, prisoners, refugees and the negotiations with Vermont. When a letter from Mathews advised him of Smyth's appointment, Justus was pleased, although the secretary warned him that Hudibras had said he would be delighted to have Captain Sherwood as his assistant.[1] On July 9, Joseph Fay arrived, and the *Royal George* came from Fort St. Johns to patrol offshore until Justus' defences were completed. Aboard her was Dr. Smyth, eager to attend the meeting with Fay.[2]

The three commissioners settled themselves in a stateroom aboard the vessel, and Joseph reported that nothing had transpired when the Vermont Legislature met. Representatives from all the states were in attendance, who asked to see all the correspondence that had been received by Governor Chittenden from Governor Haldimand. Ira put them off by saying he had left everything at home. With a chuckle Hudibras interrupted the proceedings, to Justus' annoyance. 'Let humble Allen with an awkward shame, Do good by stealth, and blush to find it fame.'

The emissaries from the other states were satisfied with Ira's excuse, but he admitted that Haldimand was willing to grant Vermont a charter like Connecticut's. That the governor had not made exactly that offer was unimportant. Joseph expected the Congress to offer its own terms, which his people were certain to reject.

Justus was perturbed. Ira should have come. Joseph was too young to shoulder the responsibility of the negotiations alone. Ira, Joseph reported, had gone to Philadelphia with his elder brother, Jonas Fay, to address the Congress and allay suspicion in that quarter. Joseph admitted that he was empowered to discuss only prisoner exchanges, and Justus stated that these had been suspended for the moment. Interrupting again, Dr. Smyth reported that Haldimand was willing to have exchanges go ahead. Fay prepared to depart, promising to send a list of prisoners the Vermonters were ready to hand over.[3]

By July 14, after some arm twisting by Colonel St. Leger, Colonel Peters dispatched Lieutenant James Parrot, of the Queen's Loyal Rangers, as well as two sergeants, three corporals, Elijah Bothum, Samuel and

Thomas Sherwood and fifteen others from Justus' company, to help at the Loyal Blockhouse.[4] At the same time, St. Leger sent thirteen men from his 34th Regiment, while Major Dundas let Justus have an engineer from Isle aux Noix to supervise construction, and a team of oxen.[5] Justus was grateful to the pompous St. Leger, for recognizing the importance of the new post.

On July 20, Justus received a letter from Joseph Fay, then at Crown Point. The schooner *Carleton* had picked Fay up near Ticonderoga, and he would soon forward a list of thirty-six prisoners, among them Major Zadock Wright, of Justus' own regiment. Justus was pleased that at last the negotiations would soon bear some fruit, and surely this would be a first step towards serious discussions on reunion. He was also delighted with the progress his men had made on the blockhouse.

Reporting to Mathews on the 29th, Justus wrote that when completed the blockhouse might be defended by fifty men against:

> 300 with small arms as two or three swivels may be plac'd in it to good advantage. ... There is not so proper a place on the Frontier as this for the residence and departure of secret scouts[6]

Meanwhile, he and Dr. Smyth had been discussing a mission which Haldimand had been considering since the doctor's visit to Quebec City. Smyth had proposed some abductions of important rebel leaders in New York State. With the Yorkers in a mood to make peace, Hudibras had persuaded Haldimand the time was ripe for a small reign of terror to assist the work being done by Butler's Rangers and the King's Royal Regiment of New York. Haldimand agreed that eight small parties of raiders be sent into New York State to carry off some of these leaders.[7] Their removal would have a devastating effect on rebel morale, as well as provide valuable prisoners to trade.

By order of the governor, each party was to include from four to six loyalists and two British regulars in civilian dress, on the strength that they were better marchers. Justus suspected that His Excellency added the regulars because he did not trust loyalists on their own. Smyth was to choose some of the kidnappers, Justus others, and St. Leger the regulars. All were to be near their intended quarry by July 31. None were to strike earlier, to allow parties with farther to travel to be in position before any other party gave the game away. Where necessary, Indian guides would be provided. At Sherwood's insistence, all were to depart from the Loyal Blockhouse, to make certain everyone understood his orders and there would be no slip-ups.

Of all the leaders, Justus had confidence in three who had proved themselves on previous occasions — John Walden Meyers, Joseph Bettys and Mathew Howard. Bettys was now an ensign in the King's Rangers, Mathew Howard a lieutenant in the King's Loyal Americans. In the others Justus had some misgivings, but Meyers' intended victim was the most important — General Philip Schuyler, the commander of the rebel military department in Albany. The Schuyler mansion, 'The Pastures', lay three kilometres south of Albany, overlooking the Hudson. Meyers knew the area well, and was the right man for the job, although Justus did not like him personally. Joe Bettys, who hailed from Ballstown, was to remove Samuel Stringer from that place. Howard's quarry was John Bleecker of Hoosic, close to his home village of Pittstown.

At that stage, Dr. Smyth returned to Fort St. Johns to choose loyalists who would accompany the party leaders, and Justus awaited the arrival of all the parties for his final briefing. By July 26 all had left the Loyal Blockhouse, with orders to memorize their instructions and destroy them. Then Justus received a letter from Hudibras, who had given Captain Azariah Pritchard permission to abduct General Jacob Bailey, in eastern Vermont, and the scout would be stopping at the blockhouse en route. Justus reacted quickly. He wanted no trouble with the Vermonters, not when Joseph Fay would soon be coming with his flag to exchange prisoners. He sent a courier to Smyth, explaining why Pritchard must be stopped.

The doctor set out hoping to overtake his man, but to Justus' dismay Pritchard reached the Loyal Blockhouse on August 1 with eight men. Justus restrained Azariah, by threatening to use force. Both men were captains on the temporary list, but Pritchard was the one who backed down. After suggesting the kidnap of Mr. Livermore, a New Hampshire delegate to the Continental Congress, which Justus rejected because the Vermonters were wooing that state, Pritchard agreed to go on a scout and to refrain from carrying off anyone of importance.

The blockhouse was by now nearly complete, resembling others built to a standard design by the Royal Engineers. It measured six metres by nine at ground level, with a large fireplace and benches round all four walls. A ladder through a trap door led to the second storey, which overhung the lower by forty-five centimetres, with slits through which muskets could be poked that had hinged covers to keep out the cold. A partition of two walls separated the officers' quarters and the second storey fireplace. The men slept on palliasses on the second floor, which was pierced with holes to allow a defence with muskets should the enemy penetrate the ground floor. The loft under the pitch of the roof, reached by another ladder, Justus reserved for his own quarters, and Dr. Smyth's when he was at the blockhouse.

Here he could talk in private, and be fairly certain no one would touch his correspondence. He asked Colonel St. Leger for an officer to be in command of the blockhouse when he had to be away, and received, with or without Colonel Peters' approval, Lieutenant John Dulmage, to command the garrison numbering sixteen men. The members of the 34th Regiment returned to Fort St. Johns once the building was nearly complete. Then, to Justus' satisfaction, St. Leger authorized a reinforcement of fourteen provincials, and he received more men from his company and some King's Rangers.[8]

These thirty men were for duty at the blockhouse. His agents, mainly officers of provincials from the temporary list, were a separate group, although he sent men from the garrison on missions in support of his scouts.

Early in August Dr. Smyth came in expectation of the next prisoner exchange. By this time five of the raiding parties sent to kidnap rebels in New York State had returned, after failing to capture their intended quarry. Worried though he was over the three parties that had not appeared, Justus was busy preparing for the flag from Vermont. On the 7th, Major Joseph Fay arrived, having left thirty-four prisoners on the Vermont shore, and he met Sherwood and Smyth aboard the *Royal George*. Justus had a like number of men under guard at the Loyal Blockhouse, and after each was searched the exchange took place. Fay complained that the men returned were in poor shape, but Justus replied in kind. He told Mathews that Major Zadock Wright was showing the 'incipid enthusiasm of a Shuffling Quaker'.[9]

Another stormy session followed aboard the *Royal George*. Over the question of reunion, Fay had nothing to offer but reassurances that the conspirators needed more time. In exasperation, Justus informed Mathews that the Vermonters were seeking 'Two strings to their bow'. His scouts reported that the Vermont leaders wanted reunion, but the general public was opposed. Penning his letter, Justus was feeling wretched, head throbbing, arms and legs numb. Dr. Smyth, complaining of stomach pains, was no comfort either. Moreover, disturbing reports that a plague of caterpillers was destroying the hay crop along the St. Lawrence Valley worried him. He was acquiring some livestock at the Loyal Blockhouse, and he was afraid he would not be able to winter them. He wanted his post to be as self-sufficient as possible. Because of the difficulties involved in bringing up supplies, his men were ploughing in preparation for planting winter wheat.

By the time Joseph Fay left, both of Haldimand's commissioners were exhausted and irritable, but they had to face more bad news. Joseph Bettys' men returned without their leader. Joe had left the kidnapping of Samuel Stringer at Ballstown in their hands, and went off to visit a girl named LeGrange, who lived at Norman's Kill, near Albany. The men had panicked without their leader and headed for the Loyal Blockhouse. Joe had persuaded the girl to run away with him, and on the heels of the men came a letter from St. Leger at Fort St. Johns.

Bettys had turned up there, and Dr. Smyth left in a bateau to question him. Hudibras reported that St. Leger had confined Joe to the garrison 'for refusing to deliver up his Desdemona', and remaining silent when Smyth demanded to know where she was hidden. Eventually the girl was found, but Smyth was reluctant to send her home, for 'I think he would not be long after her which would ruin many of his Majesty's loyal subjects'.[10] Furthermore, Bettys' arrival with what Smyth called his 'female recruit' was scandalous. Joe had a wife and children in Ballstown.

Justus wondered what had happened to Mathew Howard and John Walden Meyers, for neither had returned. Then a scout informed him that Howard had succeeded in capturing John Bleecker, but he in turn was captured with his entire party, enlarged to eighteen men because he thought the six he brought from the Loyal Blockhouse insufficient. Now all nineteen were in Bennington gaol, a rare moment of co-operation between Vermonter and Yorker.[11] Contrary to Sherwood's orders, Howard had not destroyed his written instructions and the rebels found them.

On August 17 an irate Meyers reached Fort St. Johns, and Smyth's report did nothing for Justus' headache. On July 31, Meyers had been ready, hiding in a friend's barn with a party of twelve men, for like Howard, he thought the six he had brought from the Loyal Blockhouse insufficient. He dared not strike on the day ordered because scouts he sent out told him of a manhunt for Joe Bettys, who was supposed to be forty kilometres away, kidnapping Samuel Stringer. By the evening of August 7, Meyers thought all was clear, but he did not know that Mathew Howard had been captured, nor that the rebels had Sherwood's instructions and knew other abductions were planned. Since General Schuyler was an important man he had been forewarned.

When Meyers' party broke into The Pastures, they found armed men. After a short but bloody skirmish, in which both his British regulars were wounded, Meyers withdrew, his men carrying off two of Schuyler's as they fled into the forest. Thus Mathew Howard and Joseph Bettys had spoiled Meyers' attempt to kidnap General Schuyler. Haldimand was mortified because Meyers' men had broken the gentlemanly rules of war. In their retreat from Schuyler's house, some silver — spoons, plates and tankards — went with them. The fight took place in the wide centre hallway of the Georgian mansion, but someone made a side trip into the dining-room for the valuables. Haldimand wanted the silver returned, but Meyers was able to find only the spoons. The rest had been taken by local loyalists who had joined him, and had long since been sold.[12]

At the Loyal Blockhouse Justus turned his attention to Vermont and sent David Crowfoot to Arlington with a message for resident agent Elnathan Merwin — code name Plain Truth. He wanted to know what the populace at large thought about the commissioners' negotiations, and how widespread was the knowledge that reunion with Britain was the ultimate goal of Governor Chittenden. In mid-August his cousin Thomas informed him that Seth Sherwood — Thomas' father — had been kidnapped by some of the King's Royal Regiment of New York from his home near Fort Edward and was in Montreal. Justus felt acutely embarrassed, as did Thomas. Both agreed that Seth deserved to be removed because he had entrapped many loyalists, but blood was thicker than water. Justus learned that on August 13, Sir John Johnson had allowed his uncle and several others captured at the same time to be free in Montreal, and was recommending that they be returned home on parole. To this Dr. Smyth objected:

> The Indulgence given Prisoners to return home on Parole had been detrimental to our Friends... Seth Sherwood Senr., Moses Harris and a certain Mr. Abel have not a little Contributed to the afflictions of many worthy inhabitants[13]

Justus was still pondering the implications of his uncle's capture when some of Captain Azariah Pritchard's scouting party returned from the Connecticut Valley with a rebel corporal and three civilians. On August 19, Pritchard himself showed up and reported that General Jacob Bailey appeared to be coming over to Britain's side. After hearing this intelligence, Justus brought Mathews up to date. He was afraid that many of the Vermonters were motivated by self-interest. As far as he could tell, perhaps one-fifth of the people wanted reunion in order to trade with Canada. Another fifth were genuine loyalists, but the remainder were 'mad rebels' and almost out of control.[14] Nevertheless, Justus hoped Haldimand would continue his support of the conspirators, because this was in the best interests of the loyalists. Some refugees might be turned over to authorities in other states without Chittenden's knowledge, but many would be allowed to pass on to Canada. For that reason alone the negotiations were beneficial.

Towards the end of August, Justus went to Fort St. Johns to complete arrangements for the next prisoner exchange. He resolved to put Mathew Howard and the men of his party on the list of prisoners he wanted returned from Vermont. By September 1, his miseries were beyond endurance. Dr. Smyth had a letter ready for Quebec City, and hoping that a ride might make him feel better, Justus decided to carry it as far as Montreal. Smyth's letter showed how loyalists were being helped by Vermont. He mentioned that Mrs. Hannah Brown, from Kingsbury, near Fort Edward, 'is just come in – She came through a Pass from Chittington'.[15] While in Montreal Justus added a covering letter to Smyth's:

> I drove here yesterday as hard as my horse would carry me to try and shake off a disagreeable head ache and numbess that had plagued me for some days past. Return to St. John's today, and suppose I must push off tomorrow for Skenesborough – I wish I had better health[16]

They did not leave as soon as Justus expected. Hudibras took charge to allow him a few days rest, and Thomas Smyth went ahead to inform Major Joseph Fay that there would be a delay. When Justus and the doctor were ready they left on the *Royal George* from Isle aux Noix with the prisoners and an escort of regulars. Off Crown Point, a messenger from Major Carleton, who was farther up the lake, informed Justus that the Vermont flag was approaching. Half way to Ticonderoga they sighted the Vermont party, and two officers representing Major Fay came aboard to conduct the formalities. Perusing the list, Justus found that the names of the loyalists captured with Mathew Howard were there, but not their young leader's nor those of the two British regulars in his party.

He would have to think of someone special to exchange for Howard, and find some Continental soldiers to offer for the regulars. After some discussion, the Vermonters agreed that Sherwood and Smyth should escort their prisoners to Skenesborough, while the prisoners from Vermont and their escort would proceed to Pointe au Fer. The two commissioners and their party transferred to bateaux for the journey up the narrow arm of Lake Champlain.

When they were passing the ruins of Mount Independence, scouts reported an alarming number of rebel patrols. Justus ordered everyone ashore to the east redoubt of Ty, regulars to surround the prisoners to prevent any escapes. Then he sent a scout forward to apprise Major Fay that his party was being menaced. It was raining, and Hudibras fell on the slippery boards as he was climbing from the bateau, injuring his leg. Hours passed before the scout returned with an escort and a flag from Major Fay. Back aboard the bateaux the men clambered, Smyth cantankerous because he was in severe pain.

At Skenesborough they found an elated Thomas Smyth, whose news put an end to his father's complaints. Mrs. Smyth had come, but Thomas had sent her on. She carried a dispatch from Sir Henry Clinton, and he wanted her behind the British lines with all haste.[17] His mother had left Albany accompanied by a black woman servant, and reached Bennington. The rebel faction demanded that she be searched and returned to New York, but Joseph Fay forbad either. To show his good faith he had Mrs. Smyth sent on without demanding anyone in exchange. Three members of the Smyth family were safe, but Terence still languished in Albany gaol. Before John Walden Meyers' attack on the Schuyler house, the rebels were ready to allow Terence out on parole, but after that outrage he was questioned. Young Hudibras refused to say where Meyers might be hiding, or what route he had used to leave the neighbourhood, and now all hope of parole was lost.

Also waiting at Skenesborough were Joseph Fay, Ira Allen and Isaac Clarke, with horses to take the commissioners to Pawlet for a conference with other Vermont notables. Justus hesitated. He had no authority to proceed farther into Vermont, and little desire after the uncivil treatment accorded him the year before. He used Dr. Smyth's injured leg as the excuse for not accompanying the Vermonters, and to his astonishment Ira proposed holding a meeting then and there. At last he appeared willing to negotiate in earnest. A recent election in Vermont had confirmed Chittenden's leadership, and the republic had now extended her western boundary to the Hudson River, to the satisfaction of many local residents. That made Skenesborough neutral ground and safer for the prisoner exchanges. Ira told Justus that if Governor Haldimand would send a proclamation offering favourable terms, it would greatly expedite the work of the conspirators.[18]

Justus was delighted. At last Ira had come up with something concrete. Prisoner exchange and discussions closed, Sherwood and Smyth and their escort returned to Ticonderoga where the *Royal George* awaited them for the journey back to Isle aux Noix. At Fort St. Johns, Smyth had a reunion with his wife, and on September 25 he wrote to Mathews 'Fay has behav'd well. . .. thru' his means I am possessed of my Rib again; but Alas! my poor boy; what will become of him?'

In Justus' absence Colonel St. Leger had chosen John Walden Meyers to go to New York City with the latest report on Vermont for Sir Henry Clinton. Justus had no objections, and he briefed Meyers before the hefty courier set out. Meyers had proved the most reliable of all the would be kidnappers sent into New York State that July. When his report that Ira Allen wanted a proclamation reached Haldimand, he ordered Justus to come to Quebec City immediately. The head of the secret service travelled by express again, riding almost non-stop.

After some discussions, Haldimand ordered Justus to return to Fort St. Johns. His Excellency wanted to think about the proclamation, not certain the home government would countenance a charter province. Connecticut had been one of the most rebellious of the Thirteen Colonies, and Lord George Germain might be leery of setting up any more such provinces. Back home Justus learned that Meyers had been replaced, for on the way he had fallen ill with malaria and was recuperating at Pointe au Fer. Dr. Smyth dispatched Captain John Dafoe, King's Rangers, to carry Meyers' packet to New York City.[19]

Hudibras had also written a droll account of the shortcomings of some of the secret agents. Three in particular 'haunt me like Hamlet's ghost' he claimed in a plea for instructions written September 29, 1781. 'The first is a simpleton, the second proves himself a knave, & the last, I believe unfit for anything Except weaving Lindsey Woolsy'. Farther in the same letter he moaned about men at Fort St. Johns who were not pulling their weight:

> There is a Number of Active & Able Body'd Beef devoureres here, eating up the King's Royal Bounty without thanking saying, God bless him – I wish his Excellency would permit anyone he pleased to adopt such bodily Exercise for those Gulp and Swallow Gentry as may keep them from Scorbutic and Indolent habits &c[20]

On October 10, Haldimand's proclamation arrived from Quebec City, and Justus sent a messenger to Ira Allen to arrange for its delivery in Vermont. Haldimand, too, had plans to assure its ready acceptance by the Green Mountain people. Colonel St. Leger left to occupy Crown Point with a force 1,000 strong. Major John Ross, in command at Carleton Island, was to lead an expedition from Oswego, to operate in the Mohawk Valley, avoiding the part of New York which Vermont had annexed. The same flurry of activity had been staged the year before prior to Justus' visit to Vermont, and for the same purpose. The Vermont Legislature was meeting, and Haldimand wanted to show the representatives how much better off were the people in the neutral zone than their neighbours in New York.

Although he was not feeling well, Justus was in an optimistic mood.[21] Haldimand would allow Vermont to keep the lands she had annexed, and British troops would protect her. All regiments raised in her territory would be provincial corps. Justus still had some reservations over Chittenden's motives and those of his commissioners, but surely Vermont could not refuse Haldimand's terms. Her people must know that the rebels' hold on New York was about to collapse. Johnson and Butler were doing their best to subdue the frontiers, while Sir Henry Clinton was firmly entrenched around New York City.

Many scouting parties were out in quest of information, and some were after prisoners. Ensign Thomas Lovelace, of Jessup's corps, was near Saratoga carrying a dispatch and hoping to kidnap a rebel leader. One scout informed Justus that rebel leaders were meeting in Albany to discuss making a separate peace with Britain. At Fort St. Johns, Justus was unaware that Sir Henry Clinton in New York City, and Governor Haldimand in the Château St. Louis, had received disquieting word from Virginia.

Chapter 12

The Loyal Rangers

While Justus was waiting for a message from Vermont advising him how to deliver Haldimand's proclamation, rumours spread that the British expeditionary force in Virginia might be in trouble. Lord Charles Cornwallis with 7,000 troops, many of them ill or wounded, was falling back towards the Yorktown Peninsula, aggressively pursued by Generals Washington and Rochambeault, with 16,000 men in the combined rebel-French force. Offshore cruised the French fleet under Admiral DeGrasse, which might prevent Sir Henry Clinton, en route from New York City, reinforcing Cornwallis.

This news did not alarm Justus. With the situation in the north so well in hand, a setback in the south was not serious. Canada, New York City or Florida could be used as bases from which a new expedition could be sent against the rebels. What he did not realize was that Britain, herself, was endangered. The Netherlands and Spain were also at war with the mother country, and no more troops were available for service against the rebelling colonists.

Before any message came from Vermont, Dr. Smyth received a letter dated October 5 from 'Rocks near Brown Point' at the south end of Lake Champlain. It was from the Reverend John Stuart, the Anglican missionary to the Mohawk Indians at Fort Hunter, in the Mohawk Valley, most of whose flock were refugees near Montreal or on Carleton Island. Stuart explained that he had reached this place with fifty souls — his slaves, wife and three small sons, the others mainly women and children. They were stranded until boats arrived from Canada, and in 'a most disagreeable situation. . . encamped on Shore, exposed not only to the inclemency of the weather, but an easy Prey to the Vermont Scouts if they show'd visit us'.[1]

Smyth left with the bateaux for Stuart's party. Justus wanted to wait in the hope that Ira Allen's message would come. Hudibras was not conducting an exchange, but a relief mission to bring the loyalists to Fort St. Johns. Stuart said he had had to post bail for 400 pounds, and await the exchange of a colonel. Later the rebels let him leave, but his party was not protected by a flag of truce.[2] Smyth returned on October 9 with Stuart's party, and Justus decided not to wait any longer for a message from Vermont. On the 11th he and Smyth set out from Isle aux Noix in the only available vessel, the *Trumbull*, a row galley with eight guns captured from the rebel fleet in 1776.

They stopped briefly at the Loyal Blockhouse and sailed on towards Crown Point to see whether Colonel St. Leger had any news of Ira Allen or Joseph Fay.[3] Before they reached St. Leger's encampment they took aboard Sergeant Andrew Reakley, King's Rangers, a scout and the bearer of bad news. Ensign Thomas Lovelace had been hanged, while another scout, Lemuel Casswell was a prisoner. With Caleb Clossen and Casswell, Reakley had been proceeding towards New York City, and they sought shelter with Levi Crocker, who had provided a safe house in the past. This time Crocker informed the rebels, and Reakley and Casswell were carried to Saratoga in irons. Clossen escaped, a stroke of luck because he was carrying Sherwood's dispatch, and was safely on his way to Sir Henry Clinton's headquarters.

Reakley, too, escaped. The rebels wanted to find out where the three scouts had hidden the boat they used to reach Lake George, and they sent Reakley with an escort of eighteen men to show them. He eluded them 'by knocking down two Sentries & disarming one'. Sherwood informed Mathews:

While Rikley was at Saratoga he saw Mr. Lovelace

Hang'd before Genl. Stark's door & by his order – This barbarous Murder of my worthy friend (& as true & brave a subject as ever left the Colonies) stings me to the heart! I hope in God His Excellency will permit us to retaliate either by hanging up some of the rascals we have prisoners from that State, or by taking and hanging on their own ground some of these inhuman butchers, which I know we can do.

He implored Haldimand to consider 'Mr Loveless's poor widow and family' for the dead man had been 'exceedingly Useful' to the service. When captured he was on his way to see Colonel van Vechtan, a rebel turned informer who provided Smyth with intelligence.[4] General Stark had acted rashly, for General William Heath wrote to George Clinton, the rebel governor of New York, expressing fear that Haldimand might retaliate:

I am exceedingly sorry to find by General Stark's letter that he had tried at a court martial and executed Loveless, who came with very particular written instructions to seize a prisoner from the neighbourhood of Saratoga in which attempt he and his party were taken. . . He having been armed, I think already barred the idea of his being a spy, and upon what principle he was executed I am at a loss to determine – and am apprehensive it will make some difficulty – It may be best to say as little about it at present as possible[5]

Heath's remark about Lovelace being armed and therefore not a spy showed how little he knew of the workings of Haldimand's secret service. Loyalist agents in rebel territory generally carried firearms. Andrew Reakley also reported that rebel strength at Saratoga was 400 men under General Stark. When the latter heard rumours that St. Leger's 1,000 men were crossing from Lake Champlain to Lake George, Stark began withdrawing towards Albany. Colonel St. Leger had not been there, but Major Edward Jessup had, with a detachment of King's Loyal Americans. St. Leger had sent Jessup to menace Saratoga to prevent Stark joining a rebel force that was mustering to pursue Major John Ross' expedition then in the Mohawk Valley.[6]

Near Crown Point Justus received a party of New York rebels, and he added:

I have inform'd the Captain of their Flag on board the *Trumble* of Loveless's death, & told him at the same time, that we might with as much propriety & much more justice hang him on the bow sprit of the Vessel.

After his angry outburst at the New Yorkers present, Justus decided not to carry out his threat to hang the rebel officer. St. Leger would never permit an act which Haldimand had forbidden, and Justus would not be safe under his own flags of truce. He had used Green Mountain Boy bluff to relieve his feelings. Meanwhile, where on earth was that long awaited messenger to take Haldimand's proclamation to Vermont?

Smyth had an idea. Why not kidnap a Vermont patrol? They took the suggestion to St. Leger, who gave his consent. Away went an officer and twelve men to the vicinity of Mount Independence. The following morning they encountered a patrol, a sergeant and five men. When the British officer ordered the Vermonters to lay down their arms, they raised them to firing position, whereupon one of the British regulars opened fire, killing the sergeant, one Archelus Tupper, whose name and mode of dispatch were to immortalize him far beyond his humble station in life.[7]

To everyone's mortification, the British patrol returned to Crown Point with five prisoners and a corpse. Justus knew immediately that the dead Tupper spelled trouble, and he caused St. Leger to overplay his hand. The five survivors were released, carrying Haldimand's proclamation (on reunion), the dead sergeant's clothing, a letter of apology from St. Leger to Governor Chittenden, and an invitation to the deceased's friends to come under a safe conduct and attend the funeral.[8]

Soon afterwards Justus received a letter from Ira Allen, dated October 20, describing the blockade of Cornwallis' position at Yorktown by the French fleet, which might prevent Sir Henry Clinton's reinforcements from relieving the British army. Under the circumstances, Ira asked Justus to refrain from sending the proclamation, requesting him to come to Castleton for a meeting.

Justus hesitated, apprehensive. St. Leger had sent the Vermont patrol off with the proclamation, and he could not now prevent its delivery. But he would go to Castleton for the sake of the truce, threatened by the death of Sergeant Tupper. When he reached Castleton with his escort and flag, all seemed to be in order. Chittenden wanted to keep the truce, and would use the Vermont army to enforce it. Dead set against neutrality were two men of standing — Colonel Samuel Herrick, the commandant of Fort Vengeance, and Colonel Samuel Safford, who had superceded Ethan Allen as the commander of the Vermont army.

The faction controlled by Herrick and Safford was very suspicious. One dedicated rebel wondered why 'General St. Leger was sorry that Sergeant Tupper had been killed'. Why, Vermonters opposed to reunion pondered, would a high and mighty British officer with his two gold epaulettes feel compelled to apologize for shooting a no-account sergeant in the militia?

Justus was relieved that nobody in Castleton knew that he and Smyth had had a hand in the capture of the patrol, and he did not dare raise the question of Haldimand's proclamation. No one else raised it either. For the moment, though, discussions on reunion had to be postponed, until the fate of Lord Cornwallis at Yorktown was known. If the British surrendered, General Washington would be free to turn his army towards Vermont or Canada. Reluctantly Justus conceded that Ira Allen had been wise when he told him not to send the proclamation at that time. He returned to Crown Point by way of Skenesborough, where he met some Vermont envoys whom he found very haughty.[9]

At Crown Point he reported what had transpired at Castleton to Colonel St. Leger, and with Dr. Smyth set off in the *Trumbull* for the Loyal Blockhouse. They found Captain Azariah Pritchard waiting with improbable news. Fourteen French engineers were at Ticonderoga examining the fort's walls. Justus sent Elijah Bothum to investigate, and in the interval he received a letter from the Baron von Riedesel, asking whether the report on the French presence at Ty was true.

The Baron was now the commander at Sorel, responsible for the outposts along Lake Champlain. He had been on parole in New York City, until Sir Henry Clinton had arranged to have him exchanged and returned to duty. When Elijah returned he reported that Ty was as empty as it had been for years. That rascal Pritchard had been making mischief because he was jealous of Sherwood, and wanted permission to build his own blockhouse in the Connecticut Valley.[10]

Leaving the Loyal Blockhouse in command of Lieutenant Dulmage, Justus and Hudibras set out for Fort St. Johns in a bateau, the crew fighting headwinds. The boat leaked, and neither he nor the doctor were feeling well as they helped bail. They reached the fort on November 16, cranky and exhausted, but good news soon arrived for Justus. On November 19, Governor Haldimand had signed his commission, but certain of Haldimand's decisions surprised him. Earlier, Captain Mathews had hinted that Sherwood's company might be placed in the second battalion, King's Royal Regiment of New York.[11]

Now, however, Haldimand decided to establish a new regiment, which he called the Loyal Rangers, and to incorporate into it some of the small units that had served under Burgoyne. The Queen's Loyal Rangers and the King's Loyal Americans were both absorbed into the new corps, and the Loyal Rangers were members in good standing of the Northern Department. Now Justus was a captain in that department, entitled to half pay when the Loyal Rangers were reduced. Edward Jessup was the major-commandant of Justus' new regiment.

Ebenezer Jessup, the colonel of the King's Loyal Americans, who had never impressed Haldimand, was made a captain in command of a company of pensioned men. John Peters, to his disbelief and consternation, was put in command of a company of invalids, with Thomas Sherwood as his ensign. Justus felt sorry for Peters, although he had been less than co-operative of late, and puzzled for Thomas, very able-bodied and actively scouting for him. Elijah Bothum also received an ensign's commission, and Justus was happy for his brother-in-law.[12]

Justus regretted that Haldimand had not allowed Edward Jessup a lieutenant-colonelcy, his right as a corps commander. His Excellency tolerated commissions awarded before he arrived, but he rarely gave promotions to provincials. He also avoided placing regular officers in the mortifying situation of being inferior to provincial officers.[13] Justus knew he himself deserved the rank of major, because he commanded a blockhouse, but the governor was denying him the higher rank. Although he trusted Sherwood more than others, he would not make an exception that might lead to quarrelling.

Edward Jessup was, Justus thought, a wise choice for the command of the Loyal Rangers. Born in Connecticut but raised in New York, he had the respect of the New England and New York factions in his battalion. Thanks to his brother Samuel, Justus' company was at full strength. The men were uniformed in green coatees with red facings and silver accoutrements, the colours Haldimand decreed for all provincials except the King's Royal Regiment of New York and the Royal Highland Emigrants. The latter had received red coats before Haldimand arrived in 1778, and he was gradually issuing Sir John Johnson's men with red coats as their older uniforms wore thin.[14]

The Loyal Rangers were stationed at Vercheres, but Major Jessup allowed Justus to have part of his company at the Loyal Blockhouse.[15] Because Lieutenant Dulmage was fully occupied commanding the blockhouse garrison, Jessup assigned Lieutenant James Parrot as Justus' new junior officer. His brother Samuel remained with the company, but he was also recruiting for his own commission.

While Justus was preoccupied with Vermont, prisoner exchanges and the rescue of loyalists, Dr. Smyth organized some counter-espionage at the request of Sir John Johnson. The baronet suspected that a Mrs. Cheshire, in Montreal, was aiding paroled rebels to escape and supplying intelligence to Albany. Smyth sent three counter spies to visit 'Madame Cheshire'. They carried Yankee firelocks, some paper money from Vermont and Connecticut, and a forged letter from General Jacob Bailey, the man thought to be against reunion. Dressed in shabby clothing the three agents left Fort St. Johns and called at Mrs. Cheshire's house. She received them warmly and gave them a packet and some verbal information to give to General Stark's headquarters. Upon their return to Fort St. Johns they confirmed Sir John's misgivings, for the lady was indeed a rebel agent.[16]

Brigadier Allan Maclean, the commandant in Montreal, and Johnson decided not to have her arrested. Now that they knew what she was about she could be useful. Maclean put a watch on her house and whisked her visitors off to an internment compound near the city, bagging valuable prisoners for exchange when such guests proved to be rebel agents.

Before winter closed in, Colonel St. Leger evacuated Crown Point and withdrew to Fort St. Johns. Justus stayed with his family until after Christmas, enjoying a peaceful interlude. Thomas Sherwood and Elijah Bothum came from the Loyal Blockhouse to observe the festival, and Justus' brother Samuel joined them from Verchères, still hoping for a commission. Major Jessup had permission to raise more companies, and Justus urged Samuel to try and find more recruits.

Justus was mulling over his children's future. Even if it took years more to end the rebellion, there was fine land in Canada, and Montreal had much to offer his family. The Reverend John Stuart, an excellent scholar, had received a grant from Haldimand to open a school there.[17] The clergyman was at present the chaplain to the second battalion, King's Royal Regiment of New York, and preaching to the members who were in Montreal. Occasionally he visited a Mohawk village nearby where some of his flock from Fort Hunter were housed temporarily.

The Smyths were in a house not far away which Hudibras described as 'no larger than a Racoon box' but the only one available.[18] Part of the time the doctor was at the military hospital, a mile from the fort in the barracks that housed the King's Rangers. Hudibras had a commission as surgeon to the Loyal Rangers, which would assure him a pension when the corps was reduced.

Despite rumours circulating that Cornwallis had surrendered at Yorktown, Justus was in an optimistic mood. The war had been won in the north, and while the British regulars might be out of action in the south, many provincial corps were still foraying along the coast. All was not lost, and loyalists in Canada were not depressed.

Chapter 13

In Yorktown's Wake

On December 27 Major Robert Mathews, who had received a promotion, ordered Justus to go to the Loyal Blockhouse with Dr. Smyth to send out scouting parties.[1] Haldimand wanted a confirmation or denial that Cornwallis had surrendered. If the British army had been captured, His Excellency needed to know what General George Washington and his French allies would do next. Justus and Hudibras set off in a sleigh for the outpost. Reporting to Mathews on January 16 1782, Justus wrote 'I wish you a pleasant and agreeable succession of three score and five New Years, which I think is enough for this transitory state'. This salutation was for Haldimand, sixty-five years old at the time. Justus continued:

> I mean to include the present which I hope you enjoyed with more satisfaction, and less embarrassment than the Doctor and me, poreing over our accounts or wadeing through the snow (from 7 in the morning to 11 at night) to assist the scouting parties to make ready[2]

The snow, he reported, was very deep and light. A man on snowshoes sank to his knees, and walking outdoors was nearly impossible. Once several parties were out, Justus made a journey to Montreal to purchase equipment he needed for his post. On his return he declared to Mathews that the rumours of a British surrender at Yorktown were merely a 'Whiggish plot'.[3] He soon had cause to eat those words. Scouts came in with reports of a troop build up at Albany, cannon stock-piled at Hartford, Connecticut, and a supply of uniforms at Poughkeepsie, on the lower Hudson River.

The intelligence Justus now sought was whether Washington would decide to attack Canada, turn his attention to the garrison at New York City, or coerce Vermont. However, French troops were wintering in Albany, a matter certain to alarm Haldimand. Justus urged his scouts to bring in firm information on where Washington would strike next. By February morale at the Loyal Blockhouse sagged, and a much fatigued Dr. Smyth returned to Fort St. Johns. Justus himself was exhausted and on the 7th he told Mathews:

> As most of my men expect to have little else but secret service to do, and I am not allow'd any rum to give them on fatigue, nor horses to draw provisions, I have no other way to keep up their spirits but to promise them pay for the wood and to work with them like a burly fellow, which I do every day from morning to night till I am thoroughly weary[4]

A source of dissatisfaction for Justus was the garrulity of certain scouts. At the end of January, Ensign Roger Stevens, King's Rangers, had arrived from Arlington with five prisoners. One, Joseph Randall, from Claremont, professed to be a loyalist, and Justus allowed him to remain at the blockhouse, working with the garrison, until Haldimand decided whether he would be an acceptable resident agent. Justus sent Stevens to Quebec City with a packet, and on February 14, Mathews complained that this courier was very indiscreet. The news of his presence and the content of his packet was known all over the city.[5] Writing to Dr. Smyth, still at Fort St. Johns, Justus admitted:

> It is easy to trace the source of this unpardonable conduct – Messengers arrive, and the inquisitive and impertinent flock around them for news. They sit down together to pass the evening, and over their glasses make the Business they have been upon the topic of conversation – From there they retire to their Homes and renew the subject with their wives & families – By the first post or express, it is conveyed all over the Country, no matter whether by Friends or Enemies, the effect is the Same.[6]

The fireplaces in the blockhouse devoured wood, and each day Justus detailed four men to cut three quarters of a cord each, to be measured by a sergeant and reported to the officer of the day. Officers' servants were required to help with the cutting, loading and unloading of wood and supplies from sleighs, or from boats when the lake was open. In fact, only occasionally did an officer have a servant, but Justus thought the item read well when he posted his instructions to the garrison. He wished he had someone to care for him, but Simon Bothum needed the two slaves still in New Haven, Sarah the help of Caesar Congo.

Serving in his company was Private John Jacobs, whose country of origin was listed as Africa, to Justus more diplomatic than calling him a negro, as other officers did when preparing their muster rolls.[7] One method of obtaining recruits popular with certain agents was luring slaves to desert their owners with the promise of their freedom once the rebellion had been crushed. Some officers used black men as servants, but Justus respected Private Jacobs' wish to be a soldier.

The danger of fire was a constant worry, and Justus posted this order:

> As it appears that the fires of the different rooms frequently roll onto the floor to the great danger of the garrison, a corporal of the guard will inspect the fires of the Block House & the old and new Bake rooms at 11 o'clock every evening; at one o'clock & five o'clock every morning.[8]

The cooking rooms were in a separate building to reduce the risk of setting the blockhouse afire.

Breaches of discipline were rare among the members of the garrison, for they knew they were working for an officer whom the governor held in high regard. Justus coped with minor offenses with a good scolding, a few threats, or occasionally the back of his hand, never a formal hearing followed by a flogging at the sergeants' halberts. That was for regulars, many of whom had been pressed into the service in the taverns of England.

Money was a headache for Justus, who had to send his accounts to the Château St. Louis and have them approved before he could draw public funds. Haldimand perused all the items, criticising many expenditures. In consequence, Justus' men's pay tended to be in arrears, and he was chronically short of supplies. His agents expected two shillings and sixpence a day when on missions, but Haldimand felt that this was excessive. Mathews informed him that His Excellency was displeased at 'the vast expense you have incurred on that service by paying such high wages to persons regularly subsisted and provisioned by Government.'[9] When Justus suggested the men accept less, they refused to go out, and he could not blame them. They were risking their lives, and he supplemented what Haldimand allowed from his own slender purse.

The account book he kept was a mixture of public and private expenditures. Some bills he paid with government funds, others from his own wages. Some items were payments to scouts for their expenses while in rebel territory, others for clothing such as overalls, shirts or materials — coating, binding, thread, buttons and lining. As the spring advanced, the Loyal Blockhouse was becoming the focus of a small community, and a few cabins mushroomed around the post. The residents were refugees, eager to earn a few shillings to avoid accepting government handouts, which pleased Haldimand, who wanted all who were able-bodied to support themselves. Some of the items in Justus' account book were payments to women for washing, cooking and sewing.

Meanwhile, many parties of scouts were out on snowshoes. Joseph Bettys, accompanied by Jonathan Miller and John Parker, had left the blockhouse. Bettys was to go to New York City with a dispatch for Sir Henry Clinton, the others to stay around Albany gathering information on what the French were doing. David Crowfoot had left for Arlington to visit Elnathan Merwin to find out what he knew of Washington's plans for Canada, and with dispatches for Ethan Allen. Then Justus heard that John Walden Meyers was at Pointe au Fer on a mission to Albany but temporarily halted because one of his party had fallen ill and he was awaiting a replacement. Justus sent a courier to order Meyers stopped. He had not reported at the Loyal Blockhouse. Next Justus wrote to Mathews, enquiring why Meyers had not obeyed his orders.

Mathews communicated Sherwood's displeasure to Dr. Smyth at Fort St. Johns, who replied that he thought he was responsible for scouts going into New York, while Justus was in charge of those going into Vermont or parts of New England.[10] Hudibras was being mischievous, asserting his right to send scouts out on his own initiative, when he knew which man was the deputy. He promised Justus that in future he would have all scouts he dispatched report to the blockhouse. The air cleared, Justus ordered Meyers to proceed. His mission was a worthy one, for Smyth's network of spies around Albany was in ruins. Many of his informers were in prison or had fled to Canada, and Meyers was going in search of new resident agents.

Late in March, Justus received permission from Mathews to allow Joseph Randall, who had been brought to the blockhouse as a prisoner by Roger Stevens, to return home as a resident agent. Mathews suggested that Justus let Randall escape, since a parole might make his neighbours suspicious. Randall had been staying in a hut in the woods, helping to cut wood. The man Justus sent to find Randall reported that he had already complied with Mathews' order:

> a-hunting with Joseph White from Coos he had taken the first opportunity to run away. Randel left his fuzee & ammunition at the hut and only took a pr. of Snowshoes, Hatchet, and two days provision of the King's property with him, but the manner of going away fully contradicts his pretended Loyalty. A Whining designing Yankee Scoundrel like too many others.[11]

Early in April, a scout brought word that Joseph Bettys and John Parker had been captured and were lying in the basement of the Town Hall in Albany, where prisoners were confined because the gaol was full. Jonathan Miller, who had been travelling with them, escaped and was making for the Loyal Blockhouse.[12] Justus sent an express courier to Quebec City to report to Mathews. From Fort St. Johns, Dr. Smyth wrote that he was certain Bettys would be hanged because the rebels had found his dispatch. Mathews ordered Justus to have Bettys and Parker exchanged.

Ensign Bettys of the King's Rangers was entitled to be treated as a prisoner of war, and Justus was to promise that Haldimand would retaliate if the rebels executed the two agents. 'The war,' Mathews wrote, 'has not furnished *a single instance* where a Prisoner has suffered Death in this Province.'[13] Justus sent a scout speeding towards Albany, offering to exchange any men the rebels wanted for Bettys and Parker. His efforts were in vain, and his two agents mounted the scaffold before a jeering crowd. A pall of gloom descended over the Loyal Blockhouse. Bettys was a scamp, but a lovable one whose daring the others much admired.

The circumstances of Bettys' capture were typical of the man. He stopped to visit a friend near Ballstown, and while they were seated at dinner, Joe's rifle over his arm, three men broke down the door. Bettys had not bothered to remove the deerskin cover that protected the firelock from damp and the rifle was useless, but he had presence of mind enough to ask for permission to smoke. As Joe leaned over the hearth to light a taper, his captors noticed something drop into the flames. They retrieved a small, thin metal box which contained a paper with a message in cypher and an order for the courier to receive a sum of money when he delivered it.[14] Joe begged them to let him burn the paper, and offered his captors one hundred guineas, but they refused. The combination of carelessness and wit was characteristic of Bettys; the tiny box was typical of Justus' efforts to make his packets easy to conceal. The metal box was Joe's undoing, for it preserved the message which otherwise would have been burnt before the rebels could rescue it.

That spring of 1782, Seth Sherwood returned to Fort Edward on parole, despite Dr. Smyth's objections. Justus never mentioned escorting his rebel uncle to Skenesborough, but often he simply recorded the numbers being returned. In Seth's case, his nephew's own embarrassment was sufficient reason for avoiding any reference to him. Another man sent home was Colonel Thomas Johnson, to Newbury in eastern Vermont, as a resident agent.

As the trees were turning green, Justus received more assurances that Vermont would soon declare for reunion. He tried to believe them, but he feared that the Congress might in time be persuaded to admit Vermont as the fourteenth state. In spite of all his patience, was he destined to be a lifelong exile from the pretty land he loved? The spring of 1782 was a very low point in Justus' life, yet bitterness did not surface in his writings.

The British could pack up and sail away when they

had had enough, abandoning the loyalists. On March 20 an election in Britain toppled Lord North's Conservative Ministry and brought in a flock of doves under Lord Rockingham, seeking peace at any price. Because Cornwallis had failed at Yorktown, the mother country was ready to quit, and Justus' own people would be the losers. Whatever the future held, he no longer had much cause for optimism.

Chapter 14

Undercover Activities—1782

In some theatres the war had ground almost to a halt, a circumstance that had no bearing on Justus' duties at the Loyal Blockhouse. The secret service, the negotiations with Vermont, and prisoner exchanges kept him as busy as ever, while his work with refugees became heavier. As the spring approached, rumours that Britain would soon start peace talks circulated throughout the rebelling colonies. Many loyalists who had remained in their homes, praying that the mother country would succeed, now despaired and set out for Canada, New York City or Florida. Some in the northerly parts of the colonies looked towards the outpost on North Hero Island. If loyalists could reach the Loyal Blockhouse, with its buckskin-clad commander, or find one of his scouts to guide them, they would be safe.

Amidst the heartbreak of the incoming refugees, Justus and Hudibras were cheered by the arrival of Terence Smyth. Late in February, Young Hudibras broke out of Albany gaol and succeeded in reaching Bennington, where the Fays cared for him until he recovered from his confinement. On March 26 Terence was spirited away to meet one of Sherwood's scouting parties,[1] carrying an anonymous letter from Ethan, part of which read:

> Jealousy rages high about us in the United States. The turning point is whether Vermont confederates with Congress or not which I presume will not be done. Heaven forbid it.

The Vermont conspirators allowed Terence to leave,

and at the time no one suggested that Justus send a rebel prisoner in exchange. Justus made a mental note that such a gesture would be a help, especially if he chose someone Messrs. Herrick and Safford wanted returned.

The next event that distracted Justus from the suffering refugees was the return of Lieutenant Mathew Howard, and Corporal Andrew Temple and Private William Slone, the last two of the 34th Regiment. All had been captured on August 6, 1781, after they had kidnapped John Bleecker of Hoosic. Following careful negotiations, Sherwood and Smyth had persuaded the Vermonters to exchange them.[2] Howard reported that without the knowledge of Governor Chittenden, supporters of Congress threatened to hang him if he did not reveal the strength of the royal army in Canada. Three times a halter was placed round his neck, and once he was lifted off the ground.[3] Justus knew that young Howard deserved a court martial for not destroying the written instructions as ordered, which led to John Walden Meyers' failure to kidnap General Schuyler. But Howard had suffered greatly for his carelessness, and with characteristic bluster, Justus threatened to flay him alive, then sent him to Major Edward Jessup to do duty with the regiment. Justus could not afford to have a man who was unreliable in his service.

Meanwhile, he was worrying about David Crowfoot, missing since February. On May 19, Crowfoot reached the Loyal Blockhouse and reported that after visiting Ethan Allen he had been captured by local rebels. In advance, the scout destroyed his dispatches. Towards the end of April he made good his escape, and paid another clandestine visit to Ethan, who gave him a verbal report for Sherwood.[4] Ethan and Ira Allen had treated Crowfoot well, but Ethan warned him:

> For God's sake, for his own and their safety to take care of himself, for the mob were watching every night before he came away, and offered him every assistance he should require in money, provisions, or anything else in his power.

At Arlington, Crowfoot visited Elnathan — Plain Truth — Merwin, who gave him a letter addressed to Dr. Smyth, in which he assured Hudibras that the Vermonters were trustworthy 'unless the devil is wrapped up in their skins'.[7]

Many refugees brought messages from the Allens, Fays and Chittenden — Ethan's very vague and confusing. Chittenden appeared to be holding his own against determined opposition led by Colonels Samuel Herrick and Samuel Safford. These two were fomenting mob violence against neutrality and any scheme for reunion. Nevertheless, Chittenden was offering sanctuary to loyalists, and suggesting they settle close to the border of Canada, where Haldimand might be enticed into offering them — and incidently Vermont — protection should Washington come to the aid of Herrick and Safford. An impatient Hudibras suggested that the Vermonters might be persuaded 'by the sword'.[6] Now that Terence was safe, Dr. Smyth felt more aggressive, but his relationship with Justus did not improve.

Major Mathews assured Justus that Smyth was indeed his deputy, but suggested that he be less touchy. Justus made a practice of forwarding all his reports to Smyth at Fort St. Johns before sending them to the Château St. Louis, to 'avoid uneasiness'.[7] On June 11 Mathews scolded Smyth for jealousy, and for sending out agents without consulting Sherwood, hoping to make the two loyalists work in harmony. Justus was trying hard but Hudibras remained cantankerous.

At that time Haldimand was in Montreal on a tour of inspection, which made communication with him faster, and Justus had much to report. Daily he received conflicting information from agents and refugees. Some messengers from Vermont and New York told him that loyalists should go home. All would be forgiven. Others maintained that anyone who stayed home or attempted to return was a blockhead.

Among the outcasts came Joseph Bettys' wife, Abigail, and her children, left destitute when her husband was executed in Albany. Justus greeted Abigail warmly, ordering John Dulmage to fetch milk for the children. Tactfully, Justus avoided any mention of Joe's infidelity as he poured her a glass of elderberry wine and praised her husband's bravery. On June 17, Mathews informed Joe's commanding officer, Major James Rogers, that

Widow 'Baty' could receive his pay until the 24th, and afterward a pension of 20 pounds per annum. Later, Haldimand agreed that provision be made for Bettys' children and that his widow receive 'a subaltern's proportion of Land. . . for the support of her Family'.[8]

The Baron von Riedesel ordered Justus to strengthen his command, now that his blockhouse was on the front line of the defence of Canada, and Haldimand ordered reinforcements to Isle aux Noix. Some Loyal Rangers were there, and at Pointe au Fer, among them John Walden Meyers, now a brother officer, for Haldimand had approved a captaincy for him under Major Jessup. Dr. Smyth had stopped proposing Meyers for missions, which pleased Justus. He did not fancy giving orders to the hefty German peasant, now that they were equals. Edward Jessup sent Justus enough men from his company to raise his garrison to fifty-one effectives.

The men were ploughing and planting, and in addition to some cows, Justus acquired horses and smaller livestock. In an answer to a request from Ethan Allen, Justus sent a party to destroy gun carriages at Fort Ticonderoga. The British and loyalists had sunk the guns in the autumn of 1777, but some Vermonters had resurrected them. Allen suspected the perpetrators of the salvage operation were supporters of Herrick and Safford, who wanted the guns to aid Washington if he marched north.[9]

Throughout the early summer Justus had up to forty-seven men out gathering intelligence and assisting refugees. Some were distributing copies of the *Antigua Gazette* which reported on British Admiral Rodney's victory over French Admiral DeGrasse in the West Indies, news that would put new hope into the hearts of the loyalists. With so many men out he was short-handed for routine chores around the blockhouse. He sent a request to Isle aux Noix for sawyers and tools, where Major John Nairne, who had transferred from the Royal Highland Emigrants to the 53rd Regiment, was the commandant. Major Dundas had been posted to Fort Niagara. Instead of complying, Nairne ordered Justus to send ten men to work as wood cutters at Fort St. Johns, and from fifteen to twenty to Sorel, where the Baron von Riedesel needed more help.

Justus sent von Riedesel a copy of his roster, showing only fifteen men at his post. The garrison then consisted of thirty-one men, five corporals, four sergeants, Ensigns John Dusenbury and Elijah Bothum, and Lieutenant Dulmage.[10] Soon Mathews told Justus that he need not part with any of his men, but he did not get the extra ones he wanted. He had to ask the garrison to work longer hours and pay the men extra from his own funds.

All the while Justus struggled to balance his books. Supplies for the refugees were an added burden, and he was forever sending requests to Mathews for food and clothing. Many people arrived with little more than what they wore on their backs, needing emergency relief before going on to Fort St. Johns. Dr. Smyth was receiving people from the Mohawk Valley who were piloted by scouts to Pointe au Fer.

On May 9, 1782, Justus sent Captain Pritchard and seven men to kidnap General Jacob Bailey.[11] Recent reports showed that he was against Governor Chittenden, and Haldimand ordered his removal. Pritchard was to visit resident agent Thomas Johnson in Newbury, not far from Bailey's home, to seek his advice. Returning on June 22, Pritchard reported that Bailey escaped by crossing the Connecticut River, but his party had kidnapped Bailey's son.[12] Sherwood and Pritchard suspected that Johnson had warned Bailey, although Dr. Smyth pleaded that the man they had released was not a double agent.

That month Justus deputized Elijah Bothum to take a flag and forty-two prisoners and conduct an exchange at Skenesborough. Although the Vermont leaders had not suggested sending anyone in exchange for Terence Smyth, Justus released Lieutenant Michael Dunning, of the Vermont army, hoping to pacify the Herrick-Safford faction. When the list of prisoners sent back reached Haldimand, and he learned that Dunning had been exchanged for Terence Smyth, he sent a stiff reprimand to Justus. Dunning should have been exchanged for a commissioned officer, not a refugee civilian like Terence, even though he was Hudibras' son.[13] Justus shrugged at the reproof. While there was a shred of hope that Vermont would reunite, anything was worth trying.

Then he received an order from Mathews, now back in Quebec City, to send some agents to see whether they could destroy Captain John Paul Jones' ship *America*, a vessel of sixty-two guns under construction at Portsmouth, New Hampshire. The admiral who terrorized the coast of Britain and plundered Lord Selkirk's home in the *Bonhomme Richard*, would continue his depredations once the new vessel was finished. Justus chose William Amesbury and John Lindsay, members of his company from that state, and sent them out to see what they could arrange.[14]

As August approached, Justus held his men in readiness for an attack. Throughout the exodus of refugees, over everyone's head hung the threat of invasion. He made plans to move his secret papers to Isle aux Noix, should the blockhouse be threatened. His work was interrupted by the arrival of scouts Jacob Lansing and James Breakenridge Jr., and Justus dropped everything and accompanied them to Quebec City to talk with the governor. Lansing reported that Chittenden and Ethan Allen would welcome a secret treaty with Britain that could be made public when 4,000 regulars and supplies for the Vermont army arrived in the Green Mountains.[15]

Justus' hopes were dashed again, for His Excellency refused to undertake any such aggressive moves. At New York City, Sir Guy Carleton had replaced Sir Henry Clinton as the commander-in-chief. Carleton had orders to withdraw the troops to his base, and he had begun evacuating all units along the southern coast. In July, Haldimand had suggested staging a diversion, to draw Washington's attention away from New York City, but Sir Guy forbad any further offensive operations.[16] Haldimand told Justus that he should keep on writing to Vermont proposing a cessation of hostilities, an empty gesture since there had not been any since the truce came into effect in the autumn of 1780.

The news from Vermont was vaguely encouraging. Mobs still gathered to oppose Chittenden, but the republic had practical reasons for preferring reunion with Britain over joining the Congress. The country was in an uproar. Individual states were forced to levy taxes to pay war debts, and paper money issued by the Congress was worthless. Farmers who could not pay their taxes in hard cash saw their properties auctioned off. Mobs gathered to hinder the bidding, and tax collecting was nearly impossible. Since the issue of taxes had started the rebellion, people felt betrayed. Vermont had none of these problems and virtually no debts, as she had been financing herself through the Absentee Act.

Justus could not allow himself to be overly preoccupied with Vermont. Always in the back of his mind was the state of the defences of his blockhouse. The importance of his post was brought home to him by the arrival of the Baron von Riedesel, accompanied by Dr. Smyth, for a tour of inspection. The Baron pronounced himself satisfied with Sherwood's preparations, and he departed. Hudibras remained, for another prisoner exchange was in the making. These arrangements were interrupted by the arrival on August 17 of Privates William Amesbury and John Lindsay to report on what had transpired in Portsmouth, New Hampshire.

Lindsay, the more literate of the two, wrote a report for the governor, after discussing its contents with Justus. Admiral John Paul Jones' ship *America* was being financed by France, for service in that country's line. Pretending to be privateers, the two agents were hired to work for eight weeks, until the vessel was to be launched, at four shillings a day — which was more than Justus was paying them to spy. Lindsay described Jones as 'A middling sizd man of dark complexion, dressed very grand with two gold aupelets very like Col. St Leger's'. With Amesbury, he worked on the vessel — and helped guard her! Mr. Jones feared a raid from the sea. The work was lagging because carpenters were scarce. Lindsay continued:

> We could at any time have put fire in many places on her, but as her inside work was not done & she would not burn well we thought it best to come in with our report, and go again when the General should think proper. When we came away we told Capt. Jones we must go to Boston to git some wages we had due, and we promised to return in Augt. or September and if possible to bring some ship carpenters with us from Boston.

What an audacious pair they were, Justus thought as he read what Lindsay had written. When he said the ship would not burn, he referred to her oak planking. The pine decking, once in place, would be more flammable, better suited to the purposes of arsonists. Amesbury and Lindsay assured Justus that they would be happy to try later, and if they did not succeed would not expect any pay. When the report reached Quebec City, Mathews replied that the men should be kept in readiness.[17] Justus was pessimistic. He longed to provide 'the ship carpenters from Boston' that Lindsay and Amesbury had promised to take to Portsmouth but Sir Guy Carleton had forbidden further acts of hostility. Sadly he turned his attention to the prisoner exchange.

This time with Dr. Smyth he went aboard the schooner *Maria* to Crown Point, where they met New York emissaries and traded their prisoners. By September 6 they had returned to the Loyal Blockhouse. Justus took two weeks leave while Hudibras stayed behind to command the post. Samuel was to start school in Montreal, and Justus wanted to see his elder son settled. Then he planned to move Sarah and the two younger children to the blockhouse to economize.[18] He had to pay fees for Samuel, and he was no longer satisfied with the education his son was receiving from the Reverend George Gilmour at Fort St. Johns.

The school Justus chose for the not quite eight-year-old Samuel was the classical academy kept by the Reverend John Stuart, the Anglican chaplain. There were other schoolmasters in the city, but Stuart's establishment was sanctioned by His Excellency, and many officers of provincials sent their sons to him. What young Samuel thought of being sent away from his mother by a father he rarely saw was of no importance. Justus was being the Puritan parent, surrounding his son with boys of his own class, preparing him for leadership without taking into account how a mere child might feel.

When Justus reached Fort St. Johns, he helped Sarah pack Samuel's belongings, and father and son set off in a stagecoach for Montreal. Justus stayed in the city a few days, allowing Samuel to become acclimatized to his new surroundings, and he found the social life almost as glittering as that in Quebec City. Nightly someone gave a party, and he became acquainted With Sir John and Lady Johnson, who had a house at Lachine, sixteen kilometres to the west and entertained frequently.

Back at Fort St. Johns, Justus and Sarah prepared to move to the Loyal Blockhouse, and he suggested that Samuel, his brother, and Thomas Sherwood follow this example. Both declined. Thomas, more thoughtful than his cousin, pointed out that if the rebels got wind of the presence of Sarah and the children, they might be kidnapped. Justus brushed this warning aside. His family would be safe as long as no one ventured outside the picketed area. If his loved ones wanted to go beyond these limits a few of his men would guard them.[19]

That autumn Thomas Sherwood's elder son, Reuben, fourteen-years-old and five feet (1.5 metres) tall, joined the ranks of Captain Meyers' company, Loyal Rangers.[20] When Justus discovered that Thomas had allowed young Reuben to enlist he was appalled, but his cousin reminded him that Meyers was a gentle soul, a luxury afforded large persons. Reuben would be well looked after by Meyers, whose sense of humanity had been the cause of a falling out with Dr. Smyth. At the doctor's request the big German farmer had lent him a black man from his company as a servant. While Meyers was away on a mission, Smyth took the man to Captain James Breakenridge, King's Rangers, complaining that he had been insubordinate. James handed him over to the drummers for a flogging, and when Meyers returned he was furious. Apart from the brutality, Breakenridge had not conducted a court martial.

Meyers had removed the black man from the Smyth house and returned him to duty as a soldier, since which time the doctor had had nothing to do with him.[21] For once Justus' sympathies lay with Meyers, but he was relieved that Smyth was disgruntled with the sturdy tenant farmer from the Albany area. Now Justus would not have to worry about impromptu raids such as the one on Ballstown, that might endanger his scouting parties.

By early October Justus had his family settled in the Loyal Blockhouse. When he arrived, another inconclusive letter from Ethan Allen awaited him. This time

Ethan made more of Vermont's fear of 'Sagacious Washington', the avowed enemy, and of Vermont's unwillingness to shoulder any of the Continental debt. After discussing the advantages of trade with Canada, the natural outlet for Vermont products since goods could travel by water, Governor Chittenden decided to prohibit it. Trade with the British might annoy Herrick and Safford and their followers, while Washington might seize on dealing with the enemy as the excuse he needed to invade Vermont.[22]

On November 25, Corporal Thomas Welch, of the blockhouse garrison, who had been leading a scouting party, arrived in a vessel from Vermont, escorting two visitors, Nicols and Holmes, who had three tons of beef to sell in Montreal. Justus was in a quandary, and he arrested all three men. He wrote to Major Nairne, the commandant of Isle aux Noix, for advice on how to deal with this infraction of the embargo on trade. The more Justus thought about Corporal Welch's conduct the more agitated he became. How could his man endanger all the carefully maintained relations with Chittenden? Torn by anger, and fear that one-eyed Tom might cancel the truce, sleep eluded Justus that night and he paced the floor of his quarters until dawn.[23]

A few days later Justus received an order from Major Nairne to conduct a court martial to give Corporal Welch the opportunity to defend himself. The proceedings were held on December 7, and the report was written by Thomas Sherwood, showing Captain Sherwood as the president, Ensigns John Dusenbury, Elijah Bothum and Hermanus Best as the other members of the court. Eliphelet Casswell, Henry Ridout, Adam Vanderhyder and Thomas Brown — members of Welch's scouting party when he arrived with Nicols and Holmes — were sworn and examined separately. In a legible, copybook hand, more readable than his cousin's rapid flowing style, Thomas wrote:

> the beef was brought there [Crown Point] by agreement with Capt Pritchard. . .. Corpl Welch thought he was doing his duty to take in the two men, and he did not think he should be blamed for Taking in the Beef, which he and all his party suppos'd was Brout by Agreement from Capt. Pritchard.

Justus exonerated his man, and informed Major Nairne on December 8 that Welch's:

> candid and sincere manner of making the inclosed declaration the Court were fully of the opinion that Welch thought he was doing his Govt Service in bringing in Nicols, and that he supposed he should do a favour to Capt. Pritchard.[24]

The culprits were Captain Azariah Pritchard and Holmes. Nicols had been duped, and Justus allowed him to return to Vermont. Holmes was sent to Isle aux Noix as a prisoner of war. In accordance with Major Nairne's instructions Justus would sink the beef in Lake Champlain, and he resolved to dismiss Pritchard from the secret service and return him to duty with Major Rogers. Justus paraded the garrison to the west side of the blockhouse to watch while the beef was submerged, a warning to anyone else who might be seduced into aiding Vermont traders.

That season most of the Loyal Rangers were stationed at Rivière du Chêne, a blockhouse on the south shore of Lac St. Pierre, where the stream could give the rebels access to Canada. There the regiment was to muster on January 1, and Justus dispatched Lieutenant James Parrot with as many of the men as he could spare, and a list of those he could not, so that Major Edward Jessup could make complete returns. Samuel Sherwood, a private under his brother until he could get more recruits, accompanied Lieutenant Parrot, and the men left the blockhouse on December 27.[25]

On the 30th, Justus played host to two men from Claremont, New Hampshire, the Reverend Ranna Cossitt, an Anglican clergyman, and Captain Benjamin Sumner of the militia. They were returning from a visit to Quebec City, where they had talked with Haldimand. Young Samuel was home from school in Montreal for the Christmas holiday, and the Reverend Cossitt took a liking to the lad. He recommended that Justus send him to Dartmouth College where he would be catechized by Dr. Eleazor Wheelock, the most eminent schoolmaster in America. Justus solemnly agreed to consider it, out of politeness, knowing he could never afford the expense.

Cossitt wondered about leading his entire flock to Canada, while Sumner informed Justus that General

Roger Enos, who had commanded some Vermont militia in 1776, wanted to raise a regiment for service with Britain. Enos expected to receive the rank of colonel, and to have his corps placed on the regular establishment.[26] That raised Justus' hackles. The only provincial corps so honoured was the Royal Highland Emigrants, numbered the 84th Regiment of Foot. Why should an uncertain quantity like Enos receive better treatment than Edward Jessup, whose Loyal Rangers remained a provincial corps, or Sir John Johnson, who had been trying for years to have his regiment placed on the regular establishment?

When Cossitt and Sumner were ready to leave, Justus gave them a boat and an escort from the garrison. Shortly after they set out, they found:

> the whole lake as far as they could see froze in such a manner that they dare not attempt to proceed, they therefore put the Gentlemen and the Flag on the Ice, and broke their way back to White's Camp. Corpl. Miller had the Misfortune on his way back to fall on the Ice and break his Collar bone, Corpl Welch, who pretends to know Something of Surgery, has Sett it, but we have nothing to apply to it. I wish we could have a few medicines order'd here.

Agonizing Justus finished 'It is cruel when we have a man sick or lame which is often the case that we have nothing for his relief'.[27]

Justus was playing to the gallery because he felt strongly that he should be receiving more supplies at government expense. He deliberately avoided mentioning Sarah, whose knowledge of local remedies was most useful to the garrison. She fetched willow twigs from outside, thawed them and gave them to Corporal Miller to chew, which eased his pain.[28]

Sarah also brewed spruce beer which, although no substitute for rum, was rich in ascorbic acid and prevented scurvy. When Justus could scrape up the funds, he purchased a few pairs of skates for the use of his scouts, to enable them to travel more rapidly when the surface of the ice was bare, much as Robert Rogers' rangers had skated along Lake Champlain during the Seven Years' War.

Some weeks after Corporal Miller's accident, the Reverend Ranna Cossitt wrote from New Hampshire advising Justus not to send Samuel to Dartmouth College until Dr. Wheelock had returned from a visit to Europe.[29] Justus had never taken the suggestion seriously, for apart from the expense, he did not want to entrust his firstborn to a state that was for the most part a nest of mad rebels. Justus paid a Mr. Gibson to tutor Diana and Levius, and Sarah had the company of several women who did chores for the men. He knew that his family would be more comfortable back in the house at Fort St. Johns, but he was glad to be able to save a few shillings, and he had wearied of the loneliness of duty at the blockhouse without his wife and children. The small island fortress seemed much less bleak than during the previous winter.

Chapter 15

'Behind the Cloud Topped Hill'

As the year 1783 opened, Justus Sherwood faced some cruel facts. Britain was going to give the rebelling colonies their independence. His cause was lost, and many loyalists would have to make new homes in Britain's remaining North American colonies. There was plenty of room to accommodate the refugees in Canada, and Nova Scotia was convenient for those gathered around New York City. Justus had given his best to the Northern Department, and could take pride in the work he had done assisting prisoners and refugees. Then, too, the future of Vermont was far from settled. If that state decided on reunion, he would some day be back in business with the Allens, buying more tracts from the Onion River Land Company.

Governor Haldimand wanted him to keep up the correspondence with Vermont, although now its main purpose was her continued neutrality. Justus wanted that as much as his chief, but he did not share Haldimand's conviction that the Vermont leaders were playing the British off against the Congress to avoid being coerced by either power. His Excellency went along with the conspirators because neutrality made Canada more secure, but Justus was constantly reminded of the direction of Vermont's trade. Nicols and Holmes with their beef was only one of many incidents where men came to the Loyal Blockhouse wanting to trade their wares. Lumber and grain, Vermont's main source of wealth, could not be moved cheaply by road. All her waterways north of Arlington drained ultimately to the St. Lawrence River.

Trade, Justus the hard-headed businessman knew, might be the deciding factor for Vermont. Her viable markets were Montreal and Quebec City. Timber rafts and boatloads of grain, potash and other goods could be moved economically down the Richelieu, but not towards the markets in the large population centres around New York City. If access to the St. Lawrence were denied Vermont indefinitely, her economy would be depressed. Her geography tied her to the St. Lawrence, and if she could not sell her wares there, the Allens and other frontier businessmen would suffer where it hurt most, in their pocketbooks. Frontiersmen were pragmatists as much as patriots, to whichever side, and Justus was convinced that Ethan and Ira were not deceiving him. If the Congress kept on resisting, the time might come when Vermont opted to reunite in order to have free access to the St. Lawrence.

Not long after the visit of the Reverend Cossitt and Captain Sumner, Justus played host to two other visitors. One was Luke Knowlton of New Fane, Vermont, a Cumberland County judge and member of the county's Committee of Safety. Knowlton was also a long time resident agent who had provided Justus' scouts with intelligence. He fled to the Loyal Blockhouse when he learned that Governor George Clinton of New York had offered 100 pounds to anyone who would carry him off to Poughkeepsie, on the lower Hudson River.[1] The other was Sarah's youngest brother, nineteen-year-old Lemuel Bothum, who longed to see Elijah again. After the trek through the snow in cowhide boots he was suffering from frost bitten feet.

Knowlton reported on a riot at Walpole, New Hampshire, during a sale for taxes:

> I am informed the highest Bid on the best yoke of oxen was nineteen pence and Cows some five pence. Genl. Bellows bid one dollar for a cow, which so enraged the populace that he relinquished it. After the Vendue the populace went to their Liberty pole (so called when erected) and cryed aloud Liberty is gone, Cut it down and at the fall Huzza'd aloud for King George and his Laws.

They were interrupted by the arrival of Thomas Smyth, who had been gathering intelligence in Vermont. He reported that Sergeant Moses Hurlburt, King's Rangers, attended a public dance in Arlington, got drunk and was openly recruiting.[2] Yet worse was in store. Justus learned that a recruiting party of three King's Rangers went into Vermont after stealing money in New York, and had also robbed a house near Poultney. Justus was not surprised when the Vermont leaders requested that no more recruiting parties be sent into their territory.[3] Major James Rogers had some men of dubious character in his ranks, but Justus was sympathetic to Moses Hurlburt, who had been under much strain of late. Other officers complained that he had deserters from the Continental Army in his garrison, but as long as such were conscientious Justus was tolerant of past allegiances.[4]

As soon as Lemuel Bothum was fit to travel, he and Judge Knowlton went on to Fort St. Johns, escorted by Elijah, who needed a leave of absence and time to spend with his brother. Afterward, all was quiet until late February. Then Thomas Sherwood came skating along the ice, shouting that six hundred rebels had left Albany in sleighs. When last seen they were making for Saratoga, and were commanded by Colonel Marinius Willett. Justus prepared to withstand a seige.

He posted scouts far up the lake to keep watch, then he dispatched a scout to Pointe au Fer to warn Major Carleton, another to Vermont with a message for Governor Chittenden. Next, Justus ordered all the women and children to leave for Fort St. Johns, and he helped Sarah pack before seeing her off in a sleigh with Diana, Levius and Caesar Congo. Waving until they were out of sight, Justus reflected that Thomas and Samuel had been wise in refusing to move their families to the blockhouse. Had they given up the house at Fort St. Johns, Sarah would have had to scramble for accommodation, competing with other women and children who were waiting for decent houses.

Firewood was of vital importance, for it could not be brought in if a large force of rebels surrounded his post. The work parties had to redouble their efforts since he did not dare run short of fuel in such bitter weather. One suspense-filled day followed another as Justus and his small garrison waited for news. Then the scouts returned and reported that Colonel Willett's men had turned west towards Oswego, where a detachment of the second battalion, King's Royal Regiment of New York under the command of Major John Ross was stationed.

The Vermonters, too, had waited anxiously, and when everyone knew that Oswego was Willett's objective, all relaxed, although Justus feared for the fate of the garrison under Ross. Then his scouts returned with word that Willett had failed because his advance party was spotted by Ross' scouts. The withdrawal had been frightful. Many men died from exposure, while eighty survivors were in the hospital in Albany with frozen feet.

By March 10 Justus was almost reconciled to the fact that the colonies would be granted their independence, and he wrote to Major Mathews:

> I have during the Contest Encounter'd many difficulties and dangers with Chearfulness, being always supported by my Confidence in His Majesty's Arms and my own Consciousness of the justice of his Cause; but if independence is in fact granted we have no other consolation left; than the Consciousness of having endeavour'd to do our duty, for I think no Loyalist of Principle & spirit can ever endure the thought of going back to live under the Imperious laws of a Washington and his minions.[5]

At the same time he passed on a request from Ethan Allen that Vermont be recognized as a British province in the articles of peace — a suggestion Justus himself had planted in the big mountain chieftain's mind through scout David Crowfoot. This was destined to go only as far as the Château St. Louis. His Excellency thought the British commissioners negotiating with rebel emissaries in Paris had enough thorny issues that defied solution without this baffling one.

As the snow began to melt, Justus pondered where he would find a suitable place for his family. There was plenty of good land in Canada, but the conveniently located parts were held by seigneurs. Only in the seigneury of Sorel, which the government purchased in 1780, could loyalists be accommodated satisfactorily.[6] Some

English-speaking seigneurs were seeking tenants among the refugees, in the hope that the presence of the loyalists would induce the British government to revoke the Quebec Act and institute English civil law. In Sherwood's view that would be an improvement, but it might not solve the problem of tenancy.

He had shunned renting land when he chose to settle in the New Hampshire Grants, and was no happier at the prospect of paying rent in Canada. Furthermore, as a staunch Protestant he could never be content surrounded by Canadians. He prayed that Haldimand would make more suitable arrangements, especially for the New Englanders. All would chafe if they were compelled to live among people who were apolitical and who differed from them in language and religion.

In Quebec City, Haldimand was coming to the same conclusions as Sherwood, and his plans reflected his Swiss background. Loyalists should not live among the Canadians where they might lose their identity and assimilate. They should have their own cantons, and the matter required careful consideration. His Excellency was not going to be rushed into making any snap decisions.

Throughout the month of March, the Loyal Blockhouse was as busy as a trading post. Some of Sherwood's guests were welcome, others an endurance test. One man came with shoes to sell, and was sent to New Hampshire. On the 14th, who should appear, all smiles, but Ethan Allen's obnoxious cousin Ebenezer, to enquire about trade. The memory of the march through Vermont those snowy November days of 1780 came back to haunt Justus. He was tempted to arrange for Ebenezer to vanish into the forest, with no one but a few confidants the wiser, but that was not his way. Instead, he received him, but admitted to Mathews that it was 'so painful to see him I can barely treat him with common civility'.[7]

Later in the day, Elijah Bothum arrived from Fort St. Johns, bringing Sarah, Diana, Levius and Caesar Congo. Several of the other women had returned, and Sarah wanted to be on hand to care for her husband at a trying time. On Justus' behalf, Elijah had purchased '1 pr Skaites for Master Saml' which cost six shillings and eightpence, and a slightly inferior pair for Justus Seeley, Sherwood's drummer to use while the ice remained firm enough.

Ten days later, Ira Allen wrote Justus asking him to arrange a loan of 10,000 guineas in Montreal at six percent interest. In return, Ira promised Justus a good farm in Vermont. Wearily Justus chuckled. Ira must be desperate, or he would have realized that an impoverished refugee officer whose employment was about to end had no standing with the merchants of Montreal. All the security the one time Green Mountain Boy had to offer was a piece of land in a foreign country that was in a state of turmoil.

On April 27, 1783, the preliminary articles of peace were published in the *Quebec Gazette*. As the news spread, more visitors flocked to the Loyal Blockhouse. Most were refugees, but some were rebels, smelling success and very overbearing. The latter claimed that Captain Sherwood was occupying New York territory and should be evicted forthwith. Many wanted to trade, the hostile ones to demand the discharge of friends and brothers serving in provincial corps or prisoners in camps around Montreal. Arrogant though they were, Justus felt obliged to protect them, and he informed Mathews that his men would cut such visitors to pieces if he did not keep a cautious lookout.[8]

Two loyalists from Boston named Campbell and Huntingdon came saying they had been ruined by a recent sharp decline in prices, and Justus gave them sanctuary. Soon afterwards, a man named Wait arrived, demanding that Justus hand over Campbell and Huntingdon, insisting that the Loyal Blockhouse was on land under the jurisdiction of Congress. Justus' retort was sharp. He would not surrender any man who came seeking his protection. If Wait was acting on the authority of Congress or any of that body's member states, with whom Britain was still at war, Justus would send him to Isle aux Noix as a prisoner of war. If Wait wished to go to Canada with Campbell and Huntingdon to ask Haldimand's permission to prosecute them, Justus would offer him every assistance. Wait excused himself, promising to return soon. He never did. Justus had called his bluff and Wait was relieved to escape with his skin intact.

That month Justus received his last wartime communication from Ethan Allen, dated April 18 'at a Tavern in Manchester half over seas'. Justus smiled grimly. Ethan was in his cups and misquoting Jonathan Swift. 'Independent for Independence', he declared, maintaining that Vermont would never confederate with Congress. He asked Justus to use his influence to have loyalists settle in northern Vermont — a scheme intolerable to Haldimand. The governor did not want loyalists near any border, lest their presence provoke incidents.[9]

On May 5, Mathews ordered Justus to proceed to Quebec City with seven or eight men of his detachment, or loyalists from Isle aux Noix and Fort St. Johns. Haldimand wanted him to explore the east coast, and he was to apply to Major Nairne at Isle aux Noix for a whaleboat. Mathews enclosed a passport for Sarah to visit her relatives in Vermont during Justus' absence. After asking Sarah's opinion Justus decided to take his family with him. He wanted to show Sarah Quebec City, and he had made the acquaintance of Captain Hugh O'Hara, the commandant of the garrison at Gaspé Bay. He knew he could leave the family with the O'Haras, affording the children a holiday.

Thomas Sherwood was in Justus' party when he left the Loyal Blockhouse.[19] They picked up Samuel from school in Montreal, and when they reached Quebec City, Justus rented rooms in the London Coffee House, a large stone hostelry in the Lower Town that was popular with English-speaking visitors. He conferred with the governor on his forthcoming mission, a journey to explore Gaspé Bay, Chaleur Bay and the coast as far as the Miramichi River Valley, in search of land for loyalists. Mathews told Justus that for every vacant acre there were at least fifty applicants.[11] He meant only land not under seigneurial tenure, for the seigneuries were more than half vacant.

With Sarah by his side Justus found the evenings more agreeable than on his other visits. Once Haldimand discovered that he had brought his family, he asked Justus to bring Sarah and the children for a short audience in the drawing room of the Château St. Louis.

His Excellency took a lively interest in the families of his officers and wanted to inspect Captain Sherwood's when he had the opportunity. He was fond of children, and the von Riedesel daughters adored him, calling him 'Onkel Friedrich'. In turn he referred to Augusta as 'my little wife'.[12] At the time the Baroness von Riedesel was staying in the city, recovering from the death of her infant daughter, Kanada. The child, born at Sorel, had been Haldimand's goddaughter.

Justus and Sarah went to parties with Major Mathews and his recent bride, Mary Simpson, whom the governor's secretary had long courted. From other ladies, Sarah discovered that Mathews had almost lost his Mary the summer before, when the ship *Abermarle* was in port. Her captain, Horatio Nelson, was infatuated with Mary, and when his ship was ordered to sail for Halifax, Nelson jumped ship, vowing he would never be parted from her. His crew dragged him aboard and weighed anchor, thus saving the young officer's naval career.[13]

On May 29 the Sherwoods left Quebec City and as usual, Justus recorded the type of vessel in which he sailed. His journal for Haldimand began:

> May 29th Left Quebec, in the Treasury Brig St. Peters. 7th June Arrived in Gaspy Bay, Landed My Family at Captain O'Haras where they were received with Every Mark of Civility and Politeness – Mr. O'Hara is a most worthy, sensible Man, perfectly Attached to Govt. And well dispos'd to serve the distressed Loyalists. he gave me every Assistance in his power,[14]

The O'Hara family proved compatible, and Sarah, young Samuel, Diana and Levius, now aged eight, six and five, ranked as the first tourists to spend a summer holiday in that magnificent setting. The children swam in the sea, fished with the young O'Haras, and feasted on lobsters which they caught by the tails among the shallows. Meanwhile, Justus and Captain O'Hara were fully occupied examining the land. As a farmer and surveyor, Justus knew good land when he saw it, and he found the surroundings similar to Connecticut. In his journal his New England background, the knowledge of the sea acquired during his youth in Stratford, on the coast, shone through his writing.

The country around Gaspé Bay, 'Point Peters' and

Percé he found mountainous, but there was one exception, land enough for forty to fifty families on either side of Gaspé Bay. The rivers abounded in salmon, the bay with cod, eels and lobsters. Point Peters was well situated for a fishery, but the land was not fit for cultivation. Percé he described as:

> a very pleasant place, finely situated for the Fishery. . .. if this Front was Regularly divided into Equal Lots, it Might form a very pretty Town of about 100 Houses with Land Sufficient for Fishing ground, Gardens &c.

He was picturing a New England town, overlooking the sea, and typically Yankee, he wanted the town to look attractive. Of Perboe, in Chaleur Bay, where his party arrived on June 16, he observed:

> this is an exceeding Pleasant Place, where one is in the Basin or Harbor, but the Entrance is narrow and somewhat difficult for Large Vessels. . .. the Soil is exceeding Good and natural for Grass, rye, Oats, Barley &c but I think it is in General, too low for Wheat.

Again he found the fishing excellent. Perboe would make a fine place for trade, and as he proceeded he noted other good harbours and pockets of rich soil. Captain O'-Hara turned back, and Justus, Thomas and their party continued to the mouth of the Restigouche River, where they found a harbour that was only suitable for 'Boats and Shallops'. The land was good, but the Restigouche Indians claimed it, as they did all the meadows up the river.

Setting out to explore some islands and the Miramichi River, he noted that the climate at Chaleur Bay was more favourable than on any part of the St. Lawrence below Sorel. Wheat, barley, oats, peas and grass were twenty days further advanced. He thought 1,500 families might settle there, and another 200 from Percé to Gaspé, but they would require some help for three or four years, until they could get the land cleared and houses built, and they needed to be supplied with cattle and tools. 'I am persuaded this country would in a little time become the most Valuable of His Majesty's present Dominion in North America'.

Only a Yankee from resource-poor Connecticut could have made such an optimistic evaluation of these coastal lands. Justus based his assessment on what settlers could earn by fishing and trade, but he found that land tenure was a serious drawback to creating a settlement in the vicinity:

> the settlement of this Country never can flourish while under the monopoly of a few seignury Leaders, who make it their study to mismanage the cultivation of the Lands & to keep the poor Inhabitants as much in debt as to oblige them to spend the whole Summer Season in fishing to pay up their Arrears.

On July 1, his party reached the Miramichi River, in 'the Govt of Nova Scotia'. He found it a fine river, navigable for vessels of '100 tons' for 'forty-five miles', as far as a fort, and for another 'forty-five miles' for boats. By the latter he meant a shallow draft bateau or whaleboat, as opposed to a keel boat. Again he commented on the wealth of fish, and the smoothness of the terrain, but as at Chaleur Bay he found land tenure a drawback. The land was 'monopolized by designing Men, no less than 12,000 Acres including All the good land, and most of the Salmon Fishery is own'd by two men'.

The journal concludes:

> July 14th returned to Gaspy
> 20th left Gaspy with my own family, and Capt O'-Haras Eldest Son & Daughter.
> 12 Aug't Arrived at Quebec 24 days after leaving Gaspy.
> J. Sherwood.

In his evaluation, Justus had pictured these lands populated by New Englanders, accustomed to making a living part time by farming, part from the sea. Yet the coastal setting might not suit the majority of the refugees around Montreal and Sorel. These landlocked frontiersmen from backwoods communities, although sharp traders, lacked the skills necessary to turn to the sea as an alternative to farming.

Then, too, there was insufficient land to resettle all the people, and only if Governor Haldimand would wrest the land from greedy seigneurs and establish freehold tenure. Furthermore, a goodly portion of the best land lay in the Province of Nova Scotia, where Haldimand had no jurisdiction, and where the first wave of refugees had already arrived from New York City. Sir Guy Carleton was sending his charges to Nova Scotia as soon as transports were available.

Upon landing in Quebec City, the Sherwoods left the two young O'Haras with friends, and the rest of the party hurried on to Sorel in a whaleboat to wait upon the governor. Haldimand had a summer residence there, and had left the Château St. Louis on August 7.[15]

Chapter 16

The Happiest People in America

While Justus was exploring the east coast, Dr. Smyth remained on duty at the Loyal Blockhouse. Late in July he received an emissary from General Washington — the Baron von Steuben, a professional soldier from Germany and a member of Washington's staff who had done much to improve the discipline of the Continental Army. With him travelled an appropriate retinue of aides, a secretary, a colonel, servants, and a letter from the rebel commander-in-chief demanding that Haldimand hand over the western posts to the Congress.[1]

Hudibras sent a letter by express courier to His Excellency, escorted the Baron and his party as far as Isle aux Noix, and hurried to Fort St. Johns to make arrangements for their reception there. Meanwhile, Haldimand was journeying from Quebec City to Sorel. He did not want the German officer to inspect any more of his territory than was strictly necessary, and his summer residence was adequate for the guest.

Mathews relayed news of these developments to Justus when his party landed at Sorel. His Excellency resolutely refused to hand over any of the posts, and ordered that the western forts be defended at all costs.[2] These were necessary for the protection of the loyalists and Indians and for the fur trade. Furthermore Haldimand had angrily complained to von Steuben, in German, of the rebels' many infractions of the rules of war.

They had broken the terms of the Saratoga Convention of 1777, and there had been atrocities after Lord

Cornwallis' surrender at Yorktown in 1781. Many of the provincials were smuggled past the French blockade in the only ship allowed to leave in order to carry Cornwallis' dispatches to New York City, but twenty-five of John Graves Simcoe's Queen's Rangers were shot in cold blood.[3] Haldimand had other grievances, too, not the least of which was the number of rebels who, when allowed to return home on parole, had broken their word of honour and been active against Britain. Another grievance was the hangings of Captain Sherwood's agents — Thomas Lovelace, John Parker and Joseph Bettys. The governor had taken a very tough stance, Mathews maintained, when the welfare of his province was at stake. What a pity the governor had not been as brave over the question of letting loyalists take the offensive, Justus thought ruefully.

The report on Justus' explorations convinced Haldimand that very few refugees could be sent to the east coast, and the governor's surveyor-general, Major Samuel Holland, had already begun exploring land at the mouth of the Cataraqui River, near the site of old Fort Frontenac, a ruin since the Seven Years' War. Haldimand wanted Holland to be joined as soon as possible by parties of men skilled in the art of land colonization, and Justus was to report, with a party of men, to the deputy-surveyor, John Collins, in Montreal.[4] With his cousin Thomas and his party and family, Justus left for Fort St. Johns, and they reached the Sherwood house on September 1. On the 11th, His Excellency wrote these orders for Deputy-Surveyor Collins.

He was to have a townsite laid out at Cataraqui, reserving the land around old Fort Frontenac for the garrison and 'a resort' for the Indians. Townships were to be 'six miles Square' because the people to be settled were accustomed to that method of land division. A farm lot was to be 120 acres (54.54 hectares) — 19 chains in front and 63 chains, 25 links in depth, so that each township would have 25 lots in front, plus four chains, 58 links for road allowances. To assist him, Collins would be joined at Montreal by Captain Justus Sherwood, Lieutenant Lewis Kottě and Captain Michael Grass.[5] The latter had brought some families from New York City who preferred Canada over Nova Scotia, and wanted to be resettled at Cataraqui. Grass already knew the area, because he had been a prisoner of the French at Fort Frontenac during the earlier war.

Lieutenant Gershom French, Loyal Rangers, was exploring the Rideau River and looking for a route to Cataraqui, while Captain René LaForce, of the Provincial Marine, was charting some of the coast at the foot of Lake Ontario in his brigantine *Seneca*.[6] LaForce had been commodore of the French fleet on the lake during the Seven Years' War, re-appointed by Carleton in 1776. Because he knew of LaForce's work, Justus would make no references to the quality of the harbours in his journal.

When Justus reached Fort St. Johns, he learned that Dr. Smyth was complaining that he had been in sole charge of the secret service, prisoners and refugees too long. Justus chose Thomas Sherwood to relieve Hudibras at the Loyal Blockhouse. His cousin had been on many missions, and his faithful helper at the island post since it was built. Lieutenant John Dulmage, Sherwood's dependable second-in-command, was fully occupied with his regular duties, and had never been a party to the more private aspects of the work. Thomas was well informed on the affairs of the secret service — an admirable substitute for Smyth.[7]

By September 19, Justus was in Montreal with a party that consisted of Lieutenant Solomon Johns, King's Rangers, with two privates from that corps, and Ensign Elijah Bothum and seven privates from the Loyal Rangers. The report describing their journey of exploration was entitled 'Captn Sherwood's Journal from Montreal to Lake Ontario, noting the Quality of the Land from the West end of Lake St. Francis to the Bay Kenty'.[9]

Lieutenant Louis Kotté and Captain Michael Grass had been sent on ahead but Deputy-Surveyor John Collins accompanied Justus' party. At Lachine they had to pull their bateau through the rapids with the aid of lengths of rope. They had an easy time at the Cedars Rapids, where by Haldimand's order William Twiss, now a captain in the Royal Engineers, had constructed the

Côteau du Lac Canal, forty-five centimetres deep. By September 23, the surveyors and their assistants were at the west end of Lake St. Francis, about 'sixty-five miles' from Montreal — which meant that within five days they had covered twenty-one kilometres a day in spite of the Lachine Rapids.

On the 24th, Justus sent out a party to go by land 'three miles' back from the river, and proceed 'ten miles' upstream where they would return to the shore and await the boat. That night Justus and the men who remained on the river with him camped at Mille Roches, thirty kilometres up from Lake St. Francis. There the men who had gone inland joined them and reported that they went 'four miles' from the river, and:

> the Land All the way of the best quality they ever saw, it being a mixture of black deep mould entirely free from stones, Ledges or Swamps. . .. The Land is exceeding Pleasant all along the shore, and there is a number of fine Islands in the River but is a great scarcity of Water back from the River

The following day Justus sent a party to go by land while he proceeded 'five leagues' (twenty-five kilometres) which brought him above the 'Rapid Long Sou'. Because no disaster occurred, Justus did not describe the miseries of dragging the bateau upstream — a dangerous and exhausting business, more difficult than the Lachine Rapids. Meanwhile, Lieutenant Johns and some men went inland again, and returned to report that they had never seen as fine a country for all kinds of cultivation. They had crossed a large creek that emptied into a river at the head of the Long Sault Rapids where a waterfall would make a fine mill site, one of the first requirements fOr a new community.

From the 26th to the 27th, Justus' party covered forty-seven kilometres and reached the head of the Galops Rapids, 'three leagues' below the first of Haldimand's upper posts, Fort Oswegatchie (Ogdensburg, New York), which had a small detachment of regulars. Still the high quality of the land excited Justus. By the 28th he was above Oswegatchie, and he reported that the land was somewhat stony. In general the land was of the best quality from Lake St. Francis all the way to a point twenty kilometres above Fort Oswegatchie, and would allow at least twelve townships facing the river, each 'six miles square'. Of the six lower townships, Justus wrote 'I think there Cannot be better land in America'. On the 29th, he sent three men with six days provisions to go by land all the way to Cataraqui.

The next day Justus and the rest of his party reached Carleton Island. The voyage through the Thousand Islands did not impress him, and he dismissed them as barren rock, except for Grenadier Island, which had some soil on it. Carleton Island was a bustling post, crowned at the southwest end by Fort Haldimand, built by order of His Excellency commencing in 1778. The garrison consisted of the second battalion, King's Royal Regiment of New York, a detachment of Royal Highland Emigrants, and a few other regulars. The men were busy moving the fort's equipment to Cataraqui, which would be the more important place when the settlers came.

The island also had a large refugee encampment of loyalists and Indians from the western end of the Mohawk Valley. One lady residing in a house there was Molly, a sister of the Mohawk warrior, Joseph Brant, and the widow of Sir William Johnson, Sir John's father. With Molly were several of her daughters, Sir John's half-sisters.

On October 1, Justus took part of his men and crossed to 'Long Isle' (Wolfe Island) in a bark canoe, leaving the rest of his party to take the boat the long way round to Cataraqui. This island he thought very good land, enough for two valuable townships, one east and the other west of the portage, a narrow neck of land that divided the island into two almost equal parts. At Cataraqui, Justus met with the commandant, Major John Ross. On October 2, Ross reported 'Mr. Collins arrived here last night with Capt. Sherwood'.[10] Cataraqui, too, was a hive of industry, as fatigue parties hammered and sawed to complete a new barracks. Otherwise the settlement so far consisted of a few log houses, many tents, and the crumbling ruins of Fort Frontenac. The harbour at the mouth of the Cataraqui River was large, with new docks at which many bateaux were tied.

Over the next few days Justus and his party explored as far as 'Six Nation Bay' (Collins Bay), twelve kilometres west of Cataraqui, and found the land stony along the shore, but good, a 'mile' inland. On October 6 the men who had come on foot from above Fort Oswegatchie joined him at Cataraqui and reported that for the first 'six miles' of their march the land would be suitable for settlement, a township watered by three fine creeks, one with a good mill site. All the rest of the way to within eight kilometres of Cataraqui the land was exceedingly bad 'being a constant succession of Stony Ledge and sunken Swamps Altogether unfit for Cultivation, for 3 miles, at least back from the [River]'. The last eight kilometres to Cataraqui the men found very broken, but some of the land could be improved and would allow 'a Scattering Settlement'. On the 8th Justus escorted Elijah Bothum and Solomon Johns westward, each with one assistant, and ordered them to explore up the Bay of Quinte. By the 10th, he had returned to Cataraqui and the following morning he set out in a canoe with a guide to see this bad stretch of country for himself.

Twenty-five kilometres to the east he found the Gananoque River, and was delighted by the waterfall he discovered a short distance upstream '20 feet perpendicular and the most convenient place for Mills I ever saw'. There could be one valuable township east of Cataraqui, although the land was broken, intermixed with pockets of deep soil. The lots must be picked out wherever the good land was, for 'If they are laid & drawn in a regular form many men would get lots which would be worse than none'. After making his observations, Justus again returned to Cataraqui, where he found Elijah Bothum and Solomon Johns waiting for him. He sent them out, this time to explore along the north shore of the Bay of Quinte, and on the 16th he went with two men and a canoe to 'Stoney Creek' to find its source.[11] That late in the season the water level was very low:

> this Stream is very pure water, and to affect that we were many times oblig'd to wade to our knees & draw the Canoe for an hour at a time. . . but then it begins delightful Land, and as far up as we went equal in Quality as the Long Sou. . . I began with my Compass to take the Angles of this Serpentine River guessing at the Distance from Angle to Angle, & found it as follows

He then wrote a series of compass bearings, separated by distances in miles or rods, using a method of surveying still handy for making approximate ground exploration. Justus' compass was one of two types and in either case the dial was fifteen centimetres in diameter. One had a hoop with small holes that was hinged to the face. With the hoop raised a surveyor could take elevations. The other compass had metal projections on either side that could be raised at right angles to the face. Each flap had a long, narrow, vertical slit which could be used to line up two points. The raised flaps were a simple alidade used in drawing small but fairly accurate maps.

His method of gathering information was a pace and compass traverse, wherein he took the bearing of the direction of stream flow, paced until that direction changed, and recorded the number of paces. Knowing the length of his pace, he translated the distances into miles and rods. His entry ran in part 'the Creek runs West 4° South 2 miles then SW 1 Mile to Wt 3/4 Mile then S 20 Rods then SW 10 Rods'. He found some stony places, but on the whole the soil was rich, and there was a cataract with a drop of at least three metres some 'thirty-six rods' above the mouth of the river. He was delighted with his findings. 'This is a noble stream and should be in the center of the second Township and the lots be laid Et and Wt bounded on each side of it from this'.

Justus returned once more to Cataraqui. By November 2, Elijah Bothum and Solomon Johns had joined him with good reports of the land they had visited farther west. They found some cedar swamps, but on the whole regular townships would be satisfactory. Summing up, Justus reported that he could recommend laying out twelve townships along the St. Lawrence near Long Sault, and another twelve to the west of the Cataraqui River, with a gap of about seventy kilometres in between where the land was broken.

On the 14th, Lieutenant Gershom French arrived from his visit to the country along the Rideau River, and was going on to Montreal. He agreed to take a letter for Major Mathews for Justus, and forward it on to Quebec City. Justus was enthusiastic about the land he had seen, and he told Mathews 'The climate here is very mild & good, and I think that Loyalists may be the happiest people in America by settling this Country from Long Sou to Bay Quinty'.

Until mid-November, Justus and his men concentrated on determining the boundaries of three square townships at Cataraqui. Because of the concave curve in the lakeshore, each township was separated from its neighbours by a narrow gore — a triangular-shaped wedge with its apex on the shore and its base between the northern corners. The map Justus drew shows that only parts of the first and second concessions of 120 acre lots were laid out that season, in all, 100 lots, each with 19 chains (376.2 metres) of frontage. On the map he made these notes on the potential of settlement around Cataraqui:

> Supposing 2,370 acres of land to a Township the bay quinty will admit of 3,425 families at 120 acres each, on the north side. The tongue on the South side, Suppose it to make Six Townships, one half good of which I have no doubt, will admit of settling 857 families. The Isle Tonte [Amherst Island] opposite the mouth of this Bay will make two Townships and settle at least 200 families on the above portion of Lands. The lands beyond the head of the bay at the Great Carrying Place appears equally good as far as the Eye can Extend to the westward[12]

Although Justus had scant leisure time, he did discover that rebel prisoners were confined at Cataraqui. To his astonishment one of them was Ebenezer Allen, Ethan's overbearing cousin. Ebenezer had been kidnapped from his farm by some loyalists not long after his disturbing visit to Justus' blockhouse, and escorted all the way to this post. No doubt Ebenezer would be released in due course, and in the meantime he was reaping as he had sown.[13]

On November 18, Justus departed, leaving behind two of his men who wanted to winter at Cataraqui. With the others he went in the bateau they had brought from Montreal, as far as Carleton Island that night. Some of the garrison were suffering from smallpox, but that did not deter him. There were usually cases of the dreaded disease at Fort St. Johns, and he wanted to use the better channel down the St. Lawrence. From Carleton Island

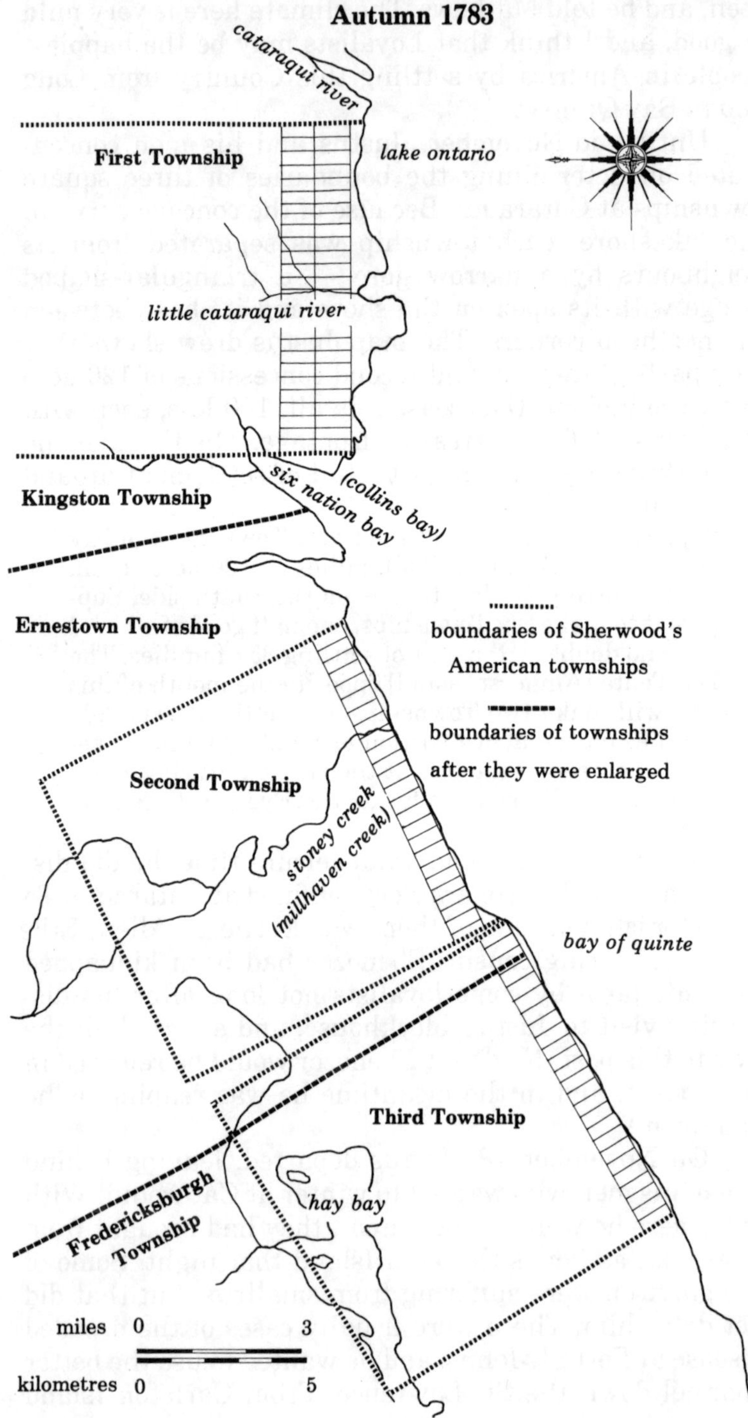
The Three Townships Sherwood Surveyed at Cataraqui
Autumn 1783
cataraqui river
First Township
lake ontario
little cataraqui river
Kingston Township
six nation bay
(collins bay)
Ernestown Township
boundaries of Sherwood's American townships
boundaries of townships after they were enlarged
Second Township
stoney creek
(millhaven creek)
bay of quinte
Third Township
Fredericksburgh Township
hay bay
miles 0 3
kilometres 0 5

the current would carry his boat swiftly due northeast. On the 2nd, Mathews had written to Major John Adolphus Harris, Royal Highland Emigrants and the commandant of Fort Haldimand, ordering him to destroy 'Smallpox matter for the purpose of Inoculation'.[14] Mathews referred to scrapings from smallpox victims that was used at that time.

Those with the disease, Mathews instructed, were to be isolated, but no inoculation programme was to be undertaken, since some men inoculated might succumb to the disease and spread it to the Indians. If any natives caught smallpox, they would claim that it was because of the inoculations and blame the British garrison. What Justus did not realize was that he himself was exhausted and vulnerable. By the time his party reached Montreal on the evening of November 23, he knew he must have some rest.

Reporting to Mathews that he had returned from Cataraqui, Justus admitted that he was thoroughly weary, but he did not know that he was incubating smallpox.[15] When he arrived at the house in Fort St. Johns, where Sarah and the two younger children were waiting for him to take them to the Loyal Blockhouse, Justus was feverish. On December 9, Dr. Smyth informed Mathews that Captain Sherwood was dangerously ill.[16]

Chapter 17

Personal Crises

The moment Dr. Smyth suspected that Justus had smallpox, he ordered everyone out of the house, an order difficult to comply with in overcrowded St. Johns. Anna Sherwood took her two younger children, Eunice her daughter Rachel, by bateau to the Loyal Blockhouse, where Thomas remained in command of the scouts. Unwilling to go so far afield, Sarah found space in the barracks for herself, Diana and Levius. Dr. Smyth found a servant who was immune to care for Justus.

Sorrowing, Sarah wondered why they had never taken the precaution of having the family inoculated, though Dr. Smyth scoffed at the idea. Inoculation with the scrapings from smallpox victims carried considerable risk. In theory a recipient developed a mild case, but in Smyth's experience, all too often he developed a serious one.

On his bed Justus tossed and turned as the fever mounted. By the third day, the servant had to tie him down to prevent him injuring himself. The red marks developed and gradually they turned to ugly pustules on his skin, inside his mouth and down his throat. Swallowing became difficult. At last his fever began to drop and he was more lucid. The acute pain in his arms, legs and back became less severe though he was far from out of danger. Dr. Smyth came to the door daily to hear the servant's report and give advice. At all costs he did not want the patient bled, a practice popular with quacks attached to the regular regiments. Anemia would only make Justus worse. Then, gradually the pustules dried up and formed scabs and Dr. Smyth was able to report to Major Mathews on December 19 that Captain Sherwood was on the mend.[1]

Smyth instructed the servant to collect all the scabs and burn them. Until every scab had been found and destroyed, Justus was a menace to other members of the family. Scabs on hands and feet tended to be deeply imbedded, and the doctor ordered the servant to dig out each scab with the tip of a sharp knife. After each treatment Justus lay weak and perspiring, but at length both the servant and the doctor were satisfied, and he was allowed to dress and sit in a chair by the fire. All his bedding was burned, and the servant scrubbed the sick room with strong soap and gave the same scouring to the rest of the house.[2]

Just before Christmas, Smyth permitted Sarah and the two children to return home, soon to be joined by Anna, Eunice and their children. The three families had more cause for celebration than in previous years; Thomas came from the Loyal Blockhouse, Samuel, Justus' brother, from Verchères, very smart in an officer's uniform. At last he had qualified for a lieutenant's commission and Justus was delighted. Young Samuel stayed in Montreal, for Sarah had asked Dr. Stuart to keep the boy in case anyone else succumbed. By the time she knew the house was safe, it was too late to change the arrangement.

On December 24, 1783, all the provincial troops on duty near Montreal, Sorel and Lake Champlain were disbanded, and Justus, his brother and cousin, became half-pay officers.[3] The Loyal Rangers, King's Rangers and the first battalion, King's Royal Regiment of New York, together with their families, were to remain where they were quartered, receiving provisions, until the spring when they could be moved up the St. Lawrence to the land the governor had chosen for them.

Three battalions remained on duty that winter — the Royal Highland Emigrants, the second battalion, King's Royal Regiment of New York, and Butler's Rangers. All were stationed at upper posts, and the order to disband came too late for Haldimand to relay it to the respective commanding officers. Meanwhile, His Excellency was busy making arrangements to resettle the refugees. He purchased large tracts from the Mississauga Indians, and was in communication with Major Edward Jessup and Sir John Johnson. On January 22, Major Mathews ordered Jessup and Sherwood to come to Quebec City to discuss the governor's plans.[4]

Edward Jessup was in Montreal completing the returns of the Loyal Rangers, and he wrote asking Justus to go ahead, taking a short memorandum he enclosed.[5] The journey was an ordeal. Justus still felt weak from his recent illness and as the sleigh passed down the St. Lawrence through air so cold it seemed to burn him, he ached for the next bed at an inn. When he reached the Château St. Louis, Mathews eyed him with concern, noting the pitted scars still so fresh they shone an angry red on the otherwise pale face. The major escorted him to the officers' quarters in the barracks he had used on other visits, and settled him in bed with a drink of hot rum. Morning would be soon enough for the governor.

During the months since Justus' work at Cataraqui, Haldimand had received his first instructions from the King through Lord North, once again the prime minister, and His Excellency was disturbed over certain provisions. These had reached him in November, though they were dated July 16, 1783. Land for loyalists was to be divided into:

> distinct seigneuries or Fiefs, to extend from two to four leagues in front. If situated upon a navigable River, otherwise to be run square, or in such shape and in such quantities, as shall be convenient & practicable. . . the propriety of which Seigneuries or Fiefs shall be and remain in vested in Us, our Heirs and Successors.[6]

Thus the loyalists were to be tenants of the Crown, and Haldimand had been informed that all tenants would pay a quit rent of one halfpenny per acre after they had been on their lands ten years. This amounted to four shillings and twopence per hundred acres per annum. New Yorkers had been accustomed to a quit rent of two shillings and sixpence per hundred acres, and the King was demanding a substantial increase.[7]

Here was news that would have shocked Justus

Sherwood. His three carefully surveyed American townships were to be swept away; loyalists were doomed to fit into the French system of land tenure. Had he been aware, he might have packed up his family and taken his chances in Vermont. However, Haldimand knew that many loyalists would be upset, and he kept the full import of his orders to himself. All Justus discovered at his first interview at the Château St. Louis was that the townships were to be larger. A few days later, Major Jessup joined him, and he learned of other provisions the British government had made that were to his taste.

Land grants were to be as follows: for every field officer, 1,000 acres (405 hectares); for every captain 700 acres; every subaltern, staff or warrant officer 500. Each enlisted man was to receive 100 acres (40.5 hectares), and in addition each member of a disbanded soldier's family whether officer or private, was entitled to 50 acres. Each civilian head of family was to be allowed 100 acres.[8]

Sherwood's captaincy entitled him to 700 acres, and another 200 for the four members of his family. Since he did not know of the restrictions the King had imposed, Justus thought he faced two choices — 900 acres (364 hectares) in Canada, or 400 acres (162 hectares) in Vermont, where he was not certain of being kindly received. The upper St. Lawrence country had more appeal because of the large land grants, and the half-pay which he could hardly expect to collect if he returned to the Green Mountains. And land was not the only compensation Haldimand planned for his refugees. They were to receive tools and clothing, and some provisions for the first two years, by which time they would be able to provide for themselves.

At the same time the governor was doing what he could to sidestep the regulations imposed in London. He wanted to give the loyalists their familiar institutions, and lacking the authority, he chose a location for the refugees that was well away from all the existing seigneuries. Those who were adamant could go to Chaleur Bay or remain at Sorel, but Haldimand was laying the foundation for a separate province where, one day, the loyalists might be permitted their rights as British Americans.

The seigneuries or fiefs ordered by the King required adjustments to the surveys. Haldimand decided on townships with 'nine miles of frontage' on navigable waterways and 'twelve miles depth' and he avoided using the name seigneury to Jessup and Sherwood. Where townships lay inland they would be 'ten miles square'. All townships would be divided into '1,000 acre concession blocks' which could be subdivided into '100 acre' farm lots. Each township was to have a townsite in the centre, or midway along its waterfront. An American section was one square mile, but a concession block measured a mile and a quarter square. Such a plan did not trouble Justus, for he would simply add two furlongs to the kind of sections he had surveyed back in Vermont.

Haldimand planned to establish sixteen townships at first. Eight were to be along the upper St. Lawrence, commencing at Pointe au Baudet, fifteen kilometres west of the boundary of the last French seigneury, leaving a gap as a buffer between anglophone and francophone.[9] The other eight would start at Cataraqui, west of the rocky portion which Justus had branded unfit for cultivation. In addition, Butler's Rangers were already establishing themselves and their dependents on land that had been purchased from the Mississauga Indians in 1781. Of the townships along the St. Lawrence, the lower five were for the first battalion, King's Royal Regiment of New York, and the upper three for the Loyal Rangers. True to his Swiss background, the governor was assigning individual 'cantons' to the distinct groups of settlers.

Of the townships being laid out in the vicinity of Cataraqui, the first was for a party of loyalists from New York City led by Captain Michael Grass. The second was for the Loyal Rangers, the third for the King's Rangers and the second battalion, King's Royal Regiment of New York, the fourth for another group who had come from New York City under the command of Major Peter van Alstyne, and the fifth for disbanded German troops who wanted to remain in Canada. The other three townships would be for stragglers, since Haldimand suspected that the migration was far from over.

He also set aside a tract along the Bay of Quinte for some Mohawk Indians, who preferred that location to the lands along the Grand River Valley that had been purchased for most of the Six Nations refugees. The Royal Highland Emigrants did not need a township. Many had been recruited in Canada and their homes were intact; those who needed land were to be accommodated with the first battalion, King's Royal Regiment of New York, which had many Highlanders in it, or near the upper posts where they were disbanded.

As his superintendent to resettle the refugees Haldimand appointed Sir John Johnson, with Major Jessup and Captain Sherwood as his assistants. Early in February the two provincial officers left Quebec City, driving along the ice of the St. Lawrence in bitter weather. Much had to be done before spring and Justus was still weak. The two parted company at Sorel, Justus to ride to Fort St. Johns on an army horse, the major to continue in the sleigh to Verchères where most of the Loyal Rangers were encamped. Twelve of Jessup's and Rogers' men were still at the Loyal Blockhouse with Thomas Sherwood, receiving more refugees, and at Fort St. Johns Dr. Smyth was issuing passports to men who wished to go into the United States and bring out their families.

When he reached his house, Justus was plunged into a crisis. Levius, then Diana succumbed to smallpox, and Sarah soon followed. Justus blamed himself until Smyth, very solicitous, assured him that Levius would have been ill much sooner if he had infected him. In Smyth's opinion, both children had been exposed outside the house, for there were other cases at the fort. Sarah caught the disease because she refused to leave the nursing of her babes to a stranger. Young children tended to suffer convulsions even with a mild case of smallpox, and they needed her.

On February 24, Justus informed Mathews that his daughter was out of danger, his son on the way to recovery, but he was very alarmed for Sarah and could not leave her even for a moment. Immune himself, he stayed with his loved ones, setting aside all other work. He thanked God that Samuel was at school in Montreal and had escaped exposure. Dr. Smyth remained at Fort St.

Johns, redeeming himself for the times when he had been a less than satisfactory deputy during the war. On March 1, Justus' vigil was drawing to a close, and he informed Mathews, 'Mrs. Sherwood is, I hope, out of danger but very weak & low. I have not been able to leave her one hour'.[10]

Now that he had time to look outside the house, Justus was disconcerted by dissent that had spread among the disbanded provincials and their families, hovering in their encampments waiting for the winter to end. For weeks dissatisfaction had been building up in the refugee camps. Many people were unhappy with the remote location Haldimand had chosen for them. The upper St. Lawrence was too far from Montreal, the market for their produce once they had a surplus to trade. While Justus was too busy to pay attention to most of the discontent, Haldimand had received reports from others. On February 2, Sir John Johnson wrote from Montreal much perturbed:

> Some evil Designing persons are endeavouring to dissuade the disbanded Men and other Loyalists from taking the Lands offered them by Government, telling them if they accept them they will be as much Soldiers as ever, and liable to be called upon at Pleasure; and that the terms are not favourable as those of the Neighbouring States, where they are not prohibited from erecting Mills – and that it will be better for them to take up Lands from Signiors in the heart of the Province.[11]

In the letter Justus wrote to Mathews on March 1, he passed on news that Dr. Smyth had deliberately kept from him until his worries over the family eased. Certain of the half-pay officers had already taken matters into their own hands:

> the people of this place seem well inclin'd for Cataraqui except for a number who are dictated by Captains Myers & Pritchard, Lt. Ruyter Lt. Wehr and Ensn Coonrod Best, these have begun a Settlement at Missisqui Bay, and (I shudder to inform you) declare that nothing but Superior force shall drive them off that land. My informer is Dr. Smyth, who I suppose will write you on the subject.[12]

Justus was not surprised that John Walden Meyers and Azariah Pritchard were the ringleaders. Lieutenant

John Ruiter and Ensign Conrad Best were Meyers' junior officers, and most of his company in the Loyal Rangers were with them.

In a more detailed report, Dr. Smyth shielded Justus, for also at Mississquoi Bay on Lake Champlain, were John Peters and Thomas Sherwood. Justus' cousin had visited the would be colonists, and Meyers informed him that he had enough land selected to raise 1,000 bushels of corn. When Justus begged Thomas to reconsider, he came to Fort St. Johns and admitted that he had a practical motive for casting envious eyes towards Meyers' enterprise. Anna was pregnant, and Thomas wanted a permanent home without delay.

Meyers was only being practical, too. At Mississquoi Bay was open meadowland that could be ploughed without the necessity of chopping down trees first. However, the motives of other half-pay officers were suspect. Pritchard was planning to enhance his fortunes with a little smuggling. John Peters was there out of spite, making things awkward because of his humiliating demotion when the Loyal Rangers were formed.

Justus sent two non-commissioned officers to inspect the illicit settlement, who reported that the officers intended to remain where they were, regardless of the consequences. They had read Lord North's declaration with respect to resettling loyalists, and were convinced that Haldimand had no right to dictate where they would live. As soon as Justus apprised His Excellency of this insubordination, Haldimand issued an order on March 4, published in the *Quebec Gazette*. All persons waiting for land, those destined for Sorel and Chaleur Bay excepted, were to assemble at Lachine by April 10, 1784, and any who failed to comply would not receive any more rations.

The governor was determined to avoid placing any refugees close to the border of Vermont. Some of the men at Mississquoi Bay were the very ones who might provoke retaliation by former rebels in New York. The location was too sensitive for John Walden Meyers, who had waged his own war around Albany. Justus thought that Meyers' performance was what might be expected from an apolitical tenant farmer from New York. He reserved his real wrath for plotters from Connecticut, whom he described to Mathews as, 'blowing the coals of sedition like two furies'.[13]

The squabbling continued as Haldimand pursued his plans to resettle the refugees. Sir John Johnson, who was supposed to be the superintendent of the loyalists, was fully occupied assisting the refugee Indians who also needed new homes. In his capacity as Superintendent of Indian Affairs, Johnson was also looking for a way to prevent American reprisals against the loyal Indians in the Ohio Valley who had been left inside the United States by the boundary settlement.

On March 4, Mathews wrote to Justus asking him to purchase food supplies. Unable to leave Sarah, he sent Elijah Bothum to Vermont to see what arrangements he could make.[14] Soon afterward Justus went to the Loyal Blockhouse, and on the 24th he informed Mathews, 'I have sold my farm at Dutchman's point to a Dr. Washburn of Vermont, reserving the Block House as King's property'.[15] Justus felt he was entitled to make the sale, although he had no title to the property, hoping that Dr. Washburn would not have difficulty establishing ownership. When the deal was made, Washburn enquired when the King's garrison would be withdrawn, a question Justus could not answer.

With his report of March 1, Justus had forwarded a letter from Josiah Cass, the schoolmaster at Machiche, who was worrying over the governor's plans. Mathews requested Justus to reassure Cass, because he could describe the lands at Cataraqui to him. The major continued, 'The journey and conveyance, you can inform him, is by no means so tedious or difficult as he conceives them to be'.[16]

His Excellency could furnish only provisions and tools. Private seigneurs were offering cattle and farming utensils, or money to purchase them, which was causing loyalists daily to take land in the seigneuries, but Haldimand doubted that such landlords could keep their promises. Furthermore, Cataraqui had advantages of climate, situation and soil over the lower St. Lawrence, and the prospect of a better agriculture than in the more easterly parts of the province.

By April, Justus was trying desperately to persuade

dissenters to accept Haldimand's plan, and to put an end to the controversy he urged the governor to speed up his preparations for transporting the refugees up the St. Lawrence.[17] The sooner the loyalists were removed from the influence of the anglophone seigneurs the better. Many of the New Yorkers wanted to accept their enducements rather than travel away to the west, but Justus expected little else of men who had lived most of their lives as tenant farmers in the old province.

Justus saw no reason why the remoteness from Montreal should be a handicap to trade. He had lived on the distant frontier in Vermont and had never found that location a disadvantage. Personally he had no desire to live among the Canadians, for he could never fit into their communities. He was still not aware of the ruling that the new townships were to be seigneuries, and he envisaged the land Haldimand had chosen becoming somewhat like Connecticut but with gentler laws — or at least the same casual disregard for harsh statutes the people of Vermont manifested — and pretty towns sited along the upper St. Lawrence. Some day his people would hold town meetings, and the governor might establish a separate province. It would have a legislative assembly, and surely an elected governor, who would be one of the people and serve their interests faithfully. Subjects who had remained loyal through the dreadful conflict deserved no less.

Justus was also making plans for his family. He petitioned for the mill site he liked in Township Number 2 beside the upper St. Lawrence, on the stream that emptied into the river just above the Long Sault Rapids. The land was poor, but the waterfall perfect for saw and grist mills. Haldimand ignored the request, because mills were the duty of the government which would in effect serve as the seigneur to the loyalists. Deputy-Surveyor John Collins had built a sawmill near Cataraqui so that the settlers could have lumber for their new homes sawn free of charge.[18]

In reward for his services, Haldimand granted Justus '200 acres' at Chaleur Bay, and a 'town lot and 60 acres' at Sorel.[19] All would be investments, since Justus intended to settle in the westerly townships. In time he planned to sell the land at Chaleur Bay, and the lots at Sorel could be leased. Some of the older refugees, among them Dr. and Mrs. Smyth, were planning to settle at Sorel, since they could not face the rough wilderness. Justus was looking forward to life in the new townships, where lumbering was the way to make money, as he knew from his days in Vermont. The St. Lawrence was a fine transport route for rafts, provided these were built strongly enough to withstand the journey down the rapids.

Meanwhile, Edward Jessup was at Lachine with some of his officers, hard at work on the preparations for the coming migration. Bateaux were under construction, flat-bottomed and small enough for the Canadian crews to manhandle them through the swift waters. Food and clothing had to be moved there from storehouses at Sorel, and axes, hoes and other tools collected. In May, Haldimand journeyed to Lachine to inspect the situation for himself, and he was disappointed that so little progress in moving the people had been made, owing to the lateness of the spring. By the end of April, lumps of ice still floated in the St. Lawrence and the governor's order to assemble by April 10 proved unworkable. There was little point in moving thousands of people to Lachine before the ice had left the river.

To Justus' satisfaction the governor was coping with the illegal settlement at Mississquoi Bay. Captain Pritchard agreed to go to Chaleur Bay, a good place for a Yankee trader, and Captain Meyers had made a deal with His Excellency. The big German had crops planted, and Haldimand agreed to let him remain at Mississquoi Bay until after the harvest, but then he must bring his family to join the other refugees in the new townships.[20] John Peters took his wife and six youngest children to Cape Breton, and John Jr. was planning to go to Cataraqui because he was enamoured of a daughter of Major Rogers. Peters' second son, Andrew, was then in Vermont visiting friends and collecting family possessions.

While Edward Jessup worked at Lachine, Justus was at Fort St. Johns gathering supplies and forwarding them. Thomas Sherwood bought some seed corn in Arlington, Vermont, while Justus' brother Samuel went in search of cattle there that belonged to loyalists in Canada. Haldimand allowed some purchases in New York, but he did not want regular trade with the former rebels. Justus proposed bringing in cattle through Oswego, owing to the difficulty of driving livestock up the St. Lawrence through the woods, with little forage and awkward rivers to cross.[21] Families were moving into Lachine, as Justus and Dr. Smyth were busy closing down the secret service. To pay their agents' arrears and other expenses they drew 79 pounds, 17 shillings.[22] All through the winter twelve Loyal Rangers and King's Rangers had remained on duty at the Loyal Blockhouse under the command of Thomas Sherwood. As the time for migration drew near, they were withdrawn and replaced by a garrison of British regulars.[23]

Once Justus had his accounts in order, he joined Edward Jessup at Lachine to help send off the bateaux of refugees to their new homes. Sir John Johnson was still preoccupied with the affairs of the Indians. Sherwood and Jessup were to organize the bateaux into brigades. The boats were about seven metres long, and each was to hold four to five families. A brigade was twelve boats that would travel together.[24] The task of sorting out who would go where, with which household goods, was a formidable one that required both patience and endurance, but by the middle of May the first brigade had started upriver bound for Cataraqui.

Chapter 18

Scapegoats to the Wilderness

After the second brigade had set out, Major Jessup asked Justus to go to Fort St. Johns and round up a party of stragglers. When Justus reached the fort he requisitioned the necessary bateaux and sailed down the Richelieu to Sorel. He reported to Mathews on May 23 that he had arrived there with '76 souls of Jessup's Corps with whom I shall proceed this day for Cataraqui'.[1] In closing he added, 'I hope to hear from you as frequently as Convenient at Cataraqui'.

At Lachine he stopped so that his people could receive their provisions and clothing. Major Jessup ordered him to wait until he had a whole brigade ready, and amidst considerable confusion Justus did what he could to help. Men argued, women tried to keep children together, babies fretted, dogs howled and fought. Justus handed out supplies and assigned people to boats. Each man and boy over ten years of age was entitled to a coat, waistcoat, breeches, hat, shirt, blanket, shoe soles, leggings and stockings. Each woman and girl over ten was to receive 'two yards of woollen cloth, four yards of linen' and a pair of stockings, a blanket and shoe soles. Each child under ten was entitled to 'one yard of woollen cloth and two yards of linen' and stockings, shoe soles, and every two children would share a blanket.

For the journey there was one tent for every five persons, and one cooking kettle per tent.[2] The families would camp until they had houses ready, then all tents were to be returned to the quartermaster's stores in Sorel. Each family was issued with one month's provisions, the rest of their food to be given them when they reached Cataraqui. Finding items the right size for the men and boys, and space in the boats was exhausting. Family size varied, as did the quantity of household goods. Dr. Solomon Jones, of the Loyal Rangers, had a grandfather clock, while others lacked such basic items as bedding. At length Justus had his brigade organized, some boats with only three families, others with six, single men and boys fitted wherever there was room.

Justus required a stiff rum once everyone was in place, and the boatmen pushed off towards the Côteau du Lac Canal. He found that the journey took longer than he anticipated. Pitching tents and settling families each night was time consuming, as was cooking for such a large group along the way. By acting like a drill sergeant, Justus got the brigade to Cataraqui by June 3, not two weeks after he had left Sorel. Major John Ross administered oaths of allegiance as required by Haldimand, and distributed hoes, axes and certificates for farm lots.

Behind Justus, Major Jessup organized another brigade and led it as far as Township Number 6 beside the St. Lawrence. Major Samuel Holland appointed Justus a deputy-surveyor at a salary of seven shillings and sixpence per day and sent him back down the river to assist Jessup. The surveyors were struggling to get enough lot lines run so that the refugees waiting there could be settled. Justus joined the now empty brigade for the journey downstream. Almost in the centre of Township Number 6 was a clearing with an old cabin that had been built by French traders years before, and there Justus found Jessup, surrounded by tents and looking frazzled. He ordered Justus to survey a town plot in the clearing before people wanting to reside there could turn it into a squatter settlement.

Justus walked over the site, envisaging where he would lay out the green, with house lots on either side of it. When he discussed his plan with Jessup, the other ordered him to lay out only a large block of house lots. Sadly Justus set to work, wondering whether Jessup was being short-sighted. This very first town beside the upper St. Lawrence might one day become an important city, and the defects of its original plan would affect generations unborn. Although Jessup, too, had been born in Connecticut, he had moved to New York when he was nine years old. He did not treasure the memory of the pretty towns of his early youth. Justus laid out the dull grid plan with no central place, a New York town, not a New England one. Where, when the time came, would people erect their public buildings?

Before Justus had finished, Jessup left for Cataraqui to see to the needs of the Loyal Rangers who were moving into Township Number 2 of that settlement. He left Justus in command of the lower settlement, and on July 2, cheered by the progress he witnessed around him, Justus reported to Mathews:

> I have been continuously Employ'd here since the 5th of last month in laying out a Town half a mile square into lots of 8 Rods square – and in laying out the second Concession; Giving the people the necessary oaths and their Certificates etc[3]

Rations and tools were short, Justus complained to the governor's secretary. He had received 487 axes, 110 hoes, 20 bush hooks, 13 grindstones, 39 frows (a tool for making shingles) and some knives. He asked for more of all these, as well as two sets of blacksmith's tools, two sets of carpenter's tools, and one set of each for the Loyal Rangers settling at Cataraqui, also half a dozen whip saws and as many crosscut saws with whatever glass and nails Haldimand was allowing for people's huts, adding, 'the Bush Hooks should be in the form of short scythes'. He begged that rations not be reduced, since his settlers could not do hard labour without adequate food:

> as they have no milk nor butter nor any kind of vegetables whatever, no fresh meat nor fish except now and then by Chance a few small pan fish taken with hook and line and even this trifling resource must fail in the winter season[4]

To help some needy people, Justus bought '100 bushels of seed' out of his own purse. The men in the ranks had received only provisions and clothing since they were disbanded. On July 7, Major John Ross at Cataraqui complained of similar shortages, blaming Sherwood for some of the deficiencies:

> there is scarce a turnip seed, if it was Sent it was em-

Loyalist Townships along the St. Lawrence and Bay of Quinte 1784

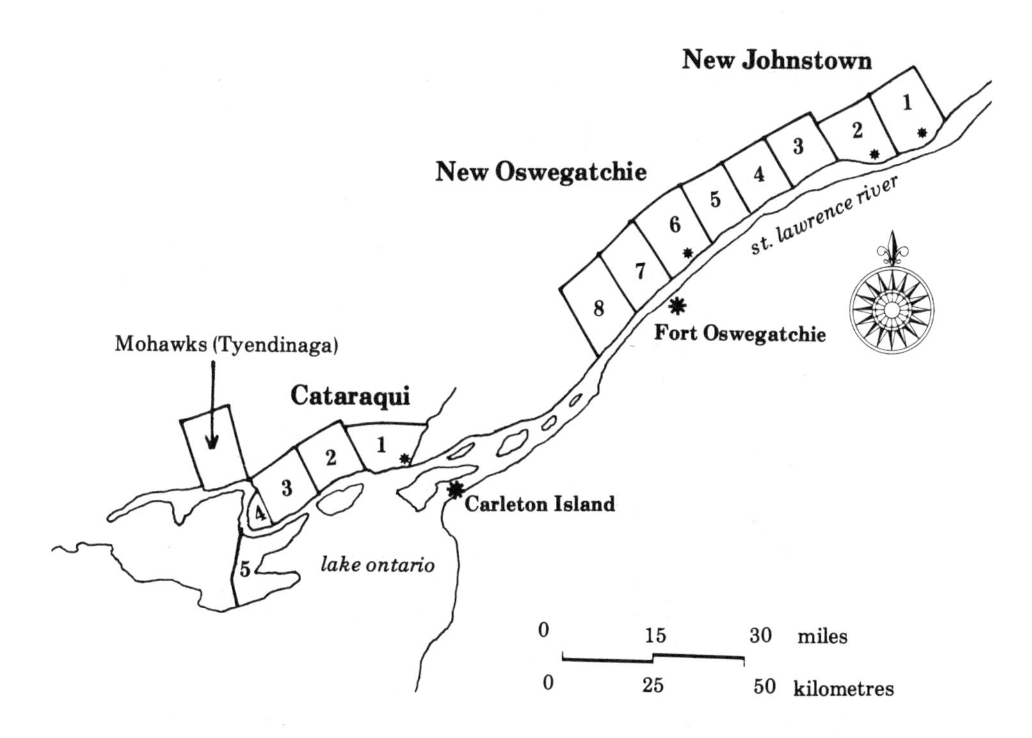

Eight townships were laid out beside the upper St. Lawrence. The lower five were the New Johnstown settlement, the upper three New Oswegatchie. The first five around the Bay of Quinte were the Cataraqui settlement. When they were named, #1 beside the St. Lawrence was Charlottenburgh, #2 Cornwall, #3 Osnabruck, #4 Williamsburgh, #5 Matilda, #6 Edwardsburgh, #7 Augusta, #8 Elizabethtown. Of the Bay of Quinte townships, #1 was Kingston, #2 Ernestown, #3 Fredericksburgh, #4 Adolphustown, #5 Marysburgh. Also shown are the first three townsites, Kingston (#1Cataraqui), Johnstown (#6 New Oswegatchie), New Johnstown (#2 New Johnstown).

bezzled on the road, they have no Seed wheat, and many not So much as a blanket to Cover them in Winter, and the wish of the great part is to return at all hazard, in Short Axes and Hoes have not yet come up for half of them, it is said Ct. Sherwood Stopp'd more than his proportion at Oswegatchie.

Apart from accusing Justus, perhaps unfairly, Ross referred to many refugees arriving by way of Carleton Island, who were not provided with clothing and food those coming from Lachine had received. Ross commented:

Disputes amongst the Loyalists frequently arise, the most material as yet between Master & Servant, where Severe Correction Seems to take place, an Evil which requires a Speedy remedy. . .. Strange is the Collection of people here[5]

The loyalists' collective personality was bewildering, even to a Scotsman whose own countrymen were not noted for their peaceable qualities. The same conditions were to be found in the townships opposite Fort Oswegatchie, but Justus was dealing with his own people and he did not feel that anything extraordinary was happening.

While Justus was busy with the settlers, the Reverend John Stuart came upriver with a brigade and called at the townsite looking for him. The clergyman was planning to settle his family at Cataraqui, hoping to be appointed the chaplain to the garrison. Anxiously Justus enquired about Stuart's school. The other said that he intended keeping the academy in Montreal open for the winter and would be glad to have Samuel as a pupil again. Stuart did not expect to move for at least a year, and when he did he anticipated re-opening his school.

Major Jessup returned from Cataraqui, too ill to carry on, and Justus continued his administrative duties. Each head of family had to take an oath of allegiance, then draw a certificate for his lot from Justus' bicorne hat. Haldimand had ordered this game of chance to ensure that the officers did not take all the best land. For himself, Justus set aside Lots 8 and 9 in the first concession of Township Number 7, and he reserved Lots 14, 15 and 16 for a town plot. Although he could not begin surveying it, he kept a list of settlers who wanted town lots in addition to farm lots. He intended to make certain that this town plot in Township Number 7 would have a green as its central place, facing the river. Seeking Haldimand's approval, Justus informed Mathews:

> I have taken my Farm at this place nearly opposite Oswegatcha, and three small Town Lots – am as well satisfy'd as I could have been in any place Except No. 2 At the Mouth of Quinty Bay.

Justus felt well within his rights in setting this land aside for himself. His captaincy entitled him to much more land. He chose Lot 7 beside his farm lots for his brother Samuel, who was still at Fort St. Johns. For Elijah Bothum, Justus selected Lots 26 and 27, also in Township Number 7, and for Thomas Sherwood he set aside Lot 1 in Township Number 8. All were in the first concession and had water frontage. Justus disobeyed Haldimand to make sure that his kinsmen would not be marooned in back concessions when they arrived with their families.

On July 23, Justus informed Mathews:

> The people have all got their farms to work, they are universally pleas'd and seem to Emulate each other in their Labour, inasmuch that almost every lot in the front of our three Townships and many of the back Concessions have already Considerable improvements and the Country begins to wear a very promising appearance.[6]

Early in August, Justus called on John Dulmage, in Township Number 6, and asked him to take charge of hearing oaths and handing out certificates to new arrivals. Major Jessup was still ailing, and Justus wanted a leave of absence to bring the Sherwood families from Fort St. Johns. He could not wait longer, because Anna Sherwood's time was drawing near, and he knew that Thomas wanted her settled soon. With an empty brigade, Justus returned to Lachine, and continued on to Fort St. Johns. There he learned that Elijah Bothum was shopping for supplies in Vermont. Mathews had warned him to be discreet since he had come on behalf of the British government, lest the locals raise their prices or refuse to sell to him.[7] Lemuel, Sarah's youngest brother, had gone with him after a lengthy visit in Canada.[8]

Their possessions packed, the three Sherwood families left for Sorel in a bateau. Justus was elated on this second journey to the settlement beside the St. Lawrence. He was introducing seven children to the new country, theirs to develop and make fruitful. Young

Samuel was nearly ten, Diana seven, Levius six. Of Thomas' brood, Reuben was fifteen, Anna twelve, Adiel five. Samuel's daughter Rachel was the same age as Adiel. Riding in the bateau, Justus was overcome with weariness. Sarah, too, was exhausted, and when walking past the rapids as the boatmen drew the bateaux upstream they set a leisurely pace. With them walked Thomas, an arm round Anna's fulsome waist, while Caesar Congo gave Levius and Adiel turns riding on his back.[9]

When they reached the town plot in Township Number 6, Justus dispensed tools and provisions to Samuel and Thomas, and they proceeded on to their respective farm lots with their families. Justus stayed to relieve John Dulmage, and Sarah and the children remained in a tent until he could find time to remove them to the lots he had selected in Township Number 7. In a few days Major Jessup felt well enough to carry on, and Justus left the townsite, which he had named Newtown. Exploring along the shore he found a spot where the woods seemed thin on Lot 9. Aided by Caesar Congo, with some help from small Samuel, he cleared a space, cutting trees and underbrush. His labour was soon interrupted by the appearance of Elijah Bothum, accompanied by the two slaves who had remained in New Haven with Simon.

Justus was gratified for he could use all the assistance available. With Elijah helping, the men cut logs six metres long for the front and rear walls, and four and one-half metres for the sides. Knotching the logs at the corners, they planned to lay them one upon another to a height of two and a half metres. Justus' brother Samuel and his slave came from Lot 7 to help raise the frame, and the others were a large enough work party to lay the walls. The roof was of elm bark, and Justus cut a door and one window on the side that faced the river. The floor was of split logs laid round side down, the hearth of flat stones.

For a chimney the men used stones from the shore, fastened with clay for mortar to the same height as the walls, and above of small sticks plastered with more clay. They chinked the logs with clay and sticks, and a blanket served as the door until Justus found the time to cut boards with a whip saw. From government stores he drew four small panes of glass, and fitted them into a rough sash. When finished, Justus thought his cabin superior to the hovels many of Vermont's settlers had built in the wilds. There the first windows were usually of oiled paper, and many had dirt floors for years on end.[10]

On August 23, Haldimand appointed Captain Sherwood a justice of the peace for the three townships beside the St. Lawrence that were occupied by the Loyal Rangers. Major Jessup had received the same appointment on November 27, 1783, but he was unwell and planning to winter in Sorel, where he had left his wife, son and daughter. Justus was gratified by the appointment, and he knew he was the logical magistrate in the townships.[11]

In September, Reuben Sherwood brought word that his mother had given birth to a son, James, the first white baby born in the three townships which people were calling New Oswegatchie.[12] For Justus, the arrival of Thomas' third son was an indication that life would soon return to normal. He was proud of the way the disbanded provincials had embraced life in the wilderness, but disturbed that the long supply lines from Montreal up the rapids had led to serious deficiencies. On October 17 he reported to Mathews:

> Our people have made a very rapid progress in Settlement but they are now much disheartened at not having received any seed wheat altho' they had sufficient Ground Clear'd I don't know what we shall do for bread another year but hope Gov't will lengthen our provisions.[13]

By the time Justus was writing his letter, Major Jessup had left for Montreal. When he reached the city, en route to Sorel, he reported that there were only six horses, eight oxen and eighteen cows at New Oswegatchie, to share among nearly 600 people. At the same time, Jessup recommended to Mathews that one man be entrusted with a liquor licence, and suggested Ephriam Jones, the commissary to the late Major Daniel McAlpin's men, as worthy of the responsibility in the three townships occupied by Loyal Rangers beside the St. Lawrence. In time Haldimand approved the appointment, which pleased Justus. Local Indians were getting rum at

Fort Oswegatchie, and while drunk were disturbing the settlers.[14]

Young Samuel returned to school in Montreal on one of the last brigades of the season, and Justus built a second cabin for his slaves, to allow the family more privacy. Elijah wanted to stay with them, rather than spend a gloomy winter by himself some distance away on his land. Afterward everyone settled down to an uncomfortable time in small quarters. Justus and the slaves spent their time cutting down trees, to prepare for planting between the stumps when the spring came. Sarah used some of the daylight hours teaching Levius and Diana their lessons. Oil for lamps was non-existent and so were tallow candles. When necessary they burned pine torches which filled the cabin with smoke the chimney did not draw. Most days the family rose with the dawn and retired when the light was gone in the evening.

Meanwhile, Haldimand had taken a leave of absence and did not expect to return to Canada. He had asked the government to appoint a successor for he wanted to retire. In His Excellency's absence, the deputy-governor, Henry Hamilton, would rule the province, and Canada was divided into two administrative districts — Quebec and Montreal. Barry St. Leger, now a brigadier-general, commanded at Montreal and was responsible for the refugees in the new townships, assisted by Major Ross, his subordinate at Cataraqui.

Many of the men who had worked in the British Secret Service, Northern Department, were not far from Justus. Although Dr. Smyth was at Sorel, his sons, Terence and Thomas, were in Township Number 8, and so was Caleb Clossen. Other scouts were near Cataraqui, while a surprising number of men from New England had settled in New Oswegatchie. James and David Breakenridge were in Township Number 7; both had held commissions in the King's Rangers, but they elected to settle among more of their own kind. Justus' long time resident agent in Arlington, Elnathan (Plain Truth) Merwin was near his farm, while a Connecticut man destined to play an important role in the development of Township Number 8 was Ensign William Buell, King's Rangers.

With the arrival of the spring of 1785, Samuel returned from school in Montreal. The Sherwoods scratched up the soil between their stumps and planted the seed the government had provided, as well as some Justus purchased. The felled trees were stripped of their branches, the logs manhandled to the side of the clearing, saved for the day when their owner could assemble a timber raft to take to Quebec City. Shifting logs and working the soil was back breaking toil and draft animals were not available. Justus resolved that before the season ended he must have some horses, and if possible a yoke of oxen.[15]

The May 12 issue of the *Quebec Gazette* showed that Justus had been appointed to the Legislative Council as a representative for the District of Montreal. This was a great honour. Brigadier St. Leger, who had recommended Justus, did not choose Major Jessup because he had left on a lengthy visit to England and would be of no use to the government for some time.[16] Sir John Johnson was also on the council, but Justus was the only half-pay captain on the list published in the newspaper.

The crop planted, Caesar Congo remained to tend it and help Sarah while the other slaves joined Justus' survey party in the back concessions of the townships. Lots were needed for the wave of settlers now coming in. Ever the businessman, Justus charged the government one shilling and sixpence per day for the labour of each slave. On September 30, 1785, for nine days of surveying, he drew three pounds, seven shillings and sixpence in salary for himself, and his account to Deputy-Surveyor John Collins showed that he drew three axes, a grindstone, and twenty-one gallons of rum.[17] He did not say how many men were in his survey party, but if it was a small one the men would not have accomplished much. West Indian rum was very high proof. Nevertheless, his workers were much more contented in the new townships than Justus' garrison had been in the austere setting of the Loyal Blockhouse — and so was their leader.

Chapter 19

In Government Circles

As soon as his family was reasonably comfortable and his farm was beginning to produce crops, Justus became once more the man he had been in New Haven, taking initiatives on behalf of his fellow settlers. In the absence of Major Edward Jessup, he was the leader in New Oswegatchie, organizing meetings that were suspiciously close to the ones he had chaired as proprietor's clerk back in the Green Mountains. A New England town meeting was hardly an institution any British official would condone, but Justus plunged ahead.

Since he was a legislative councillor and the only magistrate, he felt compelled to hold meetings to help the residents wrestle with their problems. In Quebec City, Henry Hope had succeeded Henry Hamilton as the deputy-governor. Hope would have been horrified had he been aware of such political activity. All decisions were to be made by Major John Ross at Cataraqui, or Brigadier St. Leger. Yet faced with the need for roads, schools, draft animals, supplies, clothing and provisions for settlers on their lands as well as new arrivals, Justus ignored such legalities.

He also conducted marriages, using his own copy of the Book of Common Prayer, a duty pernitted magistrates in the absence of qualified men of the cloth, to prevent couples living in sin. All the while he continued surveying more concession lines and farm lots. Once the crops were planted, Caesar Congo and the boys were able to cope with that aspect of the family's means of livelihood. Justus was so busy, both physically and mentally, that for some time he failed to notice the word 'seigneury' on certain documents referring to the new townships. Gradually, as 1785 drew to a close, the significance of the term bothered him, and he sent an enquiry to Brigadier St. Leger, who explained about the quit rents that must be paid after ten years. This robbed Justus of sleep, and he called a meeting of the officers to discuss the matter. All agreed that such a demand would be a hardship on everyone, especially the enlisted men who were not entitled to half-pay. A petition expressing their alarm was in order, but for the moment they would forbear. Perhaps this regulation would be shelved because it was an unjust law.

In May, 1786, Justus was chairing a roads committee, organizing the settlers into work parties to run a path across the front of Township Number 7.[2] He had no authority, but his people needed a means of communication by land. He was also busy surveying and at home, making his cabin more livable and worrying about the education of all three children. Mr. Stuart had closed his academy in Montreal. Justus made a journey to that city to purchase draft animals from his earnings and the half-pay of four shillings and sixpence a day. For 12 pounds each, he bought two Canadian horses, small but sturdy, one dappled gray, the other black. Later in the summer Lemuel Bothum arrived from Vermont bringing a team of Justus' oxen from the farm in New Haven where Simon was still living.

Now the Sherwoods and their slaves set to work hauling logs to the shore and building a raft to ride to Quebec City, where they would sell the logs. Justus had his slaves lash the huge logs together with lengths of willow sinew called withes, praying that their handiwork would be strong enough to withstand the battering the raft must take when passing down the rapids. Thomas Sherwood contributed logs from his land, and the men worked in shallow water since they could never launch such a heavy raft. Each log was floated once it had been drawn to the shore, and secured to its neighbour.

When the raft was ready, a bark cabin aboard to

shelter them, Justus left with Thomas and Reuben on their first venture through rapids more treacherous than those in the Richelieu River. The gentle Galops Rapids, below the townsite in Township Number 6, now called Johnstown, posed no problem, but at the Long Sault Rapids a crew of Indians from St. Regis appeared and offered to pilot the raft. They made a crib of small logs, then stationed themselves along the shore beside the whirling water. Once Justus released the crib they watched where it went. This was the safest path, they assured the raft's owners who were looking apprehensive. Aboard, each pilot steered the raft through the patch of white water he had observed, and the precious timber rode safely to smooth water.[3]

Indians repeated their performance at the Cedars and again at Lachine. From there on the men had clear sailing, past Sorel, with its many memories, down the gentle Richelieu Rapids and into the harbour of Quebec below the great rock.

Justus noticed other rafts, and a few enquiries solicited the information that most were from Vermont and New York. In bargaining, Justus found that he could not make as good a deal as he had hoped, because the miscreant Yankees and Yorkers were willing to settle for less. Canadian timber ought to take precedence for the sake of the residents. Then, cash jingling in their pockets, the Sherwoods took a stagecoach as far as Montreal.

Justus conferred with Brigadier St. Leger on the problems the settlers were encountering, and with Thomas he made some purchases. He paid 3 pounds for a cow that had been bred, a gift for Sarah. She was pregnant and needed milk to preserve her teeth. Then Justus bought a pig and a crate of chickens. Even though he could afford more animals he had to be cautious. Until he had a substantial quantity of land cleared he could not produce enough hay and grain to winter them. The upper St. Lawrence had almost no natural meadow such as existed along Lake Champlain.

Soon after Justus left Quebec City, Sir Guy Carleton arrived as the new governor-in-chief, welcome news, although his subjects must call him by a new name. Carleton had been made 1st Baron Dorchester as a reward for the work he had done evacuating loyalists and the British army from New York City in 1783. Lord Dorchester was accompanied by another old friend, Major Robert Mathews, now the governor's aide-de-camp.[4] Justus looked forward to serving the governor on the legislative council. One matter that had to be cleared up was French civil law, established under the Quebec Act.

The year 1786 brought two changes within the ranks of the tightly knit Sherwood family. Justus' daughter, Sarah, was born and Diana was thrilled to have a sister.[5] Secondly, Justus' brother Samuel announced that he was moving with Eunice and Rachel to Township Number 3 on the Bay of Quinte.[6] Samuel wanted to open a store, but Township Number 7 was the wrong place. William Buell had a store in Township Number 8, next door. Nor would Cataraqui fulfil Samuel's ambition, for Richard Cartwright had a mercantile operation there. Justus suspected that Samuel was making a declaration of independence, placing himself beyond the influence of his elder brother's dominant personality in order to be his own man, and he did not blame him.

That autumn Justus' worry over the education of his sons was eased, for the Reverend John Stuart had moved to Cataraqui and opened a new school there. Samuel and Levius were now twelve and nine, but Justus could not spare them during the growing season. When the autumn work was done, he set out with the boys for Dr. Stuart's school. Justus rode one horse, the boys the other, blankets and packs of provisions on their shoulders. Using the river shore to guide them they soon reached the tract that was unfit for settlers. They rode some fifty kilometres, and camped for the night. The following evening they reached the village at the mouth of the Cataraqui River, which people were calling King's Town. He found lodgings for the boys not far from the school house, and left them to be 'catechized' by the Anglican clergyman. Before riding back home Justus made some purchases from Richard Cartwright, who was bringing merchandise from Oswego and whose prices were lower than William Buell's.

On December 19, Justus met with other half-pay officers, and they drafted a letter to Sir John Johnson since he was their superintendent, requesting that they might have their lands 'by Grants free from any seigneurial claims or any other incumbrances whatever, The King's Quit rent excepted'.[7] This was agreed upon after a fierce argument, Justus vehemently opposed, some others in favour, fearful that trying to do away with something the King wanted might be going too far. The authors requested that the country be divided into counties with courts at convenient places, and they appealed for encouragement in the preaching of the gospel, the establishment of schools, and prohibition on the importation of lumber from the United States. Some officers wanted to specify Vermont, but Justus fought that, still hopeful that the Green Mountain people would reunite, if only to protect their commerce.

As winter closed in, Justus prayed that the petition would bear fruit with Lord Dorchester. He would never pay quit rents, and he was determined to fight this measure in Canada as earnestly as he had fought it in the New Hampshire Grants. Although he was unaware, help was on the way. Dorchester had spoken against demanding quit rents, and had recommended that men who had served their King at such cost should hold their lands without any obligations.[8] When snow blanketed the countryside Justus and his slaves cleared more land and surveyed back townships in preparation for settlers who would be arriving in the spring. He taught Thomas Sherwood to run lot lines, while Reuben was apprenticing with him to become a qualified surveyor.[9]

As the spring of 1787 began, Justus was chafing, waiting for word that Sir John Johnson had made headway with the proposals the half-pay officers had sent him in December. By April 15, after many discussions, the officers wrote a petition to Lord Dorchester, calling themselves 'the Western Loyalists' and they had eleven requests. They wanted to live under the blessings of the British constitution and to have the English system of land tenure. They asked for help in establishing churches of England and Scotland, schools at New Johnstown, New Oswegatchie, Cataraqui and Niagara, stimulation for the manufacture of potash and the growing of hemp. They needed a loan of three months' supply of pork, and recommended that clothing be given to people who had arrived since the distributions had been made to the first settlers. They wanted the surveying of new townships hastened, and a post road from Montreal to Cataraqui, with post offices along the route, and to have trade with the western Indians encouraged and supervised. They needed depots where the government would receive their surplus grain, and they asked that the commissioners then in Montreal to settle loyalists' claims for compensation be sent to the settlements. Many people could not afford the journey in order to place their claims before the commissioners.[10]

In drafting this work, two old adversaries from the Green Mountains co-operated. John Munro, the onetime New York magistrate, signed for Township Number 5, New Johnstown, the name given the townships where the first battalion, King's Royal Regiment of New York had settled. Yet Munro had not forgiven Sherwood, and he was biding his time.

Once the spring work was in hand, Justus surveyed the town plot in Township Number 7, on Lots 14, 15, and 16 in the first concession. In accordance with Haldimand's orders, these were midway along the township's waterfront. In the centre Justus reserved an oblong section stretching from the shore northward for a green, and he laid out blocks with lots on either side. Unlike ugly Johnstown, his townsite would have a proper New England symbol, where public buildings would face the green.[11] Leading the way, Justus resolved to build a decent home for his family, and it would be on the town plot rather than on his farm, only three kilometres to the east. The slaves could reside in the two cabins, close to their work.

With his slaves Justus set to work hand hewing massive logs. Then, impatient with the time this was taking, Justus went in a bateau to Cataraqui, to the government sawmill, purchased logs nearby and had them squared. He assembled a raft and floated back down the St. Lawrence to the new townsite. In the interval the slaves built two large rubble stone chimneys, with eight fireplaces — four for downstairs, four for upstairs. The

Sherwood's Plan for a Town in the First Concession of Augusta Township

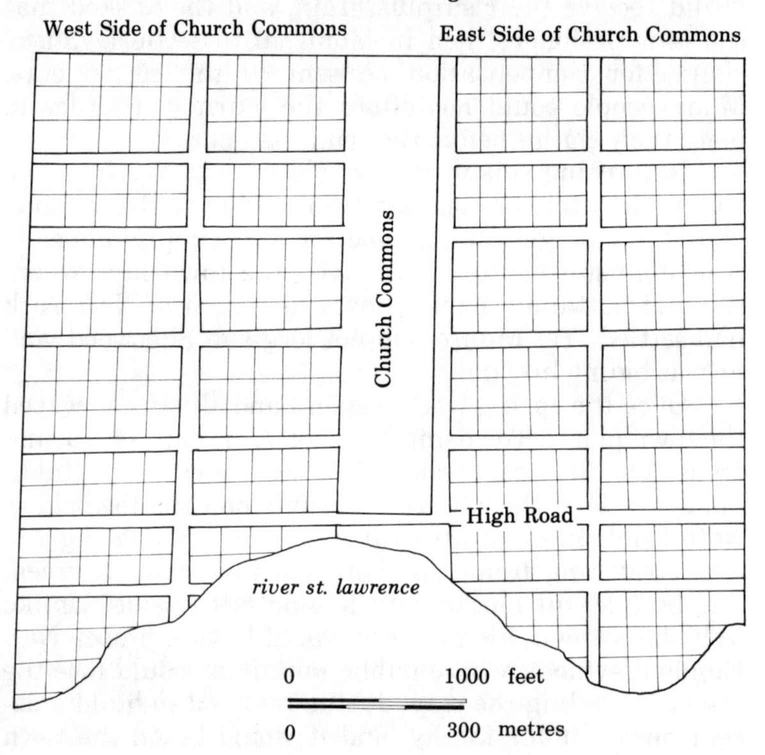

Area of Town Plot Approximately 280 acres or 113 hectares

house would have four rooms downstairs, four above. It would be symmetrical, with a wide central hallway stretching from the front door to the back. Both doorways must look impressive, since guests would arrive either from the track in front, or from the river by bateau.

Meanwhile, the spring had been very dry, and the drought was intensifying. This was serious. Only one year had passed since the first settlers coped without government rations. Many of the original settlers had enough land cleared if the harvest was normal, but relief would be needed before the coming winter was over. Justus resolved to buy provisions in Montreal as a precaution against what might lie ahead.

In May the house was habitable, and Sarah moved in, delighted with the space and airiness, both accentuated by a lack of furniture. Justus promised to buy some when he was in Montreal. The house, itself, was superior to the one they had left in New Haven, in keeping with plans Justus had treasured. Now his family had a suitable home, and he had achieved his goal. On the 21st he rode to a back concession to inspect his survey party, and when he returned Sarah told him that he had missed seeing Major Robert Mathews. Dorchester's aide-de-camp had landed from a bateau, accompanied by Major Jessup, who had recently come to the township after a long visit to England.

They waited half an hour, hoping to see Justus, but Mathews was in a hurry, on his way to Detroit and anxious to reach the fort there because Dorchester wanted a report as soon as possible. In his journal, Mathews reported that Sherwood had 'built a very tollerable House upon his Town Lot in new Oswegatchie, some distance from his Farm, and has already a Potash going forward'.[12] Justus was disappointed to have missed Haldimand's former secretary. Mathews would have been the perfect messenger to inform Dorchester of the serious consequences to be anticipated from the drought.

By late June the British commissioners hearing claims for compensation had shown no signs of coming to the settlements. Impatient over the delay, Justus went to Montreal with one of the brigades to present his claim. He needed witnesses, and he knew of several who were still in the city. He rounded up Abner Woolcot, a neighbour from New Haven, Samuel Rose, who had sold him his first farm in Sunderland, and Ensign Roger Stevens, the chatty scout in the secret service.[13] Justus was armed with some faded deeds, and a letter from Haldimand, now Sir Frederick, made a Knight of the Bath for his services in Canada.[14]

Justus saw the commissioners on July 5, and with his three witnesses he filed a claim for 1,209 pounds, fifteen shillings and sixpence. He had lost '2,985 acres of land', of which '1,000 acres' was in the Susquehanna Valley, the rest in Vermont. A secretary wrote down his testimony, received a memorial he had composed, and promised that he would hear from the commissioners soon. Leaving, Justus prayed they would be generous. Yet Haldimand had been tight-fisted with public money and he resolved not to be too optimistic. He purchased some furniture for his house, and set off in a brigade for home.

There, a disagreeable matter awaited him. Deputy-Surveyor John Collins and Mr. William Dummer Powell were in the townships investigating complaints. They reported from Kingston (in the oldest document to use the modern name) that they expected to hear:

> such complaint in the 5th Township, New Oswegatchie [more correctly New Johnstown] of the conduct of Justus Sherwood Esquire in the 3rd Township of Cataraqui against Jeptha Hawley Esqr. as tradeing Justices, but to our great surprise not a Complaint was heard in either Township and from our personal Knowledge of the Parties we are apprehensive that Complaint had been suppressed[15]

Jeptha Hawley may have been guilty of taking bribes, but in Sherwood's case the complaint originated in Township Number 5, where dwelt John Munro, magistrate in the New Hampshire Grants on behalf of New York. A contemporary definition of tradeing justices ran, 'low fellows smuggled into the commission of the peace who subsist by fomenting disputes, granting warrants and otherwise retailing justice'.[16]

Munro was venting his hatred on Sherwood, one of the few former Green Mountain Boys who was vulnerable. When the report from Collins and Powell reached

Quebec City, Lord Dorchester did not take the charge against Justus seriously. He knew enough about events in the Green Mountains to dismiss the aspersion as Munro's desire for revenge. Justus, too, ignored Munro's pettiness. Other matters preoccupied him. The crops were very thin and the harvest would be small.

Once the summer's work was done and he had gleaned what he could from the parched fields, he prepared to take another timber raft to Quebec City, and he intended to see Lord Dorchester to discuss the coming food shortage. The raft complete, he left his farm, his two sons and Reuben as crew, planning to buy supplies in Montreal on his return journey.

In Quebec City, Justus found that the governor had a new residence, the Château Haldimand, a small and cosier dwelling than the Château St. Louis. Haldimand had begun demolishing the drafty old building before he left Canada, and Dorchester was the beneficiary of his predecessor's preoccupation with comforts. Justus received an appointment with the governor, at which his deputy, General Alured Clarke, was in attendance. Justus enquired whether His Lordship could change the ruling that loyalists must some day pay quit rents. The governor was sympathetic, and emboldened, Justus asked when the province might have a legislative assembly.

Dorchester frowned, and muttered that no doubt those Yankees in the new townships would want to elect their governor. Forthright, Justus admitted that they did. The governor smiled patronizingly, and let Justus run on for some time. Alured Clarke, looked alarmed. Why had Brigadier St. Leger recommended the appointment of a loud-mouthed Yankee democrat to the legislative council? Captain Sherwood seemed a born troublemaker.

Justus enquired whether Dorchester had done anything about competition from Vermont in the timber trade. The governor was reticent. Vermont was still making overtures for reunion, and besides, Britain could use all the timber she could get. Dorchester assured Justus that he would be able to sell rafts at a respectable profit for years to come. In Montreal, Justus shopped for food, but found little to be had. Everywhere the drought had been severe. Very worried, the Sherwoods joined a brigade bound for New Oswegatchie.

During the war, many officers had belonged to the Freemason's Lodge in Montreal, but Justus had not had time to join the order. Meetings had been held at Fort Oswegatchie, but on October 19 the members convened for the first time on the north shore of the St. Lawrence, at the home of Thomas Sherwood. Justus was absent with his raft, but the November meeting was held in his house.[7] He joined, not for the philosophies embraced, but for companionship, the chance to congregate and exchange views, and to complain about the government. Principles such as religious tolerance and freedom for all men needed qualification. Justus disapproved of Roman Catholics, and owned slaves. Yet the double standard was merely part of his Yankee inheritance, that mixture of greed, acceptance of certain conditions, and good works that had been bred into him before he left Connecticut.

That autumn of 1787, Simon Bothum wrote offering to purchase "200 acres" of Justus' land in New Haven for 200 dollars. Justus agreed, for he could use the extra money. Late in November he found out just how badly he would need that money, for in a letter dated the 20th, the British commissioners in Montreal informed him that he had been awarded 229 pounds sterling for his farm in Sunderland, one house, and the furniture taken from his home in New Haven. Although Justus had calculated his losses at more than 1,200 pounds New York currency, and had expected roughly 600 pounds sterling, the commissioners were not convinced that some of his deeds were genuine, especially the land in Pennsylvania's Susquehanna Valley.[8] They had delivered chilling news on the eve of what was to be the harshest winter in Sherwood's life.

Chapter 20

Fading Light

The British commissioners were downright niggardly with Justus Sherwood. John Walden Meyers, living on the Bay of Quinte, stated his losses at 400 pounds New York, and was awarded 247 pounds sterling.[1] Since New York currency was worth slightly more than half the value of sterling, Meyers received about what he requested. Sherwood was awarded less than a brother officer who had never owned an acre of land in the Thirteen Colonies.

Sorrowing, Justus prepared to ride to Montreal to collect his pittance. That late in the season no bateau would be available to bring him home. He followed the river bank, crossing Lake of Two Mountains on a wooden ferry, and once in the city he sought out a reliable merchant with whom to invest the money so that it would grow. Retracing his steps, he felt as bleak as the cold, cheerless landscape around him. As he drew near New Oswegatchie, snow fell, fine stuff driven against his face by strong winds. Grimly he put the horse in the small stable beside his house, and he paused to look towards the grey river that separated him from his real homeland. He could survive the cold and hunger, but this time Sarah and his children would suffer with him.

The winter was remembered in later times as 'The Hungry Year'. One by one Justus butchered his precious livestock, sparing the cow, for Sarah was pregnant again. He hoped to save the horses, but the oxen he killed for his family and the neighbours. He rationed the stock of food, and to curb appetites the men did only necessary chores. Despite his hunger pangs, Justus continued fussing about the administration of justice, and the February 28 issue of the *Quebec Gazette* carried a public letter to Lord Dorchester asking for English civil law. Sherwood's signature was there along with several others.

The weeks dragged by in an endless quest for game. The family chopped holes in the ice of the St. Lawrence, and spent hours with lines lowered into the water. Whenever Justus heard of a family in severe distress, he felt obliged to send some of his own dwindling cache of food. Finally the settlers had to consume their seed potatoes and seed grains. When spring came no one had anything to plant. In Quebec City, Dorchester informed the home government that relief supplies were urgently needed, and in time a large shipment of seed arrived from Britain.

When the snow melted Justus put his emaciated horses out to scrounge, and the cow was not in much better condition. Fortunately, good climate conditions prevailed as the growing season arrived, but shortages would persist because seed was rationed to ensure that everyone got some. With money to spend, Justus and his family were not as hard pressed as the men who had served in the ranks and did not have funds to buy livestock for a fresh start. The people in the settlements were back where they had been when they first arrived and most were disheartened.

On July 24, 1788, Lord Dorchester issued a proclamation instituting more local government. The area west of the Ottawa River he divided into four new districts. Luneburg, where Justus resided, extended from the last French seigneury to the Gananoque River. West of Luneburg lay Mecklenburg, Nassau and Hesse — German names chosen to please King George.

Each district would have Courts of Common Pleas to handle civil cases. For criminal cases there would be Courts of Quarter Sessions of the Justices of the Peace, of Oyer and Terminer and General Gaol Delivery. Each district would have a land board to award grants to new settlers, and additional grants to those entitled to them.

General Gaol Delivery posed a problem since Justus' district lacked a place of incarceration. In preparation for the operation of the courts, Dorchester appointed more justices of the peace, among them Thomas Sherwood and William Buell. The governor decided it was time the townships had names, and he honoured the numerous offspring of the King. Number 7, where Justus had his farm, became Augusta; Number 8 was Elizabethtown; Number 6 with the townsite called Johnstown was Edwardsburgh, Number 5, where John Munro had built a house at least as fine as Sherwood's, became Matilda.[2]

Dorchester established a militia, and he sent a commission to Edward Jessup making him a lieutenant-colonel for a battalion to be raised in Edwardsburgh, Augusta and Elizabethtown.[3] Jessup suggested Sherwood as his second-in-command, and the governor approved. Justus was an outspoken man, but a fine soldier who would make an excellent major for the battalion.

Late in the summer Sarah gave birth to another daughter whom they named Harriet.[4] All told, 1788 was a more satisfactory year than 1787. In the autumn Lord Dorchester came to inspect the new townships, and was pleased with what he found.[5] The settlements were flourishing, and many residents assured him that they were better off than before the revolution.[6] The people along the St. Lawrence were recovering, but all had one complaint. They were upset because the 84th Regiment Royal Highland Emigrants had received larger land grants, unfair because other provincials had seen more action. Dorchester responded in a most acceptable way, by raising all grants to match those given the 84th.

After this ruling, Justus' captaincy entitled him to '3,000 acres' from the crown. Here was salve for his wounded spirits. He would soon have more land than he had possessed in Vermont and the Susquehanna Valley, although he was concerned that he might some day be expected to pay quit rents. From time to time he heard news of the Allens. Levi was at Fort St. Johns, corresponding with Justus, and Ira sent the occasional letter.[7] One day Justus received a bulky package from Levi, which contained the culmination of the philosophical studies Ethan had bragged about in the autumn of 1780 during that alarming visit to the Green Mountains. Ethan had published his book in Bennington, after printers in Connecticut refused it out of fear of the Congregational Church. Justus swallowed hard as he contemplated the title:

> Reason the only Oracle of Man or a Compenduous System of Natural Religion Alternately Adorned with Confutations of a variety of Doctrines Incompatible to it; Deduced from the most exalted Ideas which we are able to form of the Divine and Human Characters And From the Universe in General

The book caused a storm among the ministers in Connecticut, which Justus thought after leafing through it, might be its main claim to posterity.[8] Thinking over the poorly expressed doctrine of deism, Justus decided to have his two baby daughters christened. The Reverend Stuart was 100 kilometres away in Kingston, while some 80 kilometres to the east was the Reverend John Bethune, a Presbyterian minister and former chaplain to the Royal Highland Emigrants. The distance was not much less but the road was better.

On February 12, 1789, with Sarah and Diana, the babes well wrapped, Justus drove his sleigh eastward, stopping for a night in the village of New Johnstown (now Cornwall). The following day they went on to Williamstown, where dwelt the Reverend Bethune. In St. Andrew's Church, the minister performed the ceremony, and the Sherwoods began their homeward trek. Not long afterward, Justus received a letter from Ira Allen. On February 17, Ethan had died on South Hero Island while visiting his nasty cousin Ebenezer.[9] With the passing of the big mountain chieftain, one more link with Justus' past was broken.

With the spring of 1789 came the time of ploughing and planting. Samuel and Levius returned from school by bateau, bringing a letter from the Reverend Stuart. He was closing his academy because he could not meet expenses. Justus was disappointed, but not without resources at hand. Some other half-pay officers had hired a teacher, Mr. Asa Starkwather, to instruct their children, and Levius could be one of his pupils.[10] Samuel, nearly fifteen, had enough formal education and could join the survey crews as an apprentice.

Edward Jessup went on another visit to England leaving Justus to oversee the welfare of the three townships. Life moved on serenely, except for many discussions over the state of the government. The new Luneburg District Land Board began to function, and Justus was appointed to this body. So was John Munro, soon sniping again at his old foe. On June 15 the Court of Quarter Sessions convened at a tavern in Osnabruck (formerly Township Number 3). Justus attended with other justices of the peace and heard several cases.[11]

He built more rafts, and was on the road to becoming the man of property he had been before he left New Haven. While Justus was succeeding, Dorchester was making it easier for all loyalists to provide for their children. At age twenty-one, each was entitled to receive '200 acres' or in the case of a daughter, earlier if she married.[12]

Late in the autumn of 1789, Justus heard that Dr. Smyth had died. He had some unhappy memories of his association with Hudibras, but had long ago forgiven him and remembered only the Irish charm. Mrs. Smyth remained at Sorel with other elderly exiles who had not ventured up the St. Lawrence. Before the snow fell, Edward Jessup returned from England, bearing an intriguing reminder of Justus' former associates in Vermont. Levi Allen was visiting London at the same time as Jessup, who made some snide remarks. On August 12, Ethan's brother challenged Jessup to a duel, but the former commander of the Loyal Rangers refused to oblige him.[13]

As the year 1790 opened, rumours circulated that something would soon be done about the seigneurial tenure that no one wanted and that had never been enforced. Dorchester, in communication with Lord Sydney, the home secretary, was proposing the division of Canada in two parts to accommodate the aspirations of the loyalists. No one was more pleased than Justus, who had petitioned for changes in the laws. While it was not desirable to revoke the Quebec Act that gave French-speaking Canadians their rights, it was practicable to establish a separate province with English civil law in the western wilderness. And, to everyone's satisfaction, Dorchester had recommended that Sir John Johnson be the lieutenant-governor, a man whom Justus respected.

In the autumn, Master Asa Starkwather's classes became a proper school. The teacher used a cabin at the old French fort on Lot 28 in the first concession of Augusta, and a subscription list was drawn up on December 7 for the privileges of firewood around the schoolhouse. Although Justus was not one of the subscribers, he sent Levius to the school. Samuel continued his apprenticeship, and Diana worked with Sarah, learning household skills.

The settlers also started making plans for a church. They formed a committee of Justus, Simeon Colvell, Paul Heck, Daniel Jones, Asa Landon, Elijah Bothum, Thomas Sherwood and James Breakenridge. Others agreed to contribute cash, labour, food or lumber. Justus wanted to see a church overlooking the green on his town plot, but matters such as roads and land granting took precedence. Church attendance was a duty, rather than a pleasure, and having a place of worship was not of first importance.[14]

With the coming of the year 1791, Justus found that his former home, as well as his present one, had new status. The latter had been divided into the Provinces of Upper and Lower Canada by the Constitutional Act. Each was to have a legislative assembly, legislative and executive councils. Upper Canada would have freehold tenure and English civil law, but the choice of a lieutenant-governor was disappointing. The home government was sending John Graves Simcoe. Dorchester was affronted, but his superiors felt that Sir John Johnson had too much property to be an impartial ruler. Although Justus would have preferred Johnson, he was looking forward to serving Simcoe on the new legislative council. He would automatically be a member, since his appointment was for life.

That same year, Vermont was admitted to the Congress, an event Justus scarcely noticed, so busy was he, struggling to create his own version of New England in the Canadian wilderness. Yet he soon felt the effect of this change at sessions of the Luneburg District Land Board. More loyalists from Vermont made their way to Canada. Questioning them, Justus learned that they were not being persecuted. For some it was a matter of principle, allegiance to the King, while for others the appeal was cheap land. To Justus the motive was unimportant. His new province needed settlers, and frontiersmen experienced in land colonization were the best type for the life they faced.

Before the year ended, Sarah gave birth to their last child, a daughter they named Sophia.[15] The three eldest were now seventeen, fifteen and fourteen, and young adult offspring were a blessing. It was impossible to hire labourers in a community where every head of family and many single men qualified for a grant of land.

Conditions were still primitive, but people had time for some social life. Many had built more commodious homes, and dances took place at St. John's Hall in Johnstown, a new and pleasing hostelry. For the earliest families, especially the Sherwoods, life was more than mere subsistence. That August, Dorchester sailed for England on leave of absence because he did not want to be on hand to greet Simcoe when he arrived to take up his duties. Alured Clarke, Dorchester's deputy, remained in charge of both provinces until Simcoe was ready to govern. Clarke had not forgotten Mr. Sherwood's views, and he intended to warn Simcoe of that gentleman's Yankee opinions.

For Justus, the winter routine was enlivened by some not very serious sedition that brought him into conflict with John Munro once again. Two men were 'Detected in treasonous conversation. . . a design to burn the King's garrison at Oswegatchie'. After taking evidence for the crown, Justus issued warrants and had the two apprehended, and upon hearing their side of the story released them on bail. Forcing them to part with hard cash was sufficient to curb any more such talk, and besides, there was no gaol in the settlement. Munro, who was the postmaster, wrote to his superior, the Honourable Hugh Finlay, the Postmaster-General, complaining that Sherwood had acted improperly. The two men should have been sent to Fort Oswegatchie and confined. 'This embarrassed us greatly', Munro confessed 'having no Jaol'.

Munro also had objections to Justus' conduct at the land board. Neither of the two accused of treason were loyalists, and one had been a Continental soldier, yet Sherwood had admitted the latter as a settler, and allowed him '100 acres'. And, Munro added, 'Am further inform'd that he has admitted Several Suspicious Characters, who have not been qualified in his Neighbourhood'.[16] As usual, Justus ignored Munro's prating.

In the spring of 1792, Lieutenant-Governor Simcoe prepared to travel up the St. Lawrence to take command of his province. In advance he selected the members of his legislative council. They were William Osgoode, William Robertson, Peter Russell and Alexander Grant — appointed in England before Simcoe sailed for Canada. The others were Richard Duncan of Rapid Plat, James Baby of Detroit, Robert Hamilton of Niagara, Richard Cartwright of Kingston, and John Munro of Matilda.[17] Sir John Johnson's name was not on the list published in the *Quebec Gazette*, but he resided at Lachine and had been placed on the council for Lower Canada. Also missing from the list was Justus Sherwood's name. When he received his copy of the *Gazette* Justus could hardly believe his eyes. Only two men, himself and James Baby, had been members of the old council, and Simcoe had retained Baby. What did Simcoe have against him? What had that weasel John Munro manipulated to have himself on the council while Justus was excluded?

In June the Simcoes and their escort reached Matilda and were met by Munro with horses to take them to his house.[19] The lieutenant-governor had a levee at St. John's Hall in Johnstown at which the half-pay officers and their wives were to pay their respects. Justus refused to go, and Thomas resolved to spend the evening commiserating with his cousin. The prospect of watching a jubilant Munro was more than either man could stomach. Munro host to the new governor? That honour should have fallen upon Justus.

The following day the Simcoe party moved on to Kingston, where the governor held his first council meeting before passing on to his capital under the guns of Fort Niagara, which he named Newark. He soon called an election, and for electoral and military purposes he set up counties. Edwardsburgh and Augusta were part of

Grenville County, and entitled to elect a member to the assembly. Justus decided not to run because he might be wasting valuable time in an assembly doomed to impotence. Ephriam Jones stood and won the seat.[20] Justus prayed that Simcoe would prove an able ruler. The province needed to be developed as much as its people needed a voice in their affairs. Meanwhile, he would do his share of the developing. He had timber to cut, his three little girls to enjoy, and the future of Diana and his sons to plan.

That September, the first Parliament of Upper Canada met at Newark. In keeping with his policy of converting the wilderness into a carbon copy of England, Simcoe changed the district names to Eastern (Luneburg), Midland (Mecklenburg), Home (Nassau) and Western (Hesse). Under the Constitutional Act, one seventh of the land was reserved for the support of a Protestant clergy, and another seventh to provide revenue for the crown. Simcoe decided that the lot size for all farms would be '200 acres', and the reserved lots would be scattered through the townships in a regular pattern, not set aside in blocks.

When Justus heard this news he was livid. Thank heaven his land board had awarded lots side by side, so that the townships could be filled in, avoiding empty spaces that interfered with road building. Men were willing to work on a road past their own farms, but they felt imposed upon when chopping down trees across vacant land that had no owner to share the labour. The land board members had made certain that the farm lots were awarded to form a continuous community.[21]

Simcoe delivered two more snubs to Justus Sherwood. When the governor wanted a district court judge, he appointed John Munro, despite the fact that Justus was the most experienced magistrate in the neighbourhood.[22] Then when he organized the militia by counties, Simcoe followed the English practice of appointing lieutenants to raise the battalions. For his lieutenant in Grenville county he chose Peter Drummond, another half-pay captain from the Loyal Rangers.

War had broken out between Britain and France, and Simcoe feared that the Americans might renew their alliance with the enemy. Upper Canada, thinly populated and nearly impossible to defend, was the most vulnerable part of British North America. Despite the threat, Simcoe also ignored Edward Jessup, who had commanded a regiment. Furthermore, Justus had been senior to Drummond when both men were captains in the Loyal Rangers.

Brooding before the fire in his house, Justus wondered again what Simcoe had against him personally. He had served Governor Haldimand faithfully and was only too willing to do the same for Simcoe. Not only that, Justus was forty-six years old and working as hard as he had done all his life. He had no way of knowing that Alured Clarke and certain of John Munro's friends in Quebec City had damaged him in Simcoe's eyes.

At the height of the alert a letter came from Ira Allen, one more typical of him than his request that Justus raise a loan for him in Montreal. He proposed a truce along the Vermont border if war broke out between the two countries, and begged Justus to use his influence.[23] Justus' reply was only a matter of courtesy. He had no influence to wield now that he had been excluded from government circles. He continued living beside the St. Lawrence, improving his farmland, selling his timber rafts. The Constitutional Act and the arrival of a governor to take a real interest in his province now seemed a hollow victory. Justus Sherwood, with his Yankee political ambitions, had been set aside.

Chapter 21

Founding Father

While Justus cultivated his garden, the legislature met for a second time at Newark and voted to legalize town meetings. Simcoe was horrified, but under pressure he agreed to compromise. He empowered justices of the peace to issue warrants for the election of township officers, such as clerks, supervisors of highways, pathmasters and fence viewers.[1] To Justus this limited form of town meeting was an improvement.

Next, Simcoe moved his capital to the Toronto Carrying Place. Negotiations were afoot to surrender Fort Niagara to the United States, and once that occurred the legislature at Newark could be bombarded if further disturbances took place between the two powers. From York, the governor handed down a ruling distressing to the half-pay officers, the main slave-owning group. Slavery was to be abolished, which caused an uproar among the officers. Again Simcoe agreed to compromise. Owners could keep their slaves, but no more could be brought into the province. Children born to slaves were to be free at age twenty-five, all grandchildren free from birth.[2] Justus' most reliable source of labour was saved.

While he believed in liberty and self-determination for freeborn men, he saw no reason why men born into slavery should not remain in that condition. Pre-destination died hard. Not long after Simcoe's ruling, Justus sold Caesar Congo to Elijah Bothum.[3] Caesar had been Sarah's loyal attendant, but Elijah needed him. He had recently married Molly Hurd and was working his own land in earnest. Justus had two other slaves, and two nearly grown sons to help him. He knew Elijah would be good to Caesar, and the transaction, Justus felt, was in keeping with his kindly nature.

Little was happening near the Sherwood house on the town plot in Augusta. Although it was centrally located, as ordered by Haldimand, the water in front was shallow, unable to accommodate schooners. Since Justus knew the importance of a good harbour for the successful development of a town, he had been too obedient to Haldimand when he might have used his own judgement. At the eastern end of the township was a good harbour, and there, under the direction of Edward Jessup, a village was growing, on a dull grid plan.

Johnstown, too, was a failure, for the harbour was shallow. That gave Justus some solace, for its plan was uninspired. He continued improving his property, serving on the land board and in the courts, preparing his sons to be successful in life. He knew that surveyors were badly needed, but neither Samuel nor Levius was taking kindly to the training. Samuel suggested he would be happier studying law, and Justus sent him to Montreal to apprentice with James Walker, a lawyer who sometimes appeared before the Court of Quarter Sessions in the Eastern District.

For convenience, Justus built a small windmill on Lot 26 in the first concession of Augusta. The land belonged to Elijah Bothum, and lacked a stream suitable for a waterwheel. This mill was not a commercial venture, but a help in grinding grain for relatives and friends in the vicinity. At the same time, Justus was looking for a good waterfall where he could build large mills, and when he found one he intended to apply for the tract of land on which it stood as part of his military grant.

He threw himself wholeheartedly into acquiring all the '3,000 acres' his captaincy had earned him — and more. In March 1793, with Roger Stevens and two unbelievable associates, Justus petitioned for two townships on the Rideau River. Stevens was in the neighbourhood for he had moved from Montreal recently. He had explored the Rideau country and built a mill on a waterfall before any townships were surveyed there. The other partners were none other than Joseph Fay and Samuel Safford.[5] Shades of the Onion River Land Company! Only two years after Vermont joined the United States, Justus was on friendly terms with Fay, who had confounded him during the Vermont negotiations, and Safford, so overtly hostile to reunion with Britain. Truly Justus was a man who could forget, or forgive, when money was to be made.

Nothing came of this plot. Simcoe was not a governor of New Hampshire promoting real estate deals in someone else's backyard. Justus also missed the opportunity to acquire '800 acres' on the Gananoque River that had a mill site.[6] When he applied in 1794, this tract had been granted to Roger Stevens' brother Abel, a Baptist elder who had brought some of his flock from Vermont to Leeds County, to the west of Grenville. Not often did a man get the better of Justus, but Abel was tarred with the same brush.

On one matter Simcoe and Justus were in accord. The province needed settlers. The governor offered extra land to inhabitants who assisted him in attracting newcomers. In June, 1794, Justus and Thomas Sherwood each received '200 acres' for settling twenty-two families from Vermont in Leeds County.[7] Justus' last petition for a grand scheme was sent to the governor in August, 1795, when he joined other men in petitioning for '30,000 acres' on the Rideau.[8] This came to nothing. More successful was a petition read on July 8, 1794, before a committee of council at York. The members recommended that Sherwood be awarded 'whatever Military Lands may be still due to him, as a reduced Captain may be assigned to him by the Surveyor General to whom the location thereof is referred'.[9]

From the land board he received a few tracts at a time. Some of his land was unsuitable for farming, but well located for timber rafts. He received some land in the broken front of Yonge Township, and some in the broken front of Escott. Both these townships were within the area Justus had deemed unfit for settlement in the autumn of 1783, but were on the waterfront where hauling logs to the shore was easy.[10] His land at Chaleur Bay was a gift from Haldimand and not part of his military grant, and the land at Sorel he sold to Francis Hogel, his fellow captain in the Queen's Loyal Rangers.[11]

In 1794, Simcoe abolished the land boards and decreed that all petitions were to go to his executive council. In future the governor would have the last word on who got land. Justus' only remaining public duty was as a justice of the peace, and never once did Simcoe call upon him to perform any task in the interests of the new homeland he had explored with such enthusiasm for Haldimand.

In the spring of 1796, the British garrison evacuated Fort Oswegatchie, and among the other posts handed over to the Americans under Jay's Treaty was the Loyal Blockhouse. In jig time, American land speculators were buzzing up and down the south shore of the St. Lawrence. Reuben Sherwood began laying out townships to the west of the fort, acquiring knowledge of the lie of the land that he would exploit in 1812. Towards the end of July the Simcoe family passed by in a bateau. The governor had asked for a leave of absence, and Peter Russell, the receiver-general, was acting governor. Soon afterward Lord Dorchester resigned, and his successor was General Robert Prescott, for whom Edward Jessup's village at the east end of Augusta would be named.

With Simcoe absent, young Samuel Sherwood received good news. Peter Russell allowed the legislative council to take action on the lack of lawyers in Upper Canada. Sixteen men of some education were chosen to become what Adiel Sherwood called 'Heaven-born Lawyers' and one was Justus' elder son. Someone in the government knew that Samuel had trained under Lawyer Walker in Montreal, and was better qualified than others selected to practice law by divine inspiration. Samuel opened an office in Edward Jessup's village, rather than on his father's town plot. Justus had no objections, for his son had to be where merchants and traders came and went. Levius joined his brother in the winter, for Justus needed him during the busy season.

In the spring of 1797, Diana Sherwood married Samuel Smades, a farmer with land on the Rideau.[12] At Justus' suggestion Diana petitioned for Lot 16 in the first concession of Augusta. It was part of the town plot, but no town was ever going to develop. The land was more valuable than any in the back townships, and Diana's petition was successful. Her wedding was a community affair, second in importance only to a funeral.

The family celebrated, and Samuel came from the Bay of Quinte with three children, Rachel, now nineteen, John and Samuel Harris, but without Eunice. Samuel was a widower, for his wife had died in November, 1795, after giving birth to their second son.[13] Closer at hand were the Thomas Sherwoods and Elijah Bothums and their children. Thomas performed the ceremony while Justus gave the bride away. Despite the Reverend Stuart's disapproval, Simcoe had entrenched the right of magistrates to officiate at weddings where a Church of England clergyman was not resident within 'eighteen miles', which was the case in Augusta.

That summer Upper Canada had a second election, and Edward Jessup Jr. won the seat for Grenville. Justus was tempted to stand, now that Simcoe had left, but he did not want to challenge his friend's son. For the Sherwoods, life moved along serenely, but discontent was mounting in the townships. Early in 1798, the government announced that Grenville and Leeds Counties would be separated from the Eastern District to form the new District of Johnstown, effective in 1800. The arrangement gratified Justus and his fellow Yankees. Soon they would not be outvoted by Yorkers. Whenever a group of New Englanders congregated, heated discussions took place, and the Sherwood house was the focal point for dissenters wanting to change the government. Another vocal man was William Buell of Elizabethtown, whose mother, Mercy Peters, was a cousin of John, Justus' onetime commanding officer.[14]

At times the St. John's Hall in Johnstown bore a striking resemblance to the Green Mountain Tavern in Bennington. Yet caution prevailed. No one wanted the community branded a nest of wild radicals, or worse, republicans. Even Justus, the former outlaw and Green Mountain Boy, agreed that dissent must stop short of sedition. He could not risk being forced into exile a second time in his life for swimming against the tide. Most of the others insisted that the place to talk reform was in the assembly. The government must be modified, not overthrown.

In that part of Upper Canada, the seeds of the reform movement that would soon dominate the politics of the province were being sown. Reform in the Johnstown District was destined to have its own flavour because of the strength of the Yankee componet. New Englanders believed in government by discussion, and they enjoyed argument and debate before voting and agreeing to abide by the outcome.

By the summer of 1798, Diana had made Justus a grandfather. She named her son Elijah Bothum Smades, after her favourite uncle, but she promised to name the next boy after Justus and he was well pleased.[15] When he had two timber rafts ready, with Levius, the slaves and some hired hands, Justus set off down the St. Lawrence, leaving Samuel to man the law office in Edward Jessup's village. When the rafts were floating past Trois Rivières, tragedy struck.

Before the horrified eyes of Levius and the crews, Justus staggered, tumbled from his raft and disappeared.[16] While Levius ordered the clumsy rafts to the shore, watchers set out in small boats to search. In the wake Justus sank. Panic, agony, a struggle to reach the surface, then euphoria and peace overwhelmed him. His time had come and in his dying moments he was aware of voices of others who had gone before him. The thunder ringing in his ears was Ethan, summoning him to a wolf hunt, but his companions were agents the rebels had murdered — Thomas Lovelace, John Parker and Joe Bettys — as he sank to a watery grave.

In a small boat a near hysterical Levius peered into the deep blue waters, but could find no sign of his father. The crews thought Justus had drowned, but Levius was convinced that a sudden heart attack had overtaken him. Justus was far too agile and experienced at riding rafts to fall off unless there was another problem. He had been exerting himself all his life. The back-breaking toil he had performed in the New Hampshire Grants, the years of privation when he served His Majesty's cause, the struggle to re-establish himself and provide for his family in the manner he planned from the day he married Sarah — all had conspired to carry him off at age fifty-one, robbing him of his three score and ten years.

The searchers never did find Justus' body.[17] After waiting several days in the hope that someone would locate his father, Levius hired a horse and rode back up the St. Lawrence, to let Samuel know that he was now the head of the family. His thoughts turned to his mother, and to little Sophia, only seven years old. Yet Sarah was a strong-minded woman who would take this loss in her stride. Their father had many noble accomplishments to his credit, but he had died unfulfilled, frustrated in his desire to see his new community thrive, guided by the better traditions of Connecticut. Now the torch passed to younger hands.

Epilogue

For some time after Levius reached home, Sarah sustained a hope that Justus would be found. When he left her during the war years, he had always turned up safe. Surely this was possible once more. Gradually she came to accept that he would not be coming. She mourned him, but she had three girls to raise and the farm to run. Samuel and Levius were capable men and willing to help, but they were fully occupied with the law office and the timber rafts.

One piece of unfinished business was the '200 acres' in Vermont that still belonged to Justus. In 1801, Levius sold Simon Bothum '150 acres for 150 dollars' and he gave his uncle the remaining 50 acres — the farm Simon occupied.[1] Simon had been working the land ever since Justus fled to Crown Point in 1776, and since the title to this piece was in Elijah Bothum Sr.'s name, Levius did not want to press a claim to it.

Samuel became the Member of the Legislative Assembly for Grenville County at the election of 1800. The other member for the District of Johnstown was William Buell, representing Leeds County, who declared himself in opposition to the government.[2] Buell, rather than Samuel, carried Justus' torch. Samuel had lived most of his life under a military regime, and his knowledge of Connecticut institutions was second-hand. Little is known of Samuel's later life, although he opened a law office in Montreal before the War of 1812. He served as a major in the militia, and in 1818, with Levius assisting him he successfully defended two of the men accused of murdering Governor Semple of the Hudson's Bay Company.[3] He was in the Lower Canada Assembly, and indicted for libel in 1816.[4]

Levius had a distinguished career in the law and politics in Upper Canada. In 1803, he was called to the bar, by which time he was the Registrar of Leeds and Grenville. He opened his law office in Elizabethtown, where a village was growing on William Buell's land. In 1812, when the country was on the verge of war, Levius was elected to the assembly representing Leeds County.[5] That year, he was appointed the lieutenant-colonel of the first battalion, Leeds Militia. On February 7, 1813, a force of American riflemen raided Buell's village, then called Brockville after the slain hero of the Battle of Queenston Heights. They carried off fifty-two men, including Levius' second-in-command, Major Bartholomew Carley, and Captain Adiel Sherwood. Levius was away at the time and he reported on the effects of the American incursion when he returned.[6]

The attack on Brockville affected Levius' political views and his subsequent actions. When party lines were drawn between reformers and conservatives, Levius favoured the latter. Like other thoughtful people, Levius feared that too strident demands for home rule might induce the British government to withdraw the garrisons of regulars, without whose protection the country could not survive.

William Lyon Mackenzie accused Levius of being in the Family Compact.[7] He was married into it, for his wife, Charlotte, was Ephriam Jones' daughter. Loyalists from New York, the Joneses were accustomed to a landed gentry and determined to be the backbone of the Upper Canadian aristocracy, but in Levius' case Mackenzie's charge was misplaced. Prior to the union of Upper and Lower Canada in 1841, the governor of the day, Lord Sydenham, had gone to great lengths to break the power of the Family Compact. Yet Sydenham appointed Levius his Speaker of the Legislative Council, which he would not have done had Justus' second son represented the interests of a discredited ruling clique.

Levius was a moderate man, diplomatic and with a talent for keeping out of trouble which his father lacked. This younger son displayed his tolerance in his choice of a wife, for Charlotte Jones' mother was a French-speak-

Levius Peters Sherwood, 1777-1850. Courtesy: Judge Livius Sherwood

ing Canadian who raised her daughters in her own faith.[8] Levius agreed that he and Charlotte would follow this example. His four sons (Henry, George, Samuel and Edward) were Anglicans, his three daughters (Charlotte, Helen and Amelia) were Roman Catholics.

Of Justus' daughters, Diana lived in Augusta after she and Samuel had pioneered on the Rideau River. Sarah married Andrew McCollom, also of Augusta, while Harriet married Dr. Benjamin Trask of Montreal. Sophia's life was tragically short. She married Jonathan Jones at age nineteen, died three years later, and was buried in the cemetery on the town plot in Augusta, where in 1809, the settlers erected a church. After Sophia's passing, Justus' widow Sarah moved to Montreal, where she died in 1818 at age sixty-four.[9]

The kinsman who most closely emulated Justus was his cousin Reuben. The surveyor of the next generation, Reuben laid out many townships and lots in eastern Upper Canada. When the War of 1812 broke out, Reuben was a Captain of Guides from Côteau du Lac to Kingston, and he did some spying on the side, keeping up that family tradition. In the summer of 1813, he was near Cape Vincent, New York, a village opposite Kingston, travelling in a canoe with his lieutenant and nine men. Landing the men on an island, and taking his lieutenant, Reuben paddled to the American shore, and found some militiamen building a blockhouse. Boldly he told them that an invasion had begun and asked to be taken to their commanding officer.

They led Reuben and his lieutenant to Major John B. Esselstyn and his deputy, a captain whose name has been lost. Reuben told the privates they could go home on parole, but the officers were prisoners of war. When the enlisted men took to their heels, Reuben marched his captives back to the canoe and escorted them across the St. Lawrence. Later the major was exchanged for Major Carley, the captain for Adiel Sherwood. Reuben was decorated after the Battle of Crysler's Farm, and in 1814, he piloted gunboats down the St. Lawrence. He also recaptured some supply bateaux that had been taken by the Americans.[10]

Justus' dream of a New England town in Augusta

was doomed to disappointment, and the only public building to stand on his town plot was the Blue Church. Yet the Johnstown District would not lack a central place. In 1808, the government ruled that the village of Johnstown, hitherto the administrative centre, was too far to the east, and a new district seat would be chosen in Elizabethtown. William Buell hired Reuben Sherwood to lay out a townsite on his property, and it had a square. Named Brockville in 1812, it grew into what one traveller called 'the prettiest town I saw in Upper Canada'.[11] Through the foresight of another Connecticut Yankee, Justus' community had the kind of focus he cherished.

Tantalizing glimpses of later Sherwoods flit through source materials, and most pertain to Levius' descendants. His eldest son Henry — dark and handsome, more Jones than Sherwood — helped smash Mackenzie's printing press, and chased the rebels up Yonge Street at the head of his militia company. Despite three Roman Catholic sisters, Henry was the darling of the Orangemen, and mayor of Toronto. For ten months, in 1848, conservative Henry was the Premier of the Province of Canada.

George represented Brockville in the assembly for twenty years, and was Commissioner of Crown Lands and Minister of Public Works in the Macdonald-Cartier Ministry prior to Confederation. Samuel was the Registrar of the City of Toronto. Edward, the youngest, was expelled from Upper Canada College for striking the mathematics master, a man famous for harshness.[12] This abrupt halt to his education did not interfere with his later life, for Edward was the Registrar of the City of Ottawa. Levius and Henry were occasional visitors at Dundurn Castle, near Hamilton. Lady MacNab's mother, Sophia Jones Stuart, was Levius' sister-in-law, and her daughters called him Uncle Sherwood.

In Bishop Strachan's letter book is a note to Miss Christina Sherwood, Samuel's daughter, complimenting her on her verses. The cleric was being kind to a delicate child who only lived fourteen years. Her brother, Captain L.P. Sherwood, rode at the head of a company of Queen's Own Rifles to chase away the Fenians in 1866. Edward's son, Percy, was the Commissioner of the Dominion Police, and he was knighted.

A modern echo of Justus himself is his great great great grandson, Livius Sherwood, who was Director of Sailing at the 1976 Olympic yachting events in Kingston. Sailors from all over the world were protected by a high mesh wire enclosure. Patroling offshore was a Canadian destroyer, while overhead whirred watchful helicopters. The setting, amidst tight security, was reminiscent of the Loyal Blockhouse, separated from the rest of North Hero Island by pickets, the *Royal George* patroling offshore.

Certainly, Justus Sherwood qualifies as a hero and not just because he died young and not in his own bed. If at times Justus Sherwood seemed a trifle too land hungry and sharp in his business practices, he was a man of his own time. This steady, energetic man lived according to the example he found around him. A dedicated fighter for a cause, he was quick to forgive his enemies, whether loyalist or rebel. Despite personal suffering, the American Revolution did not leave him an embittered man. He was a colourful character, a pimpernel figure in his blockhouse, the loyalists' rescuer, and a hard driving pioneer in what became the Province of Ontario.

Appendix A

Memorial of Justus Sherwood to the Commissioners appointed by Act of Parliament for enquiring into the Losses and Services of the American Loyalists. June, 1787

The Memorial of Justus Sherwood formerly Resident in the New Hampshire Grants in the Province of New York and County of Charlotte late Captain in His Majesty's Provl Regiment called Loyal Rangers —

Shewith.

That your Memorialist at the Commencement of the late unhappy Rebellion manifested his Attachment to His Majesty and the British Govert by Exerting his Influence to prevent the people in his Vicinity from taking Arms agt His Majesty for which your Memorialist was in Augt 1776 taken by order of the Committee by an armed Compy of Men from his House and Farm in New Haven who wantonly destroyed and took away the Household Furniture Wearing Appl and provisions &c belonging to your Memt breaking open his Chests taking tearing and trampling under foot all his papers and writings which they could get hold of, your Memorialist procured Bail at that time and permission to go to his Family and Continue under certain restrictions untill further Orders from the Committee, But the same night on which your Memorialist came to his Family he was taken out of his Bed by an Armed Force, who kept him under a Guard of Insulters for some time obliging him to bear his own and their Expences your Memorialist was then ordered to prison by a Committee for the Crime as they alledged of being Enimical to the Country Refusing to take the Oaths required by the Committee and sending Intelligce to Genl Carleton in Canada. After about a Months Imprisonment your Memorialist was brought before the Grand Committee (as they called it) and by that Committee Condemned to be shut up in Simsbury Mines during Life But before they could Execute this shocking Sentence (worse than Death) Your Memorialt had the good fortune to break away from his Keepers, and fly to the Mountains where, in a few days abt 40 of the Loyal Inhabits (distressed) for their Loyalty joined him, whom your Memorialist piloted abt 200 Miles thro the Wilderness and joined Genl Carleton at Crown Point in the Month of Octr 1776 the first body of Loyalists in America that Joined His Majestys Army — in March following your Memorialt went with five Men by Order of Genl Carleton in a private Scout as far as Shaftsbury opposite Albany for Intelligence and returned in the beginning of May to Genl Philips at Montreal with an Account of the Rebell Troops from Albany Northward and a Sketch of the Fortification at Ticonderoga and Mount Independent, their Number of Artillery &c your Memorialist was 41 days on this Scout and lost two of his party taken prisoners by a Rebel Scout on the Coast of Lake Champlain and your Memorialt escaped with the rest of his party by seizing the Rebel Boats which lay on the Shore and pushing into the Lake — Your Memorialist commanded the Loyalists after Col Festers Death in the Battle of Bennington and was employed in various Scouts and services under Genl Burgoyne and was in every Action a [nd] Skirmish thro' that Campaign at the unfortunate conclusion of which your Memorialist became a prisoner at the Saratoga Convention and suffered many Insults and abuses by the Rebels who happened to know him — In 1778 your Memorialist was again employed by order of Genl Carleton to procure Intelligence &c and Continued in that and various other services by order of Genl Haldimand untill the Conclusion of the War during which time your Memorialt had the Honour to serve under the Command of a number of Experienced and brave Officers in various Expeditions and Actions Viz — Major Genl Powell — Brigr Genl St Leger, Col. Carleton, Major Carleton, Major Jessup, Major Rogers and many others — In Consequence of the above recited Attachment and active Services for His Majestys Govt your Memorialist was attainted and outlawed by the Rebels and of course his little property which he had accumulated by honest Industry was forfeited and sold or otherways taken for the use of the Rebels.

Your Memorialist therefore prays &c &c
Justus Sherwood

Schedule of Loss sustained of Justus Sherwood

1000 Acres of Wild Land at Susquehana	£ 175. –. –
630 Do in Dorset an old settled Townsp	£ 250. –. –
50 Do in New Haven a good River Lot	£ 50. –. –
50 Do in Burlington a good River Lot	£ 50. –. –
365 Do in Racock wild Land	£ 50. –. –
65 Do in Tinmouth 3d Division	£ 16. 5. –
365 Do in New Huntington wild Land	£ 65. –. –
300 Do in Middlebury good Land	£ 112.10. –
160 Do in Sunderland an old Townsp	£ 100. –. –
10 Head of Cattle	£ 50. –. –
House Furniture & Moveables Destroyed	£ 100. –. –
Farmg Utensils taken away after my Impt	£ 60. –. –
12 Acres of Harvested Wheat & Do of Oats	£ 45. –. –
15 Tons of good Hay in Stacks	£ 18.15. –
10 Acres of Indn Corn, Pots & Garden &c	£ 40. –. –
	£1182.10. –
Omd in my former Acct 17 Hogs, 1 Barl of Choice side pork, 1½ Acre of Flax	£ 27. 8. 6
Lawf. Money	£1209.18. 6

The source of the above is the Public Record Office, London, from the Audit Office Records AO 13-22 pp. 351-360, and is published with the permission of the Controller of H.M. Stationery Office, London, U.K.

Appendix B

A Report by Mary I. Duncan, Handwriting Analyst

Justus Sherwood's letters, written with a quill pen, form the basis of this Graphoanalysis report. His rather flourished writing style was typical of the penmanship of his era, but within that style there was a simplicity and lack of ostentation which showed an unpretentious person and one not given to 'putting on airs'.

He was methodical in his thinking and when he had a problem to solve he did it in logical steps, one at a time. He was a fluid thinker and his thoughts flowed smoothly and easily from one subject to another, and as he was creative, he utilized his past experience by blending it with new ideas and brought a fresh approach to the solution of a problem.

He had excellent organizational ability and his manner of planning what he had to do helped him keep a very ordered life. Yet at the same time, he was flexible and would have been able to adapt and adjust to new or unexpected changes in plans.

In temperament he was a friendly, outgoing person and was quick to respond to others and their interests, but he constantly guarded against being overly expressive of his feelings. He was rather shy and would not have been one to draw undue attention to himself. He often felt insecure, and perhaps even inadequate, but he hid any such feelings behind a mask of calm self-assurance.

He was energetic and seemed to possess a good mental attitude and the strength to do a good day's work. He was decisive, and as his goals and his identity were clear to him there was strength in his decisions and he could be firm without being offensive. He had strong determination and carried through on things despite ordinary obstacles and problems; he was resolute and had learned that a job must be done regardless of his feelings.

His highly legible writing indicates a frank, open person, one who not only had a desire to be understood but one who was able to communicate his ideas to others clearly. At the same time, he was somewhat on the defensive and wary of being taken advantage of in any way. He was not one to take people at face value but instead waited until he was sure that they could be trusted.

He was selective and most at ease in the company of a few special friends and on the occasions he chose. He had diplomacy and while it was not a strong trait, the indications are that he was able to get along in harmony with others, and his generous, co-operative spirit made him a good worker and a fine friend.

Intelligence and strength of character gave him a maturity that made for effective leadership. He was tolerant and able to defend his ideas without completely ignoring different viewpoints. At the same time, he had very definite opinions about things, and on some points he could not be swayed.

He had a quick temper but had so much control that it would have taken a lot of provocation for him to 'lose his cool'. He disliked restrictions upon his freedom of action and did his best work when he was on his own, so it seems likely that he was happiest when in complete charge of a situation.

He had such excellent co-ordination that he could well have been noted for his athletic prowess. The combination of rhythm and manual dexterity indicated a person who was skilful in creating or fixing things with his hands — a skill that doubtless stood him in good stead in handling the firearms of the day.

The fact that his signatures are so very much like the body of the letters indicates a harmony between the official and the private person. He was very much as he appeared to be and all the indications are that he was a genuine and straight-forward person.

All in all, Justus Sherwood was a man of talent and ability. One can well imagine him being highly respected by his men and trusted by his superiors.

Mary I. Duncan.
Master Certified Graphoanalyst.

Bibliographical Essay

Most of the material for this work was drawn from the papers preserved by Governor Frederick Haldimand following his tour of duty in Canada, from 1778 until 1784. The originals are in the British Museum. Handwritten transcripts known as Series B are in the Public Archives of Canada, and identified in my footnotes as PAC. I have referred in these notes to both the originals and the transcripts. Midway through my research, the Public Archives of Canada put Series B in storage, and purchased copies of the British Museum collection on microfilm, which have different page numberings. An attempt to have all my footnotes conform to the British Museum numbering involved too much eye strain to be worth the effort.

An invaluable source, also drawn from the Haldimand Papers, is the many published works of the late Brigadier E.A. Cruikshank, who spent years transcribing documents. The work of two earlier biographers of Sherwood was most helpful. One is I.C.R. Pemberton's doctoral thesis for the University of Western Ontario, dated 1972. It is scholarly, but the author did not make use of War Office records, and he was misled on certain aspects of Sherwood's military experience. Pemberton saw Sherwood as non-violent, and temperamentally unsuited to intrigue. I see him as capable of using his fists, and probably the best man Haldimand had available for the secret service. The other biography, by Colonel H.M. Jackson, is short, and his reporting on the years prior to 1778 is not very accurate. He left room for a more comprehensive treatment of the subject.

Other useful sources were the Audit Office records, in the Public Record Office in London. These are the memorials of all the loyalists who filed claims for compensation, and is the second most valuable source on loyalists. The War Office records contain muster rolls, lists of officers, and some information on the activities of the regiments and individuals, and copies are in the Public Archives of Canada. Other sources in the Public Archives of Canada are the Upper Canada State Papers, Land Petitions, the Land and State Book, survey records, Lower Canada Land Records, the Quebec Land Book, Quebec Executive Council Minutes, Military Series C and Q, and Public Accounts. The Vermont Public Record Office in Montpelier provided some information on Sherwood's lands and on his in-laws, the Bothums.

In the Ontario Archives in Toronto are the Jessup Papers, Sherwood's Original Notebook, and a card catalogue with information on births, marriages and deaths of many early families. Some American repositories yielded useful detail. The papers of Sir Henry Clinton are in the William L Clements Library, University of Michigan, Ann Arbor. Some of John Peters' papers are in the New York State Library, Albany. The Vermont State Library has manuscripts relating to Ethan Allen. The letter books of Richard Cartwright are in the Douglas Library, Queen's University in Kingston. An account book kept by Sherwood is in the Metropolitan Toronto Library.

Some Vermont sources, and others drawn from New England and New York, were marginally useful for the more obscure phases of Sherwood's early life. But the Vermonters wrote him out of their history, or molded him to their own ends. The post-1784 years are also illusive. Had Lieutenant-Governor Simcoe given Sherwood any public appointments, some of his letters might have been preserved in the former's correspondence. Rounding out the early years, and the later ones, required considerable detective work. Such would have been nearly impossible had I not in advance re-created the life of another loyalist whose story has even more gaps, that of John Walden Meyers.

By the time I began Sherwood's biography, I had more than a nodding acquaintance with many of his associates. In fact, I did not like Sherwood until I understood the Connecticut upbringing that had shaped him. At first, the lack of private letters worried me until Mary I. Duncan, a certified graphoanalyst, undertook a study of Sherwood's handwriting. Her observation that his signature indicated 'a harmony between the official and the private person' gave me confidence. She convinced me that private letters would have shed no more light on the man than his public writings.

Where the documentation was weak, I made use of occasions when Sherwood's viewpoint was evident. If he felt one way in a situation, he reacted in the same manner under similar circumstances where sources are missing. This technique was necessary, or there could have been no biography of Sherwood, nor of many other loyalists beyond the few such as William Smith, who left diaries and private letters. Smith was a civilian whose story is quite different from the men who fought the war, whereas Sherwood was a soldier.

Notes

Prologue: From a Fate Worse Than Death

1. Jackson, H.M. *Justus Sherwood: Soldier, Loyalist and Negotiator*. Published privately 1958. p. 2. Other sources show Sarah's surname as Bottum. Justus spelled it Bothum.
2. Public Record Office, London. Audit Office AO 13-22, pp. 351-359. *Memorial of Justus Sherwood.*
3. Lapp, Eula C. *To Their Heirs Forever*. Picton, 1970. Parts I-IV, pp. 2-114, on the families in the Camden Valley.
4. Leavitt, Thad. W.H. *History of Leeds and Grenville*. Brockville, 1879. p. 18. Memoir of Adiel Sherwood, shows that Caesar Congo was very young in 1776.
5. P.R.O. Memorial of Justus Sherwood.
6. Thompson, Judge D.P. *The Green Mountain Boys – A Historical Tale of the Early Settlement of Vermont*. New York, 1839. Foreword; p. 328.
7. Koier, Louise B. *A November Journey. Vermont's Debt to Captain Justus Sherwood*. Vermont Historical Society, Montpelier, Vt. News and Notes VI. Nov. 13, 1954.
8. Pemberton, I.C.R. *Justus Sherwood, Vermont Loyalist*. Doctoral Thesis, University of Western Ontario, 1972. Pemberton discovered that there were two Justus Sherwoods; the other one's dates of birth and death are 1752-1836.
9. PAC *Haldimand Papers* B 177 pt. 1, p. 36. Sherwood to Mathews, Feb. 14, 1782.
10. Duncan, Mary I. Graphoanalyst. Report on Sherwood's handwriting.

Chapter 1: Outlaw, Rebel, Loyalist

1. Pope, C.H. *Pioneers of Massachusetts*. Baltimore, 1965. p. 413. The family reached Massachusetts Bay April 30, aboard the *Francis of Ipswich*.
2. Stratford Historical Society; from Orcutt's *History of Stratford*.
3. Newton, Connecticut. Register of Deeds, vols 9, 10. Quoted in Pemberton. p. 8.
4. Bushman, Richard L. *From Puritan to Yankee: Character and Social Order in Connecticut*. Cambridge, Mass. 1967.
5. *Ibid.* p. 45.
6. O'Callahan, E.B. ed. *Documentary History of the State of New York*. Albany, 1851. pp. 776-777.
7. Coolidge, A.J. and Mansfield, J.B. *History and Description of New England, General and Social*. Boston, 1859, vol. 1. p. 110.
8. Mathews, Hazel C. *Frontier Spies*. Fort Myers, Fla., 1970, p. 8.
9. Stuart, E. Rae. *Jessup's Rangers as a Factor in Loyalist Settlement*. Toronto, 1961. p. 5.
10. P.R.O. AO 13-22. p. 355. Testimony of Roger Stevens.
11. Three accounts describe the Green Mountain Boys. Van De Water, F.F. *The Reluctant Republic*; New York, 1974; Pell, John. *Ethan Allen*. Boston, 1929; Allen, Ira. *The National and Political History of Vermont*. London, 1798. Pemberton suggested that Sherwood was only a business associate of the Allens. Proof that he was committed to the struggle with New York is found in his purchase of 1,000 acres in the Susquehanna Valley, where Connecticut settlers were battling Pennsylvanians and their royal governor.

12. Allen, Ira. *History of Vermont.* p. 15
13. Pell, p. 72.
14. Justus could have been in the first assault, but nothing in the record supports this. No list of Green Mountain Boys exists prior to 1776.
15. Pell, pp. 112-113.
16. Mathews, p. 42.
17. Smith, H.P. *History of Addison County.* Syracuse, N.Y., 1886. p. 526.
18. Several secondary sources claim that Sherwood sent a message to Tryon, but he never admitted this, nor spying for Carleton. An approach to Tryon was the usual way of becoming involved, and Carleton had prior knowledge of Sherwood before he reached Crown Point in October, 1776.
19. Hemenway, Abby Maria. *The Vermont Historical Gazeteer.* vol. 1. Burlington, Vt., 1867. p. 130.

Chapter 2: Secret Mission

1. Hadden, Lieutenant James N., Royal Artillery. *Journal and Orderly Books.* Albany, N.Y., 1884. p. 69.
2. *Ibid.*
3. Haldimand Papers, British Museum. Add. Mss. 21841. Sherwood's report is folios 50-51. PAC Haldimand papers, B 181, p. 62. Report dated April 7, 1777.
4. Haldimand Papers, British Museum Add. Mss. 21841. Folios 50-51. Sherwood's report.
5. The stockade is shown on a map of Albany made for Lord Jeffrey Amherst. Albany Society for History and Art.
6. P.R.O. AO 13-22. Memorial of Justus Sherwood, to which is appended a list of his lost property.
7. Stuart. Jessup's Corps. p. 27.
8. Thompson, Zadock. *History of Vermont. Natural, Civil and Statistical.* Burlington, Vt., 1842. Pt. III, p. 92.
9. Toronto Globe, July 16, 1877. Narrative of John Peters, June 5, 1786, written in Pimlico, England.
10. Stuart, Jessup's Corps, pp. 25 and 27. PAC Haldimand Papers, B 167, p. 11. Subsistence Account for the Loyal Volunteers, October 24, 1777, after Pfister's death.
11. P.R.O. AO 13-14. Memorial of John Wilson.
12. Smith, Paul H. *Loyalists and Redcoats: A Study of British Revolutionary Policy.* Chapel Hill, N.C. 1964, pp. 63-65.
13. Lewis, Paul. *The Man who Lost America. A Biography of 'Gentleman Johnny' Burgoyne.* New York, 1973; p. 25.
14. Stuart, Jessup's Corps, p. 24.
15. O'Callahan, E.B., ed. *Orderly Book of Lieut.-Gen. John Burgoyne.* Albany, N.Y., 1860. Map of Burgoyne's line of battle in the appendix.

Chapter 3: Rattlesnake Hill

1. Burt, A.L. *Guy Carleton, Lord Dorchester, 1724-1808.* Revised version. The Canadian Historical Association. Historical Booklet No. 5. p. 11. Some secondary accounts state that Howe was to bring an army north to effect a junction with Burgoyne. Burt points out that this is incorrect. Howe notified Carleton that he would be in Pennsylvania. Burgoyne knew, when he left Canada that he was on his own, although he later asked Clinton for reinforcements.
2. The credit for placing the guns has been given to Twiss in every source, and nothing beyond the fact that Sherwood reconnoitred the forts was ever said about his part. The task Twiss faced was enormous. If he had had to explore on his own and select the place to make his path, he would have needed more time. Years later Twiss asked for Sherwood to guide him along Lake Champlain, which suggests that he already knew him.
3. Hemenway. Gazetteer. vol. I, p. 749.

4. *Ibid.* vol. I, p. 719.
5. *Ibid.* vol. I, p. 749.
6. Mathews. *Frontier Spies.* p. 17. Here was proof that in 1775 Sherwood's interests lay with the rebels. Skene represented New York, and would have tried to control the Green Mountain Boys.
7. Later Burgoyne blamed his failure on the lack of loyalist support. Yet more loyalists came forward than other writers usually admit in secondary sources. A conservative estimate is that 1,000 loyalists joined Burgoyne.
8. Toronto Globe. Narrative of John Peters. War Office 28, vol. 4, p. 271. Appointment of Officers within Mentioned, from PAC collection.
9. PAC Haldimand Papers. B 161 p. 10. Return of the Corps of Royalists Commanded by Colonel Ebenezer Jessup.
10. *Ibid.* B 167, p. 374. Payroll of the Queen's Loyal Rangers.
11. P.R.O. AO 13-15. p. 415. Memorial of Patrick Smyth.

Chapter 4: Bennington Bloodbath
1. Almon, J. ed. *The Remembrancer, or Impartial Repository of Political Events.* 17 vols. by year, 1775-1784. London, 1777, pp. 392-394. General Burgoyne's instructions to Colonel Baum. Parke, Joseph W.R. *The Battle of Bennington.* Bennington Museum, 1976. Map on back cover.
2. Peters Papers. New York State Library. Albany, N.Y.
3. Several sources refer to a Tory officer only, but Sherwood was the man scouting near Bennington, and Burgoyne referred to him.
4. War Office 28, vol. 4. p. 271. Wright's appointment was made on August 6, 1777.
5. Stevens, B.F. *Facsimilies of Manuscripts in European Archives Relating to America 1773-1783.* London, 1889-1895. No. 1665. Philip Skene to Lord Dartmouth, Aug. 30, 1777.
6. In secondary sources only three positions are given for Baum's force, with all the Tories at Pfister's redoubt. A map on the back cover of Parke's booklet shows two positions for provincials. It was prepared by Lieutenant Durnford, Royal Engineers for Burgoyne.
7. New York State Library. MSS 3591. Return of the 3rd Company, Queen's Loyal Rangers after the Battle of Bennington.
8. O'Callaghan, Orderly Book of Lieut.-Gen. John Burgoyne. pp. 153-154.

Chapter 5: Saratoga
1. PAC War Office 28, vol. 9. p. 95. Memorial of Justus Sherwood to Sir Guy Carleton. Mar. 9, 1778.
2. Hadden. Journal and Orderly Books. p. 113, footnote.
3. PAC War Office 28, vol. 4. p. 103. Report of Colonel John Peters. Oct. 1, 1777.
4. PAC Haldimand Papers. B 167, p. 37. General Order at Battenkill. Aug. 25, 1777.
5. Riedesel, Mme. de. *Letters and Memoirs.* New York, 1827. The letters are useful sources for the events that followed her arrival at Fort Edward.
6. Pemberton. p. 57.
7. Stone, William L. *Life of Joseph Brant.* Cooperstown, N.Y. 1845. vol. 2. p. 211.
8. That Sherwood was wounded is not found in any primary source. The information was passed on by his sons.
9. PAC War Office 28. vol. 4. p. 103.
10. Lunt, James. *John Burgoyne of Saratoga.* New York, 1975. p. 335. Article 8 of the Saratoga Convention.
11. PAC War Office 28, vol. 4. p. 266. Present State of Several Detachments of Royalists who Returned from Lieutenant Genl Burgoyne's Army to Canada after the Convention. May 1, 1778.

Chapter 6: Under Convention

1. Walton, E.P. ed. *Records of the Council of Safety, State of Vermont.* Montpelier, Vt. 1873. vol. 1. p. 192.
2. No information on where Sarah was dropped along Lake Champlain has survived, but leaving refugees some miles off to make their own way was typical.
3. Hadden. Journal and Orderly Books. p. 72. footnote.
4. Sherwood's second son's name is given as Livius in some secondary sources. Sherwood's handwriting is responsible. His great great grandson was named Livius after his mother misread the name in the family Bible.
5. The description is based on a photograph of Levius. The Reverend Henry Scadding described him as slender and spare; John Morgan Gray, in his biography of Lord Selkirk, referred to Levius as Samuel Sherwood's 'lean, sharp faced younger brother'.
6. PAC War Office 28, vol. 9, p. 95. Memorial of Justus Sherwood to Governor Carleton. Mar. 9, 1778.
7. Confiscations, Albany County. New York State Library, Albany, N.Y.
8. Nye, M.G. *State Papers of Vermont.* no date. vol. 4. p. 17.
9. Ontario Archives. Jessup Papers. Edward Jessup's Receipt Book.
10. PAC Haldimand Papers. B 83, p. 97. June 1, 1778.
11. *Ibid.* B 181, p. 106. Sherwood to Carleton, July 10, 1778. Evidence that he went on the mission is found in the report he wrote on his return to Fort St. Johns.
12. Pell. p. 161. Ethan did confiscate Levi's property later.
13. Van De Water. *Reluctant Republic.* This is a colourful account of the birth pains of Vermont, which omits British machinations.
14. Katcher, Philip. *The American Provincial Corps, 1775-1784.* Osprey Men-at-Arms Series, Reading, England, 1973. p. 11. Katcher identifies the loyalists as Jessup's; they were Peters' corps.

Chapter 7: A Pimpernel Emerges

1. Leavitt, Thad. *History of Leeds and Grenville.* Brockville, 1879. p. 20. Memoir of Adiel Sherwood. The family moved to Canada in the summer of 1779.
2. PAC Haldimand Papers. B 181. pp. 106-110. Sherwood to Carleton, July 10, 1778.
3. The evidence that Sherwood had been negotiating with the rebels is not found until he was conducting the exchange of prisoners in the spring of 1779. Clinton Papers, University of Michigan, No. 2019. Deposition of Andrew Stephenson, one of the prisoners.
4. Enys, Lieutenant John. *The American Journals of Lt. John Enys.* Elizabeth Cometti, ed. Syracuse, N.Y. 1976. p. 24; Bredenberg, Oscar. *Military Activities in the Champlain Valley after 1777.* Champlain, N.Y. 1962. pp. 14-20.
5. PAC Haldimand Papers. B 83, p. 112; McIlwraith, J.N. *Sir Frederick Haldimand.* Toronto, 1929. p. 132.
6. PAC Haldimand Papers. B 54 pp. 266-269. Haldimand to Germain. Nov. 1, 1779; Fryer, M.B. *King's Men.* Toronto, 1980. Chapters 4 and 5, the histories of the two regiments.
7. Cruikshank, E.A. *The King's Royal Regiment of New York.* Ontario Historical Society Papers and Records. vol. 27 (1931) p. 391.
8. McIllwraith. p. 89.
9. PAC Haldimand Papers. B 54 p. 30. Haldimand to Germain, Oct. 15, 1778.
10. Mathews' name first appears on The Army Lists in 1778.
11. From the letters that passed between Mathews and Sherwood, most of the rest of the biography has been pieced together and the documentation is stronger. No document indicates that Sherwood met Haldimand at this time, but Haldimand would not have returned Sherwood to Fort St. Johns unless he had had the opportunity to form an opinion about him.
12. PAC Haldimand Papers. B 214, pp. 69-70. Memorial of Captain Sherwood

to Governor Haldimand. Nov. 16, 1778.
13. *Ibid.* B 54 p. 30. Haldimand to Germain. Oct. 15, 1778.
14. Joseph Bettys is brought in at this point because he becomes crucial in later events, and needs to be emphasised.
15. PAC Haldimand Papers. B 214. p. 81. Petition to Haldimand. Nov. 12, 1778.
16. *Ibid.* B 54. pp. 267-268. Haldimand to Germain. Nov. 1, 1779.

Chapter 8: Banished Yankee
1. Wardner, H.E. *The Birthplace of Vermont.* A History of Windsor to 1781. New York 1927. p. 489.
2. The date of these appointments is not documented. By 1780 Sherwood is referred to as the commissioner for both duties, and he carried out his first prisoner exchange in the spring of 1779.
3. Cruikshank, E.A. *John Walden Meyers, Loyalist Pioneer.* Ontario Historical Society Papers and Records. vol. 31 (1936). p. 12.
4. Jane Goddard, a descendant, provided the description of Meyers, based on information handed down through the family.
5. Mathews. *Frontier Spies.* p. 78.
6. Haldimand Papers, British Museum. Add. Mss. 21819. p. 17. Haldimand to Sir John Johnson, May 25, 1779.
7. Cruikshank. *John Walden Meyers.* p. 14. Meyers to Mathews, July 1, 1779.
8. Cruikshank, E.A. *Butler's Rangers.* Lundy's Lane Historical Society, 1893. pp. 68-75.
9. Hadden. *Journal and Orderly Books.* p. 72. footnote.
10. Cruikshank. *King's Royal Regiment.* pp. 223-224.
11. Cruikshank. *John Walden Meyers.* p. 15.
12. Leavitt. p. 20. Memoir of Adiel Sherwood. Judge John Deacon of Brockville, a descendant, has an oak chest that Thomas Sherwood brought from Fort Edward.
13. McIlwraith. pp. 125-126.
14. PAC Haldimand Papers. B 175 p. 19. Beverley Robinson to Ethan Allen, March 30, 1780.
15. *Ibid.* B 176 p. 131. G. Smyth to Haldimand. June 15, 1781.
16. McIlwraith. pp. 125-126.
17. Pell. p. 192.
18. Cruikshank. *King's Royal Regiment.* pp. 239-240.
19. PAC Haldimand Papers. B 182, quoted in Pell. p. 234.
20. Sir Henry Clinton Papers. No. 2891. Joseph McCracken to Colonel van Schaik. May 16, 1780, relaying information on prisoners who escaped.
21. Smith, Paul. *Loyalists and Redcoats: A Study of British Revolutionary Policy.* Chapel Hill, N.C. 1964. p. 74.
22. Haldimand papers, British Museum. Add. Mss. 21820, pp. 2-15. Letters of James Rogers and Robert Mathews.
23. Pell. p. 188, from PAC Military Series 'Q'.
24. Burleigh, H.C. *Samuel Sherwood's Account Book.* Kingston, 1975. Preface.
25. PAC War Office 28, vol. 10, part 3, p. 347. A muster roll dated Feb. 17, 1782, listing Samuel Sherwood as a volunteer in Justus' company.
26. Vermont State Library, Montpelier, Vt. Manuscripts relating to Ethan Allen. p. 407.

Chapter 9: With Fife and Drum
1. PAC Haldimand Papers. B 182 p. 284. Sherwood to Mathews, Aug. 24, 1780.
2. *Ibid.* p. 264. Report of Samuel Sherwood. Sept. 23, 1780.
3. Enys. Journal. p. 35.
4. Sherwood was fascinated by ships and knew how to sail a boat. He used sailor's terms and was careful to specify what type of craft he was aboard when travelling by water.
5. PAC Haldimand Papers. B 180 pp. 42-58. Sherwood's complete journal from

October 26, 1780 until he reached Quebec City.
6. Ontario Archives. Haldimand Papers. Envelope 7, pp. 157-8. Haldimand to Major Carleton. Nov. 9, 1780.
7. Enys. Journal. p. 50.
8. Justus dated his arrival in Quebec City as Nov. 31. England switched from the Julian to the Gregorian calendar in 1752.

Chapter 10: Justus Smells Success
1. PAC Haldimand Papers. B 176 p. 27, Sherwood to Mathews, Jan. 6, 1781.
2. Sir Henry Clinton Papers. Haldimand to Sherwood, Dec. 20, 1780, enclosed with a letter from Haldimand to Clinton, Aug. 2, 1781.
3. McIlwraith. p. 223. Describes the social life.
4. The appointment was verbal. Sherwood's letters subsequent to his visit in Quebec City indicate that he was in command of the scouts.
5. Ontario Archives, Jessup Papers. Military Order Book. Item for Dec. 5, 1780.
6. PAC Haldimand Papers B 176 p. 53, Sherwood to Mathews Jan. 18, 1781.
7. Jackson. *Justus Sherwood.* p. 18.
8. Ontario Archives. Jessup Papers. A list of the members of the Board of Officers.
9. PAC Haldimand Papers. B 180 p. 31, Sherwood to Mathews, Feb. 19, 1781.
10. *Ibid.* pp. 4-6. Sherwood to Mathews, Mar. 10, 1781.
11. *Ibid.* p. 7. Peters to Sherwood, Mar. 20, 1781.
12. Fitch, Dr. Asa. *Manuscript on Washington County, N.Y.* New York Genealogical and Biographical Society, N.Y. vol. 3, p. 137. Account of Abner Squires; p. 88. Account of Belus Hard.
13. PAC Haldimand papers. B 180 p. 102. Report of Samuel Rose, undated.
14. *Ibid.* p. 9. Sherwood to Mathews, Apr. 9, 1781.
15. Cruikshank. *John Walden Meyers.* p. 17.
16. PAC Vermont Papers.
17. PAC Haldimand Papers. B 83 p. 140. General Order from Headquarters. Sept. 4, 1780.
18. Stuart. p. 44.
19. PAC Haldimand Papers. B 83 p. 140. Sept. 4, 1781.
20. P.R.O. AO 12-53. Claim of Jeremiah French. July 5, 1787. With the claim is a letter from Sherwood.
21. PAC Haldimand Papers. B 176 p. 91. Sherwood to Mathews. May 8, 1781.
22. *Ibid.* B 175 p. 70. Sherwood to Mathews, May 8, 1781.
23. *Ibid* B 180 pp. 28-29. Sherwood to Mathews, May 11, 1781.
24. *Ibid.* p. 38. Sherwood to Mathews, May 22, 1781.
25. *Ibid.* p. 36. Sherwood to Mathews May 18, 1781.
26. *Ibid.* B 179 pt. 1. p. 40. Mathews to Sherwood, May 21, 1781.
27. *Ibid.* B 180 pp. 107-108. Sherwood to Mathews, June 2, 1781.
28. *Ibid.* B 176 p. 123. Sherwood to Mathews, June 2, 1781.
29. *Ibid.* B 179 pt. 1. p. 72. Mathews to Sherwood. June 5, 1781.
30. *Ibid.* B 178 p. 142. Sherwood to Mathews, July 1, 1781. The agreement reached with Haldimand was verbal. The first reference to it is found in a letter Sherwood wrote on July 1.
31. *Ibid.* B 176 p. 131. Smyth to Haldimand, June 15, 1781.
32. Paltsitz, Victor Hugo ed. *Minutes of the Board of Commissioners for Detecting and Defeating Conspiracies.* Albany, N.Y. 1901. p. 479 and p. 721, vol. 1.
33. Cruikshank. *John Walden Meyers.* p. 19.
34. PAC Haldimand Papers. B 167 p. 378, quoted by Stuart.
35. *Ibid.* B 176 pp. 142-143. Sherwood to Mathews, July 1, 1781.

Chapter 11: The Loyal Blockhouse
1. PAC Haldimand Papers B 176 p. 213. Smyth to Mathews, Aug. 14, 1781.
2. *Ibid.* B 180 p. 112. Smyth to Mathews, for Sherwood, July 8, 1781.

3. *Ibid.* Smyth to Mathews, July 9, 1781.
4. PAC War Office 28, vol. 4, p. 286. Muster Roll of the Corps Royalists Commanded by John Peters Esquire, July 14, 1781.
5. PAC Haldimand Papers. B 176 p. 213. Smyth to Mathews, Aug. 26, 1781.
6. *Ibid.* p. 183. Sherwood to Mathews, July 27, 1781.
7. *Ibid.* B 176 pp. 189-190 Memorandum by Captain Sherwood, July 30, 1781; B 179 pt. 1. p. 57. Mathews to Sherwood, July 4, 1781; pp. 304-305, undated, but with other letters for July.
8. *Ibid.* B 176 p. 251. Sherwood to Mathews, Aug. 26, 1781.
9. *Ibid.* p. 205. Sherwood to Mathews, Aug. 9, 1781.
10. *Ibid.* p. 247. Smyth to Mathews, Aug. 25, 1781; p. 270. Sept. 4, 1781.
11. *Ibid.* p. 284. A list of men, their regiments and ranks, captured with Mathew Howard.
12. Cruikshank. *John Walden Meyers.* p. 11; PAC Haldimand Papers B 175 no page number. Haldimand to Schuyler, Nov. 8, 1781.
13. *Ibid.* B 176 pp. 359-361. Smyth to Mathews, Nov. 21, 1781.
14. *Ibid.* B 180 pp. 120-121. Sherwood to Mathews, Aug. 19, 1781.
15. *Ibid.* p. 125. Smyth to Haldimand. Sept 1, 1781.
16. *Ibid.* p. 124. Sherwood to Mathews, Sept. 2, 1781.
17. *Ibid.* B 176 pp. 289-290. Smyth to Mathews, Sept. 25, 1781. Mrs. Smyth's given name is not known. She signed her letters R. Smyth.
18. Jackson, *Justus Sherwood.* p. 32.
19. Cruikshank. *John Walden Meyers.* pp. 29-30.
20. PAC Haldimand Papers. B 176 pe 293. Smyth to Mathews, Sept. 25, 1781.
21. *Ibid.* B 180 p. 136. Sherwood to Mathews, Oct. 27, 1781.

Chapter 12: The Loyal Rangers

1. PAC Haldimand Papers B 176 pp. 299-300. Stuart to Smyth Oct. 5, 1781.
2. Talman, J.J. *Loyalist Narratives from Upper Canada.* Toronto, 1966. pp. 341-344. Stuart to the Society for the Propagation of the Gospel. Oct. 11; 1781.
3. PAC Haldimand Papers B 176 pp. 314-315. Sherwood to Mathews. Oct. 18, 1781.
4. *Ibid.* p. 258. Smyth to Mathews, August 31, 1781.
5. Sir Henry Clinton Papers No. 4061. Gen. Heath to Gov. Clinton. Oct. 11, 1781.
6. PAC Haldimand Papers B 134 p. 171. St. Leger to Headquarters. Nov. 2, 1781.
7. *Ibid.* B 176 p. 326. Sherwood to Mathews. Nov. 2, 1781.
8. *Ibid.* B 180 p. 123; Pell p. 281.
9. PAC Haldimand Papers B 176 p. 355. Sherwood to Haldimand. Nov. 2, 1781.
10. *Ibid.* B 177 pt. 1. pp. 614-617. Sherwood to Mathews. Oct. 14, 1781.
11. *Ibid.* B 179 pt. 1; p. 116. Mathews to Sherwood. July 27, 1781.
12. *Ibid.* B 167 p. 398. Return of Officers in the Loyal Rangers.
13. *Ibid.* B 54 p. 29. Haldimand to Germain. Oct. 14, 1778.
14. The coat worn by Jeremiah French, a lieutenant in the second battalion, after serving as a captain in the Queen's Loyal Rangers, is in the Hamilton Military Museum at Dundurn Castle. It is red with blue facings and gold lace.
15. Justus Sherwood's Account Book. Metropolitan Toronto Library. The Baldwin Room.
16. PAC Haldimand Papers B 176 p. 344. Smyth to Mathews. Nov. 7, 1781.
17. McIlwraith. p. 235; Talman, p. 344.
18. PAC Haldimand Papers B 177 pt. 1. p. 323. Smyth to Mathews. May 25, 1782.

Chapter 13: In Yorktown's Wake

1. PAC Haldimand Papers B 179 pt. 1, p. 163. Mathews to Sherwood. Dec. 27,

1781.
2. *Ibid.* B 177 pt. 1, p. 1. Sherwood to Mathews. Jan. 2, 1782.
3. *Ibid.* pp. 12-13. Sherwood to Mathews. Jan. 16, 1782.
4. *Ibid.* p. 36. Sherwood to Mathews. Feb. 7, 1782.
5. *Ibid.* B 179 pt. 2, p. 181. Mathews to Sherwood. Feb. 14, 1782.
6. *Ibid.* p. 185. Sherwood to Smyth. Feb. 14, 1782. Sherwood was aware of the problem before he received Mathews' letter.
7. *Ibid.* B 56 p. 454. Muster Roll of Sherwood's Company. Jan. 1, 1783 at Rivière du Chêne.
8. Sherwood's Account Book. Item for Nov. 12, 1782.
9. PAC Haldimand Papers B 177 pt. 1, p. 182. Mathews to Sherwood and Smyth. May 14, 1782.
10. *Ibid.* B 179 pt. 1, p. 205. Mathews to Sherwood. Feb. 20, 1782.
11. *Ibid.* B 177 pt. 1, p. 161. Sherwood to Mathews. Mar. 28, 1782.
12. *Ibid.* p. 170. GX to XX. Apr. 3, 1782.
13. *Ibid.* B 179 pt. 2, p. 8. Mathews to Sherwood. May 17, 1782.
14. Stone, William Leete. *Life of Joseph Brant.* Cooperstown, N.Y. 1854. vol. 2, p. 213. Stone claimed that Bettys was to receive thirty guineas, but Haldimand would never have agreed to so large a sum.

Chapter 14: Undercover Activities 1782

1. PAC Haldimand Papers B 177 pt. 1. pp. 25-28. Report of Terence Smyth. Feb. 6, 1782; Ethan Allen to Haldimand. Mar. 4, 1782. p. 264.
2. PAC War Office 28, vol. 5, p. 168. Undated, the next document is May 5, 1782.
3. PAC Haldimand Papers B 178 p. 102. Deposition of Mathew Howard. Mar. 1, 1783.
4. *Ibid.* B 177 pt. 1, p. 303. Sherwood to Mathews. May 19, 1782; Pell, p. 224. Vermont sources claim that Crowfoot had eighteen recruits, for whom Sherwood handed over twice that number of rebels in a prisoner exchange. Sherwood told Mathews that Crowfoot escaped.
5. PAC Haldimand papers B 177. pt. 1. p. 27. Plain Truth Merwin to Smyth. May 8, 1782.
6. *Ibid.* p. 229. Smyth to Haldimand. Apr. 28, 1782.
7. *Ibid.* p. 112. Sherwood to Mathews. Mar. 18, 1782.
8. *Ibid.* p. 346. Smyth to Mathews. June 12, 1782; Haldimand Papers. British Museum. Add. Mss. 21820. p. 140. Mathews to James Rogers. June 17, 1782; PAC Haldimand Papers B 63 p. 239. Mathews to Sherwood. Apr. 26, 1784.
9. Jackson. Justus Sherwood. p. 39.
10. PAC Haldimand Papers B 177 pt. 1. pp. 289-291. Sherwood to Mathews. May 15, 1782; p. 282. Weekly State of the Loyal Blockhouse. May 12, 1782.
11. *Ibid.* p. 274. Sherwood to Mathews. May 9, 1782.
12. *Ibid.* B 177 pt. 2. p. 371. Smyth to Mathews. June 22, 1782.
13. *Ibid.* B 179 pt. 1. pp. 129-130. Mathews to Sherwood and Smyth. June 24, 1782. Reprimand re Dunning.
14. *Ibid.* B 177 pt. 1. p. 443. Report of John Lindsay. Aug. 17, 1782.
15. *Ibid.* B 179. pt. 2. p. 50. Report to Headquarters. Undated.
16. *Ibid.* B 125. pp. 41-42. Haldimand to Ross. July 7, 1782. Re cessation of hostilities.
17. *Ibid.* B 179. pt. 2. no page number. Mathews to Sherwood. Aug. 22, 1782.
18. Jackson. *Justus Sherwood.* p. 47.
19. Justus Sherwood's Account Book.
20. PAC War Office 28 vol. 4. pp. 458-459. Muster roll of Meyers' company. Jan. 1, 1783 at Riviere du Chene.
21. Cruikshank. *John Walden Meyers.* p. 36.
22. Pemberton. p. 248.
23. PAC Haldimand Papers. B 177 pt. 1. p. 601. Sherwood to Mathews. Nov.

16, 1782.
24. Haldimand Papers. British Museum. Add. Mss. 21821. p. 421. Findings of the Court Martial held at the Loyal Blockhouse. Decm 7, 1782.
25. *Ibid.* p. 339. Return of Gentlemen who wish to recruit men for His Majesty's Service... Verchères, 27 January, 1782.
26. PAC Haldimand Papers. B 175. pp. 185-186. Cossitt and Sumner to Haldimand. Dec. 30, 1782.
27. *Ibid.* B 161. p. 474. Sherwood to Nairne. Dec. 31, 1782.
28. The bark of willow trees contains acetysalicylic acid, a fact known at the time.
29. PAC Haldimand Papers, B 178 p. 135. Cossitt to Sherwood. Mar. 31, 1783.

Chapter 15: 'Behind the Cloud Topped Hill'
1. PAC Haldimand Papers B 178 p. 22. Knowlton to Haldimand. Jan. 10, 1783.
2. *Ibid.* pp. 15-16. Thomas Smyth to Mathews. Jan. 9, 1783.
3. Jackson. Justus Sherwood. p.50.
4. PAC Haldimand papers. B 178 p. 112. Sherwood to Mathews. Mar. 10, 1783.
5. *Ibid.* p. 120. Sherwood to Mathews. Mar. 10, 1783.
6. McIlwraith. p. 183.
7. PAC Haldimand Papers. B 178 p. 133. Sherwood to Mathews. Mar. 14, 1783.
8. Jackson. *Justus Sherwood.* pp. 52-53.
9. PAC Haldimamd Papers. B 178 p. 173. Ethan Allen to Sherwood. Apr. 18, 1783.
10. P.R.O. AO 13-22. pp. 360-361. Memorial of Thomas Sherwood.
11. Jackson. *Justus Sherwood.* p. 55.
12. McIlwraith. p. 301-302.
13. *Ibid.* p. 244.
14. PAC Haldimand Papers. B 169 pp. 6-14. Sherwood's journal.
15. McIlwraith. p. 259.

Chapter 16: The Happiest People in America
1. PAC Haldimand Papers. B 175 p. 211. Washington to Haldimand. July 12, 1783.
2. *Ibid.* p. 219. Haldimand to von Steuben. Aug. 6, 1783. Written before Haldimand left for Sorel.
3. Van Steen. M. *Governor Simcoe and His Lady.* Toronto, 1968. p. 24.
4. PAC Haldimand Papers. B 169 pp. 15-30. Sherwood's journal from Montreal to Lake Ontario.
5. *Ibid.* B 126 pp. 43-44. Haldimand to Collins. Sept. 11, 1783.
6. *Ibid.* p. 90. Haldimand to Ross. Sept. 7, 1783.
7. P.R.O. AO 13-22. p. 361. Memorial of Thomas Sherwood.
8. Haldimand Papers British Museum. Add. Mss. 21820. James Rogers to Mathews. Jan. 7, 1783.
9. PAC Haldimand Papers. B 169 pp. 15-25. Sherwood's journal.
10. *Ibid.* B 124 p. 44. Ross to Mathews. Oct. 2, 1783.
11. From Sherwood's description this was Millhaven Creek.
12. PAC National Map Collection. F/412 – 1783.
13. Haldimand Papers. British Museum. Add. Mss. 21822. p. 131. Petition of Ebenezer Allen, filed with correspondence for December, 1783; p. 132. Ebenezer Allen to Haldimand. Aug. 31, 1784, from Cataraqui, asking for a trial or release.
14. PAC Haldimand Papers. B 128 p. 125. Mathews to Harris. Nov. 2, 1783.
15. *Ibid.* B 178 p. 316. Sherwood to Mathews. Nov. 23, 1783.
16. *Ibid.* p. 321. Smyth to Mathews. Dec. 9, 1783.

Chapter 17: Personal Crises
1. PAC Haldimand Papers. B 178 p. 321. Smyth to Mathews. Dec. 19, 1783.
2. In the Sherwood household all these measures were taken, for no one else contracted the disease before the incubation period — seven to sixteen

days — had ended.
3. PAC Land Petitions. R.G. 1 L 3, S Bundle, vol. 469, p. 92. Petition of Samuel Sherwood. 1790.
4. PAC Haldimand Papers. B 65 p. 1. Mathews to Sherwood. Jan. 22, 1784.
5. *Ibid.* B 162 p. 171. Jessup to Mathews. Jan. 29, 1784.
6. Cruikshank, E.A. *The Settlement of the United Empire Loyalists on the Upper St. Lawrence and Bay of Quinte in 1784.* Toronto. 1934. p. 35.
7. Stuart. p. 5.
8. PAC Haldimand Papers B 169 pp. 121-122. General Order from Headquarters.
9. The first township, Lancaster, was surveyed later for Roman Catholic settlers, and was not one of the original eight.
10. PAC Haldimand Papers B 162 p. 190. Sherwood to Mathews. Mar. 1, 1784.
11. *Ibid.* B 115 pp. 223-224. Johnson to Mathews. Feb. 2, 1784.
12. *Ibid.* B 162 p. 190. Sherwood to Mathews. Mar. 1, 1784.
13. *Ibid.* B 178 pp. 293-294. Sherwood to Mathews. May 13, 1784.
14. *Ibid.* pp. 324-325. Smyth to Mathews. May 20, 1784.
15. *Ibid.* B 162 p. 220. Sherwood to Mathews. Mar. 26, 1784.
16. *Ibid.* B 63 p. 119. Mathews to Sherwood. Mar. 8, 1784.
17. *Ibid.* B 178 p. 285. Sherwood to Mathews. Apr. 15, 1784.
18. *Ibid.* B 65 p. 30. Mathews to Sir John Johnson. May 20, 1784.
19. *Ibid.* B 63 p. 254; B 162 p. 295.
20. Cruikshank. *John Walden Meyers.* pp. 42-43.
21. PAC Haldimand Papers. B 64 p. 30. Sherwood to Mathews. May 20, 1784.
22. *Ibid.* B 178 p. 309. Sherwood to Mathews. May 20, 1784.
23. P.R.O. AO 13-22. p. 361. Memorial of Thomas Sherwood.
24. Leavitt. p. 18. Memoir of Adiel Sherwood.

Chapter 18: Scapegoats to the Wilderness

1. PAC Haldimand Papers B 162 p. 295. Sherwood to Mathews. May 23, 1784.
2. PAC M.G. 4, S. 28, p. 116. A list signed by Captain John Barnes, Deputy Quartermaster-General at Sorel.
3. PAC Haldimand Papers. B 162 p. 329. Sherwood to Mathews. July 2, 1784. The townsite is shown on a map of the United Counties of Leeds and Grenville. 1861-2. Putnam and Walling, Publishers. Kingston, C.W.
4. PAC Haldimand Papers B 162 p. 338-339. Sherwood to Mathews. July 23, 1784; p. 330. Sherwood to Mathews. July 2, 1784.
5. Cruikshank. *King's Royal Regiment of New York.* p. 313.
6. PAC Haldimand Papers. B 162 pp. 338-339. Sherwood to Mathews. July 23, 1784.
7. *Ibid.* B 65 p. 44. Mathews to Ensign Bothum. Aug. 5, 1784.
8. Vermont Vital Records, Montpelier. Lemuel died on Mar. 12, 1858, aged fifty-one. The cause of death was 'old age'.
9. Leavitt. pp. 20-21. Memoir of Adiel Sherwood.
10. Pringle, G.F. *Lunenburg or The Old Eastern District.* Cornwall, Ontario. 1890. pp. 35-36.
11. Cruikshank. *Loyalist Settlement.* pp. 136 and 155; Ontario Archives. Jessup Papers. Nov. 27, 1783.
12. Leavitt. p. 31.
13. PAC Haldimand Papers. B 162 p. 381. Sherwood to Mathews. Oct. 17, 1784.
14. *Ibid.* pp. 383-385. Jessup to Mathews. Sept. 14, 1784.
15. Leavitt. p. 20. Adiel Sherwood said that the only animal that accompanied the Sherwoods was a small dog called Tipler.
16. Ontario Archives. Jessup Papers. Mathews to Jessup. Jan. 22, 1787. Jessup had recently returned from England.
17. PAC R.G. 1, E 1, 5 A. Oswegatchie. Nov. 12. Account for work done as a deputy surveyor of the expenses for survey party submitted to John Collins by Justus Sherwood.

Chapter 19: In Government Circles

1. Old county histories refer to town meetings in the 1780s, although these were not legal until 1793.
2. Ontario Archives. Justus Sherwood's Notebook. No. 375. A Return of Settlers, New Oswegatchie, Augusta Township 1784-1787.
3. Haddock, J.A. *The Picturesque St. Lawrence River*. Watertown, N.Y. 1896. p. 68.
4. McIlwraith. pp. 331-332.
5. Ontario Archives. Biographical card catalogue. Sarah was baptised by the Reverend John Bethune on February 13, 1789, at the same time as her younger sister, Harriet.
6. Burleigh, H.C. *Samuel Sherwood's Account Book*. Kingston, 1975. Preface.
7. Shortt, A. and Doughty, A.C. *Documents Relating to the Constitutional History of Canada, 1759-1791*. Revised edition. Ottawa, 1918. pt. II, p. 945.
8. PAC Haldimand Papers. B 146 pp. 63-64. Carleton to Haldimand. June 4, 1783.
9. Leavitt. p. 20. Memoir of Adiel Sherwood.
10. Shortt and Doughty. Pt. II, p. 949.
11. PAC Map Collection. 1784-1789. Identified as Maitland, but the shoreline matches the New Oswegatchie townsite.
12. PAC M. G. 23 J 9. Journal of Major Robert Mathews.
13. P.R.O. AO 13-22. p. 360. A list of Sherwood's lost property.
14. McIlwraith. p. 313.
15. Preston, R.A. *Kingston Before the War of 1812*. Toronto. 1959. p. 123. Report of John Collins and William Dummer Powell. Aug. 18, 1787.
16. Grose, Francis. *A Classical Dictionary of the Vulgar Tongue; 1785-1788*. Revised in 1811. Northfield, Minn. 1971. Definition of a tradeing justice.
17. Robertson, John Ross. *History of Freemasonry in Canada*. Toronto. 1899. pp. 291 and 297.
18. Pemberton. p. 313; Audit Office Records, Public Record Office, London. 1783-1790. XXXII pp. 413-414.

Chapter 20: Fading Light

1. Cruikshank. *John Walden Meyers*. p. 43.
2. PAC R.G. 1. Quebec Executive Council Minutes. May 14, 1788. p. 33. Draft Patent for Forming New Districts.
3. Stuart. p. 119.
4. Ontario Archives. Biographical Card Catalogue.
5. Craig, G.M. *Upper Canada, the Formative Years*. Toronto, 1963. p. 13.
6. Leavitt. pp. 22-23. Leavitt dates the Hungry Year as 1787, with the worst of the famine felt before the harvest of 1788.
7. Vermont Historical Society, Montpelier. Manuscripts relating to Ethan Allen; Pell p. 316.
8. Pell. pp. 228 and 256.
9. *Ibid.* p. 316.
10. Stuart. p. 144.
11. Pringle. p. 46.
12. PAC R.G. L, 1, vol. 18. Quebec Land Book. Minutes of the Executive Council, Province of Quebec. Nov. 9, 1789.
13. Jesup, Rev. G. *Edward Jessup of West Farms, Westchester Co. New York and his Descendants*. Cambridge, Mass. 1887. p. 236.
14. McKenzie, Ruth. *Leeds and Grenville; Their first two hundred years*. Toronto 1967. pp. 75-76. McKenzie stated that a church was built by 1790, but on Feb. 11, 1795, Rosseter Boyle wrote to Major Littlehales, Simcoe's secretary, enquiring what Messers Sherwood and Jones had done with the money collected for a church. E.A.Cruikshank, ed. *Simcoe Papers*. Ontario Historical Society 1923. vol. 3, p. 291.
15. Ontario Archives. Biographical Card Catalogue.

16. Cruikshank. Simcoe Papers. vol. 1, p. 103.
17. Scott, Duncan Campbell. *John Graves Simcoe*. Toronto, 1910. p. 79. A list of the members of the legislative council.
18. Bradley, A.G. *Lord Dorchester*. Toronto, 1926. Revised Edition. p. 269.
19. Innis, Mary Quayle. *Mrs. Simcoe's Diary*. Toronto, 1965. pp. 68-69.
20. Leavitt. p. 98.
21. *Ibid.* pp. 16, 162, 109-110. List of land grants.
22. Armstrong, F.H. *Handbook of Upper Canadian Chronology and Territorial Legislation*. London, Ont. 1967. p. 104.
23. Wilbur, J.B. *Ira Allen, Founder of Vermont. 1751-1814*. Boston. 1902. pp. 60 and 395-396.

Chapter 21: Founding Father
1. Craig. p. 30.
2. Scott. pp. 89-90.
3. Leavitt. pp. 20-21. Letter from Adiel Sherwood to Dr. Canniff. Mar. 10, 1868.
4. Ontario Dept. of Lands and Forests. Survey Records. Surveyor's Letters held in the PAC. W. Chewett. 1792-1796. No. 17. Niagara. Oct. 31, 1796.
5. PAC Upper Canada Land Petitions. Series C. vol. 1793. F Bundle. 1793-1795. No. 52.; Wilbur. *Ira Allen*. vol. 21 pp. 395-396.
6. PAC Upper Canada Land and State Book A. 1792-1796. p. 134; Cruikshank, E.A. *The Activities of Abel Stevens as a Pioneer*. Ontario Historical Society Papers and Records. XXXI (1936) pp. 60-62.
7. Upper Canada Land Books. Series C – 101. vol. D. p. 348.
8. Pemberton. p. 327; from Eighteenth Report, Ontario Bureau of Archives. 1929. p. 148.
9. Cruikshank. *Simcoe Papers*. vol. 5. p. 216; from Book B. Reports of Committees of Council held at York from the 5th to the 28th of July, 1796.
10. The land records for Leeds and Grenville show a total of 2,750 acres bearing the names of Justus and his children. Of this, 100 acres may have been his brother Samuel's first grant, and 186 acres was Diana's at the time of her marriage. Sherwood never did receive his full 3,000 acres.
11. PAC Quebec Land Records. 'Justin' Sherwood owned Lots 11 and 12 in the Seigneury of Sorel, and J.B. Lemoine purchased them from Francis Hogel on Nov. 3, 1796 for 40 pounds.
12. Leavitt. p. 162.
13. Burleigh. Preface.
14. Toronto Globe. July 16, 1877. *Narrative of John Peters*; Leavitt. p. 181.
15. Ontario Archives. Biographical Card Catalogue.
16. *Ibid.*
17. Pemberton. p. 332. Records show that Sherwood was not buried in the Blue Church cemetery. Archdeacon R.L. Gourlay of St. James Church, Trois Rivières, wrote to Pemberton on June 7, 1972, informing him that Sherwood was not buried there.

Epilogue
1. Vermont Public Record Office, Montpelier. New Haven Deeds and Records. IV. no. 31.
2. Armstrong. Handbook. Samuel Sherwood, p. 84. William Buell, p. 88.
3. Gray, John Morgan. *Lord Selkirk of Red River*. Toronto, 1963. pp. 293-301.
4. PAC *Quebec Gazette*. Mar. 23, 1813; Sept. 19, 1816.
5. Armstrong. *Handbook*. pp. 89, 121, 146.
6. PAC Military Series C. 678, p. 82.
7. Guillet, Edwin. *Life and Times of the Patriots*. Toronto, 1933 and 1963. pp. 244-245. Mackenzie's article on the Family Compact.
8. Leavitt. p. 181.
9. Ontario Archives. Biographical Card Catalogue.
10. PAC Military Series C. 679. 25-8, p. 487; C 703. p. 13.
11. *Bartlett's Canada*. Toronto, 1966. p. 182. From E.T. Coke. *A Subaltern's Furlough*.
12. Howard, Richard B. *Upper Canada College 1829-1979 Colborne's Legacy*. Toronto, 1979. p. 82.

Bibliography

Printed Documentary Material

Armstrong, F.H. *Handbook of Upper Canadian Chronology and Territorial Legislation.* University of Western Ontario. London, 1967.

Army Lists (The) *A List of General and Field Officers.* 1775 to 1784. Metropolitan Toronto Library.

Hadden, Lt. James, Royal Artillery. *Journal and Orderly Books.* Albany, 1884.

O'Callaghan, E.B. ed. *Documentary History of the State of New York.* Albany, 1851.

Paltsits, Victor Hugo ed. *Minutes of the Board of Commissioners for Detecting and Defeating Conspiracies.* Albany, 1901.

Peters, John Toronto Globe. July 16, 1877. *Narrative of John Peters.*

Preston, R.A. *Kingston Before the War of 1812.* Champlain Society, Toronto, 1959.

Quebec Gazette Issues in the Public Archives of Canada.

Shortt, A. and Doughty, A.G. *Documents Relating to the Constitutional History of Canada. 1759-1791.*

Talman, J.J. *Loyalist Narratives from Upper Canada.* Champlain Society. Toronto, 1946.

Walton, E.P. ed. *Records of the Council of Safety.* State of Vermont. Montpelier, 1873.

Secondary Sources

Allen, Ira *The National and Political History of Vermont.* London, 1798.

Anbury, Thomas *With Burgoyne from Quebec.* Toronto, 1963.

Bartlett's Canada Toronto, 1968. Quotation from Lt. E.T. Coke. *A Subaltern's Furlough.*

Bradley, A.G. *Lord Dorchester.* Makers of Canada Series. Toronto, 1926.

Bredenberg, Oscar. *Military Activities in the Champlain Valley after 1777.* Champlain, N.Y. 1962.

Bushman, Richard L. *From Puritan to Yankee: Character and Social Order in Connecticut.* Cambridge, Mass. 1967.

Burleigh, H.C. *Samuel Sherwood's Account Book.* Kingston, 1975.

Burt, A.L. *Guy Carleton.* Canadian Historical Association. Historical Booklet no. 5

Cappon, Lester J. *Atlas of Early American History, the Revolutionary Era. 1760-1790.* Princeton, N.J. 1976.

Cooledge, A.J. and Mansfield, J.B. *History and Description of New England: General and Social.* Boston, 1859.

Craig, G.M. *Upper Canada, the Formative Years.* Toronto, 1963.

Cruikshank, E.A. ed. *The Simcoe Papers.* Ontario Historical Society, 1923.

Cruikshank, E.A. *Captain John Walden Meyers, Loyalist Pioneer.* Ontario Historical Society Papers and Records XXXI (1936).

Cruikshank, E.A. *The King's Royal Regiment of New York.* Ontario Historical Society Papers and Records XXXIII (1939).

Cruikshank, E.A. *The Settlement of the United Empire Loyalists on the upper St. Lawrence and the Bay of Quinte in 1784.* Toronto, 1934.

Delderfield, Eric R. ed. *Kings and Queens of England and Great Britain.* Newton Abbot, Devon, England. 1970.

Dupuy, H.E. and Dupuy, T.N. *The Compact History of the Revolutionary War.* New York, 1963.

Enys, Lieut. John *The American Journals of Lt. John Enys.* Elizabeth Cometti ed. Syracuse, N.Y. 1976.

Fitch, Dr. Asa Manuscripts on Washington County, New York. New York Genealogical and Biographical Society, New York.

Fryer, Mary Beacock *Loyalist Spy*. Brockville, 1974.
Fryer, Mary Beacock and Ten Cate, A.G. *Pictorial History of the Thousand Islands*. Brockville, 1978.
Gray, John Morgan *Lord Selkirk of Red River*. Toronto, 1964.
Grose, Francis A. *A Classical Dictionary of the Vulgar Tongue* 1785 and 1788. Reprint of an 1811 edition. Northfield, Ill. 1971.
Guillet, Edwin *Life and Times of the Patriots*. Toronto, 1933 and 1963.
Haddock, John A. *The Picturesque St. Lawrence River*. Watertown, N.Y. 1896.
Hemenway, Abby Maria *The Vermont Historical Gazetteer*. Burlington, Claremont, Montpelier, Vt. 1867-1891.
Howard, Richard B. *Upper Canada College 1829-1979: Colborne's Legacy*. Toronto, 1979.
Innis, Mary Quayle *Mrs. Simcoe's Diary*. Toronto, 1965.
Jackson, H.M. *Justus Sherwood, Soldier, Loyalist and Negotiator*. Published privately, 1953.
Jackson, H.M. *Rogers' Rangers*. Published privately, 1958.
Jesup, Rev. H.G. *Edward Jessup of West Farms, Westchester Co. and his Descendants*. Cambridge, Mass. 1887.
Katcher, Philip *The American Provincial Corps 1775-1784*. Osprey Men-at-Arms Series, Reading, England, 1973.
Koier, Louise B. *A November Journey: Vermont's Debt to Captain Justus Sherwood*. Vermont Historical Society, News and Notes VI. Nov. 31, 1954.
Lapp, Eula C. *To Their Heirs Forever. Picton, 1970.*
Leavitt, Thad. *History of Leeds and Grenville*. Brockville, 1879.
Lewis, Paul *The Man who Lost America. A Biography of Gentleman Johnny Burgoyne*. New York, 1973.
Lunt, James *John Burgoyne of Saratoga*. New York, 1975.
MacNutt, W.S. *New Brunswick: A History. 1784-1867*. Toronto, 1963.
Mathews, Hazel C. *Frontier Spies*. Fort Myers, Florida, 1971.
McIlwraith, J.N. *Sir Frederick Haldimand*. Makers of Canada Series. Toronto, 1926.
McKenzie, Ruth *Leeds and Grenville: Their First Two Hundred Years*. Toronto, 1968.
Nye, M.G. *State Papers of Vermont*. No date.
O'Callaghan, E.B. ed. *Orderly Book of Lieut.-Gen. John Burgoyne*. Albany, MCCCLX.
Order of Colonial Lords of the Manors in American Publications. Columbia University Press. No date.
Parke, J.W.R. *The Battle of Bennington*. Bennington Museum, 1976.
Pell, John *Ethan Allen*. Boston, 1929.
Pemberton, I.C.R. *Justus Sherwood, Vermont Loyalist*. Doctoral Dissertation. University of Western Ontario. London, Ont. 1972.
Pope, Charles Henry *Pioneers of Massachusetts*. Baltimore, 1965.
Pringle, J.F. *Lunenburgh or the Old Eastern District*. Cornwall, 1890.
Remembrancer, The, or Impartial Repository of Political Events. London, 1775-1784.
Robertson, John Ross. *A History of Freemasonry in Canada*. Toronto, 1899.
Scott, Duncan Campbell *John Graves Simcoe*. Makers of Canada Series. Toronto, 1910.
Smith, H.P. *History of Addison County*. Syracuse, N.Y. 1886.
Smith, Paul H. *Loyalists and Redcoats: A Study of British Revoluntionary Policy*. Chapel Hill, N.C. 1964.
Stevens, B.F. *Facsimilies of Manuscripts in European Archives Relating to America. 1773-1783*. London, 1889-1895.
Stone, William Leete *Life of Joseph Brant*. Cooperstown, N.Y. 1854.
Stratford Historical Society. Orcutt's *History of Stratford and Bridgeport*.
Stuart, E. Rae *Jessup's Rangers as a Factor in Loyalist Settlement*. Three History Theses, 1939. Toronto, 1961.

Tharp, Louise Hall *The Baroness and the General*. Toronto, 1962.
Thompson, Judge D.P. *The Green Mountain Boys: A Historical Tale of the Early Settlement of Vermont*. New York, 1839.
Thompson, Zadock *History of Vermont, Natural, Civil and Statistical*. Bennington, 1842.
United Empire Loyalists' Association of Ontario. Annual Transactions. 1901-1902.
Van De Water, Fred. F. *The Reluctant Republic*. New York, 1974.
Van Steen, Marcus *Governor Simcoe and His Lady*. Toronto, 1968.
Vermont Historical Society. Proceedings of
Wardner, H.S. *The Birthplace of Vermont. A History of Windsor to 1781*. New York, 1927.
Wilbur, J.B. *Ira Allen, Founder of Vermont 1751-1814*. Boston, 1902.

Index